Praise for Alden Reimonenq's
The Upside-Down Tree
* * *

"The presentation of a community under siege in Alden Reimonenq's *The Upside-Down Tree* immerses the reader in an unforgettable and unflinching novel about the rapacious consequences of the virulent racism in the Deep South after Reconstruction. The impressive evocation of place, character, and circumstance of this difficult and shameful period in American history begins to fill a gap in our literary canon and remains with the reader long after the last page, feeling both enlightened and a little wiser about the sins of our American past."

—Ernesto Mestre-Reed, author of *The Lazarus Rumba*, *The Second Death of Única Aveyano*, and *Sacrificio*

"If Barack Obama hadn't already used the title, *The Audacity of Hope* could be the title of Alden Reimonenq's first novel. From its opening pages, *The Upside-Down Tree* immersed me in a time, place, and culture I knew nothing about, in which racism and homophobia threaten and destroy, yet hope persists.

Characters of diverse races—Black, Choctaw, Creole, White—drew my sympathy or hatred as I read the fast-moving narrative. Joyous community scenes of making gumbo and preparing a crab feast unite diverse individuals, transcending the severity of the problems they face.

Catholicism and African religious beliefs blend and clash as interracial relationships develop. At the heart of the novel an interracial gay relationship moves tentatively yet feels foreordained.

The novel exposes racism and homophobia as not merely ugly but deadly in personal and moving ways. As I neared the conclusion, I realized that *The Upside-Down Tree* was deepening my understanding of the Black Lives Matter and the LGBTQ movements while underscoring the audacity of hope."

—Carol Beran, PhD (UC Berkeley); Professor Emerita (St Mary's College of California); published widely on Alice Munro and Margaret Atwood

"With *The Upside-Down Tree*, Alden Reimonenq has crafted must-read historical fiction for any reade᠎ ᠎᠎᠎᠎᠎᠎᠎᠎᠎᠎᠎᠎᠎᠎᠎ly years of the Jim Crow era.

Mystical, powerful, and ima᠎᠎᠎᠎᠎᠎᠎᠎᠎᠎᠎᠎ ᠎᠎nq's *The Upside-Down Tree* pushes b᠎᠎᠎ he racial prejudice and persecutions of the early Jim Crow era in Louisiana. A must-read for Louisiana Creole descendants, African Americans, as well as readers of historical fiction and southern and resistance literature.

Unique, mystical, powerful, and unforgettable, Alden Reimonenq's *The Upside-Down Tree* is one of the most impactful novels of the year."

—Chris Helvey, author of *The White Jamaican*,
editor in chief, *Trajectory Journal*

"Alden Reimonenq's *The Upside-Down Tree* is a remarkable achievement—a riveting, richly textured journey to rural Louisiana at the turn of the twentieth century that also helps explain our present day. It's a novel of ideas that also never fails to breathe life into its complex, original, and fully human characters. Highly recommended."

— Lou Berney, author of many novels, winner of the
Edgar Award for *November Road*

The
UPSIDE-DOWN
TREE

Alden Reimonenq

 Aubade Publishing
Ashburn, VA

Edited by Joe Puckett

Cover design and book layout by Cosette Puckett

Illustration by Cosette Puckett

Library of Congress Control Number: 2021947964

ISBN: 978-1-951547-17-2

Published by Aubade Publishing, Ashburn, VA

Printed in the United States of America

Inspired by James Baldwin

and for

Darrick DeWitt Lackey

Contents

Author's Note

When enslaved people from Yorubaland in West Africa arrived in various "new world" countries, they carried with them their cultures and religions. The enslaved and their descendants suffered religious oppression and were forced to adopt Christianity and to filter out or hide their own faith practices. Consequently, in the African diaspora, we find a plethora of adaptations of original religious forms and concepts. One religious entity found commonly throughout the African diaspora is the Orisha—a spiritual being originating in ancestor worship. Orishas appear in a variety of forms and contexts, with many different names, in diverse black populations. For example, Orishas are present in Brazil's Candomblé religion, in the Caribbean's Vodoun, and in Louisiana's Voodoo or Hoodoo. Depending on the strength of traditional cultural practices or religious beliefs, the Orishas' presence and influence are boldly drawn, silhouetted, or faded.

Although there are many Yoruba Orishas, two spirits inhabit *The Upside-Down Tree's* pages: Eshu and Yemanja. Their attributes explain who they are and trace their influence on the lives of this novel's characters.

Eshu is a trickster, a messenger, who thrives on accident and indeterminacy. Exercising his wit or whim, he can be benevolent or malevolent. His messages often carry double entendre rather than clarity. He enjoys helping those he inspires, but he will puzzle and trap them as well—always imparting hidden wisdom. Eshu is considered the cleverest of Orishas, motivating humans to grapple with more than they can see. In *The Upside-Down Tree*, he resides mostly in trees and uses them to speak for him. He can also move rapidly from place to place to do good or fatal harm. In Yoruba tradition, he is often pictured as Janus-faced.

Yemanja is the Orisha of the sea—a creative power associated with motherhood and life-giving and life-affirming forces. She is traditionally known as a protector of those connected to the sea: sailors, fishermen, divers, etc. She is among the most powerful Orishas and is dedicated to the actualization of womanhood, fertility, and all aspects of family life—especially the care of children. Yemanja suffered intensely in her lifetime, but her survival, through her female prowess and intellect, gained for her a place of universal honor and respect. She has many qualities but is mainly associated with birth, rebirth, creativity, growth, forgiveness, and resolution effected through natural acts. Yemanja is a water figure in complex ways, who is determined to cleanse naturally what is soiled in humanity by unnatural acts. She is often pictured in a blue dress, white apron, and jeweled-studded crown.

I wish people were all trees and I think I could enjoy them then.

Georgia O'Keeffe, 1921

Easter Sunday
April 13, 1873

EVIL HURRICANED ITS WAY through all the open spaces in Colfax, Louisiana. It burned houses and shook black lives; it brutalized children, caused them to go missing. It lynched fathers and brothers, raped mothers and sisters, and emptied churches. Whites held runaway power that engaged Colfax in a long-standing battle that pinnacled in a bloody massacre that left only those few black survivors who sheltered themselves in homes with barricaded windows and doors. This evil was slow and menacing; its fury lingered, careful and deliberate, disposing of black bodies as if litter from the town's square to the countryside. Evil is not a consort with peace; therefore, Colfax's town history was marked forever with black blood that dripped mercilessly from false white hands celebrating Christ's resurrection that Sunday. But evil can be too good at being itself, and that massacre fueled its energy in a destruction that crossed generations that day and into the future. Two Colfax citizens participated in breeding and cultivating this evil.

Feverish Avery Barjone stumbled into an enormous pine silhouetted by weak moonlight. He heard the hammering of horse hooves, but that was not nearly the worry the bullet in his chest caused. He turned his back to the pine and sat buttressed by its strength. With raised arms, he cried, "Eshu. Eshu. Eshu. I need fire." The tree, still dripping from an earlier rain, shook itself, enkindling energy in him. "Fire! And light, Eshu!"

At just twenty and already full of arrogance and contempt, Carl Keller found Avery. Sitting erect on his horse, he drew his gun, ready to riddle Avery's skull with bullets. He hesitated. "Daddy would've killed you by now for destroying our peace. Ain't enough we saved your black ass before?"

1

"You too young to know yo' daddy. He was too evil to 'bide the law."

"Well, Sheriff Nash won't be taking no surrenders at Grant Parish courthouse. They all burning. Because of you niggers, there's fire everywhere."

"Gonna be fire here. Ain't nobody owning me no more. Eshu, fire! Eshu!"

"Call your spirits, nigger. They don't scare me."

The pine shuddered its reply, and a branch flamed over. Its force knocked Carl off his horse and threw his gun inches from Avery. The horse sprinted into the woods. The blaze lit the metal, and Avery grabbed the gun and pointed it at Carl.

"You, listen! I'll die under this tree, but you gonna walk like death if you don't do like I say. This fire's my curse on you. Go to the church graveyard and look for my boy Kebbi. If he's there, his mama's dead. Care for him till he can care for hisself. Do good by him, and you'll find some peace. You don't, my curse will hang 'round your whole life like misery. If Kebbi ain't in that graveyard, forget us."

Carl eyed the burning pine branch, mystified that nothing had fallen. The fire was a fierce and cacophonous burst of orange and gold luminosity that transfixed him. His gasping and heaving broke his gaze. The gun's weight pulled Avery's arm to the ground, and a weak moon cast a pale, angry light on his corpse. Slowly, the branch extinguished itself. Carl picked up his gun and headed to the church, now ablaze in the Colfax town square.

Easter Sunday

April 15, 1900

CARL WALKED SLOWLY ACROSS his front porch, drawing heavily on his cigarette while spitting loose bits of tobacco. He scanned the bank of pines across the road and scrutinized the biggest. Several times, he had planned to raze them and plant pecans. His butler echoed his groundskeeper's caution against this, claiming that too many young men played with their whores in those pines, which kept "that sinning" out of sight. "Pecans don't grow dense enough to hide all that," the groundskeeper pronounced. Carl, who never intended to marry, respected a man's right to whore around unhindered—no matter the location.

Carl inherited his father's height. Even in a sitting position, he resembled a column—capped with a face chiseled in a scowl. His aquiline nose elongated his face, slenderized his lips, and made his eyes squint into slits. This long head was covered with red hair, streaked with gray and perfectly parted down the middle—groomed against any attempt to muss it. There was, in his shoulders, a broadness that seemed unnatural: he was not a muscular man, but shoulders that resembled armor framed his chest. No matter the weather, he always wore a suit that fit like wet sheets on a clothesline. His constant grimace was perhaps caused by his belt's tightness— despite which he was constantly tugging upward, fearing his pants would fall. This gesturing produced pinched pleats in his trousers and kept him in perpetual agitation against himself. Very little moved him to peace or contentment other than his satisfaction in making others feel small in his presence. Hence, the best company he kept was his own.

The evening's coolness, the sky's clearness, and the jasmine's fragrance reminded him of longed-for peace. After twenty-seven years, his fear was that he had allowed Kebbi too much latitude, trusted him too much, and defended him too often. Colfax whites

3

had lost their patience. In worsening economic times, whites had no will to lose control *and* money. For most, these were the same. Avery's curse spurred Carl's adherence *and* threatened his standing.

As he stubbed out his cigarette on the porch railing, he watched the moon's lazy rising—the same lazy moon that had accompanied him, the previous night, when he had knocked on Kebbi's front door. As if giving an order, he said, "I know it's late, but we need to talk."

Kebbi stepped onto the porch and closed the door. His body hardened at the sight of Carl, who always read this anger-ridden face as on the verge of rage. Carl heard voices inside the house.

Conversations with Kebbi were always short. He began, "They know what you're planning for tomorrow night. Get out of Colfax before you get killed like your daddy. You fucking insist on making pigs squeal around here. Think of your boy. You can't win, and people have had enough."

"Maybe we can't *win*, but we *can* fight. One day, we might win. Don't know about no plans. Go now, Carl."

Even standing below Kebbi, Carl was eye-to-eye with his enemy. Still, Kebbi felt his position on *his* porch gave him power. He peered into Carl's eyes. Maybe for the first time, Carl noticed just how black Kebbi was, how perfect his white teeth were, and how brilliant his eyes. Although Carl would deny it, there was intelligence and beauty in this man that was unquestionable. His muscled body was an outward sign of the strength within. Even the fullness of his lips seemed formed by a power bent on creating perfection. Around Carl, such lips functioned not for smiles but for tightness ready to spew hatred when provoked. It could not be ignored that Kebbi possessed an astounding representation of Africa in color, strength, and hot energy. His masculinity diminished Carl's, who appeared whimpering in Kebbi's presence. Carl's focus was how bull-like Kebbi appeared—this notion invigorated by Kebbi's anger, always expressed in a loud air-filled snort.

With meekness subduing him and rage pushing him, Carl had walked away in an envelope of tension. Hearing Kebbi's door slam signified an inevitability. He thought, *Nigger, you'll die like your daddy. His curse will curse your stinking life. Your nigger son will pay for what you stole.* Peace proved impossible if Kebbi would not leave Colfax. Carl determined that to release himself from the curse demanded Kebbi's death. He also knew that recovering the stolen money was impossible in the current climate. He vowed to deal with that later and cautioned himself, *One step at a time.*

He left Kebbi's house and his contempt directed him headlong into the quarters to Ike Singleton's. Two weeks earlier, after the bank had declined his mortgage application, Ike had begged Carl for a loan to buy the place he rented for his blacksmith shop. Carl refused to loan him the money then, knowing Ike remained allied to Kebbi. Fueled by Kebbi's arrogance, he thought, *Ike's a desperate nigger with the right kind of collateral. He'll talk.* That very night, Ike Singleton had unwittingly signed for the loan with Kebbi's blood.

On the moonlit porch, Carl recalled his history with Kebbi. He never believed him to be honest; it was hard for anyone like him to survive by honesty. He could suffer dishonesty if Kebbi had not made public his malicious and uppity ways. He had given him acres to farm, a small house, and a reasonable sharecropper's rent that some thought too generous. Kebbi had, in Carl's view, abused this generosity by denouncing the rent as equivalent to enslavement. If the argument had been kept between them, there might have been some reconciliation. Kebbi, however, used the rent as a cause to unite all black tenant farmers to demand livable terms for the lands they farmed.

If that had been the only problem Kebbi caused, Carl might have been able to endure. Kebbi, however, renewed his appetite for resistance with any perceived gain. When Carl had had enough ridicule from his peers, he strategized that it would be best to send Kebbi away for a time. The family pecan business in southern Louisiana presented an opportunity. Hébert Bellocq had provided a contact who was interested in buying enough pecan trees to create a grove. The client was also willing to pay for the installation, for which Kebbi was perfect. Carl hired a lawyer to draft the contract that was agreed to by all sides. Even with his suspicions against Carl, Kebbi agreed to perform his part of the bargain, including collecting and returning cash payments to Carl. When he returned from the installation to Colfax, bloody and injured, without any money, Carl faced a barrier he could not cross. Kebbi claimed that he had almost lost his life, having been robbed of all the money he was carrying.

Carl was forced to lie to convince whites that Kebbi had *not* stolen his money. He also repeated what he knew to be Kebbi's lie that white trash outlaws had robbed him. This only fueled the town's anger. These lies bolstered Kebbi's lust for power and money. Limits were dangerously tested and ignored because Carl's fear gave continuous life to Avery's curse. Carl tried to hide his trepidation, but Kebbi sniffed it and made it a weapon. Whites' suspicion against Carl was fortified with Kebbi's frequent and public agitation in the black part of town.

Kebbi also pressed limits by organizing blacks to demand higher wages, land ownership, and, their right to vote. Black Colfax made Kebbi their leader, and whites depended on Carl to manage this because the Kellers had owned the Barjones as slaves. Yet, the present warred with the past, and peace was always on the brink of fracture. In fact, Kebbi was gaining control over Carl. Both knew that they had reached a line that only one winner could cross. Kebbi's recent plotting against white farmers was the last test of their fictional trust. Carl, therefore, feigned protection for Kebbi whose banishment or death he wished for and planned.

Nagged by anticipation, Carl sat, equestrian-like, smoking till he heard a horse in a gallop approaching his house. He reached in his suit pocket for a fold of bills fastened with a rubber band. The henchman was winded and stood on the bottom step. Before he could report anything, Carl held up his hand to silence him, handed him the money, and turned away. The rider pocketed the money and faded into the night. He stared at the moonlit pines in a deep cast of yellow. *The curse and Kebbi are dead.* Too hungry to sit longer, he headed inside, ate leftover Easter capon, and went to bed. He hoped to sleep peacefully, something he craved since he pulled twelve-year-old Kebbi from behind a tombstone twenty-seven years earlier.

By midnight, all black neighborhoods were swallowed up by a terrifying silence. Meffre, Kebbi's son, hid in the crawl space under the house. He shivered with April's chilly dampness and the prospect that his father had been killed. He waited there for over an hour until the slow thudding of an approaching horse startled him. He knew that the rider was Ossi, the Choctaw, who would bring dreaded news and carry him on a long journey to southern Louisiana.

Straight Smoke and Noise

July 1900

THE PIPE SMOKE ASCENDED in a straight line, not a whit of air moving it. Femme sat in uneasy stillness. Dragging her rocker across the garret to its far corner, she yearned for just a whoosh of air. As she inhaled deeply and blew smoke toward the old oak shading the house's north end, she caught how quickly the rocker had stopped when she picked up the chicken crate table for her lemonade and pipe holder. Men and boys walked home up and down the footpath from the Coulon lumber mill and sugarcane or strawberry fields. She thought of Pichon and Percie, Aunt Velma's twins, as she fixed on the pipe and its matching holder. They had made them for her. The insipid stillness returned to control the pipe smoke, reforming its line more rigidly than before. She thought, *Too much stillness; noise is coming.*

The peace fled as quickly as her thought. In quick but gentle movements, the old oak awakened. Femme drew on her pipe and smiled, saying, "Eshu, that oak has no bother for you. What do you see?"

The oak went still. She set her pipe down as wavy smoke reached upward and wiggled away. The chickens pecking near the magnolia looked up and fell back to their scratching. A fat pig raised her head from a pine's narrow shade and found too much sun in her eyes. With a grunt, she sighed and fell asleep again. Except for the oak, stillness returned. When the oak stirred again, and no other tree moved, she suspected that Eshu was at work.

Femme stood. "Eshu, just tell me." Then, she heard, *New boy.* She laughed heartily. "You're teaching that oak tricks? Don't know how y'all do it, but we need men for babies. Anyway, I'm too hungry for riddles. Let me check my lima beans. Those two-legged bother-ations are on their way—ass and face as usual."

As she turned to go inside, the oak blasted agitation, and Labas, the beagle, bayed loudly. It was such an unusual commotion that Femme waited until the rustling stopped. Eshu repeated, *New boy.*

The oak waved its branches westward, and she thought, *Albion would understand.* She remembered her father reading this tree's movements. Silence was necessary, thoughts unimportant. "Daddy, what does Eshu want? This puzzling can't be about me."

After adding ham chunks to her bean pot, she sat on the porch until the oak's movement stopped, the stillness returned, and Eshu whispered, *New boy.* She muttered her father's orisha mantra, "Accept in silence." With her hands on her hips, she muttered, "The twins are late. Five more minutes, and they'll eat alone."

After ten minutes, it was time to check the lima beans again. From the kitchen, she spied Pichon and Percie coming through the side barn gate. It was clear why folks called them the mismatched twins. Pichon was tall, slender, and muscular. Percie was short, plump, round all over, and two shades lighter than his brother. Percie trotted behind, trying to compete with Pichon's long strides. They intended to sneak up on Femme, but she frightened them by standing right behind them.

"Why y'all in my yard?"

"Jesus-and-a-half, Miss Femme! Wednesday lima beans called us." Pichon sighed and nudged Percie to say something else. Percie kept his eyes fixed on the ground.

"Well, they ain't done yet," she lied, "and you two need a bath. Smelling like rotten chicken skins and whiskey. Don't put your feet on my garret. Come back when you're respectable. And, don't mess up Aunt Velma's house. . . ."

Percie had already made his way toward the barn, laughing and taking off his shirt and shoes as he ran. Pichon said boldly, "We'll be back for those beans."

Dusk turned into night and, after eating her dinner alone, Femme sat praying to Eshu. The fat pig's squealing startled her. She also heard a male voice. Then, Labas set to barking as an afterthought. *They're not back that quick.*

After five quiet minutes, Femme was certain it was not the twins. She opened the big drawer under the table and felt for her pistol. A dim light grew brighter in the barn loft. Labas barked incessantly now, and she heard commotion. Horses neighed. The cow beckoned gently to her calf. The chickens scattered and clucked. The old, confused rooster crowed.

She put the pistol on the table and pulled a thin piece of kindling from the wood bucket. Peering out of the window toward the barn, she opened the stove and thrust it in to disturb the embers. At the sink, she pumped a glass of water. She prayed: "Eshu, fire for candles." The embers awakened with a pop and a deep orange glow. The kindling match threw up a flame, and Femme, with fire and water, stepped into her bedroom.

She lit candles in a tangle of moves and approached the oratory in the spare bedroom's eastern corner. Yellow candlelight revealed two wooden statues with gifts at their feet. She bowed slightly to each. With a wide smile and lungs full of air, she said, "Yemanja. Water for you. I need your hands in mine. Show me how to be steady with this pistol—if I have to be." Femme eyed the water, which remained still. She chanted, "Yemanja. Yemanja. Life in Yemanja." She smiled and held her arms open around the oratory. Its heavy doors, always open, allowed her to rest her arms while she prayed. She stopped suddenly as the water rippled. She smiled again, putting camellia petals at the base of Eshu's statue. Heavy footsteps dragging across the garret pulled her back to the kitchen. She picked up the pistol and sat at the table.

Ossi stood at the front door and looked in and then down at the blood on his clothes. They stared at each other long enough for her to feel that no danger dwelled behind his peaceful eyes. Still, she kept the gun in plain view. He smiled an awkward assurance, and she walked to the screened door.

"Please, you *must* come to him. In the barn," he said, pointing without much emotion.

Femme said without fear, "You *must* bring *him* in here."

"We're looking for Mr. Lucien Coulon, but first we got to get someone to tend to a bad cut in the boy's leg."

"Then he needs a bed. Fetch him." Ossi left running. Femme pumped a pot of water and set it on the stove. She threw wood into its belly and watched the fire's color change with loud, happy chatter as if in celebration.

Ossi returned with Meffre. Femme said invitingly, "Oh, now. Who are you? Come in." She turned to go to the bedroom and thought: *Yemanja, my hands need you. And water. And the twins.* Meffre stood like a stone guardian beside Ossi. Deep sadness spread across his face as he mumbled his name. Ossi held him and guided him toward Femme, who said, "This way." Meffre limped—his right leg a burden.

Ossi helped him to the bed. Femme approached them with a handful of towels, Meffre's face awash with fear. Still, he tendered a weak smile. He held his leg and suppressed a cry, focused on Ossi and what he carried. Femme noticed the valise. "Meffre holds this close. Please, save it for him." He focused on Meffre's bloody pants, and Femme followed his eyes.

Before Ossi left, she asked, "Were two stinky boys sleeping in that barn?"

"No. But, I saw two boys raking pine straw around a house not far on the footpath. They watched us long and hard as we rolled by in our rig."

"If you can find either one or both, I need them. Tell them Femme said to go get Aunt Velma in my buckboard. Scare them to make them move fast." Ossi turned to go. Femme had a thought. "Actually, tell them the lima beans are almost gone." Ossi nodded.

Femme turned to Meffre. "First, we have to change those clothes and clean you. I'll get a nightshirt. We need hot water. Can you manage?"

"Big slice in my leg, but I'll try, miss."

She spun around the kitchen, gathering hot water and more towels. She returned to find Meffre, dressed in the nightshirt, under the sheets with his right leg exposed. He studied how delicate her face was, full of prettiness. The pain abruptly pulled his thoughts elsewhere. His whimpering caught her attention as she gently wrapped a warm wet towel over the wound. "I hope you're hungry. I have lots of experience with hungry men. Aunt Velma's coming. She's a midwife. When we can't get a doctor, we call her."

Meffre's eyes filled unexpectedly. Femme said softly, "It must hurt really bad. Let me put a pillow under your leg." His face loosened. "Better?"

"Yes, my leg ain't so stiff now. Thank you." She followed his eyes as he looked to the foot of the bed. With barely enough breath, he said, "That valise is the promise made to Daddy by Mr. Lucien Coulon."

Femme's surprise was evident in her fidgeting. "I know Mr. Lucien Coulon very well. We call him Papa Luc. I'll put the valise here where you can see it. As soon as Aunt Velma comes, we'll clean and bandage you up." She gently washed his face and hands, trying to avoid moving his leg. There were small abrasions all over him, and the towel covered a deep and long diagonal cut. Meffre withstood Femme's washing with only the slightest movement.

Labas barked at mysterious sounds. Aunt Velma treaded up the garret, knocked on the front door, and rustled into the kitchen. She was a tall but thin, chocolate-colored woman, who always seemed hot. She moved constantly, but she moved slowly and deliberately. She was reputed to be one of the best cooks and seamstresses in Lacombe. However, no praise came her way for how she dressed. Gossips had it that she wore a broadcloth uniform of unattractive solid colors too dark for her. On special occasions she wore stripes or tiny flowers on a dark background. Her signature accessory was a headband she covered in fabric matching her dress. It held back her shock of thick curly hair. Her apron was always impeccably white and starched. She marched to the bedroom, set a big leather bag down, and walked back out to the garret. There, she yelled obscenities at Labas, asked Jesus's forgiveness, and returned. Labas ran under the house, growling.

Aunt Velma was in the mood for fussing. The twins had not worked steadily in some time, which meant misery controlled her house. "I need quiet for this kind of work. Jesus help this child if *you're* taking up nursing. Move," she ordered Femme. Aunt Velma studied Meffre's eyes. She kicked the dirty and bloody clothes under the bed and immediately assessed the wound. Femme went to the kitchen.

"I got more hot water out here!"

"Who *is* this child, Femme? And why my boys all in a hurry and can't talk civil? Didn't say a word to Papa Luc. Lawd today: look at this." She rushed to the door and called Femme with her hands. "I'll take care of cleaning this, but you got to get that jackass doctor in here tonight or tomorrow early. He needs stitching. Bring the water."

"We won't fight tonight," Femme insisted. "I've only known the sight of these people for two good hours. You know nearly as much as I do."

"Hmm! Sorry, cher. My damn no-count boys make me bossy. Nervous today, and now more so for this child. Lawd." She glared at Femme and remembered how she had called her a "pretty sassy wench" when, just after her daddy died, she had stood up to Papa Luc

11

over how the chicken business should be run. She warned Femme that men get riled when questioned. Femme responded with a grunt. Aunt Velma admired this independence, and it was the start of their connection as family—a tight, unsaid connection they depended on. Because her house was within walking distance of Femme's, Aunt Velma entrusted her with watching out for Percie and Pichon. She kissed Femme, holding her shoulders firmly and letting her eyes say the rest. She went to Meffre, wiped his forehead, and slowly washed the wounds. Meffre gritted his teeth and moaned. Then, he blurted out, "Mama! Daddy. Help me. Jesus. Eshu."

Hearing the mention of Eshu, Femme went to the oratory. She smiled at Yemanja's statue and put it in her apron pocket. Returning, she found Aunt Velma unwrapping the last layer of the large, bloody bandage. "Holy Joseph, the carpenter, give me strength." Femme brought water from the oratory and poured it into a roasting pot of clean water. Throwing suspicious looks at Femme, Aunt Velma smiled and muttered, "African holy water. Lawd today." She carefully cleaned and redressed the largest wound. Femme gave Meffre a small glass of brandy. When he finished, Aunt Velma sat next to him and held him. Finally, Meffre became quiet in her arms. He fell into a snoring, deep sleep.

They moved quietly to the kitchen. Aunt Velma stood, lips tight, arms folded. She said, "I seen this kind of healing shit before. One time, Percie came home with a twig bandage. He'd been crabbing with Julien Broyard and somehow sliced his finger bad. A Choctaw woman, down the bayou, put twigs under a rag and wrapped it tight. Fucking Choctaw women. They try to help. God bless them. But hell, twigs and herbs and shit in an open cut? Jesus and St. Jude, help this child." Her eyes were damp and shiny.

"Devil did a dance on him, but a Choctaw brought him here."

"I don't know, cher. Sometimes Choctaws give me gas. Maybe a sip of brandy will help."

After an hour, Femme and Aunt Velma became certain that Meffre would sleep through the night. Ossi, Percie, and Pichon remained in the kitchen eating their second bowl of lima beans and rice. Ossi had pushed the ham aside. Femme came to the kitchen with soiled towels and Meffre's bloody clothes. Ossi jumped to his feet; the twins did not budge. "That Choctaw was hungry for lima beans. He don't like good meat," Percie said, eyeing the ham hocks.

"Percie! Pump me two buckets of water to soak these towels. Burn the clothes. That'll keep your mind busy," Femme said, never taking her eyes off him. He meandered toward the pump still fully engaged with the last of his beans. Pichon eyed the ham hocks. She smiled at Ossi. "You don't eat meat?"

He looked up with outright confidence. "Don't care for any tonight, miss."

"When you're finished, check on our sleeping boy." Ossi ate slowly, eyeing the door. When he finished, Femme said invitingly, "See for yourself: a swig of brandy's got him sleeping soundly." She glared at Pichon, who had snatched the meat off Ossi's plate and was heading out the door grinning.

Aunt Velma stepped aside as Ossi entered. "He's calm now but needs a doctor to stitch that big cut. I wrapped it tight, but that won't hold but till overnight. Don't wake him." Ossi moved quietly, leaving the door ajar. Aunt Velma looked at him, then at Femme, and then at Meffre.

Femme whispered, "He brought him here. Asked for help with his leg and said they're looking for Papa Luc. That's all I know."

Aunt Velma frowned and said slowly, "That boy's sick. He's done bled like a stuck pig in August. I don't like all this in your house. Papa Luc won't either."

Femme bristled. "I got up this morning without this, and I'm going to bed with it." She regretted that her tone was too direct and might offend. She also feared how Hébert could manage to make this episode grow arms and legs to spread a vicious version of it around town.

"Like I said, I don't need to know. But I can tell you right now, you better send for that jackass Hébert or you'll need Father Lorquette. That poor ass . . . I mean that poor soul is lucky he ain't fucking dead. Got to go. Papa Luc won't pay me till Saturday. Can you send a ham or three chickens to tide me over? The twins feed like a school of croakers."

"They can pass by tomorrow. Thanks, my friend. Pichon! Percie! Come take your mama to Papa Luc's and tell him I need him and Dr. Bellocq here early tomorrow."

Aunt Velma sipped the last of her brandy and headed for the porch. "Yeah. The old porker's the only doctor you can get quick. Let's go, boys."

13

"He's a spy. With Papa Luc here, Hébert won't cross me." Femme nervously ushered Aunt Velma and the twins out. They mounted the buckboard and drove slowly toward Lake road. Ossi went to the barn to sleep, and Femme turned to the oak. "So, 'new boy.' Eshu, you've been pushing good on bad and bad on good. I puzzled out your meaning." She flopped into her porch rocker and lit her pipe.

✝ ✝ ✝

The past invaded her present on such evenings. Her father, who lived on slavery's borders, told vivid stories. Few had known her mother; she died giving birth to Femme. Until she was sixteen, she and her father had lived in New Orleans. The Sisters of the Holy Family schooled her well, infusing her education with the Catholic catechism; her father taught her to talk to African Vodun orishas.

From Yorubaland, he claimed that he freed himself in America. When full of Muscadine wine, he prattled on nostalgically about his capture and enslavement on a ship bound for Salvador, Bahia. All versions featured a French merchant who swore he never bought or sold slaves. He shipped goods and provided transport for all kinds of cargo. He never interrogated his ships' captains. He only used paid laborers wherever and however he found them. How clients or captains got their laborers had, he said, nothing to do with him. This Frenchman, named Labat, owned cargo ships that trafficked from Africa, to Brazil, and to New Orleans.

Femme's father maintained that he was intent on escaping, but he met a woman from Angola—the escape was postponed. They lived together till they sold her and took her to Rio de Janeiro. Any reminiscence of Salvador included descriptions of "wretchedness," for there he lost his love and was sold—despite Labat's protest—to a slaver named Albion, bound for Louisiana. From Salvador, he spent months curing his shackle wounds until he boarded a Mississippi River steamer. This story changed slightly on every telling, but the common refrain was that during a sudden murderous storm, he plunged into the river before it turned northward past the crescent in New Orleans. Muddy rocks, with which he blended naturally, sheltered him. He ambled along the rocks just below the French Quarter and waited till nightfall. Then, the orisha Yemanja led him—through a cleansing rain—to the market, where scattered

14

crates of half-rotten fruit provided his first meal in American freedom. That day, he named himself Albion Labat. After menial work loading, unloading, and carrying fruit, he found a job making cigars on St. Peter's Street. The owner, an old, sickly French naval officer, sold them in his Vieux Carré shop. When he died, he left the shop to Albion, surprising him and other shop owners. Owning property made him the target of poor Créoles and newly arrived Europeans, especially the Irish, who looted his shop constantly. He met and married Femme's mother, who worked in an antique store on Royal Street. He lived in the upstairs living quarters of the cigar shop and needed a bed. His neighbor, the owner of the cutler shop next door, referred him to the shop where "pretty and petite" Zoie Payée was a clerk. He bought the first bed she showed him with the proviso that she would go to dinner or lunch with him. Their eventual courting, much to Albion's dismay, was done mostly at Sunday Mass and lunch in the Vieux Carré. After two years, Zoie gave Albion a beautiful daughter at the expense of her life. He raised Femme alone with the help of the Sisters of the Holy Family at John Birchman's orphanage and school.

When Papa Luc happened into the cigar shop one day, he and Albion became friends as Papa Luc mentioned selling a chicken-and-egg farm in Lacombe. Albion sold the cigar shop and settled in Lacombe. Femme watched attentively and learned the business from her father and Papa Luc. She also visited the Coulon mansion, where she met Alinnie (Papa Luc's wife) and Aunt Velma (their cook). The mansion was on a stretch of thirty acres adjacent to the meager three her father owned, but Albion was content to protect and provide for Femme there. He lived three more years and left Femme an auspicious future, the pledge of Papa Luc's protection, and a solid grounding in her African heritage. Femme allowed that this history's truth rested with the Vodun orishas.

At first, Femme was apprehensive about running a chicken farm. For a while, Papa Luc cared for daily operations—an unintended result of which was her frequent, inquisitive visits to the Coulon place. Papa Luc preached that inside knowledge of Lacombe was critical for protecting her interests and ensuring her success. Her inquisitiveness annoyed Papa Luc—especially questions about the farm's revenue. Yet, Papa Luc always acquiesced, believing this was his obligation to Albion. Femme had never forgotten the conversation they had had in her presence. Albion asked, too servile for Femme's liking, that Papa Luc promise to protect his daughter's interests. "You have my word that I'll watch over the girl and chicken farm. I'll make sure she's protected," Papa Luc had said, looking directly at Femme.

Albion was already frail, but his mind was on Femme's future. He said, "You know his secret. Keep it as long as his promise holds." Femme perceived that Papa Luc was only mildly annoyed. He ended the conversation with: "Well then, she's got a way to keep me honest."

Femme thought her independence required breaking free from Papa Luc. She learned, however, that such a breach was futile and at cross-purposes with the reality of existing as a young black woman in rural Louisiana. Too often, gossip circulated that luck followed young women who could pique the interest of men like Papa Luc. Femme fumed: "Luck will never play that plaçage game with me." Over the years, she also realized Papa Luc's sole interest in her was his steadfast obligation to protect her. She came to believe that even the secret was insurance but never a wedge between them. This was tested once when Papa Luc had tried to exert authority over her. It had started with her decision to sell chickens and eggs from her barn rather than just through delivery.

Papa Luc had heard about this through one of his clients. He rode over to Femme's in a huff and, without getting off his horse, shouted, "What you doing, girl? Having people buying produce from your barn and front gate will have all kinds of folks trafficking around your property. Your daddy never wanted this. You're a single woman inviting trouble—"

Femme held up her hand to stop the tirade. "Been selling like this for over a month. Business is good. Folks walk down that footpath every day to and from work at your mill or on their way to and from town. I only need one hired hand now to deliver all over Lacombe. This is my new way to more profit. How can you argue with that?"

"I promised your daddy to protect you."

"Then, protect me but let me run my business. Y'all need some eggs or chickens over at the mansion?" Papa Luc left in the same huff he arrived in. Femme had felt comfortable with this small win and hoped that eventually Papa Luc would be proud of her.

When yellow fever gripped Alinnie, Papa Luc suffered immensely. He took little interest in women, except for Aunt Velma, who became responsible not only for cooking but also for caring for their son, Lucien. During this time, Papa Luc's meddling bother-in-law Hébert inserted himself into the Coulon household as an overbearing nuisance. This was a dark period at the Coulon mansion, and Femme had felt an obligation to stand by Papa Luc and Lucien. Alinnie's death yoked Papa Luc and Femme through an empathy linked to losing beloved kin. She recalled one happy moment in all this suffering. Aunt Velma had told her that the Coulon's favorite dessert was crème brûlèe. Femme interrupted their dinner one evening having baked the dessert as a gift to honor Alinnie. "Femme, this is a beautiful gesture," he said with watery eyes. He hugged her, and she did not hesitate to kiss his cheek before moving on to serve the dish. That was the first time she remembered eating at the Coulon table. Although their relationship had been tested occasionally, now, at thirty, Femme trusted Papa Luc fully.

+ + +

The day's busyness brought on fatigue. She went inside to turn off kerosene lamps and ready herself for bed. There was movement where Meffre slept, but she did not disturb him.

Eshu stirred Meffre from a turbulent nightmare. The brandy had numbed his leg's pain. With Eshu's nudging, he willed himself awake and, with wide eyes, he searched through the darkness for the valise.

The Valise

PICHON'S LONG LEGS DRIPPED with sweat when he reached Femme's garret the next morning. He saw a croaker-sack bundle next to the front door and knew he had to carry it to somebody. Settling butt-first on the bottom step, he knew his rest would be short, but he loved sitting in Femme's yard. The live oaks circled her house and provided calming shade and coolness even on the hottest, wettest days. The one magnolia and big sprawling pine seemed out of place in the circle of oaks, but each had a role.

That pine, in the middle of the chicken yard, provided low branches as perches for those who did not sleep in the barn. It also dropped enough pine straw for the barn-nesting house. The old pine did not mind its association with chickens, but it was confounded by a fat pig, which had rooted a hole close to its trunk. When the sun got too hot in the chicken yard, the pig slid, squeaking, under the fence to nap by the oak. At night, she slept in the barn.

The magnolia occupied a special place in the middle of the front yard. It was a people-tree, planted for admiration and, in this, no one was disappointed. It grew perfectly straight and provided an umbrella for shade-loving azaleas and camellias in a garden rarely without bloom. Femme, with the twins' help, saw to that. Pichon admired the begonias and said, "It's hot as the devil's ass today. Y'all got it made in the shade."

"Hey, Pichon. Take this croaker sack home. I put two pullets in there. Didn't have time to clean them. So, y'all get to plucking. Aunt Velma asked for a ham for later in the week. I'm frying fish this evening. Y'all stop by."

Throwing the croaker sack across his shoulder, Pichon asked, "Miss Femme, you know any up-the-bayou girls who might want to wink at a good-looking buck like me?"

"Oh! Smelling yourself, huh? Your mama said you were eyeballing Julien Broyard's girl Charmaine. Those high-yellow ones can be trouble."

"She done changed fast. I saw her creeping down the sawdust pile. Lawd! Everything was moving up and down. Ornery, but pretty. I had to catch my breath—"

"Get out of my yard! Dumb as dirt. What makes you think she'd . . . ?"

Pichon moved quickly. He had grabbed the croaker sack and fled past the magnolia. From this comfortable range, he said over his shoulder, "I think she winked at me."

Femme laughed and said, "Eshu, help him."

All the windows stood open to cool the room for Meffre. Femme tried to move the chamber pot quietly, but her stirring woke him. "Oh, Miss Femme, I wish I could do that."

"Shush. Go back to sleep, doctor's coming." With that, she closed the door.

Her father built the house with many windows to ventilate against Lacombe's heavy heat. With a lake and bayou, tolerating humidity was a daily trial. The windows carried the coolness passing through the oaks and whatever breezes they hurled and chased around the yard. Femme enjoyed that the windows offered views from all sides. Every room opened onto the big porch that girdled the house. With various vantage points and the animals as sentinels, it was nearly impossible for anyone to surprise her.

The kitchen was still cool, and she prepared cabbage, broccoli, and carrots to go with the fish she expected. She had seen Ossi leave with a cane pole at daybreak. She sang through her kitchen routine and enjoyed the quiet that surely would not last.

In a noisemaking flurry, Labas barked, chickens clucked and screeched, the fat pink pig oinked, and horses answered. Femme watched Ossi stride across the yard carrying a sack and cane pole that pulled just enough to reveal his defined muscular arms. He opened the side barn door and let the horses out. The cow and calf followed in a queue that soon unraveled as the horses galloped away. Femme met him on the garret, full of girlishness. She looked up and took note of the comfort in his dark eyes. She could not avoid the contours of his face, shiny with rich gold color and strong with pronounced bones. His thick eyebrows were the only hair on his face, but his head was crowned with jet-black hair that fell down his back. She, at that moment, wondered what it would be like to be gathered up by those arms, broad shoulders, and massive chest. She caught herself staring and purposefully fidgeted with her apron and pretended to bat away mosquitoes.

"Morning. What you got for me? Hot already," she said, noticing his seriousness.

"That bayou could use a good flooding. Only caught croakers, but they're big enough to filet," he asserted, his eyes fixed intentionally on the sack. In side glances, he caught the natural contrast between her deep brown skin and her exquisite smile. Her thin lips formed a tiny, pursed mouth that betrayed the strength in her voice. He liked how she moved her petite frame with ease. She stood a full head shorter than he, and he had to lower his eyes to meet hers, which he was trying to avoid.

Femme liked him, warmed by his presence and enticed by his easy questioning. He held the fish sack gift-like. "I never knew a croaker I couldn't murder in a skillet. Any way you send them will do. I see you ate the gift I left you."

"Oh! Thank you. I ate your gift and brought gifts back." He raised the sack and smiled.

He turned to go, and Femme interrupted him. "On second thought, please filet them. There's a pump and trough back there for cleaning fish. I keep the leavings in a big bucket of water for my azaleas and camellias."

He did not slow his stride but turned his head slightly. "I washed there last night and this morning." Femme thought, *He knows my place after just one night? Yemanja's welcoming him.*

Meffre cried out and arrested her attention. She bolted through the house and found him with his fists balled up. His breathing was erratic; his eyes were weak and red. "Meffre, I'm sorry. Dr. Bellocq's coming soon. You asked for Eshu last night. Call on him to run the pain out." She sensed that Meffre was losing his will to fight. He fell back on the pillow, gasping and looking at the ceiling.

Femme picked up a tiny bowl of water from the oratory. "Yemanja, let this water in against the pain." She washed his face, which seemed to calm him.

An hour later, the yard exploded with voices and roaring animal chatter, especially Labas. She could hear Ossi talking. She saw Papa Luc and Hébert making their separate ways toward the house. To her surprise, Lucien followed them. He was as tall as Papa Luc and walked with the same confidence.

Papa Luc and Hébert said "Morning, Femme" simultaneously. Papa Luc made way for Hébert to enter. Ossi stood on the porch until Femme waved him in. He went immediately to the farthest corner of the kitchen and looked out of the window toward the pasture. She invited Lucien in.

"Femme, very busy, so can't stay long," said Papa Luc, frowning.

"Take your hats off; y'all making my house poor." Femme pointed to the bedroom. "Aunt Velma washed and cleaned his wounds last night. She said he needs stitching and thinks there's an infection. He's really weak." Femme directed Hébert to the bedroom.

"Let me see. Privately, please," Hébert ordered. He patted his chest and belched. He was overweight and bald—the potbellied sort of man who gasped with the slightest activity. His horn-rimmed spectacles provided little assistance as he struggled to get his girth on a straight course. He wore only white long-sleeved shirts that barely covered his bulk. The most useless accessory in his attire was a wide-buckle belt. His pants hung just below his protruding navel as if glued there. The zipper never made it to the top of his pants, and he feared any fix for this would result in a disastrous pop that would be far too exposing. A bulbous strawberry nose betrayed any attempt to hide that damnation waited for him, earned by sinful fixations in gluttony for food and liquor. He was a quarrelsome man, who had never acquired a healer's temperament. Worst of all, he was a shameless gossip, an interfering nuisance, who was connected to Lacombe's most nefarious citizens.

Femme turned to Papa Luc, who followed her. "I know you don't want to talk in front of Hébert. Stop here and listen: the Choctaw brought that poor boy here. All I know is his daddy told him to find *you*. I don't know how he's been hurt. He's too weak to talk much, and the Choctaw says even less. I didn't want Hébert in my house with all this—"

Papa Luc mustered an agitated smile and said, "Femme, he's an ass-ache, but looks like you need him. Anyway, I don't know these people." He put his hat on, pulled it off, and finally hung it on the back of a chair. He did not look at Femme. Instead, he poured himself a glass of lemonade he did not want.

Femme squinted, and Papa Luc regretted his sharp tone. He put the glass down, took her arm and said, "Don't get miffed. I'm just picking at you. Hébert ain't never gonna get along with you or Aunt Velma. I'm always insulting him and telling him to go home to Small House, but he pops up all the time. Anyway, I'm busy today. The sawmill and the produce stand in Mandeville are giving me grief." He pushed his hands in his pockets and asked, "Where y'all from?" Lucien flinched and Ossi turned around slowly.

Although he and Papa Luc stood equal in height, Ossi seemed to dwarf him. He stretched out his massive arms bearlike and cracked his neck and back. He stepped slightly forward and spoke directly to Papa Luc. "Colfax."

Papa Luc's face turned stony. "Well, there's some confusion about any business with me. Don't remember any coloreds or Choctaws from Colfax."

Ossi moved closer to Papa Luc and said, "He'll tell you. If not, I will."

Knowing Papa Luc's fixation on protecting her, Femme slid between them, facing Ossi. She looked into his eyes. "We owe Meffre some peace. Let's drink lemonade. Papa Luc, sit and rest your nerves."

Ossi moved back to the window, and Femme poured lemonade. Papa Luc drank in sips after turning his chair to the front door. "Told you I'm busy, Femme."

Ossi whispered to Femme, "I've got a trough to clean." Lucien followed him out and sat on the porch, biting his fingernails.

"Now listen. You promised Daddy you'd look after me and mine. This is me and mine time." He fanned his hat in her direction. She smiled and asked, "How's Hébert doing with Lucien? Aunt Velma says he's been showing up to help the boy find Jesus."

Papa Luc stretched out a frowning smile. "Oh! Femme, my house is a mess of shouts right now. Hébert don't approve of Lucien's drinking and taking off to New Orleans. Lucien says he ain't looking for Jesus or a wife, and that sets Hébert to fretting. I never should've asked Hébert to come here."

Papa Luc knew that from the start, there was competition. Hébert had imagined Lucien as Sacred Heart's organist; Aunt Velma had taught him blues songs to play on the piano. Hébert really feared that Lucien was absorbing Aunt Velma's culture. He refused to accept that she had won Lucien's soul with the blues. Too often had he found her dancing with the boy, way to close for his approval.

Once, he had even scolded her, in the name of Jesus, about teaching Lucien to shake like a devil. That scene was made worse when he caught Lucien mocking him to incite Aunt Velma to laugh uncontrollably. Papa Luc had to intervene. Thinking about this caused the tightness in Papa Luc's lips to slacken, and Femme had a lot to ask him but was also relieved to see Percie sprinting past the gate.

"Mama sent this tonic for that boy. Morning, Papa Luc." He paused, looked down. "Mama said I'm looking for a job." Papa Luc laughed and nodded in Percie's direction. He looked at the tonic bottle he held out for Femme to take. When she did, he left quickly on his short legs.

Femme offered, "Tell him to stay at Small House or down with Pike drinking at Mudbug's. Hébert *and* Aunt Velma are too big a mule for one man to whip."

Papa Luc nodded. A satisfied smile beautified Femme's oval face, and this set his weakness for her in motion. She moved closer. "At least, let's keep *our* peace." She stroked his face and kissed the top of his head.

Eshu shook the oak, and Papa Luc's two-sided heart fluctuated: full of love for Alinnie, who was now a memory; full of regret for not being firmer with Hébert by putting him out of his life sooner. He tolerated Hébert because he was the only family Lucien had. He finished his lemonade and stood as Hébert puffed his way out of the bedroom, full of disgust and belching loudly.

"Femme, that dumb boy wants to talk to you and Luc. Did what I could. He won't let me stitch that lash any tighter. He's got a nasty infection and talking won't stop it from spreading. Won't take medicine. Won't cooperate. I'm done."

Hébert went to the sink, washed his hands, and headed for the porch. Papa Luc seemed to want to protest, but Femme guided him to the bedroom, which held the heavy air of sickness and sadness. The sight of Meffre filled Papa Luc's face with pity. Femme shoved him gently to the footboard. He had no will against such suffering.

"Where's Ossi?" Meffre asked.

Femme looked out of the window. "They're coming now. He cleaned some fat croakers for dinner. Sit, Papa Luc."

Ossi and Lucien appeared in the doorway. Lucien bit his fingernails and slid next to Papa Luc. Ossi stopped Femme at the door and said, "I don't think that man is going to believe us. The son is good, but the father is angry and doesn't know why."

Femme whispered, "Papa Luc is good man through and through. He can't show who he really is around this town. That makes him *seem* angry. Now, Meffre is all our worry." Ossi stared at her, and she interpreted his gaze as disapproval. He, however, put her at ease by nodding approvingly.

Meffre sat upright to accommodate his pain. He found some comfort in Lucien's smile as opposed to Ossi's eyes moving from the bed to floor in jerky glances. Femme, suspicious of Hébert's eavesdropping, closed the bedroom door. She moved near the bed's edge and gave Meffre a nod to start. With a whimpering voice and eyes fixed on Lucien's smiling face, Meffre told the story of his last days in Colfax:

Three Saturdays before Easter, Kebbi had yelled enough to send chickens flying and the devil running. His fury raised the same kind of tornado when Meffre's mother died from an illness they called "bad blood." The house was only quiet when Ossi came to bring food and check on Meffre. This latest rage was over how turncoat blacks had informed Carl Keller of Kebbi's plan to lead a work boycott for full wages. Carl paid blacks to spy on Kebbi, and their fear was betrayal's price. Soon afterward, Kebbi had seen Carl coming to town from the river. Carl scolded him and warned that by Easter, "dead niggers gonna be as common as floating river mullets."

Meffre had asked about his father's plan. Kebbi had a dog-mad look in his eyes and told Meffre, "They fear blacks going north to work. They lose us. They lose profit. We gonna fight. I ain't picking cotton; you ain't neither. Nobody gonna pick cotton or cut cane for free."

The next day, Ossi warned that he heard there was going to be trouble if black people kept up secret meetings. Kebbi knew this and told Meffre about Luc Coulon in Lacombe and plans for Ossi to escort him. He emphasized that Coulon would remember he had planted his pecan grove and promised help if he needed to leave Colfax. He gave Meffre the leather valise as proof of the promise.

Kebbi woke irritable the next day, Easter Sunday, because his daddy died on that day. Meffre went to church and returned to find Ossi and Kebbi standing roadside. Mass was short; only a dozen parishioners attended. At home, Meffre and Ossi could tell Kebbi was dog-mad again. He sat on the porch waiting in a quiet that made everyone nervous—like scared spiders before a flood.

Around sunset, Kebbi went to town and returned soon. His face was full of worry. He spoke softly to Ossi to ensure, that if anything happened to him, Ossi would take Meffre out of Grant Parish to a Choctaw village on the Red River and then to Lacombe. He grabbed the leather valise, put money in it, and secured everything they had worth stealing in a wooden chest. He put clothes in a croaker sack and gave Meffre firm instructions where to hide. With the buckboard loaded, Kebbi embraced Meffre and got on his horse. That's the last time they saw him.

At two in the morning, Ossi drove south on the Red River Road with horses tied to the wagon where Meffre slept. They rode all night till dawn and stayed on the parish border in a Choctaw village. The next day, the news came that Kebbi died fighting. The sheriff had scores of armed white men helping him to shoot all violators. They killed and burned Kebbi's friends publicly in the town square and threw their bodies in the river.

Ossi and Meffre rushed to reload the wagon, knowing they would be followed. They had traveled only three miles when Carl's henchmen arrived. Ossi put one down with a large hunting knife. Another went after Meffre, knocking him down and slashing his leg. He landed on top of Meffre about to cut his throat when Ossi sliced him down like a stalk of sugarcane.

Spent from retelling the ordeal, Meffre gazed pleadingly at Lucien. Lucien smiled and nodded an approving smile. Lucien's blue eyes held Meffre, but his gaze became too large for the small room and its discerning onlookers. Lucien resumed his nail biting, and Meffre turned his eyes to Papa Luc, and through his suffering managed to say, "Mr. Coulon, I've got that valise and your promise. You knew my daddy. Look. There. Your initials."

Papa Luc stared at the old leather valise. He knew it well, for it had been his father's. He remembered Kebbi too, for he had never seen a man work with such pride about perfection. His pecan grove was a sign of that pride. He said, "Those pecan trees matured three years ago. When your daddy was here, he always carried a croaker sack. I went to pay him one day and, out of curiosity, asked why he held that sack so close. He laughed and said it was his past and future because it held his dirty and clean clothes. On his last workday, I gave him that valise for his clothes and promised him help. That was my word, and I am my word. I never met Carl Keller. Hébert put me in contact with Keller's family business in Covington. They sold me the trees your daddy planted."

Papa Luc felt connected to Meffre because their stories grew from the bond of one man's word to another. He knew, however, that Hébert still waited on the porch. He signaled to Lucien that they were leaving. He said, "Well, I've got shipments for New Orleans. I'll come back here as soon as I can. Femme, please tell Percie I want to see him today. I can use him to man the produce stand in Mandeville." He started toward the door, but Femme blocked him. "Not now. I'll be back—soon," he whispered, nodding toward the porch. She moved aside.

Papa Luc walked out and down the steps in a rush, bypassing Hébert without a word. The doctor rushed behind him. "Luc!"

"I got papers to sign in Covington for a shipment to New Orleans."

"What was he telling you? You don't mean to bring more niggers begging in Lacombe, do you? He told me he was from Colfax. Everybody knows the trouble they've had."

"I'm not afraid of my shadow like some people. Stay out of my damn business."

Hébert shouted, "What happened in Colfax could happen here. Did you see that Choctaw? Stone-faced and breeding trouble."

Lucien went straight to mount his horse as his father said, "You charge these poor people double. Then, you sit your fat ass in Sacred Heart, singing and praying with the rest of those hypocritical bastards. Go to hell!" Papa Luc tipped his hat to Femme and rode swiftly away with Lucien.

Hébert struggled to mount his horse and tugged angrily at the reins. He decided to go to Mudbug's to talk to Reginald and to wire Carl later. Femme watched him riding away full of worry for what the infection would do to worsen Meffre's condition. She sat on the steps and prayed to Yemanja for a cleansing rain.

✝ ✝ ✝

The rain Femme prayed for came steadily for the next four days. During this time, the infection had fevered Meffre, and Femme gave him only cold water. They became close enough that he expected her to hold his hand and tell him about her life. He especially enjoyed her stories about Eshu and his tricks. One day, she would have him laughing; the next, he was in too much pain to walk to relieve himself without Ossi's help.

The day the rain stopped, near nightfall, he had weakened and vomited often. The stitches burned. Femme washed his face with water from the oratory. When he revived, she said, "I'm sorry for your people. We've had trouble here but not like that. Papa Luc is a generous man, and I'm glad you told him everything. He'll help you."

Meffre shifted in the bed, groaned, settled back on the pillow, and held out his hand. "Miss Femme, I didn't tell him *everything*. I couldn't. Ossi told me more."

Meffre added that after the pecan trees were delivered, Carl sent Kebbi to design and plant the grove and return with the payment. Kebbi did this work as part of his plan to leave Colfax. At that time, it seemed Carl trusted Kebbi, given they were at peace. But Kebbi never trusted Carl and wanted revenge for his father's death. He invented a story of being robbed along the Red River. Carl sent the law to investigate in every town and Choctaw village along the river. Ossi corroborated Kebbi's story and told the Colfax sheriff that Kebbi was unconscious when they found him. Carl never believed that. He sent letters to Papa Luc but got no response. Carl's kitchen boy destroyed every letter he was ordered to post. Everybody on Carl's place hated him and trusted Kebbi. Even the Créole man in the telegraph office despised Carl. He never sent a word as Carl dictated it. Carl, however, never trusted Kebbi after that. Whites believed Kebbi had betrayed Carl, who was too fearful of blacks and their curses to take revenge.

Nearly seven years later, Kebbi confided in Ossi that he had saved enough money to leave and pay for the trip south to Lacombe. It was around this time that confrontations and rioting in Colfax started. Blacks said they would not pay for freedom they already had. Kebbi refused to pick cotton on premises and moved from Carl's place. Blacks started to claim him as their leader, and eventually this exploded into rebellion.

Meffre's eyes shuddered with the weight of exhaustion. Femme said, "Rest, son. Tomorrow, I'm taking you to a doctor in Abita Springs or Covington."

He closed his eyes and turned his head away. Femme left quietly. She found Pichon and Percie rummaging through a sack of fruit. She startled them. "Who sent me that fruit?"

"Papa Luc," Percie answered. "Pretty pears. Thought we'd test for sweetness."

"Did Papa Luc send a produce shipment to the New Orleans market today? Or, did he go himself."

Percie answered, "Yes, ma'am. Mama said he went on the boat this morning. I helped him load the wagon. And Papa Luc gave me a job running the produce stand at Mandeville pier."

"I didn't know him to make market on a Thursday."

"When summer fruit is ripe, he'll go to market three times a week. He left from Covington," Pichon said, grabbing a pear from Percie.

"I just wanted to be sure he wasn't making excuses today. Seen Ossi?"

Percie had a mouthful of pear. Pichon realized he had to respond. "In the barn tending the horses. Nice horses. I like him. Showed me how to sharpen knives. I invited him to sleep at our house but looks like he wants to stay close to Meffre."

"Well, tell him food will be ready soon."

Femme set the table, fully in conversation with Eshu. *Eshu, whisper the riddles; I'll make them out. And watch those twins, young with old souls. What about Ossi?*

The big pine, the sole magnolia, and all the mossy oaks responded by cooling a damp, hot July breeze and blowing it through the yard. Each tree, in turn, caught the breeze and pitched it to a neighbor until the biggest oak caught it and hurled it gently around Femme's neck, turning her focus to Papa Luc and the pecan grove.

The Pecan Grove

PAPA LUC'S FACE BORE a handsome element, beauteous still with marks of his youth. Age failed to erase the brightness of his azure eyes, the chisel of his nose, the fineness of his lips, or even the glimmer of his shiny teeth. He was built to be a presence, with an imposing muscularity and boulder solidness. Tall and agile, never given to stooping, his gait was a prideful stride. On his horse, he seemed to pose as a statuesque rider ready for an artistic rendering. Yet, for all his visual appeal, he was, when alone especially, the picture of man with firm inner peace and unmovable self-esteem. That is, until the world invaded his peace. After years of volleying, he and Femme marked mutual boundaries to ensure tranquility. He had even accepted Lucien's erratic male behavior, which often brought an anxious joy over which Aunt Velma presided, Papa Luc allowed, and Hébert loathed.

Peaceful survival in Lacombe depended on owning substantial commerce. Most folks simply raised and grew what they ate. That was never his objective, and he intentionally passed his business savvy to Femme. What he raised and grew would, by necessity, sell at market in Covington, New Orleans, and Lacombe. Finding that *one* lucrative commercial commodity motivated the Coulons to experiment in pecans, strawberries, peaches, and, of all things, Muscadine wine. Affording a pecan grove was feasible for only those moneyed like the Coulons.

Papa Luc rarely feared failure because strawberries, for years, had done well enough to enable him to buy more land to invest in pecans. Both sold in local markets and were in demand up the Mississippi as far as Detroit. Peaches and strawberries starved many folks, but Papa Luc made them a profitable sideline by selling them to preserve factories in Georgia and Alabama. The Muscadine wine, however, filled in empty spots consistently at every market. And, there was the lumber mill, the most lucrative and consistent of his holdings. It required only meager oversight from Papa Luc, who hoped it would provide business experience for Lucien, who seemed more interested in drinking Muscadine wine and playing jazz and blues in the bungalow in the pecan grove. Papa Luc taught Lucien the importance of responsibility; yet, he felt obligated to allow his son's youth to thrive. Thus, Lucien enjoyed his father's protection as an inspirational license to play.

At times, however, the peace he enjoyed depended on Papa Luc's taking risks most white men would not venture into. On the very evening that Femme's father died of a consuming cough, he had sat with her and Aunt Velma waiting for the inevitable. Femme had held Albion's hands, praying to Eshu for a peaceful surrender. Aunt Velma said her rosary, and Papa Luc, against all bigoted social protocol, would not leave them. He had remembered holding Alinnie's hands and said to Femme, "They always say stay strong. Last thing you need now is some rule. Feel what's true for you and him." His eyes were shiny, and he pounced his hat from knee to knee.

Femme smiled and went back to praying until she could feel life's retreat from Albion's hands. Papa Luc acknowledged the passing by taking Femme's hands. She placed her head on his chest and closed her eyes, sobbing gently. Aunt Velma closed Albion's eyelids and pulled the sheet up to his neck. Papa Luc's greatest power was found in such moments when his soul swelled with a holy humanity borne from a satisfaction fulfilled in caring for others. That evening held the memory of the embrace of a father and friend. That evening, she loved a man, other than her father, for the first time.

He had already championed fulfilling the promise to Meffre because it was how he invested in the peace he wanted for Lucien and himself. Femme and Aunt Velma questioned that Papa Luc permitted Hébert to have any proximity to the mansion after Alinnie's death, but this too was drawing to its close because Lucien found the meddling fool repugnant. In her present turmoil, Femme's calling on Papa Luc was normal, and Hébert's despicable behavior was just as normal. Soon he would call on Femme to initiate a future for Meffre that would help secure a peace they all longed for.

✝ ✝ ✝

30

Femme took Meffre by stagecoach to Dr. Congete in Covington. He immediately trusted the doctor, who smiled and called him "son." He spoke directly to Meffre, telling him that he was healing too slowly and had to start fighting the infection "like a man." After scrubbing the wound clean, he warned Meffre that his weakness came from the infection, which could only be destroyed fully with prescribed medicine. This visit sparked Eshu's spirit in Meffre. When they returned home, he began to improve and ate with more gusto. Femme sensed this and called on Eshu for strength and Yemanja for creativity to forge the will in Papa Luc to keep his promise. She also thanked the orishas for Ossi.

Ossi took over the egg collection, packaging, and loading for market. He had learned quickly how to sell eggs to front gate customers. He nearly replaced Pichon and Percie for chores, and there was never a shortage of rabbit, squirrel, fish, or crab for meals. Femme eagerly awaited his return from hunting. When the yard signaled his return, she eagerly greeted him on the porch.

"What's the surprise for today. That croaker sack is mighty full."

"If you can guess, you can have it." He smiled and held the sack over her head.

"Well, I've been daydreaming about stuffed crabs. That sack is gyrating up a storm. Those are some blue crabs begging for a stuffing." She walked down the steps, pushing her curls behind her ears.

He backed up and dangled the sack in the air, preventing her grabbing it. He wore a light blue, sleeveless shirt with small wooden peg buttons down the front. His gray overalls were a patchwork of pockets—all filled with something necessary for hunting or fishing. Lead sinkers weighed down the top pockets while a variety of twine and cord spools bulged in the lower ones. The sun dropped sparkles across his bronze-colored skin, using his sweat to create a luring sheen over his brow and muscled shoulders. The sheen was hypnotic, and she had to blink the sack back into focus. "How you know you're right? I might have live rabbits I trapped." He pretended a stern look, and she pretended to pout.

"But I wanted stuffed crabs for dinner. Do some magic and turn the rabbits into crabs." He could not suppress his laughter as she drew nearer, grabbing after the sack but landing her grip on his arm. His body carried the natural smells of the lake and woods; this, she found irresistible as she lunged repeatedly for the sack. He never disconnected his eyes from hers. He raised and lowered the sack until she stood still with her hands planted on her waist in defiance. Her curls had worked their way into a pretty disarray. He relented.

"Crabs it is, then. Just this time. Next time, you have to do the magic yourself."

They quickly grew accustomed to such occasions and enjoyed the stability that began as a crisis. Papa Luc visited—often with Lucien—to check on Meffre but said little about how he would fulfill his promise. Ossi's presence, for Femme and Meffre, eased some of the anxiety about the future.

The beginning of August brought morning suns that carried with them sheets of steam and swarms of mosquitoes. Femme sat on the steps and watched Ossi load the last crate of eggs on the wagon. He walked slowly toward her. She often wondered why he held back *his* story. She would not pry. Yet, she wanted to know him. Something in his very movements connected their spirits. He said, "Thirty-one dozen. Not one cracked. Brown separated from white. I'll eat before I take these to that lake boat."

"Well, you've got time. Boat won't get there till noon. Come in. Fried chicken and biscuits."

"I want to talk to you. About things. Let's eat on the porch."

He went to wash behind the barn, and when he returned, Femme had set the porch table. He nodded gratitude.

"I know Meffre told you what he knew about his daddy. I need to tell you more about Kebbi and what he planned."

Ossi questioned whether Kebbi cared about death because he took too many risks. He preached the necessity of fighting whites incessantly to achieve complete revenge. He manipulated Carl to gain advantage piece by piece; then, he used money or power to plan his next fight. After the confusion over the pecan trees died down, Carl offered to rent Kebbi land to farm to keep field hands in Colfax. Five years later, Kebbi wanted papers on the land. He insisted he had bought the land by farming it and giving Carl profits. Again, his powerful threat of taking all the field hands north forced Carl to concede. Still, he wanted his family to be free, far from Colfax—his sole objective.

The fullness of Ossi's story raised questions for Femme, not the least of which was how Kebbi and Ossi became close. When she asked about this, Ossi grew sullen and said only that Kebbi saved his brother's life; afterward, their families became one. "We're like brothers. Taking care of Meffre repays Kebbi. He paid me to carry Meffre here, so I wouldn't feel obligation, but I do. I never wanted to live in a village with a wife and children. But I know duty to family. Meffre's family."

Femme fiddled with the dishes, moving and stacking them. This chat confused her. Ossi's openness about not wanting a wife and children but accepting Meffre as family sounded like a caution to her. She put silverware in a glass and smoothed the tablecloth's wrinkles. Ossi grabbed her arm. "Meffre's living against his will and won't let anyone save him, won't try. I felt heaviness from everything in this yard when that fat doctor touched him. Looks like Papa Luc means to do right by the boy, but he wants me to leave."

Femme was baffled—the orishas had sent no warning. Again, full of curiosity, she asked sadly, "Meffre seems better after taking the medicine. Why do you think he's giving up?"

"Too many eggs for July and August. These chickens should be heat-lazy by now. The yard is too still. Blooms and buds are too tight. Death signs."

She pulled the napkin from her lap, folded it, and dropped it atop the dirty dishes. She tried to hide her dismay and asked, "Ossi, do you hear? How do you know this? What talks to you?"

"Nothing. I sense when something is different. That's all."

"My orishas *speak* to me. Meffre, too. After going to the doctor, I sensed his wanting to get better." She wanted a quick answer but knew that his responses came without rushing. He finished his chicken through soft chewing and slow swallowing. Femme held her head in her hands, her eyes fixed on him. His eyes held no pain or sorrow. He knew she waited for an answer, but his answer might make her remove her gaze. He pushed his plate aside, looked more deeply into her eyes, and then slowly landed his other hand on hers. "Tell Meffre you won't let that fat doctor near him again."

He pulled his chair back. She let her hands fall to her lap. "Kebbi saved the money he gave to Meffre. He took the money Papa Luc paid for the grove payment; Carl never saw that money. Kebbi never admitted he stole it. He said it was owed to him and his daddy for being slaves. When he came to my village, he had very little money. He told me that Meffre would find his inheritance in Lacombe. I believe that valise and pecan grove will tell him how."

"The valise and the pecan grove?"

"Kebbi begged me to keep Meffre with that valise. We'll have to tell him this if—"

"Ossi"—she pleaded—"promise to stay till I figure out—"

"I'll stay," he said quickly. She took his hand; his covered hers. "I'll stay, but now I've got eggs to take to Mandeville. Then I'm going to stop in Abita Springs to see my people who helped us get here." She stood and looked down on the stacked dishes, sighing to register her protest against his leaving. He opened the kitchen screened door and winked at her as she carried the load into the house.

He closed the door and faked a cough until she blew him a kiss through the screen. He knew he was crossing boundaries he had set. For this, he willed himself to move slowly.

She smiled and said, "Percie's running the produce stand in Mandeville. He'll help load the crates and arrange the shipment. Tell him it's mine."

"I sold a mess of speckled trout through Percie. Pichon said he's the handsome twin and Percie's mouth looked like a perch. It did. But, Percie can handle a horse better than most men I know, including his brother."

+ + +

For three days, Ossi stood guard as Aunt Velma and Femme nursed Meffre. On the fourth day, Meffre asked Femme to record his parents' names in a bible. Femme said, "Sure, son. Years ago, Sister Bernadine gave me a bible I use just for that." She took the bible from the oratory's bottom shelf. "I wrote everything. Here's my birthday from thirty years ago: 'Numa Labat'—that's me. There's Daddy's death date; here's Mama's." She handed the bible to Aunt Velma, who sat frowning. Femme searched for a pen and ink in the oratory. "Aunt Velma's a church lady, so she can write what you want." Aunt Velma snatched the pen from Femme to feign annoyance at being bossed around, though she looked at Meffre with moist eyes.

"Kebbi Barjone. Daddy was thirty-nine when he died. Can I have a line like that? His daddy was Avery Barjone. I'm Meffre Kebbi. I need to be baptized. Mama stopped fighting Daddy for that. My mama was thirty-five when she died. Only name for her is Yana."

Aunt Velma wrote slowly and cautiously. "Of course, cher."

"I don't know what day Daddy was born. He said the year was 1861. His daddy died Easter, April 13, 1873, and he died this Easter," Meffre said feebly. He struggled to reposition his leg, and the scene unsettled Femme. She recalled Ossi's fear that Meffre might die and asked, "What day were you born?"

Meffre slid in Femme's direction and answered, "January 15, 1883."

Aunt Velma seemed overwhelmed and said she had to get back to Papa Luc's. She kissed them, loaded three dozen eggs in her basket, and left. Femme started to ache for Meffre. Even asleep, his leg trembled with slow spasmodic jitters. She went to the oratory, touched Eshu's statue and trembled as she held it. Meffre turned to her, his eyes glistening. He held out his hand, and she handed him the statue. "I'll never allow that Dr. Bellocq near you again, promise."

He smiled and held Eshu tightly. "These oaks don't keep secrets, huh? They told me to fight." Femme embraced him and left him alone to pray.

After four hours of working in the barn, Ossi met Femme on the porch with a cheerful look. He said, "The clouds have released the sky! Won't rain. Quiet breezes in the trees." Femme held his face affectionately. "Meffre is better, stronger." He moved away to avoid her hold on him. Still, her joy emboldened her to take his hand and lead him inside. They felt gentle breezes invading the house.

Meffre raised his head and allowed his parents to take his pain into an echo that marched through the house and out into the wind. He felt Kebbi's and Yana's spirits leave on a warm agile breeze, out the window, and through the oak branches toward the pecan grove.

+ + +

After two months, Meffre was up and working diligently on delivering chickens and eggs. His recovery, he wanted to believe, was due to his washing his leg with Yemanja water, not because of the doctor's salve or pills. With his first walk across the porch, his spirit changed. Soon, Ossi became his teacher; he learned quickly.

"You have to remember your orders. Some folks want only brown eggs. Those ladies beyond Papa Luc's house want a mixed bucket. They never change their order, so remember to put in two pullets even if they don't ask for them." Ossi looked at him for signs that he had absorbed the lesson. Meffre nodded but rearranged the buckets to organize them into his system.

Femme came out with folds of newspaper. "Use these for wrapping the chickens. I wrap them on a diagonal to make them fit, but you'll find your own way."

Meffre happily took on the work. His smile featured his contentment even when the pushcart was heavy and hard to manage. His limp had disappeared, and he claimed Femme's cooking gave him back his strength.

Pichon had taught him the north and south delivery routes along the footpath that stretched behind the pecan grove to the sawmill. Meffre loaded eggs in small buckets the night before delivery because the morning occupied him with killing and cleaning chickens for standing orders. With a loaded pushcart, he dispatched the orders along the southbound footpath beyond Percie and Pichon's house. This allowed him an empty cart on the way back home when he would rest and eat before loading and delivering along the north route between Femme's house, Papa Luc's, and the sawmill.

After eating his lunch, he prepared the afternoon northbound load and said, "Miss Laurent don't want chickens on the foot no more. Since her husband died, she don't use the feet. So, I'll need three plucked, no feet. All other orders are on the foot." Femme and Ossi smiled at Meffre's diligence.

Meffre set out on his northbound delivery route, which he liked most because he passed the pecan grove where Lucien could often be heard playing the piano. He always wanted to stop but would not—unwritten prohibitions were too real. During his recovery, he had heard Papa Luc relating a story to Femme that he heard down at Mudbug's. Pike, the bartender, said two men had been caught doing "nasty stuff" behind the Mandeville Hotel barn. They were both found beaten bloody with broken bones over most of their bodies.

He had looked forward to Papa Luc's short visits, mostly because Lucien was often with him. He got to ask about Lucien's music, which Papa Luc took as a cue to let them talk privately. The day Papa Luc had told the brutal story, he had come alone and spent most of his time talking to Femme in the kitchen. The story troubled Meffre and came to occupy a dark place in his memory. That day, the story erased his yearning to hear news about Papa Luc's promise.

Over time, he became expert at his work. One day in late October, after his deliveries, he was on his way home when he approached the grove house surprised by shouting. He saw Lucien tussling with someone on the porch. Parking his cart near the fence, he hopped over and stood behind a pine. He could see Lucien struggling and punching, but it was clear that he was losing. Lucien's next scream triggered Meffre's immediate motion. A reddened brute dragged Lucien, shirtless, down the steps and across the yard, where a hatchet was wedged in a stump.

The boy was thick and sturdy with wet red hair. He easily pinned Lucien down against escape. "You gonna pay me."

Lucien tried to grab at the boy's legs to trip him, but each time, the brute swung at him with a kitchen knife and dropped it when he saw a hatchet lodged in a nearby stump. He pulled at the hatchet. Lucien pleaded, "Todd, you'll get caught. Stop! I'll pay you more tomorrow."

"*Lucy*, you ain't never gonna play piano with two hands again." Lucien struggled to rise, but the brute slammed him to the ground and put his foot on his chest, planting his right arm against the stump.

With eyes on the hatchet, Meffre gauged his power to strike and delivered a fierce blow that knocked the assailant face-first into the dirt. Lucien grabbed the knife, and Meffre jumped up and found the hatchet. He stood over the big red face and said, "He won't lose his hand, but you need to run."

He got to his feet in a rage. "Nigger, you gonna die. Maybe not today, but it's coming." He ran headlong through the grove toward Lake Road.

Lucien was bleeding from scratches in several places, and the worst was across his stomach. He was breathing heavily, could barely walk. "Let's go inside, Meffre. My uncle is home. I can't go there now." The bleeding from the cuts pushed him to the ground.

"Stay here," Meffre said and rushed back to the fence. He opened the gate and rolled the pushcart to the house. He dumped empty buckets on the ground and ran inside the bungalow. He came back with a bedspread, which he used as a cushion in the cart. He helped Lucien to lift himself into the cart and covered him. "I'm taking you home."

Aunt Velma was in the yard putting sheets out to dry, singing: "Y'all been sentenced. I'm just hanging you." When she saw them approaching, she bellowed, "Sweet Jesus. What happened? Get him into the house. Baby, you covered in blood. Thank Lucifer, Hébert's here! What happened?"

Lucien looked pleadingly at Meffre. "I was robbed," he uttered. Meffre busied himself lifting him. They took him through the kitchen and upstairs to his bedroom. Aunt Velma yelled for Hébert, who came sluggishly. His girth took up the entire door space, where he puffed momentarily and said to Aunt Velma, "Hmm! Girl, go get my bag downstairs and bring back towels. You, boy, go get hot water. Run!" Downstairs, Aunt Velma told Meffre to saddle any horse in the barn and go to the sawmill to get Papa Luc.

Hébert had finished tending to Lucien when Papa Luc arrived. He stood next to the bed and became furious to see blackened eyes and bruised skin. The lower part of his stomach was swollen and held four bloody-black stitches. Tight white bandages covered several places on his right arm and shoulder. He held Lucien's forearm, looked up at Hébert, and asked, "He'll be fine, right?"

Hébert shouted, "Why is that nigger in here? Lucien won't talk. For all I know, that nigger did this."

Papa Luc shouted, "Hébert, get out. Go to Small House. Go now!" Aunt Velma collected bloody towels and cotton balls. She smiled and winked at Meffre. She left, telling Lucien she was coming back with soup. Hébert marched out after her, slamming the door. Papa Luc invited Meffre to sit.

"Lucien, what happened?"

He sat up and looked at Meffre and then at Papa Luc. "I got into a fight with a guy from the Bend-in-the-Road in Mandeville. Yesterday, I lost a bet in a poker game and owed him a dollar. Only had half that much when he showed up today. He got the best of me. Don't even know his name. Probably not even from around here."

"I'll go to Sheriff Blake—"

"No! Please. I don't want folks talking. I'm all stitched up. I'll be more careful next time. Just stupid."

Papa Luc thought it was Meffre's presence that prevented Lucien's saying more. "Well, just rest. I'll be back from the mill in an hour or so. Meffre, you can stay, if you like." He closed the door, calling for Aunt Velma.

Meffre moved his chair closer to the bed. "I could never lie to my daddy. Why lie? Why did that boy, Todd, call you 'Lucy'?"

Lucien said, "Thank you, Meffre. I'll owe you forever. Please, never talk about this. Todd is an Eaton, and his family is dangerous—especially his daddy, Reginald. He's Uncle Hébert's good friend. What I did was dumb. I'll never do it again. Please?"

Meffre recalled the troubling story Papa Luc had told Femme about the "nasty stuff" behind the Mandeville Hotel. He stared into Lucien's weakened blue eyes. *I'd never put you in danger.* Agreeing so readily felt odd to him, but something between them roused him to say, "I'll just say I saved you." Lucien held out his hand, and they shook. Meffre was entranced with Lucien's blue eyes. He stared at his hands and asked, "You bite your nails all the time. You nervous?"

"Piano playing is easier with short nails," he said laughing. He enjoyed Meffre's closeness, but his eyelids were getting heavy. Soon Lucien closed his eyes and, in minutes, dozed off.

When Aunt Velma came with soup, Meffre sat watching him sleep, full of hatred for Hébert and Todd. Sitting in Lucien's room also inspired a need to protect someone as he had been protected. He could feel his heart's strong rhythm, which produced something stronger than hate. He did not even sense Aunt Velma's presence, but he was certain that this incident knotted him to Lucien.

+ + +

Eshu spent the next two days annoying Meffre with a buzz that said "Lucien" as a constant sizzle fluttering from one ear to the other. No matter what the self-imposed distraction he concocted, Meffre failed to jettison the buzz. He completed his delivery and was on his way home. The buzzing resounded as he approached the Coulon mansion. He parked his pushcart and sat under an old oak tree surrounded by dainty white and red camellia bushes. He stared at Lucien's window and wondered whether he should visit. The buzz eased and then exploded into a fury circling his head. "Eshu. Give me peace!"

As he climbed the steps, he saw Aunt Velma at the stove. He waited at the screened door and tapped gently to get her attention. He took off his straw hat and picked at his hair. "Aunt Velma. I was wondering . . . I mean, if Lucien is here, I might pay a short visit. Don't want to disturb him." He spoke through the screened door and saw Aunt Velma's broad smile, which put him at ease.

"Come on in. We're here by ourselves. Lucien's gonna be happy to see you."

Lucien was sprawled on his bed reading. Aunt Velma walked in without knocking and clapped her hands. "Get rid of that book. You got company. Somebody to keep you from moping in that bed. I got apple fritters to finish. Meffre, I think he's faking all his pain." She winked at Lucien and pulled the door behind her.

Lucien propped two pillows behind his head but did not sit up. He smiled and gestured for Meffre to come closer. "Looks like you're getting ready for some serious jazz playing, judging from those fingernails." Meffre stood next to Lucien, who offered to shake hands.

"Thanks for coming. Been thinking about you."

Meffre looked around for a place to hang his hat and then just let it fall next to the bed. "Been thinking about your stitches. Must be tightening up cross your stomach. They say it's a sign of healing. Hurts, though. I remember."

"Well, I wish I could sit longer and get out of this bed. The tightness aches worse in this bed."

"Let's get you up, then. You can sit in that big soft chair."

Lucien welcomed getting closer to Meffre. He pulled up and rested on his elbows. Meffre directed him to swing his legs around to the side of the bed and to lift his arm onto his shoulders. Lucien obeyed but moved slower than he had to. Meffre slid his arms under Lucien's, and their firm chests connected in a strong embrace. Meffre pulled Lucien up gently until his feet hit the floor. Then, Lucien owned the moment and held Meffre tighter. His small half-hearted grunts cautioned Meffre to guide him slowly backwards toward the chair.

Lucien planted his head on Meffre's shoulder and smelled the naturalness of a working man's body. Meffre, for his part, turned his face to Lucien's neck and inhaled cleanliness accented by the scent of fragrant soap.

As they approached the chair Lucien's warm breathing on his neck aroused Meffre. They stopped in front of the chair, and Lucien kissed his neck. "Thanks for this." Meffre pulled them apart just enough to take in those blue eyes. He nodded and smiled.

A knowing onlooker would have observed dancers doing a two-step, agile and solid limbs performing keenly youthful desire. To their mutual surprise, their erections had blossomed past deniability. Meffre loosened his hold, positioned Lucien in front of the chair, and grabbed a robe from the chair's arm. He held it up to

Lucien but looked down on the swelling in his undergarments. They both laughed full-throatily as Lucien put on the robe and slid deeply into the chair's cushions. He said, with satisfaction, "Seems you've cured what really ails me!"

This was expected boldness from Lucien. That Meffre felt no shame for his own bulging overalls surprised even him. Calm and laughter overcame him. Freedom and contentment uncoiled and erased, momentarily, any fear of danger. These feelings rendered Meffre incapable of looking beyond this moment in this room. He listened to Lucien rattle on about his cuts until Aunt Velma tapped on the door with tray of lemonade and warm apple fritters. She left as quickly as she came and said only, "Be friends. That's rich nowadays."

"She can't possibly know how much I want that to be true. A friend to you. That's a richness."

"Back in Colfax, two men who were 'like that' would end up dead. Ever worry about that?"

"Sure, I do. Lacombe and Colfax are surely the same. Friendship, to me, is worth the risk, though." Lucien said this, knowing Meffre avoided looking in his direction. He extended his hand.

Somehow those words made the blithe scene inside the room turn into something too real for Meffre. For too long, he had anguished over admitting to himself that he was 'like that.' The guilt he always felt returned. Without any reaction to Lucien, he gobbled the apple fritter and slurped the lemonade down in one gulp. He said, "Got to get that pushcart loaded for tomorrow's delivery. Don't let those stitches keep you in that bed." He swiped his hat up from the floor, shook Lucien's hand, and headed for the door.

Lucien bit at the apple fritter full of complacency. *Visit was too quick moving for Meffre. But we share a deep secret.*

Aunt Velma came in to collect the dirty dishes and was happy to see Lucien still sitting in the chair. He looked at her slyly, and she knew questions were coming. "How do you know when you're in love, Aunt Velma, like you and Papa Luc?"

She put her tray down and sat on the bed, searching for the right words. "Don't judge love by what I got with your daddy. We got a secret, *dangerous* kind of love." They both laughed. "Like I see it and always say: love is like a big ocean wave. It'll kill you or put you safe on shore. You'll know love when it washes right up on you. Ride it

41

like a wave, son." Lucien held his arms open, and she held and kissed him. She picked up her tray and left saying, "Don't tell me why you asked about love. I know already."

+ + +

Lucien dusted and polished the upright piano in the bungalow until he could see his reflection in the wood's high-satin finish. He lifted the bench seat to select sheet music from among his favorites—Schumann, Liszt, or Chopin—when he came across a bill advertising jazz bands back in 1896. He had forgotten Reynaud had given it to him with the promise that when he was old enough, he would take him to Funky Butt Hall for a jazz fête. This inspired him to abandon the composers and instead play some music *he* had composed from Aunt Velma's singing.

Meffre had a long day packed with deliveries, but this was the first time in a while that he heard music in the grove. Since the experience in Lucien's room, Eshu had nagged him about visiting Lucien. He had resolved that anything beyond friendship with Lucien was a complicated risk he could not take. Still, he wanted to see him, to hear him play, and to see if their friendship were possible. He parked the pushcart off the path near the gate and walked toward the music.

Lucien played loudly, and Meffre's knocking had competition against the jazz riffs. He waited for a break in the music to bang the door frame harder. He could hear Lucien approaching the screened door and stepped out of view. To frighten him, he shouted, "Jazz," as soon as Lucien poked his head out of the door. He jumped back but was excited to see Meffre. They hugged with distance between them until Lucien invited him in. "Sounds like all that nail biting paid off. Could hear you a long way up the path."

"Today's the first day I've been here. My hateful uncle took the stitches out two days ago. I had to come here to get out and to play. Come, sit on the bench here, and I'll play one of Aunt Velma's favorite dance songs."

Meffre was wary of the closeness. He had no will to resist though. He tapped his feet and bobbed his head to the music's beat. He brushed against Lucien and pulled away only to be lured by those blue eyes once again. Lucien was fused to the keys, and Meffre felt the connection between the sound and player. He surmised that being there with Lucien, with his music, was the only way to know him and to be his friend.

To take a break, Lucien offered Meffre a glass of Muscadine wine. Meffre frowned and claimed it was weak. They sipped the sweet wine and enjoyed its warmth. Meffre went back to the piano bench and sat so that he could face Lucien. He was not sure what he would say, but knew he wanted to talk frankly. He downed his wine and said, "I like what Aunt Velma said about friendship. I want that but different from the way . . . different from when I helped you to sit in the chair. I mean, we can't be friends like that here. You understand?"

"I know. There are too many eyes in small towns like Lacombe. Even the most loving eyes can burn holes in you. Give me a chance and tell me when I've gone too far."

He walked over to Meffre, sat, and put his head on his shoulder. Meffre did not move immediately. He wanted to put his arms around Lucien but feared what would follow. He rose slowly and walked to the table to get more wine. He walked back to the piano bench and stood in front of Lucien. Then, he mussed his golden, straight hair and said mockingly, "You gone too far already. Don't allow my friends to put their heads on my shoulder."

"Sorry. I'll be more careful." He laughed and turned to bang out an upbeat ragtime tune.

The ragtime chords served adroitly to change the subject and restore comfort between them. They knew, without voicing it, that establishing and maintaining limits on their kind of friendship would test their mettle. By the time Meffre left the grove that evening, they also knew that music was a conduit through which they would always have freedom to speak the truth.

Tied and Untied Knots

P ICHON DISLIKED GOING TO the Coulon's. It always gave him a feeling of doing some inexplicable wrong just to cross the ditch and pass through the gate. The air grew heavier, trees shuffled warnings, and his hands never moved freely. He carried caution with him, even against Aunt Velma's saying otherwise. She loved Papa Luc and Lucien and often told Pichon that Hébert was the only enemy.

Everyone knew that Papa Luc and Hébert were estranged; few cared. Hébert's periodic presence at the mansion was as common and annoying as gnats and mosquitoes. After Alinnie died, Hébert boldly maneuvered entrance under the pretense that he had promised his sister to care for young Lucien. This was less than a half-truth. Hébert frequented the mansion for the free meals Aunt Velma prepared. More importantly, taking advantage of the meals allowed him to sponge any information that could bolster his ambition to establish and lead a band of regulators. His undercover role as a regulator, near Papa Luc, also signified to other regulators their need to be ubiquitous as a force to intimidate blacks and their supporters. When Papa Luc traveled, Hébert would invite Reginald Eaton, a principal regulator, over to drink, which unnerved Aunt Velma. More frequently, he and Reginald met at Mudbug Saloon. There, they often received telegrams from Carl Keller, who sent directives or inquiries related to apprehending Meffre or Ossi. More than once, Hébert opined that Carl was too slow in his "patient approach" to ferreting out "those two Colfax outlaws." Reginald's take was the same as Sheriff Blake's: "As long as Keller pays, we'll be as patient as he is." Hébert's presence at Mudbug's and the mansion, he believed, advantaged him over the others in Carl's eyes. To him, this was genius.

Pichon's bad feelings for the mansion intensified whenever his mother recounted the story of his father's lynching, which took place in the woods directly behind the Coulon's property line. As the twins got older, Aunt Velma had elaborated on the details of their father's death. Recently, given the frequency of lynching in St. Tammany Parish, she had decided to tell the full story during their favorite meal of codfish cakes, cabbage with smoked pork, and broccoli rice.

She set the table while examining their hands and popping the hats off their heads. "Y'all know better. Coming to my table with hats. Just to rile me." They smiled at each other, waiting for her to bless the table. She did so and cautioned that they had to be serious for a while. "I got to tell y'all parts about of your daddy's dying that's new to y'all. Was Papa Luc that found your daddy." She passed them heaping plates of food and spoke slowly and solemnly.

On that unforgettable day, Papa Luc had found Edgar Baptistte hung and burned. His murderers protected his face so that he could be identified. They nailed a note to the tree: *This is payment for the sow this bastard stole.* Papa Luc took it upon himself to inform Aunt Velma and Sheriff Blake. The sheriff started an investigation that no one expected to arrive with guilty suspects.

Papa Luc sent Edgar's body to the black undertaker and paid for the funeral. A week later, unbeknownst to Papa Luc, Hébert insinuated to Aunt Velma that she owed the Coulons $44.00 for the newly installed tin roof on her house. After Aunt Velma mentioned this to Papa Luc, no one said another word about it.

The twins were two years old when their father died, and Aunt Velma insisted that retellings of this tragedy might keep nooses from Pichon and Percie's necks. Though the twins rarely spoke of their father, his memory had never been lost. This time, the story held them longer in their seriousness than before. Aunt Velma had reached them and broke the silence. "Looks like y'all don't like my food tonight." That signal was enough to animate them into a dive for more codfish cakes.

Aunt Velma's small house sat at the southern end of the footpath along which Femme's modest but spacious house lay at a midpoint between the Coulon mansion and sawmill. Even as boys, Pichon and Percie walked the footpath to the Coulon mansion and then to the sawdust pile to play. This lumber mill proved to be Papa Luc's best financial and humanitarian investment. When slavery had ended, competition for laborers was the prime cause for white landowners fighting each other. The Coulons had avoided that fight. Keeping the mill from being torched, either by those who envied their success or who had been enslaved by it, proved battle enough. Yet, the Coulons persevered by being the first to pay wages to freed slaves. This garnered support from black and Créole people while white competitors sneered and left the Coulons alone. The tradition continued when Papa Luc offered Pichon a job at the mill as soon as it was clear that he was not going any further in school.

Pichon remembered how Aunt Velma had insisted that he go to the mill to ask Papa Luc for a job. He smiled now at how simple the conversation had been. "Mr. Coulon, Mama don't trust me staying home doing nothing now that school's out. She says work would keep my mind out of the devil's workshop."

"Well, all young men need school or work. You look strong enough to carry timber. Come early Monday, at six, for your first day." The easy conversation bolstered Pichon's confidence in Papa Luc. He smiled as Pichon thanked him, full of promises that he would be a good worker.

Pichon knew his family's history, but mistrust invaded his feet's thick skin every time he neared the property. Schooled to be Femme's mouth and ear to and from the Coulons, he delivered messages either early in the morning or after work. The sign for transmitting messages was Aunt Velma's red dishrag, hanging outside the kitchen's windowsill.

As he neared the gate, he saw Hébert sitting on the porch swing. Even the immensity of the house and the porch's expanse could not dwarf Hébert. *Lawd, today. I don't want to have to deal with that mean white man this early.* He walked directly up to the porch, took off his hat, and was about to speak when Hébert looked up from his newspaper, as if to talk to the sky, and said, "I don't care why you're here. Go around to the kitchen."

By the time he said "kitchen" Pichon had already started walking across the length of the long veranda. "Morning, sir," he said and kept walking. *That's a prayer answered.*

Aunt Velma saw Pichon coming and smiled a big welcome. Without thinking, she pushed her headband back and said, "I dropped a fork this morning, so I knew you'd be here. Come eat a fast biscuit. *He* didn't want biscuits. Thinks I'm gonna poison him. I ain't poisoned him yet because Lucien asked me not to. Anyway, poison ain't cheap."

Pichon laughed and said, "He sent me back here."

"Yeah! He got into it with Lucien, who's smelling himself and that's giving the porker a time. Boy children, without mother love, sometimes spin like tops and fall wrong. See? My love is saving y'all. Anyway, Lucien's a man now. He don't need that porker. Never did."

"I heard Lucien's spending time in his 'office' in the pecan grove, at Mudbug's, in New Orleans, Covington, and some hotel in Mandeville."

She pushed her headband toward the middle of her head. "The porker told Reginald Eaton that. So what? His daddy ain't fussing. Lucien's got a softness 'bout him, a good soul. What you got for me today?" She guided Pichon in and handed him a plate of biscuits with Muscadine jelly and butter. She watched him eat and wipe butter from his lips. It reminded her of Lucien in tender moments with his mother. She had been brought to tears more than once when she had spied the boy crying while sitting in Alinnie's sewing chair, one of her favorite spots. Once, he had just had a row with Hébert over missing Mass. When Lucien finally came home, clearly exhausted from a night of carousing, Hébert towered over him. "You're digging your mother another grave, burying the future she wanted for you." Lucien could not accept the reprimand and started a tirade of cussing. He went into the sewing room and locked the door. After his uncle left, he let Aunt Velma in and talked about missing his mother. She had held him as he heaved his grief forward as if his mother had just died.

Pichon sensed his mother's sadness and put the empty plate in the sink to pull her back to the message he was carrying. "Femme wants Papa Luc to ask, down at Sacred Heart, will they christen Meffre."

"Papa Luc? He's as bad as Femme. Seldom goes to church. Lawd. Now listen. Me and Lucien going to buy fish from Julien Broyard today. *I'll* ask Father."

Aunt Velma had never remarried. She claimed she had had her husband and did not want to suffer through the horror of another "love" being lynched. She held that she could keep men scared by appearing to be just meat and bones. She also mused that skinny women, with mean looks and crooked smiles, could keep black bucks guessing and running.

When Pichon walked past the Coulon's that evening, there was no dishrag. Although surprised, he kept walking. He took the footpath behind Femme's house through the woods home. After feeding the animals, he and Percie washed, and headed out to Femme's. He was surprised to see Papa Luc's horse. Ossi and Meffre sat on the front steps, a sign that Papa Luc and Femme were inside talking.

"Evening. Y'all awful quiet out here," Pichon said.

"Been talking for nearly two hours. I want to know what they going to do with Meffre," Ossi said, scraping his knife against a post that supported the railing. He tightened his lips.

Percie asked, "Did you know Miss Femme keeps brandy and wine in the barn?"

Ossi laughed at the twins. "You two are young with good thinking already. Sometimes I like whiskey, and wine, and home brew, but not now."

Pichon looked at Percie askance and lied. "Oh! We know. Just wanted to show you where she keeps it." Meffre shook his head.

The front door banged open, and Ossi jumped up. Papa Luc popped on his hat and hopped down the steps. He nodded at them and mounted his horse. As he rode away, he noticed Femme waving with a broad smile. He waved her away and sped down the road.

"Y'all, come in and eat. Pichon, after supper, I need you to tell your mama that the christening is tomorrow at Sacred Heart. Ask her to bring her choir so the church won't look empty. Tell her, I'm even going to be there. Let's eat."

Percie ate six crab cakes, four biscuits with butter, three portions of onion potatoes, and three ears of corn. Pichon ate half that much, and Meffre and Ossi laughed at Femme's useless reprimands against their eating too much. Pichon, then, protested that there was no dessert except strawberries. Femme got up slowly, pulled Pichon out of his chair, and said, "Go try and get your dessert at Julien Broyard's." Everyone laughed loudly at this, no one more than Percie.

After Pichon, Percie, and Meffre went to tend the horses, Femme pulled her chair closer to Ossi. "Yana wanted Meffre christened. Will you come?"

"Yes. What did he say about Meffre? I'll take Kebbi's boy with me—to Abita."

"Don't worry. He's good on his promise. He can't take Meffre to live at his house. That'll raise too many eyebrows in Lacombe. Besides Hébert is always underfoot. I got plenty room. You and Meffre can live here."

The tension left his face. She explained that Papa Luc was worried that trouble could come to Lacombe. There were rumors that Carl Keller hired regulators to go after money he claimed Kebbi stole. Sheriff Blake found out that there's a search for whoever killed the white men whose bodies were found outside Colfax. He said Reginald told Hébert this so that Aunt Velma could overhear it. Papa Luc had only done business with Carl by letter and telegram. Still, he felt responsible for this trouble from Carl.

Ossi looked at his hands. "I'm more responsible. Papa Luc doesn't want me here."

Femme gently raised his chin, connecting his eyes to hers and said, "Papa Luc and I love each other in a way that's hard to understand, even for us. He protects me and mine as an obligation. Like family. That valise is as good as his signature that he'll keep his promise."

The good news made her eyes glisten. Ossi wiped her face and stood. She stood and faced him, and they let the necessary time pass that eyes need to reflect emotion. She could see a softening, even an understanding, revealed in the relaxing of his facial expression. Time passed—time enough for understanding without words. He put his large hands in the small of her back and pulled her against his chest. And they kissed, long and hard and with a quick-born love that has no care to restrain itself.

Ossi smiled gently and said, "I guess I should thank Papa Luc for that kiss."

Femme chuckled and held him tightly. She then pulled away slightly. "We should thank each other for kisses and what we feel. Papa Luc's like a father. I'm sure he and I have confused each other about that. Now, after all these years, we know who we are to each other. You're right though: He's miffed you're here. It's not about me. It's the Colfax mess. I told him I didn't ask you to come and won't ask you to leave. Believe me, he left here angry about lots of things, but not about you. He's worried about his businesses. You're my concern, not his."

Ossi nodded. "I want to stay with Meffre *and* you." His frankness made him uneasy. "Well, I'll go out to the barn to get some nets ready."

Femme stopped him. "Ossi, starting tonight, I want all of us to sleep in this house. We've got Colfax threatening us. I depend on the twins and Meffre but, for now, I hope you'll stay with *me*."

He opened his arms to embrace her and said, "I'll sleep inside in the room next to Meffre. But I still need nets for tomorrow. I'm going with Meffre for soft-shell crabs."

In girlish fidgeting, she wrapped loose curls behind her ears. "Good, I have a taste for blue crabs."

That night, Meffre and Ossi sat with her in the living room to hear the details of the day's good news. Papa Luc offered to let Meffre work the pecan grove given that Lucien had very little interest in it. He planned to have legal papers drawn so that when Meffre succeeded at the pecan business, he could take over the land legally. Papa Luc thought that stretch of land would be a good place for Meffre to start, living on the premises at first while he learned the business. The land, sandwiched between the Coulon place and Femme's, would keep Meffre close.

Meffre became overwhelmed with the news and believed he had honored his father. This moved Ossi immensely. He hugged Femme and kissed her in gratitude. Without a word, he headed to the barn to get his things. The danger of returning to Colfax haunted him. Just the idea of staying in Lacombe inspired a preferable uneasy calm.

✝ ✝ ✝

Femme and Meffre arrived at Sacred Heart and found Aunt Velma and her choir. She slapped this one and pinched that one to keep some order with the dozen-load of misbehaving children. She pulled on one of the girl's long braids just as Femme approached her. "Can you believe these li'l bastards? They're about to tear the pews apart. I'm glad christenings are short. Don't have souls yet. Demons."

"Thank you. All we do for Meffre's parents will rest their souls. Let me find Father."

Aunt Velma called Father Lorquette "a pretty li'l man." He was tall and lanky with a head of thick, soft jet-black curls. His deep blue eyes set back in a pale white face that always appeared in need of a shave. For a priest whose profession demanded sermonizing, he was soft-spoken and genteel. The parish women gossiped that Father was always clean but never well-groomed. He walked up to Femme and said, "Miss, let's have the service now. I don't want folks complaining because the boy's not a parishioner. Hello, Aunt Velma. Meffre, come with me." He guided Meffre to the baptismal font in the sacristy and bent him over to apply water to his head, saying words in Latin no one, except Femme, understood. The choir sang Schubert's "Ave Maria" while Father administered communion. With his back to them, he said more Latin prayers no one could hear and turned to bless them.

Ossi, the twins, and four of Aunt Velma's choirboys walked out before the blessing. Father Lorquette eyed Ossi curiously and nodded. Femme stared intensely enough that his gaze shifted from Ossi to her. *What did that nod mean?* Their stares broke as the altar boy brought the incense burner. Father Lorquette circled the pews, waved it, and left pungent smoke trailing him. With more quick Latin prayers, the christening ended, and the priest and altar boy left. Meffre stood silently next to Femme, his tears falling steadily. His breathing intensified, and Femme pulled him to her and said, "Cry some happiness for your people."

After corralling her choir, Aunt Velma ushered them all toward Femme. She looked startled and commented hurriedly, "Quick christening. Might be a blessing, looks like rain. Come on y'all. Percie, come drive the rig. Pichon, watch these heathens, smelling like rusty nails." Percie drove away slowly with the choir crouching behind Aunt Velma's hollering.

Ossi took Femme's hand and guided her to the buckboard. He helped her up as Aunt Velma looked back at them warily. Meffre sat in the back with his head in his hands. Ossi drove slowly toward Church Road. Femme thought of Yana and Kebbi but was pulled from these feelings when she saw Father Lorquette walking toward the church with Hébert.

"Ossi, look, there's Hébert." Ossi looked askance at Femme and grunted in disgust. She found comfort in his silence. His mysteriousness exuded the confidence she interpreted as alluring and tinged with sexual play.

Father Lorquette sat in a pew with his back to the altar. He faced Hébert, who fumed, and said, "Dr. Bellocq, Velma Baptistte asked me to baptize the boy."

Hébert bristled and, as if searching for lost hair, raked his fingers across his bald head and shouted, "It's bad enough we have to worship with niggers and Choctaws. But to have them christened here? I should write the bishop?"

Hébert's shouting and railing unnerved the priest. He stood directly in front of him. "Dr. Bellocq, the boy was born and raised

Catholic. I christened him with blessings a child of God deserves. This should not upset a good Christian like you."

Struggle as he might, Hébert pulled himself up braced by the pew in front of him. He shouted even louder: "Upset? I know too well how this can destroy a place." Hébert kicked the kneeler up with a bang and rocked the pew. Huffing all the way, he lumbered down the aisle and yelled, "If you won't stop this, there are people who will!" He wobbled to the front door. The short walk had him gasping for air; his efforts ended in a loud belch.

Father Lorquette dealt frequently with such hatred. He turned toward the altar, knelt, and prayed: "Lord, transform this hatred into the kind of love you've shown this poor boy. Use me, Lord, to help your children." He knelt in prayerful solitude until he heard the door open again. Hébert stood drenched in the vestibule.

"Dr. Bellocq. What happened?" he asked, rushing toward him.

"That stupid stable boy's late. Rain's coming down in a vengeance," he said in complete annoyance.

"Would you like to come to the rectory till he arrives?"

"No, I'll sit here."

Just then, the door opened, and Femme walked in, putting on her chapel veil. "Father, I knocked at your house. No one answered. Sorry to interrupt. Hello, Hébert," she said in a feigned cheerful voice.

"Is there a problem?" Father asked.

"No, not at all." She looked down on Hébert. "You and I didn't talk about some certification for Meffre Barjone's christening. He'll be attending this church, and I want to do everything right. Before I got all the way home, I asked Ossi to carry me back."

Femme said this loudly and clearly, which incited Hébert to puff up. "Well, Father, you have nigger business, so I'll just go out in the rain"—he punched at his chest with his fist.

"You won't be in the rain; Yemanja's stopped it already. Just enough rain to bless the christening. Sorry you missed it, Hébert," Femme said, swelling with confidence.

"Femme, I wouldn't come to no nigger baptism. Don't traffic *superior* qualities with me. I'm not to be played with." He made to walk away, and Femme stood directly in his path.

"Hébert, you need to traffic in prayer instead of devil's work. If rain has riled you, you better get ready for a fight. You can't live with people, but you better try to live with nature. Love the sun, the lightning, and the rain!"

"Swallow your African dirt. Out of my way." He grabbed at his chest and winced.

Femme moved gently to let him go by and said sweetly, "African spirits won't stand in your way; nor will I."

Hébert pushed at the door violently. They could hear his screaming at the stable boy. Femme turned to Father Lorquette and smiled. "I just want to register Meffre, Father."

"Of course. For a baptism, we put a registry notice in the church record book." Father Lorquette had pleading eyes that Femme found encouraging and irresistible.

"You were late, boy. That made me late. Bet I missed Reginald. Stop at Mudbug's and hitch the rig in the back. Hear me?" Hébert did not wait for a response.

He unloaded himself from the rig and dodged rain puddles all the way to Mudbug's entrance. In the corner, where his favorite table stood, the saloon was in shadows just as he liked it. He dusted off the chair with his handkerchief and looked around for Pike, who was nowhere to be seen. He yelled, "Pike!"

Mudbug had one owner who claimed to have escaped from an Irish prison. His name was Pike O'Neal, a short, scruffy, skinny man with gapped teeth and thin red hair. Gossip had it that Pike claimed he would never spend money to put up signs for White and Colored because he only saw one color: "money green." The truth was Pike knew blacks would never enter Mudbug's; thus, the unwritten law kept his bar segregated. He took advantage of this bigotry and spied on regulators who frequented Mudbug's. He was a stalwart Catholic, in league with Father Lorquette and Sheriff Blake.

"Wasn't expecting you today, Doc. Bourbon or brandy?"

"Brandy. In a clean glass. Double your pour. I'm in a foul mood. I missed Reginald Eaton, huh? Sick of niggers, Créoles, and Choctaws."

Pike was expert at siphoning information—much of it gossip—from Hébert. He never showed any eagerness; nor would he ask anything before a third or fourth shot. By then, Hébert, who might have come in taciturn suddenly transformed into someone jolly and animated. Today, Pike was not sure of his chances for success. He trotted over with two glasses and a brandy bottle. "Yeah. Mr. Eaton was here. Gone an hour ago. Doc, only with you I'll break my law and have a drink. Here, let's suck one down for the Irish."

Hébert downed the brandy and swiped the bottle from Pike's hand for a second pour. "I'm French, Pike! Hate this town. Before I came here, I had a career and life and everything. Coming here was my sister's idea. Then she died. I told you all that."

Pike started to feel lucky. "What went wrong, Doc?" He poured Hébert another double.

"Ugly bastard with money took my wife. Found out years later he was Créole. Tried to tell the stupid bitch he was *passé blanc*. She wouldn't listen. I come here and still got to fight niggers and Créoles. That bitch Femme too. Don't' worry, Pike. We're watching her black ass. We'll bring her down." He banged a belch out of his chest and wiped sweat.

Someone called Pike at the bar. He left the brandy and said, "Doc, you got God on your side. The church too. I'll be back." Pike knew Hébert had crossed into babble territory. Talking to him further might waste time.

✝ ✝ ✝

On the way home, Femme explained to Ossi and Meffre that, in Lacombe, they needed to fight little battles with insecure whites like Hébert. She mentioned this as a warning of Hébert's Colfax history. Femme's caution filled the buckboard with seriousness until they neared the road leading home. Ossi's stomach growled loudly. "See, all I need is food, work, and rest. Sometimes it's hard sleeping in the room next to Meffre. Talks loud when he sleeps sound. To Jesus *and* Eshu." He looked affectionately at Meffre and then at Femme as he rubbed her hand. "You talk when you sleep?"

Femme felt a tingling in the soles of her feet that sent her into an uncontrollable fit of grinning and giggling. She held Ossi's hand in both of hers and then kissed his neck gently. He smiled proudly at getting it right—with words, which were hard for him. Words filling this moment tied them together against Hébert's unraveling hatred. A happy, loving moment, even in its being entirely ordinary. *Yemanja, I'm moving to the other side of some hill. Watch that I don't fumble, stumble, tumble, or worst, fall on the other side.*

+ + +

Over the last few months, as she and Ossi grew closer, Femme noticed that Meffre had distinct sides to his personality. At times, he was moody or petulant for no clear reason. Sometimes, she tried to engage him, but he showed his preference for solitude. Nothing soothed him more than sitting close to the old oak next to the porch. This tree was a favorite haunt of Eshu's, and Femme observed a growing connection between the two. Meffre was often full of mischief with Labas—brought on, no doubt, by Eshu's antics and nudging. Femme assumed that Meffre prayed to Eshu, sitting under the oak, hands knotted together, eyes closed, and completely at peace.

Meffre did not share his reasons for his personality vicissitudes: he yearned to hold someone as he saw Ossi hold Femme. What others saw as moodiness was often his daydreaming of holding and kissing Lucien; this conflicted with real prohibitions around him. Thus, he embraced hope and confusion: hope for love with Lucien and confusion over obstacles against such love. He and Lucien stayed within the limits they set, but Meffre ached to test those limits. Ossi surmised that Meffre was maturing—that brought with it some confusion and hurt. Ossi helped him greatly by teaching him to hunt, fish, and tend to small crops. Meffre enjoyed fishing best and proved an excellent and patient fisherman. They caught nearly everything that became their meals. Seafood was a specialty with constant surprises, and rabbits became a staple Femme and the twins had never enjoyed so much.

Everyone settled into roles that knitted together as a finely woven familial net. Their first night together brought Femme and Ossi to a closeness that seemed just the oblivion brought on when raw sexual satisfaction runs amuck. The closeness was not satisfactorily explained by sex, however. They knew that by deliberately staring into each other's eyes, without talking, they engendered a tight knot that was felt deeper than youthful play. On this first night, Ossi struggled to shelter his thoughts. He wanted to fall in love with Femme and knew he would. The danger he brought from Colfax was an obvious obstacle they could not deny. His bond with Femme was pulled taut several times during the night. He said to her, "You've never been near a man you loved before. Your heart's beating tells me."

Femme found a comfortable place for her head on his chest, just low enough to look into his eyes. "Daddy told me I'd know love when my soul talked. Maybe you're hearing that."

Ossi kissed her lips and forehead and said, "I bring you more than love. I bring danger from Colfax. I don't want that for you." He turned to face the window where the oak rested still. He smiled at the moonlight shining boldly through the branches. Femme closed his eyes and gently kissed his lips. He fell asleep quickly. She remained awake long enough to hear Meffre talking in his sleep to Eshu.

+ + +

Ossi was a man of self-control and determination. Their intimacy was hers first, then, and only then, his. He never ended his passion without first hearing, with great pleasure, her complete, vulnerable release. He waited for that moment when she was at her weakest and most euphoric—when she was dependent on him. He waited for her to stop taking and to simply give him what she had never shared. At these moments, he practiced a slow skill and gently and kindly released himself into her. His body became a solid block of muscles smoothly moving in unison to a tightness within her and then a gradual, barely noticeable looseness. He became, almost at once, solid power and then tenderly, with agility, embodied peace. These harmonious moments were held in the embrace of his thick arms that cradled her while, at the same time, they begged her respect.

The frequency of their loving forced its maturity. Their days and nights were punctuated so, yet Ossi never missed bringing home variety and abundance for the table, which Femme delighted in preparing. The twins were their evening entertainment.

One quiet evening, Femme fried rabbit when the animal orchestra erupted in the front yard. Only Labas's baying was absent; he and Meffre were with Ossi. Femme waited for the noise to abate, but she heard Papa Luc yelling for her at the gate. "Femme, don't you set that hound on me."

"He's with Ossi," she said proudly noticing his grimacing. "Papa Luc, what are you doing here this time of day?"

"We had a big argument with Hébert early this morning. Telling Lucien he had blue eyes just like Jesus. Lucien cussed him and said his eyes are his mother's. He's spoiled and ornery like me, and he's headstrong and full-spirited like her."

Papa Luc made his way clumsily to the porch. He had been drinking and walked boldly right into Femme's arms. She hugged him firmly. He smiled. She smiled. She grabbed his hand and led him into the house. The yard went silent.

"Well, now listen. Sounds like Hébert is getting pretty powerful getting you to leave your own house."

"I ain't done a snatch of work today. Hébert stayed around drinking my whiskey and gossiping with Reginald." He sat at the kitchen table and picked up the lemonade Femme poured. She went back to her rabbit frying, and he reached into his pocket for a small thick-paper satchel, which he put on the table, tapping it to get Femme's attention. "I really came here to deliver a promise to Meffre's daddy. I had that Waddell lawyer in Covington draw up these papers. Two copies for you, and I have a copy in my safe."

Femme finished taking the rabbit pieces out of the frying pan, covered them with a clean white towel. Her curiosity made her movements all the quicker. She put her hand on his shoulder and said, "He's been here four months now. I've grown to love him like Aunt Velma's twins."

Papa Luc put the satchel in her hand and kissed it. "The papers make legal Meffre will get two acres and the bungalow when he's eighteen. I initially thought I'd just employ him in the pecan grove, but Lucien reminded me that he saved his life. So, I deeded it to him outright. Luckily, for him, the grove is part of that acreage and carries his daddy's memory. Lucien talked me through all that. Seems like they've become good friends. We should keep this from Hébert, who'd raise hell a shovel at a time. I hope Meffre will see this as gratitude too, for saving Lucien's life. If only I could untie myself from Hébert."

"Meffre's working in the pecan grove is good. He can live here till he's eighteen. Ossi will be here too. Papa Luc, thank you." His expression changed. He plopped his hat from one thigh to the next. *What has irritated him now?* He stood and faced her.

"I promised Albion to protect you. I'm being replaced? So that Choctaw *is* living with you? He's running it around here now? I heard he done took up with Créoles in New Orleans—watch it. If all that's true, it ain't good. Lacombe people don't like it. They fear what they don't understand. Then, they destroy it. Fear is not the *worst* part of them. It's the *only* part. Especially Hébert." He tightened his lips, clenched his teeth, and turned away from her. He put his hat on, took it off as if to speak, and pushed his chair under the table.

She was about to deliver a flippant, hurtful response when the oak tree started to fuss. Quickly turning him around, she kissed him on the cheek sweetly, and said, "Thank you for everything. From now on *the Choctaw* is living and sleeping wherever he likes in my house—by my invitation. Ossi cannot replace you in my heart or in my life. But we both knew a man would come into my life to love me in ways you can't. May I have this happiness?" Papa Luc's face slackened and showed a father's reluctant acquiescence. He kissed her forehead and headed for the porch. He mounted his horse, looking back on her smiling in the doorway, and rode away, respecting her independence and bravery.

She stood at the end of the porch close to the oak. *Eshu, Ossi cannot know what I know. He must tell me about New Orleans and the Créoles. "Testing trust ruins trust," Daddy told me.* The old oak responded with one large shake, which pitched enough brown leaves to the ground to rouse the fat pig and send her running. The entire yard started shuffling again. She picked up her pipe and pulled tobacco out of her apron pocket, never taking her eyes off the oak. She sat in her rocker smoking and thinking of Ossi.

✝ ✝ ✝

Two weeks later, Aunt Velma appeared at Femme's barn door with a basket. As always, she yelled from the yard for Femme, but one was never where the other was at the same time. This yelling created a commotion and, finally, Femme, stood in the middle of the yard and screeched, "I'm tired running after you."

"Well, by the time I find you, I'm gonna forget why I came. Lawd, what I wouldn't do for a chair."

"Let's sit on the porch. What's in the basket?"

"Nothing but my excuse to come here. I need some eggs I don't need. Pichon won't be coming by because the porker figured out the meaning of my red dishrag. He told me he knows it means more than eggs and chickens. You know, they say 'evil is smart.' Anyway, no more red dishrags. Pichon ain't seen it. He looked right at me this morning, nodded, and before I could wave, he was gone."

"Charmaine Broyard."

"Not already? Well, let that be. Ain't ours to mess with. Yet. Pichon's two shades darker, in the devil's direction, than her daddy's gonna see fit for Charmaine. But that young heifer got her own mind. Julien's got a stubborn old soul. Acts like Charmaine is all he got."

"Pichon's stopping by Julien's for no good reason or really too good a reason. That's why you haven't seen him."

Aunt Velma was silent and took her time putting her basket on the table next to Femme looking at her, looking away, looking at the barn unnecessarily, and finally settling into a chair. She took a deep healthy breath. For five uninterrupted minutes, she relayed how, since Lucien was robbed in the pecan grove, he had started taking off to Mandeville, New Orleans, and elsewhere. Hébert, with God as witness, held that the boy was destined for hell. Lucien was not the prime cause of Hébert's visits though. After registering disgust, she arrived at the crux of her message: Hébert had made an announcement that he would never take another meal at the mansion "because too many ears" take his "words, one by one, to Femme." She was visibly sad and grunted. "He has also set his mind to running Ossi away. My heart was in my mouth when he told that other porker, Reginald. Said too many people talk about Ossi and what he's stirring up in New Orleans." Hearing Ossi's name, Femme turned to the oak as if someone had called her. She sat transfixed, listening to two conversations. She was in spirit with Eshu when Aunt Velma pinched her.

"Tell me I ain't talking to myself," Aunt Velma snapped as Femme recoiled.

"I heard you. I'm just angry. Can't I have a future? Ossi brought me *more* than Colfax trouble. I love him. Like you love Papa Luc. Small minds can't handle that."

Aunt Velma sat again and took Femme's hand. "Right! So-called Christians turn their noses up on me and Luc and look away. Been doing so since slavery. It's normal for them and maybe us too. You and Ossi together is too new for hypocrites." The conversation rattled and disgusted Femme. Seeing this, Aunt Velma rose to go as Femme went into the house. *Jesus, she really loves that Choctaw. Too quick. Gonna make her grieve.*

Femme linked Papa Luc's censure about Ossi to Aunt Velma's warning about Hébert. Kneeling at the oratory, she called on Eshu to reveal those who conspired against her love for Ossi and Meffre. Yemanja's water bowl trembled, and Femme heard, *Ladies.*

59

Ladies of the Altar Society

AS SHE WENT THROUGH her chores, Aunt Velma found reminders of happiness everywhere. The dining room table-cloth, with Alinnie's intricate lace patterns, resurrected memories of excited chatter before Lucien was born. As she dusted the breakfront, she recalled when Lucien started walking. Alinnie doted on him but wanted to return to teaching Choctaw and black children at the Catholic school. She turned little Lucien over to Aunt Velma's kitchen, where it was safe for him to play under her watchful protection. Always welcoming an audience for her singing and dancing, Aunt Velma enjoyed the company. Julien Broyard made a rocking floor cradle for Lucien. She had very little time to hold him but passed him often singing blues songs and rocking and dancing. The cradle was a percussion accompaniment as she shuffled through the kitchen to tap his cradle. He enjoyed and whined for foot tapping, songs, or simple whistling.

If anyone looked at pictures of Lucien and his parents, it would be easy to opine that they were happy. Aunt Velma's dusting brought to her the rigid contrast between Alinnie and Hébert. Her surmise was simple: Hébert had no soul.

Alinnie's most enjoyable day was Sunday because Lucien escorted her to the very front row of Sacred Heart for Mass. This routine pageant was a necessary show for the congregation. Alinnie became an enormously respected parishioner, who had been elected as the head of the Ladies Altar Society. On many occasions, after berating Papa Luc for not attending Mass, she snarled, "Sacred Heart Church is vital to Lacombe's peace. You should come to church, too."

When Lucien started enjoying his first rash of independence, Alinnie noticed that he would nod at people as they entered Sacred Heart. He also became fond of smiling and nodding at Choctaws and black people, who sat in the back and in the choir loft. She was proud of him. Yet, she knew the imposed limits of public displays. Her every attempt to caution him pushed his independence further. Then, she became careful of too much protesting—especially knowing that she and Aunt Velma had instilled this humanity in him.

One Sunday morning, Lucien held his mother's arm and walked her slowly and methodically toward the first pew when he spied Aunt Velma with an armful of large candles. She was too holy to drop a candle, but Lucien did not know that. He let go his mother's arm and darted to help Aunt Velma. The church sighed its consternation. Aunt Velma was as surprised as Alinnie, and the two eyed each other until Lucien took his seat. Alinnie's disdain landed in a strange place between Lucien's decency and Lacombe's self-annihilating hatred.

It was less than six months later that Alinnie died of yellow fever. Shortly afterward, Hébert began his vigilance over Lucien. Every confrontation with Lucien had to do with his not being where he should be. Aunt Velma was constantly accused of not watching him—even after he turned fifteen.

A few years later, Lucien deliberately missed accompanying Hébert to Mass—something he abhorred doing. On that Sunday, Hébert lost his prayers and writhed in anger. Lucien had turned eighteen the night before in Mandeville at the Bend-in-the-Road Bar and at the Pirogue Saloon, both full of blues players, mostly blacks from New Orleans. His independence had grown yards, and the company of like-minded and free-spirited people was much more a lure for him than religion. The shouting that Sunday still echoed in Aunt Velma's memory—so much so that she missed Hébert's thumping into the kitchen.

He sat uneasily waiting at the table. It was taking too long, and his impatience went intentionally unnoticed by Aunt Velma, who sang a favorite blues song as she set out biscuits and coffee. She stopped singing to ask if Hébert had seen Lucien. Hébert pursed his lips as if he were loaded to spew venom. She retreated to the stove for eggs and ham.

Hébert slid his chair back and stood with his hands on his hips. "Can I, for one morning of my miserable life, eat breakfast without that nonsense you're screeching? Puts me in a foul mood. Girl, I'm talking to you."

"I hear you, sir. But, my agreement with Papa Luc says I can sing in the kitchen to keep my head right. I don't sing in the dining room. I can send word for Papa Luc to come settle this. Again!"

With as much vehemence as he could muster, Hébert knocked over his chair and pushed his bulk toward the dining room.

"I'm right behind you, *sir.*" She muttered to herself, "Stay out of my kitchen. Coming in here to spy. You ain't getting nothing to blab down at church or Mudbug's today." Then, to him, "Enjoy your breakfast."

In quick fluid moves, Aunt Velma left, and Hébert sat fussing. She knew he would complain that the coffee must be cold; she appeared with a fresh cup and the coffee pot.

"Is that chicory coffee?"

"It sure is, *sir.* Just like yesterday and the day before."

"Full of lip this morning, girl?"

Aunt Velma walked very slowly to the kitchen, smiling. She started singing loudly as soon as she crossed the threshold. Hébert's hate intensified as he thought about losing his influence on Lucien. He detested whites like Alinnie and Papa Luc who eschewed their superiority. In his view, such eschewal was throwing away the position their money afforded. He thought Lucien followed their lead. *Just like his pecans: hard shell and soft center.* Voices and laughter in the kitchen took him out of his reverie and stiffened his spine. Papa Luc came in and nodded his greeting, forewarned of an impending tirade against Aunt Velma.

Hébert said, "She runs this house but won't rule me. This sickening episode is seen all over the South: colored women think they rule houses they clean. Problem is, they think they *own* those houses."

Papa Luc said, "Good morning, Hébert. *You're* eating in the dining room. Looks like Aunt Velma *does* rule here. Look, I don't know a white woman in this parish who doesn't tangle with colored or Créole women they've hired. Count on Aunt Velma winning. Or, get your own cook and take your meals at Small House. You said you'd never eat here again, and there you sit. She'll be here longer than you ever will. Anyway, Eva Doucette said the Ladies Altar Society is meeting down at Sacred Heart this evening. They want you there to represent the usher board."

"I know. Mary Eaton's coming to fetch me." He scrunched up his lips childishly.

"Why can't they meet the same day every week like they did when Alinnie ran it?" Papa Luc fiddled with his hat and stared out the window.

"People are busy. I've got questions, too. What's going on between you and *that* Velma? You take up for her like she's your wife. People ask about *that*. Where's Lucien?"

"Celebrating his birthday with his friends." He put his hat on angrily. "Keep Velma out of your filthy mouth. We're trying to keep watch over those church meetings. Things are getting bad again. Two lynchings last week in Mandeville. I got to get back to the mill. If you want Aunt Velma to stop singing, tell her you love her songs."

Aunt Velma overheard the conversation and smirked through the dining room door in Hébert's direction. She was emboldened by Papa Luc's angry defense, which she interpreted as an expression of his true feelings for her. The love relationship between them surprised them both. Her moving into the Coulon mansion after Alinnie died was normal and expected. Her moving into Papa Luc's bed three years later had been the result of an unexpected gift: a gramophone she had wished for in a casual conversation with Lucien. Papa Luc surprised her with the gift and records on her birthday. Her happiness and excitement shooed her composure away and she kissed Papa Luc on the lips before he could pull back. When he embraced her, passion took over and became part of a secret history. Even at an early age, Lucien absorbed the scene with happy and approving eyes. He promised them their secret was safe—especially from Hébert. In return, he was given the latitude young men hope for. Aunt Velma became his emissary to Papa Luc, a role she played with aplomb.

She recalled with satisfaction the times Lucien had come home after piano practice at the Carmelite convent. Papa Luc had made a deal with him that he had to learn to read and play classical music before he "graduated" to improvising in jazz. Lucien had excelled in his classical lessons with the Carmelites, but Aunt Velma was his jazz teacher. Papa Luc approved fully because the music helped heal Lucien from losing his mother. During this time, interfering Hébert had become a watchdog and had too often reprimanded Lucien for not practicing scales or refining his technique on sonatas. He also forced Lucien to play religious music, for which Lucien had had no appetite.

One evening, Hébert had hidden just outside the parlor and heard Lucien playing jazz. He slid the door open just enough to witness Aunt Velma singing in her brassy voice as she danced and shook wildly. She fanned her feet with her skirt as if to put out some flame. Every deep note she hit, every suggestive move she made, and, worst of all, every accompaniment Lucien conceived and delivered impelled Hébert into the realm of utter disgust. Aunt Velma smiled remembering how he had flailed his arms and shouted for them to stop their "devil's work." From that day to this, the battle over jazz raged, and she was happy for a slight win.

Hébert pouted and hissed. "Just so you know, *I* decided to eat in here; that kitchen *girl* didn't decide it." Papa Luc nodded mockingly and left. Hébert stared at the enormous oak tree that shaded most of the front garden. Its slow easy movements lulled him into a calm. He nibbled at biscuit crumbs. *Nothing much is easily given, but, as they say, "a lot can be easily taken."*

✝ ✝ ✝

Going to the Broyard's house became Pichon's favorite chore. Messages and parcels from Femme and Aunt Velma gave the trips legitimacy, but that was not *his* purpose. He planned a history with Charmaine and thought constantly about his next chance to steal a quick, practiced snatch of her. Still, these impulses were slowed by Femme's warning: to even court Charmaine, he had to win favor with Julien Broyard. He pushed the gate open with his foot, caressing a small wooden bucket of eggs, and saw Julien moving fast toward his work shed. To win Julien, he thought he had to appear manly, smart, and holy. He knocked gently and spoke through the door. "Good morning, Mr. Julien. This is one of those mornings I like to start with a prayer for more mornings like this one. I hope you're feeling very well," he said gallantly.

"Pichon, why you talking so damn formal? Why you here?"

"Eggs Femme sent. She also sent word that those altar society ladies are meeting tonight. I guess Charmaine ought to know. Your house sure is quiet this morning."

"Charmaine's getting ready for school. Thank Femme for the eggs. I'll carry Charmaine to the church this evening." Julien walked toward the door, a sign for Pichon to leave. Mentioning Charmaine's name set him to grinning in his silly-boy way. He sensed that Julien's opinion against him had not swayed. Still, he welcomed his patting him on the shoulder and saying, "Don't never be a stranger, Pichon—when it comes to news from Femme or your mama." To

Pichon, this was progress, and he nearly danced out of the yard singing "thank you."

Julien found Charmaine eating breakfast. In a few strict words, he delivered Pichon's message. After cleaning the kitchen, she went to the large hall closet and counted out five starched altar cloths. She pulled down several altar napkins while her father sipped strong black coffee. She asked, "Did he say anything else?"

"No, cher, come straight home," he said, examining how perfectly she stacked the embroidered white altar napkins. "I'll be driving you down there. Things getting crazy again."

"That *was* Pichon you were talking to, right?"

"Yes, and it was nothing to do with you. You're getting hotter than Good Friday fish grease, miss. Aunt Velma's boys come here to see me, go fishing, and carry messages. Nothing about you." Charmaine turned her eyes down and smiled. This reprimand was just another version of the many restrictions Julien declared daily to ensure that she was "raised right." She acknowledged that her father was strict, but she also loved him and his overbearing ways. She could differentiate between his love and his responsibility for her honor. They had had only one blistering argument over her wanting to step out of his boundaries. She had once been bold enough to go to a picnic after church without permission. Even his severe punishment, which took away her privilege of reading romantic novels, did not lessen her love and adoration for him.

+ + +

Sacred Heart Church had a horseshoe driveway and sat far back from the road. The old wood frame church looked as if it could hardly hold itself up. It was worn and battered from too much heat, humidity, and hurricanes. Its weatherboards always seemed to need a new painting even after it had a fresh one. The blue trim had grayed to dullness, and the doors never extended welcome. It was a church that had not known loving parishioners. It was a church constantly fueled by strife. Even the sanctuary's wallboards held strife's venom. Its smell was not one of flowers from past marriages or baptism celebrations. Instead, the last argument or controversy stunk like thick August swamp gas over the aisles and pews. Even the colorful stained-glass windows struggled to retain enough sunlight to show their luster.

Father Lorquette took a long swig from a flask, pocketed it, and went back to sweeping the center aisle. The pinched folds of facial skin signified that he detested the taste of whiskey. The smell served as a necessary, nasty part of his disguise. While waiting for the Ladies Altar Society, he always kept to an assumed routine: sweep the church, smell of liquor, and appear subservient. He timed these tasks perfectly to arrive at the front doors as the bells tolled five o'clock. He put the broom in the front closet and heard wagons. Pike supplied him with cheap whiskey from Mudbug's and—more importantly—regulator information his clients spoke loosely about. Father took another quick swig and opened the front doors.

Portly Mary Eaton and corpulent Hébert gave the wagon a good shaking and were already down as women arrived in twos and threes, with stable boys but no husbands. Father Lorquette stood on the church porch and bade them all good evening. Mary led everyone to the first pew and sat glancing back as others arrived.

Father Lorquette followed them and said, "As usual, ladies, I'll leave you. If you need anything, I'll be in the rectory." He said this leaning over the pew, with great flourish, as the women frowned and pinched their noses against sniffing whiskey breath. He depended on his feigned drunkenness to ease their tongues into careless antagonistic chatter that revealed secrets often about their regulating husbands and sons.

He had almost reached the door when Mary called him with echoes reaching the rafters. She was a big-boned, agile, chunky woman, who stood tall above the others. She said, "Father, please lock the front doors and leave through the side door. I want to start taking necessary precautions against all of this danger we're hearing about."

This surprised Father Lorquette, but he complied. He locked the front doors noisily and left, slamming the side door that led to the rectory. He stood just outside to listen attentively until Charmaine and Julien arrived.

"Is everyone here? No. Where's Pauline?" Mary asked, surveying two full pews.

"I passed by her house. She's gonna be a little late," Olga Glapion offered.

Mary shrugged. "Well, let's get started and finished before that drunk returns. He's sure stinking tonight. Last time, we talked about what happened in Colfax and how we won't let niggers do it here. My husband, Reginald, has been talking to other men—those who'll listen," she said, looking at Hébert, "and, everybody agrees we need to prepare. Lacombe niggers will do worse than in Colfax. They got Créoles and Choctaws helping them. Reginald told me Femme's got a Choctaw and a nigger boy, whose daddy died in Colfax, living with her.

A buzz arose from the pews. Hearing his name, Hébert grew agitated. To silence them, he held up his hand. "I don't mean to suffer abuse about what Luc Coulon will and won't do about these niggers. I got no control over him. Reginald gives me information. I circulate it to our advantage. Luc Coulon is weak. But I'm loyal to you camellias. The *only* way to nip nigger trouble is not allowing it to bud. Femme and that Choctaw are planning something."

"I heard they came to church *together?*" Olga said, full of dramatic outrage.

Mary retook her position. "They did. Listen. Our men question if they can trust this priest or even Sheriff Blake. The men say they're not ready to go after Femme because Luc Coulon protects her. But they mean to go after the Choctaw and Velma's twins. She controls Coulon and got him to hire her boys. We're watching them, but they're watching us too. Reginald says those twins are a big easy target they need to hit to send our message. My Reginald always says that fearless niggers are the most dangerous ones." A loud assent spurred Mary to continue. "Our men have become regulators to break up any resistance. We're getting help from as far away as Colfax and Shreveport. The best way to start is lynching niggers regularly."

Hearing this made Father Lorquette stand erect in disbelief. He swallowed hard and listened, peering through the doors' crack. Hébert nodded, taking in a bellyful of air, and said, "Femme answers to no one. I agree we can't worry about her now." He was poised to continue the rant, but an impending belch arrested him.

One of the younger women, comely and unspoiled, stood and pulled back her chapel veil. She said timidly, "My sister and I came to talk about safety and how to keep peace. Our husbands sent us. We're new, but I can't forget we're in the Lord's house. I mean no disrespect to Dr. Hébert or Miss Mary, but I'm compelled to say I'm completely offended and feel like we're sinning when people use such language."

Father Lorquette recognized the young women and was dismayed that they had joined this group. They were among his most decent and faithful parishioners. Hopelessness started to take a hold of him. He heard movement in the front pew. Before Hébert could respond, Mary folded her arms in defiance and pronounced with great calm, "This is just a building. Some of you were raised to believe it's more. Believe what you want, but this has been the only place to meet and not be discovered. But eyes are on us. This church is our enemy till we take it back, which we aim to do. We can pretend to be good Catholics, but don't forget why we're here. This ain't no prayer meeting. We're organizing to fight."

The young woman repositioned her chapel veil and sat embarrassed. There were several women who were angry at Mary's unladylike behavior, but they simply murmured to each other. Two crossed themselves and mumbled prayers, but most nodded assent to Mary's rallying speech.

From the second row came the booming voice of Amelia Plachette. "I need to talk on this." Amelia was a tall woman, who had been lied to about how marrying a farmer was marrying well. She was also the clichéd white southern farmer's wife: buxom with a tiny waist; minimally educated but inept in domestic affairs; pretty, but in a flimsy way; and, prideful because no other vice was acceptable or tolerated. Amelia had been married for ten years to an old Lacombe family. Without Mary's acknowledgement, she said, "These girls, as they say, are new. Girls, I know you and your good-looking husbands, because y'all are some of my kin. Let me tell you something: colored girls can grab and hold your husband faster and longer than you. You'll learn *that* when he comes home to find you powdered and primped, and he's already been lured and tired out by sweaty, hot brown tits all day in the fields. I'm thirty and haven't carried one of my husband's babies, but colored girls in Mandeville parade Plachette's bastards in front of me like the spoils of war. For ten years, it would've been easier to take bullets and survive. Y'all need to listen!" Amelia, her face wet with angry tears, sat exhausted. She glared at the young sisters, who cringed.

The conversation meandered in and out of perilous subjects until a hard, loud knocking shocked them into jerking their collective heads toward the front door. Father heard the banging as well and took off to the rectory.

"Must be Pauline Breau. We're almost finished. I'll call her to the side door." Mary walked quickly and spoke through the door's cracked wood, "Come to the side door; this one's locked." She pranced back to the front just as the side door opened.

"Good evening, ladies. Why are the front doors locked?" No one responded. "Anyway, I just have a change of altar clothes. Don't mind me. Doing the Lord's work, you know," Charmaine said, smiling and counting altar napkins.

"I thought you came on Wednesdays, Charmaine?" asked Mary.

"Daddy's been really busy lately, so I come when he can bring me. Got work to do in the sacristy. Don't want to interrupt y'all."

"Oh, you ain't interrupting. We're finished, girl. Let's go." Mary ordered.

"Finished? Well, good evening." Charmaine walked into the sacristy and closed the door. She quickly put the altar linens on a nearby table and fled back to listen.

Mary turned her back to the sanctuary and whispered, "I'll send word for the next meeting. From now on we're keeping them short."

After the echo of shoe shuffling quieted, Charmaine opened the door. She looked puzzled. *They always finish by saying the rosary. Not one of them was kneeling or had any rosary beads. Why was Dr. Hébert here?* She snuffed out candles and worried she had arrived too late. She stuffed the week's soiled linens into a pillowcase and went to fetch Julien to meet with Father Lorquette.

Father sat on a bench on the rectory's screened porch smoking his pipe. Charmaine, full of anxiety, spoke plainly. "There were three more this week than last. Two were those sisters married to the two brothers. They go to Mass every Sunday and sit together in the third pew on the Blessed Mother's side—"

"The Pellicer girls," Julien interrupted. "Good folks. I don't know their husbands. The Pellicers are rich from sugar cane. Charmaine says they didn't end with the rosary. This ain't good, Father."

Julien and Charmaine owned Father's adoration and trust. Tonight, their faces showed slithers of fear. He confessed *his* fear and told them he overheard plans against Percie and Pichon. "They also talked about more 'regular' lynchings. They'll be watching Femme and Ossi too."

Charmaine said, "Mary Eaton stopped the meeting when I got there. She was red as hot pig blood. They weren't expecting me. Oh! I found it funny that that old doctor was there."

Father used the bench to tap the burnt tobacco out his pipe. He set it aside and pulled uneasily at his collar. "They never end without the rosary. Come to think of it, they never asked me to lock the front door before. Always changing the day they meet. Dr. Bellocq there.

Bad signs." His head was full to spinning. His whiskey-tiredness dragged on his voice. "When they set the next meeting, I'll send word. Pichon passes by here every Friday morning early to deliver the sacristy flowers he picks up from the Slidell stagecoach. He goes directly to work after and can carry word to Papa Luc, Ossi, and Percie." Charmaine's head pricked up. The men noticed her interest, especially when she averted her focus to the pillowcase of soiled linens.

"We'll talk to Femme tomorrow," Julien said.

Father put his pipe in his cassock pocket. He patted Charmaine on the shoulder and thanked them for their vigilance. He sighed and said, "This will be hard on Aunt Velma. I'll need to pay her a visit. I'll talk to Sheriff Blake and Pike too. Oh! I'm still invited for red beans and sausage on Mondays, right?"

Julien smiled and said, "Don't be late, Father. I'll have more children than Moses this Monday. Aunt Velma's holding choir practice at the house, and after they sing, they eat like field hands. You're welcome at Guinea Beach anytime." They left, and Father Lorquette went inside to nurse his complaining, whiskey-aching stomach.

As was his ritual, he woke the next morning for Mass and went to light church candles for early risers who came to pray before work. Pike was a fixture at Mass every morning and often helped Father light candles and ready the church for Mass. As he set out along the cobblestone path, he could make out someone running in his direction. Pike was waving his arms and shouting, "Go back, Father. You don't want to see this."

Father met Pike just at the bend in the walkway that turned toward the side church door. "Pike, I smell smoke. What is it?"

Pike tried to block the priest from proceeding. His big green eyes puddled over. "A big cross!"

Father Lorquette turned the corner and did not get near the church. A ten-foot burning pine cross lit the steps to the side entrance. In the faint morning light, the pine's sap crackled angrily as golden fire ominously revealed black amorphous hands clutching against Sacred Heart's walls.

Guinea Beach's Squeaky Sand

WORD OF SACRED HEART'S cross-burning ran headlong through Lacombe. Pike informed Sheriff Blake, who went immediately to the rectory. Pichon delivered the sacristy flowers from Slidell and raced his horse over to the Coulon mansion to let his mother know. Then he went to the sawmill to tell Lucien and Papa Luc. Charmaine and Julien arrived for Mass that morning and gasped at the charred cross. They drove down Lake Road to Femme's where Ossi and Meffre were eating breakfast. When she saw their rig outside her gate, she braced herself.

Papa Luc arrived home early that evening. Aunt Velma wept through supper preparations and looked helplessly at him. "They coming for my boys. I feel it in my soul."

He held her close, rubbed her back, and gently kissed her neck. He pulled away slightly and said, "Look at me, Velma. You know how much I love you. I'm doing everything I can to prevent trouble. I pray I'm trusting the right people. Lucien and I are watching and listening. For now, that's all we can do." Neither said anything else.

After stopping again at Sacred Heart to commiserate with Father, Charmaine and Julien went home confused and bewildered. No one knew the entire story about Guinea Beach, but the part told consistently was that an old man—long gone—named it. He lived just up the trail from the Broyards. He raised guinea hens, the world's best noise sentinels. Folks also claimed that the ugly hens, parading around Julien's yard, were part of the old man's spirit. Julien claimed the old man told him he named the beach after those "damned" chickens. When Julien could not find work, they roasted well for dinner. They also protected against intruders.

Julien's house set back from the bayou on a rise full of oaks and magnolias. A solitary man, he had built a large work shed—a retreat from the nearly inescapable noise of guineas and children running across the squeaky sand down to the bayou to swim. Everyone understood that this was *his* shed, where work benches lined the center of the building. He stored finishing lumber—mostly staples of oak and pine—in long racks along the east walls for building cabinets. The shed's west walls were covered with varieties of fishing nets, poles, and other boating equipment. The shed housed— most importantly—large crocks, hidden from view, in which he made a potent homebrew.

Although he worked building cabinets and painting houses, his house was Lacombe's most disagreeable dwelling. He rarely invited clients to visit because his house could never do justice to his excellent carpentry. He blamed this all on being married to a Catholic woman, who volunteered his services for free too often to poor people. Between that and the truth was the fact that he was often mellowed by the homebrew he drank. He and his "sainted" wife Sadie—and later his daughter Charmaine—had made a history of agreements that they constantly fought over. The one they abided by religiously, however, was that his shed was off limits. Sadie sent things to him there, including messages, but she had not seen the shed's interior for eight years—that is, eight years before she died in a hurricane flood. She tried to get home from the dell chapel she was cleaning, but the water rose too quickly, and she could not swim.

As their only child, Charmaine inherited her mother's place serving in the church and participating in Julien's rules about his privacy. She could stand at the door and yell for him as long as she did not enter. This uncontested rule governed their home life, and mostly, there was peace.

Julien sat on a stool sharpening a sickle with a file. His daddy had given him the file the day he finally learned to sharpen knives "the right way." With only the shrill repetition of the file's grating, he mused on the futility of ever repairing his house. It looked ownerless though Broyards had lived there for more than a half century. He and his eleven brothers and sisters had done nothing more for the house than upset its insides and weaken its shaky foundation. They had used the house like worn but thick-leathered brogans—useful though worn past useful looking. The tin roof was streaked with bands of rust that seemed to grow in opposite directions from orange roofing nails. The rafters had not been boxed, so they projected like monotonous spikes from under the tin. When the house was built, the rafters had all been cut the same length, but no one would believe that now. Uniformity seemed to have just walked away from all sides, including the top. The outside walls reneged on their duty to warm anything. They covered the house in defiance, even defense. To call the house used-up or unloved would be calling far too much attention to its lack of self-respect. This house lived and thrived on its shame, sitting, as it did, amidst laughing oaks and prissy magnolias. This house was not neglected; it was tired. Tired of trying to be a house for too many for too long. Julien knew this and resigned himself to just live there long enough to raise Charmaine till she married and left. He vowed to build a small house nearer the road afterward. In his plan, there would be no shed.

His one pleasure, after his homebrew, involved retreating to his shed to fix things, build things, and give fixed things to those in need. Reflecting on the disaster that was his house fueled his depression over the cross-burnings, lynchings, and threats to Aunt Velma's twins. Even the the shed's confines did not provide customary peace. His participation in the resistance that endangered Charmaine nagged him. She was his prize. All the neighborhood children went to the church school, and Charmaine was, by all counts, the smartest. She was an ordinary-looking olive-skinned Créole girl: plain, pretty, and even voluptuous, but not beautiful. She inherited her mother's *passé blanc* complexion and her father's sturdiness. She was not stout and certainly not thin. There was a thickness about her body that put her midway between shapely and plump. She wore her straight auburn hair pulled back severely into a chignon without adornment. Her oval face was animated by greenish-brown eyes. All in all, most saw her as a lovely and devoted young Christian woman.

At times, Julien saw her differently: she was willful, arrogant, and calculating. He loved all of these as attributes he cautioned against. To be sure, he was proud to have fathered her. She was his unyielding obligation and a cherished reward. He was pulled, just then, from his sharpening by the sound of the guineas followed by a stampede of school children, running to the beach. It started to rain heavily just then, and Charmaine called, "Hey, Daddy. It was raining down-the-bayou. You better come in." Julien knew she would not wait for an answer, but he put the file and sickle down and started closing the shed. He thought: *Time's coming for her to leave.*

Charmaine was enormously popular at school because she was the herald for the condition of the Guinea Beach: water temperature, the location of the swing rope, and where the best secret places were. Black and Créole families came to picnic along the bayou beach, famous for its white, squeaking sands. Julien was often asked why the sand squeaked as folks trafficked across the beach to the bayou below. He would invariably give the same answer: "The sand is sassing back at those loud guinea hens." Once a geologist from Tulane had told him that the sand was round with quartz particles and that caused the squeaking sound. Julien shrugged and went back to his shed to drink beer.

Folks gossiped that Julien never spoke more than a hundred educated words because he was too busy cussing about his misery. In contrast, Charmaine, spouted, offshoot fashion, into a net of complex relationships puzzled over by everyone who knew her. She was proud to show her intelligence. It made her independence natural.

She turned seventeen refusing to mark the occasion because Julien had made it clear that he was not going to have Pichon "dusting his black off" all over her. Aunt Velma tried everything she could to stop the fight between them, mainly because she knew that Charmaine would win by getting, in all the wrong ways, what her father denied her. She sympathized more with Charmaine, given the cross-burning at Sacred Heart and Pichon's being a target. In Aunt Velma's opinion, Julien's prejudice was a story too common in Louisiana—one that "ain't worth the damn telling." It was Pichon's blackness that attracted Charmaine as wildly as it repulsed her father. Everyone, even Julien, knew this.

Through all this, Pichon, undaunted by the Altar Society's threat, sent messages to Charmaine through Aunt Velma and Femme. It was now clear that he was not welcome to court Charmaine at the Broyard's. This he accepted but was dismayed that Charmaine did not speak to him after Sunday Mass. He asked Femme to inquire if he had offended her. When Femme reported that Charmaine had only responded with a smile, Pichon asked Aunt Velma to deliver a flower for him. Aunt Velma had no fear of Julien and after Mass she handed the flower defiantly to Charmaine in front of her father and said, "Here's a rose from your admirer." Charmaine blushed, folded the flower into the soiled altar clothes she carried, and flung the bundle in the back of the rig. Julien was silent all the way to Guinea Beach.

After several such failed episodes, Pichon's envoys abandoned helping him. By then, he realized that her father was fencing

Charmaine in an impenetrable blockade over which he presided and guarded. Lacombe proved small enough for battling wills to present themselves in a public fight that everyone could enjoy. Soon enough, the town was taking bets that Pichon would win the prize despite Julien's boasts otherwise.

On the third day in December, a Friday, in the year of her seventeenth birthday, Charmaine woke well before dawn. Julien had left to buy crab bait and his absence allowed her to walk nearly three miles to the road leading to the sawmill just off Cold Branch Road. At the road's edge, she sat on a stump as men turned their horses to the mill. Singing to herself, she waited for Pichon. She remembered that he always delivered the sacristy flowers to Father on Friday mornings before he went to work. She decided to risk waiting. She thought about how beautiful he was—especially that he was tall and coal black. A few times, she had confessed to Father Lorquette her impure thoughts about Pichon. Yet, at this very moment, she imagined his muscled embrace and was embarrassed at her sighing. Father had given her penance of prayers to the Holy Mother for purity. She sang aloud about the Holy Mother and May's flowers, thinking: *I only imagine, and it's a sin. For what I'm going to do, my soul's damned.*

Whenever Julien hinted that his daughter's going to the convent would be a good life for her, Aunt Velma laughed and said that Charmaine had breasts "shaped for breastfeeding" and hips "framed for saddling babies." Still, there was no denying that Charmaine's appearance tended toward severe and nunlike. Her dresses always had high collars even in the enervating summer heat. It was rare that she showed her arms' skin below the elbow. Yet, no matter the dress she wore to suggest modesty, her prominent breasts protruded and placed her comfortably between well-figured and mildly corpulent. Some gossips even opined that her attire was a sign of some dire penance she was doing. For Charmaine, the truth was simple: those exterior extravagances mattered very little.

Just then, an old armadillo, which stopped at the road's graveled edge, sank heavily into the ditch, and emerged just in time to halt its maneuvers against an unfamiliar and rare sight: a loud, shaky double rig, drawn by two horses and full of cut firewood, plodding up Lake Road. The armadillo was incensed at the intrusion, and Charmaine thought it hilarious that plans, no matter how well laid, can be squashed so easily. The rig passed slowly, and she said to the armadillo, "It's a good thing you're old and slow. Like Daddy says, 'Young folks kill themselves with youth.' Watch out."

Soon enough, Pichon rode up fully astonished to see Charmaine standing on the stump waving. "Pichon, meet me Sunday at Guinea Beach at dusk. Don't be late. I have to get home before Daddy gets back." She left Pichon speechless, staring at the stump as if he had just awakened. By the time he reacted to speak, Charmaine was headed up Lake Road.

"Wait. I can ride you home."

"No. You can't. Go to work before someone sees us." She grabbed the chignon as if to tighten it. "We'll have time to talk plenty on Sunday." She smiled and smacked a kiss toward him. He hopped off his horse, hoping to prolong the visit. She raised her arm in protest and kept walking.

With the reins dangling in his right hand, he waved her away with his left. He smiled heartily and jumped back on his horse. He turned toward the sawmill and smiled his way through his work all day. Meeting her could be good or bad, but the risk she took was a hopeful sign.

Pichon thought of little else except Charmaine, Ossi's frequent absences, and Femme's worrying about all of them. Aunt Velma's caution to "watch things" made the twins anxious when Femme talked about taking a trip alone to New Orleans. The trip took five hours one way by train, and her going was far too mysterious. These all had become daily distractions for Pichon. Percie enjoyed far fewer complications. He was always courting a new girlfriend, training a horse, or finding happiness in a large plate of food. His work at the Mandeville pier sustained him and his simple tastes.

Pichon and Percie had grown to care deeply for Meffre, and they knew Femme and Ossi expected such closeness. Just whistling blues songs perked the boy up, but the twins always had jokes ready to create levity to ward off Meffre's moodiness.

Meffre began his apprenticeship in the pecan business, and Femme always found a way to smile and see happiness in their developing relationship. But Pichon knew that she remained troubled. His only respite from all of this involved anticipating time with Charmaine.

By the time she was fourteen, Charmaine started dreaming of Pichon. She had made the mistake of telling a choir girl that Pichon was good looking. That noise found its way into after-Mass gossip.

Later it filled her house and set Julien to preaching to the walls every time Charmaine appeared. Julien believed that black skin was a prediction for a horrible life full of hatred. He meant to prevent his daughter from being so cursed and set a course to moor her away from it. His prejudice was couched in the cautionary line: "Like should marry like." He could not swallow criticisms of his being "color-struck." His defense of preserving Créole heritage was mocked even by his closest friends. Most of all, he despised Charmaine's flippant comparisons of him to Hébert Bellocq. Such comparisons felt like a heavy rock in his chest. What he believed to be tradition he refused to see as prejudice.

For Charmaine, this was a challenge birthed by her dreams and avaricious reading of love stories. She especially liked Shakespeare's lovers, who rarely loved without obstacles. That kind of love, she believed, was the only love that could survive in Lacombe, where alternatives were scarce or prohibited.

She did nothing, of course, to realize her fantasy till she dreamed that she was old and still cleaning Julien's house. She saw herself scrubbing floors and cooking. She shivered in her sleep, in the dream dressed in long, dirty aprons. In every corner, there were buckets of dirty, sudsy water, with rags hanging from them. The buckets were identical and seemed to get bigger, the longer she dreamed. Awake, she vowed to lure in Pichon before she turned sixteen. At that age, her father would start, in earnest, to arrange her meeting some Créole she would surely detest.

She had often tried to get news about Pichon from his mother, who would only pull her to her breast and tell her gently, "Forget it, girl. He won't allow it." Aunt Velma knew Julien well. As much as she would like to see this grow into a strong love and marriage, she also feared the pain it could cause. Thus, she set about protecting them from the love match. She told Pichon that Charmaine stopped asking for him and that her father had put fear in her soul. She lied to Charmaine that Pichon was keen on a girl in Slidell. Aunt Velma, who claimed that she only trafficked in gossip out of necessity, told Femme about "this thing trying to fix itself 'tween Pichon and Charmaine." Full of guilt, she prayed for forgiveness for lying and keeping secrets. She admonished herself: *You hypocrite. Loving Papa Luc in secret while stopping this young love.*

Still, Charmaine was as savvy as she was intelligent. Gossip moved through Lacombe at a spiritual speed: quick, unnoticed, and full of blessings and danger. She surmised that Pichon's lack of attention meant that her father's stubborn reticence was stronger and more effective than her ladylike hinting and curiosity. After the haunting dream, she decided she had to resort to a plan to move her life forward. Sixteen made her anxious, and seventeen made her determined, especially after learning about the plotting against Pichon by regulators.

Saturday passed too slowly. Her father commented a dozen times about her being too quiet and moody. At one point, Aunt Velma accused her of being too detached from ironing Sacred Heart's altar clothes to have anything but sin on her mind.

She slept very little Saturday night. For this, she was glad given the possibility that the haunting dream would recur. Remembering it, however, strengthened her resolve. Through Sunday morning preparations, throughout the Mass, through dinner, and in and out of the slow afternoon, she only thought of Pichon.

Julien rarely changed his Sunday pattern of sequestering himself. He cut lumber for cabinets while Charmaine sewed children's clothes to deliver to clients after church. It was easy for her to slip away unnoticed. She walked quickly along the path that led to the bayou, humming to herself as she noticed how the light pried its way through the tree branches to fall easily on the floor of pine straw or oak leaves.

As she neared the bayou, she saw Pichon sitting with his head thrown back resting on the trunk of a huge pine, the one she adored for its canopy of branches. He fiddled in his satchel for grapes he brought her. He set them on a blanket beside him. She had spent many days under this pine, resting or hiding from the sun. Not wanting to disturb him, she walked slowly now. She believed that this pine demanded respect for its long life, generous shade, and peace. She believed this more now because Pichon was a part of the scene. She ambled up to him, without his noticing her, and put her hand on his head. He did not show surprise but simply put his hand on hers and gently pulled it to his lips. She knelt next to him and let him hold her hand over his heart. Then she said, "All of this must be done fast so we can have a life together." With this, she turned Pichon's head and kissed him hard and passionately. He responded with warm gentleness and was led by her.

The evening light was weak on the bayou, but it provided enough glow for Pichon to see Charmaine undressing. "Oh my God,

Charmaine! Not that kind of 'fast.' No, we can't. I mean this is too much for here, for now. I don't mean to die this young. Your daddy—"

Charmaine looked at him, without emotion, and with her mind set on a mission. She did not smile or frown. She simply pulled off his shirt and pulled him on top of her. For as ready as Pichon was, he was also fearful. He said, "I brought grapes."

Her expression turned serious. She held his broad shoulders and said, "Look, Pichon. My daddy won't allow your courting one of those guinea hens. Forget courting and romance. What we give each other today is not love. It's necessity. If we're to be together, you need to father our child tonight or soon. Daddy will force you on me if I'm carrying your baby. Your mama will see to that. It's the only way."

"I can't. It's wrong and against everything holy. I haven't told you I love you," he said, pleadingly.

"You *don't* love me. We can't love each other yet. That happens later. Finish this now so one day we *can* love each other. Take your pants off."

She watched his jittery struggles as he pulled at his underclothes through snatches that revealed his muscles' contours before he was naked. She lifted her slip over her head and sat before him, looking at her hands. When he sat beside her, his flaccid manhood hung longer than she had imagined. He moved to kiss her, but she focused on the obvious might of his ebony chest. With her palms completely open, she stroked his chest and planted her head there. He took her face in his hands and kissed her. Their hearts thumped until her awkwardness unintentionally touched his erection. He smiled and gently handed her his satchel for a pillow. Then, he allowed his nature to rule. He tried not to push when she squirmed. Instead he fondled her full breasts and kissed them tenderly. When she succumbed to his pulsations, he kissed her neck and breasts until she moaned softly and called his name. His strength and weight excited her, and, in an aggravated series of fumbling and graceful glides, they negotiated, in their novice way, pain and intermittent pleasure. "I can't wait anymore. Now. Now. Now." And then some rest came as the pine rustled its branches into a slight breeze.

The breeze was a sign for Charmaine to clean herself. She washed away blood with the fresh and clear bayou water and cried as Pichon knelt nearby consoling her. They dressed silently and held each other against waves of guilt and bliss.

"Meet me here next Sunday and every Sunday till you don't see me here." Pichon had no time to respond. She ran up the path, leaving him confused. The night had fallen hard around him, but he could not move. He reached for his satchel and pulled out a candle, which he lit and then prayed: "Femme prays to you trees. Pine tree, grow my love for Charmaine."

+ + +

The next time, Pichon committed to bringing some romance. "I brought you chocolates."

She took the candy, put it in the pocket of her dress, took his hand, and said playfully, "I have something to *give* you that can't fit in your pocket."

Their secret place, under the huge pine, on Guinea Beach, seemed to shrink, as their maturity and lovemaking grew. Charmaine never told Pichon she loved him, and he never missed his Sunday chances to tell her that his love was stronger than the week before. His previous fears abated as Sundays passed. And this one place that was, for others, the most open and public, the most used for summer fun, and the least sought after for lovemaking, was now their secret, loving pine tree. They often remarked, later, that their lives were created by the majesty of the lone, longleaf pine. They saw it as a natural blessing that the pine witnessed their love. Eshu smiled and rustled pine branches in approval.

+ + +

In the middle of January, a cold Sunday arrived, and Pichon sat alone for an hour until he surmised that he was going to be a father, which gave him even more reason to stay alive. Time stretched out long enough for him to realize how badly he missed Charmaine. That longing forced him to imagine not having her. That imagined absence engendered an internal quarrel. He grappled with fear tearing apart all hope for his future family. After kicking the squeaky sand, punching the air, and scratching his head, he thought of fatherhood and spurred a germ of happiness that overpowered the fear. He stood, faced the pine, and said gleefully, "I'm gonna be a daddy."

Soul Seed

THE THREATS AGAINST OSSI and the twins invaded Lacombe households like an observed intruder that no one acknowledged. Strangely, the threat emboldened Pichon. For Ossi, it was an accustomed threat he treated as ammunition to fire against enemies.

Except for candles in the oratory, Ossi came home to darkness. Femme was on her knees praying. Pointing in the direction of the barn, she signaled that Meffre was there. Ossi touched her shoulder lightly and left. Praying was difficult, more so after Ossi appeared. Yet, pray she must. The coolness of early March felt odd to her: it held a peculiar slowness, stasis even. Nothing seemed to want to sprout out thick and green, and the usual retreat of winter was not easily detected. Even the wetness was sloppy and ugly, without purpose. The rain had not been satisfied to beautify the few noticeable leaves with drops of crystal. To Femme, it all felt like signs of deliberate neglect and uneasiness.

Ossi had not mentioned his trips to New Orleans. Although they talked constantly about what Hébert and others were conspiring, she had not broached the subject of his absence. She worried that questioning him would be an affront. His secretiveness tormented her; yet, the orishas had impeded her will to confront him. With a bowl of water and a floating night jasmine in the oratory, she had asked Yemanja to create the best moment to question him. The water remained still; the jasmine's petals turned brown. Yemanja had responded against questioning.

Whenever Ossi returned, his presence calmed her; yet, there was still something wedged between them. Aunt Velma had tried to reassure her. "Choctaw men are different. They keep to themselves. Don't talk much. Femme, maybe it's best to quiet yourself. Accept his ways. He ain't gonna deceive you. He's protecting you and Meffre."

She gazed on Eshu's small wooden statue. Her father had carved it and told her to put it in light that felt right. She was eight the first time she heard Eshu speak. Albion had heard her talking to the old chinaberry tree behind the cigar shop. He stopped his work, and his elation erupted in knowing that she had inherited his spirituality. Years later, she had dressed this statue as her father had described it. Eshu's pants were white lace lined in silver ribbon. His upper garment was scarlet trimmed in the same white and silver lace. A thick and wide embroidered white ribbon crisscrossed his chest and served as a belt behind. White and scarlet tightly threaded beads hung around his neck. His head was adorned with an intricate silver crown that covered his ears, almost helmetlike, and peaked in a sharp point at the top. The entire crown was bejeweled in diamond-like stones, sparkling like stars. Eshu's dark facial features were uncovered; his black eyes were pronounced.

She put her right hand on the statue. "Eshu, something is right but wrong too. It's hard to pray for peace. What's happening? Aunt Velma calms me talking about Ossi and frightens me talking about Hébert. Nothing has slowed him down, and he is bound to destroy us."

Days later, she poured water into the bowl next to Yemanja's statue, just enough to create a ripple for another white jasmine to dance. Praying, she stood and lit candles and could hear Ossi and Meffre in the side yard chopping wood. She moved to go to them just as Pichon and Percie created a disturbance in the front yard, teasing Labas.

After supper and a lean rendering of Pichon's bad day at the sawmill and Percie's great day at Papa Luc's produce stand, Ossi and Femme gave them a look that said, "good night." The twins helped Meffre carry wood in and left. Everybody sensed that something was nagging Pichon when his joking turned to seriousness. Meffre assured them that it was all about Charmaine. In truth, it was his being a regulators' target and the shadow that cast over his impending fatherhood.

For Ossi, supper passed too quickly and without the usual conversation about keeping peace in Lacombe. Suppertime was a constant sharing of news from hungry mouths to craving ears, creating a labyrinth of information—helpful and dangerous. Yet, this night, Femme moved too quickly from the table to the kitchen sink with an armful of dishes. Meffre carried leftover bread and the bowls with uneaten vegetables. He smiled and tossed his eyes over the twins' plates of bones. Ossi caught his smile, hoping to use it as a segue into what might be miffing Femme. "Pichon never leaves fish even for a cat," he said, putting his plate next to the sink and holding her around her waist. He gently put his head on her shoulder and waited.

"Ossi, my sweet, Ossi. Just stay there. Don't move. Just listen to my nervous heart. I'm worried to shaking about Hébert."

Meffre knowingly grabbed a bucket of food slop for the pigs and said, "I'll go lock the barn."

Ossi turned Femme around and said softly, "You want to wash those dishes and come to bed with me? Let me calm you. Finish your work. Then, I'll come back and put you to sleep."

Femme felt herself moving from tightness into the peace that heralds passion. She remembered Aunt Velma's talking about men and what they want and why they want so much of it so often. She had also issued a caution: "Remember to complain about it, or they'll find out that you always want it too." Femme laughed and caught herself. She looked over her shoulder for Ossi, who had disappeared into the bedroom. *I guess Aunt Velma's right: it's good to have a man around two or three times a week.*

Ossi's singing in the bathroom found its way into the kitchen as a wordless humming. Femme put a thick blanket against the bottom of the front door—a common and practical precaution. The night's chill would become a cold breeze. She did the same for all the outside doors, turned off all the lanterns, and took two candles into the bedroom. Meffre's room was in darkness.

Ossi lay stretched out across the bed. His long, black hair was shiny and lay strewn across and down his broad chest. The room's dwindling light colored his torso bronze. Lying naked, he expressed himself in natural pride. Femme loved his unbraided hair and its natural smell against his manliness. She eyed every inch of him, from the tip of nose to his thick muscled legs. He was a prize for passion. "Turn over. Let me braid your hair so it doesn't get in my way." He registered a mild, playful protest and turned onto his stomach. She used only her fingers as a comb and braided the long strands with strength and tenderness. She loosened her own hair by untying a small leather strap. At the end of Ossi's braid, she tied the leather strap into a bow and made a curl using her finger. "Don't fall asleep. I have to clean this kitchen off me," she said, turning him over.

"I want to get really tired tonight before I go to sleep. And, I'm not tired yet. I'll just sing my song till you get back." He sang, in low, mellow, prayerful tones. He sang about love of women, the sun, and the land. As he sang, he watched the old oak sway in a breezy accompaniment.

The washing was timely and spiritual for Femme. She soaked in the warm tub, praying away her worry and fears. She begged Yemanja to clean away the angry thoughts against Hébert. *No loving should happen with a dirty soul. Clean my soul, Yemanja. Let me love.*

When she appeared before Ossi, she repaid his nakedness by dropping the damp towel that covered her. The oval shape of her face was fit for a porcelain cameo, the fine features inherited from her mother. Perhaps the finest of all was the perfection of her lips, just full enough to reveal a smile, designed to be precious. Her blackness complemented the light's attempt to accentuate its naturalness. Hers was a velvety ebony, smooth and enticing, made to arouse and incite begging. In generous waves, her hair fell protectively over her breasts but was ineffective in hiding her sensuality. Femme exaggerated nothing. Just standing there in sensuous light, she effortlessly imbued the scene with élan.

That night's loving was special because each released power to the other in passionate volleys. Ossi did for Femme everything she could want without asking. She marveled in how he gave so much more than he took by tender, soft movements that ensured her satisfaction against his. She reciprocated by demonstrating her pleasure for all his slow and easy effort. Together, they allowed their spent energy a slow easy creeping away. The bed's heat started to cool with a sneaky, creeping chill, and Ossi pulled Femme closer. "Now you keep me warm. There's enough fire in you."

Femme held him tight across his chest, looking at him with eyes full of puzzlement. Her mind drifted to his secrecy about the New Orleans trips. As was his custom, Ossi turned to the window and looked out on the old oak to muse on nature in nighttime. She pulled her arm from him and held herself with happiness and apprehension. She could feel joyous warmth while she could also feel her restraint diminishing. Her heart started beating differently. Slowly, with practiced determination, she said, "Ossi, I believe in you. Please look at me. When will we talk about where you've been going? I'm afraid for you."

When he turned to her, she saw his wet cheeks glistening through eyes that held a cool distance. His being annoyed frightened her. He pulled himself up and sat looking down on her. He had rehearsed, many times, what he would say. He knew she would react in a way that would allow him to leave although, in his soul, he never wanted to go. Yet, their lives depended on his absence.

The room filled slowly with a piercing chill. He put his heavy hand on Femme's forehead and said dispassionately, "When I take the eggs and chickens to market, I don't always deliver them to Percie in Mandeville. I take them all the way to Covington and twice, when I told you I hunted overnight, I took the shipment to New Orleans. Those two times I went to the Vieux Carré Market and then to the St. John Birchman orphanage. I carry news and money and weapons in both directions so we can be ready. I've left much of this with my people in Abita Springs. There will be no Colfax massacre in Lacombe." As he spoke, he could see a mourning look coming across her face. He was troubled that his quick explanation was insufficient. He pushed himself up against the headboard, crossed his imposing arms, and stared at a wall, full of regret for his inadequacies.

Femme sprung up vexed. As he expected, she questioned him. "You lied to me? You did this without telling me? You left me here helpless? Ossi, I don't want to lose you in a fight against Hébert and those Eatons. *Why* didn't you tell me?"

Her joy had flipped into the anger she had tried to control. In that moment, she also knew that Ossi was remarkably unlike Papa Luc. Yet, it was clear, she had gone too far. Yemanja's not answering her prayers and Aunt Velma's warnings echoed in her mind. To question his absence was to question his integrity, his constancy, his motives, his thinking, and his judgment—maybe even his love.

Why did she do it? It was impulsive and foolish. But she wanted the assurance of her central place in his life. Ossi moved away and had nearly dressed himself by the time she finished a rant against Hébert. He walked to the other side of the bed, away from the window, pulled the covers toward the head of the bed, and found a comfortable place to sleep on top of them. Femme moved to make room. Her every attempt to sidle next to him produced rigidity. Finally, tired by his belligerent silence, she slept and dreamed of fires in the swamp.

A spear of bright morning sun, coming through the oak's branches, awakened her. She found coldness where he had slept. It startled her to find eight dollars on the pillow, probably from the egg shipments. She looked quickly out into the empty yard and moaned incoherently to the unresponsive oak. Then, she walked to the bathroom and immediately recognized Ossi's curl bound by the leather strap on the sink.

Shortly after seven, Meffre found Femme in the kitchen setting out breakfast. She continued moaning, deep in mourning and regret, after the twins came in. They knew immediately that there was wrong everywhere. For different reasons, Pichon and Percie knew it was a time for listening, though they were desperate to talk with her. Femme looked at Pichon directly. She reached for his hand, took it and said, "Looks like a lot will change around here. I'll need you to help Meffre here after work. Percie, I'll probably need to go to New Orleans. I'll let you know. Meffre, just work here and in the grove as you always do." She paused, then added, "I'm depending on y'all."

She faced Meffre and said, "I don't want you to know the misery your people had. But I pushed your life in that direction last night. I ran Ossi off. I don't know if he'll come back. Hébert started this, and I helped by saying too much. I knew better. Aunt Velma told me that Hébert was agitating again and meant to stop Ossi by running him off. It'll be hard for us to make it in Lacombe—too much for me to work against alone. We must all be careful and smart and loyal. We're stronger than anything they can do to us." She cried into her apron, sad and embarrassed for her weakness.

Meffre stood close to Percie, who looked down on his shoes because he did not know where to settle his eyes. Meffre looked directly at her, wanting to tell her what he could not say now. Pichon said nothing but moved closer and held her. They knew what Ossi was doing in New Orleans; protection depended on silence. They knew this time would come and had sworn to Ossi that whenever he left, they would protect Femme. These thoughts pounded against their skulls rhythmically with Femme's sobbing. At that moment, all Pichon's play and foolhardiness settled into a corner of his spirit and made way for maturity. Meffre willed himself into a resignation to replace anger. Sadness invaded Percie's face and elongated his round features. He went to Femme and hugged and kissed her; then, he left for work. Assured that Ossi would never abandon them, Meffre went to the oratory to pray.

Femme had to tell Pichon some of her plans. She dried her eyes and took in a deep breath. "Pichon, pass by Aunt Velma's this morning. Tell her Ossi left and to make sure Hébert knows. With

Ossi gone, maybe he'll stop trying to hurt him. Then let Papa Luc know everything. The two of them will take care of the rest. It'll take me some time to get ready for what I need to do. For now, I want you to bring me candles—new or old. I need forty-three. Later this spring, get me three moccasins from the swamp—thick hungry ones we can feed till we need them." She delivered these directions deliberately, and Pichon knew not to question.

With this, Femme kissed his hand. She left him there and went to her bedroom to sit at the foot of her bed. That day was the first Pichon had been near Femme without his playfulness. That day, he knew her differently. That day, he knew she was something beautiful and powerful. That day, he loved her, without qualification, as his kin. He walked to her bed, knelt beside her, and let his head fall into her lap. He whispered, "I'm gonna be a daddy, and I have no fear of the regulators."

Femme pulled a small vial of water from her apron pocket and raised Pichon up to face her. She said happily, "Yemanja told me about your little soul seed. Spread this water around your house to bless it for you *and* Julien."

Eshu's Seesaws

PICHON WORKED STEADILY AT the lumber mill getting as many extra hours as he was allowed since January. It was difficult to focus on work, avoid fixating on regulators' threats, and endure not being able to interact with Charmaine. Desperate to see her, he became a frequent attendee at Mass just to trade glances. Julien's constant presence and perpetual scowling were barriers. He vowed he would not go anywhere near up-the-bayou or Charmaine's house, but one Saturday, having heard that Julien went crabbing on the Lake, he decided to risk a visit to Guinea Beach. When he saw Julien's rig parked in the yard, he turned away defeated. He constantly nagged Femme and his mother about Charmaine, but the news was slim.

In his spare time, he cleaned pots, kettles, and skillets in his yard. Meffre loved this work and earned a little money too. He especially liked getting the fire "red and blue" hot. Every kitchen in Lacombe had an iron skillet or kettle that accumulated hard black scales from packed-on grease. Pichon mastered making a fire hot enough to burn the pots clean. Afterward, he polished and seasoned the pots with enough oil to restore their dark lustrous shine.

Meffre enjoyed Pichon's joke-songs. On a day when Pichon had five big skillets in the fire, he entertained Meffre by singing about "Cooter Brown."

> *Old folks surely say*
> *Cooter Brown slid this way.*
> *He surely slid this way.*
> *To get his swaying attention,*
> *Slew-footed Elzora made mention*
> *That Johnnie Walker was in her kitchen.*
> *So, Cooter slid that way.*

Swaggering, he slid that way.
Then, Johnnie Walker slipped away:
Sloshing in glasses, sipped all day.
Then slew-footed Elzora couldn't play,
'Cause snoring Cooter had no play.
Ain't nothing sadder
To make you madder
Than a slew-foot woman,
A bad plan, and
a soft drunken man.

Meffre laughed and begged for more, and Pichon, who had a repertoire, gladly indulged. Meffre learned the songs quickly and made them his own. He told Pichon he was going to sing them so Lucien could put them to music.

On his way to the sawmill, Pichon often delivered pots, kettles, and skillets to his customers. They paid twenty-five cents or more, depending on size. He had Julien's frying skillet to leave with his mother at the Coulon's. Yet, she had left no signals for him. With Ossi's leaving, the quiet in Lacombe grew furiously against Hébert's threats. Aunt Velma and Femme were ever vigilant. This was especially taxing for Aunt Velma, who had to endure Hébert's spying early mornings and late evenings, just when she looked for Pichon.

One rainy Wednesday, and against too many failures that week, Aunt Velma tested her creativity to lure Pichon. On Monday, she had hung a yellow sweater out to dry, with magnolia leaves pinned to it, but the wind took it away before he saw it. Tuesday's rain washed away a red flowerpot with celery stalks in it. Finally, on Wednesday, she resolved, sun or rain, to get him to stop by enlisting the help of an ornery old rooster who frequented the back porch because he was too lazy to peck for his own food. Instead, he made himself a nuisance by crowing loudly on the porch railing. Aunt Velma took this as a sign that the good Lord was helping her. She made several tiny rice balls and set them all over the railing. The old rooster watched her, but he did not see the string hanging from her apron pocket. "I'd burn every pot in this house trying to cook yo' old tough neck. So, let's see if you good for something else. Want this rice, ole fool?"

The rooster eyed where the sun was trying to peek out behind the rain clouds. He let out a hoarse attempt at crowing and leapt to peck at the rice. He let Aunt Velma know that he was not afraid of her crowding the porch. She, for her part, pulled the string out in plain view and waited for him to bend his scrawny neck. In one quick and surprising second, Aunt Velma tied one of his legs to the railing. As soon as she was inside the screened door, he stopped his fussing and wing flapping and went back to pecking. "That'll get Pichon in this yard. You much better than a sweater or a flowerpot, ole fool."

When Pichon walked past the Coulon fence and saw the rooster, he laughed enough to bring Aunt Velma out. "Mama, times are hard if you got on the good side of that hateful old rooster. I got Julien's skillet here."

"Get in here, boy. Julien done pitched all his fits. I been over there every day last week. You can't go over till he comes to our house first. It's got to look like he's forcing you to marry Charmaine. I'm working on him, but you and Percie get the house clean and ready. It better look like the White House."

Pichon's eyes bucked and mouth gaped. He shifted from one leg to the other and broke out of the kitchen, sprinted over the porch rail, and ran into the adjacent woods. He fell on his back and yelled to the sky, "Thank you, Lawd Jesus for giving me one happy day." He rolled in the shade of the pines, clapping his hands to beat of a song. When he finally picked off the pine straw stuck in his overalls, he ran back to Aunt Velma and, out of breath and grinning, said "We'll have the house looking like President McKinley just got home."

"Boy, go tell Femme Papa Luc is likely to pass by there soon. The altar ladies got a meeting tomorrow night. They riled up about cross-burnings that the porker said ain't their doing. Oh! Tell her we getting a gas stove. And take that skillet to Sacred Heart. Charmaine'll pick it up." She smiled just seeing his satisfaction.

Pichon's head was full of chaos. "Old rooster, you got a lifetime of wives, so this ain't new to you. I'm getting married and having a baby. Here, I'll let you go." The rooster flew off the porch as Pichon left. The quiet lured him to the rail, where he perched, pecking at more rice balls.

+ + +

Meffre sat beneath the oak in the front yard. The fat pig took exception to this, especially because he shooed her away. He found comfort there because Eshu spoke to him from the branches. This was also his shelter to daydream about Lucien. Their friendship deepened after the rescue, but the physical distance they imposed between them created longing for Meffre. He often surprised Lucien with unannounced visits to the grove to hear his piano playing. Often, he regretted the closeness because he feared a sexless friendship would not last. Sitting on a piano bench together triggered awkwardness. He fidgeted constantly not knowing where to put his hands and arms. His stopovers became less frequent. In solitude with the oak, the only other company Meffre had was Labas, who was mischievous and full of devilment Meffre and Eshu found perfect.

On a day, when Eshu played trickster, Meffre spent hours training Labas to steal Femme's pipe, by hiding pork rinds in his pocket. Labas was a nosy, lazy hound with a nuisance baying. Such a nose and pork rinds were made for each other; mischief planned by an idle eighteen-year-old made the scheming effective, and Eshu provided inspiration.

After repeated attempts of baiting the beagle with morsels of pork, Labas finally learned the pipe-for-rind fetch, and Meffre held the pipe and laughed: "Took you too long to learn how to bring it. You're too dumb to take it back. Go on, sleep, dream about pork rinds." Labas plopped down next to him.

His best times, under the oak, were when Eshu filled his head with Lucien's piano playing. Labas slept soundly and suffered Meffre's pretended piano playing on his long fat body. He passed time this way until Labas left, annoyed by some nagging scent. Meffre mulled over Lucien's willingness to take risks compared to his own torment of being exposed. These idle times gradually matured him into a guiltless introspection on who he was. He prayed to Eshu for self-acceptance.

In the weeks ahead, everyone noticed that Meffre, Labas, and the oak were a threesome. After missing her pipe several times, Femme had no doubt that Meffre's orisha was Eshu. Had she time to worry, she might have, but her mind fixed on Ossi and the gossip circulating around town. Papa Luc had turned his attention to controlling the fighting between Lucien and Hébert. Charmaine had overheard little of consequence from the sacristy. Mary, at several altar society meetings, gave credit to Reginald for policing Femme and running Ossi off. Father Lorquette visited Femme, warning that Mary had emerged as the leading camellia. He was concerned about what might happen now that she and Reginald were leaders with connections to networks outside Lacombe.

Femme's biggest worries, however, were Papa Luc's absence, frequent cross-burnings, and lynchings in Ponchatoula. Two such cross-burnings were close to Percie and Pichon's house. She had always known the orishas kept her place safe: Yemanja and Eshu gave warnings that she became expert at reading. Yemanja made water ripple in pots, pans, and buckets—often with the solitary expression: *calm water.* Such rippling put her on her guard.

Her preoccupation with Ossi's absence kindled an unaccustomed fear. Grieving over him was not only a complication but also a distraction. Although she sometimes believed he would not return, she also feared that he would. His return could mean his death, or Meffre's, or both. The success of Hébert's regulators spurred revenge in her. She envied Papa Luc's tolerance in keeping Hébert close. It was an effective way to spy furtively on the regulator's moves, but watching evil succeed was difficult. She called on Eshu's guidance. What he provided was far less subtle than Yemanja. Whenever she tried to grapple with a decision about Ossi, she would light a candle and pray to Eshu. During her prayer, the candle would snuff itself out. Other times, with eyes closed, she prayed without candles and asked for Eshu's wisdom. She would open her eyes to find the oratory candles burning bright. Too often, she walked through the house haunted by worry and fear, only to hear buzzing and to find no insects. Standing in the kitchen, looking out the screened door, she would yell to Eshu, "Stop nagging me!" Invariably, Eshu shook the oak's flimsy branches in defiance.

She had also made a habit of frequenting the oratory to make sure the valise was still there. Whenever she did so, she also checked on the small satchel of Meffre's legal documents Papa Luc had given her. She looked at Eshu's statue and immediately felt relieved and said, "Daddy always said you're the warrior of self-control." She felt a spurt of happiness and grabbed Eshu's statue. As she turned around, she saw Meffre in the doorway. "Meffre, son, I didn't know you were here."

"Miss Femme, you call on the orishas. Daddy did too. He taught me. Mama wouldn't let me talk about loas or orishas. She made me go to Mass. Still, I talk to Eshu because he talks to me." Now that he was fully healed, Femme noticed that he smiled much more and always stood tall and straight. His chest formed a defined impression through his shirts, the sleeves of which were taut against his broad pecs. She admired his beauty and wondered whether he recognized how attractive he would be to Lacombe's young ladies.

"Sit here, son. Living with the orishas is hard. From slavery, so much has been taken from African people that they don't know what to believe." Meffre sat in a big chair next to the oratory. It was the first time he carefully examined the statues' faces. Femme knew she had to make this real. She pointed and asked, "Son, how well do you know these orishas?"

"I've never seen statues before. Daddy always talked about orishas and loas, telling me they're good for our souls. He thought Eshu was going to be my orisha. I believe in Eshu. But I'm afraid of going to hell, like Mama said."

"Do *you* believe you'll go to hell?"

"No. What I feel about Eshu is good." He paused, never taking his eyes off the statues. "It's funny. He makes me peaceful. Helps me remember Mama and Daddy. Helps me think. When I get angry, he talks me out of it. Even when I want to trick you or the twins, he helps me."

Femme smiled. "Meffre, these orishas come from a religion in Africa that the slaves brought with them. Many believe this is ancestor worship. It's called Vodun, but it's real. Believing keeps them alive to guide us. Believe this if you want to. You're old enough to make that decision. I was raised Catholic, too. Daddy believed only what he experienced. Our parents had their beliefs—we have ours. It should be right for us and make sense to us. I believe the trees possess the orishas' spirits."

He admitted excitedly that he believed too. He said Eshu had guided him inside just then. He hesitated then said, "Eshu tells me to fight to keep my soul. I felt him in the Red River steamboat when we came here. I talked to him about my leg's pain on the Mississippi freighter trip. I feel him now." Femme embraced him. She could feel his spirit enjoining hers. He hugged her until he could feel her tears wetting his shirt. He spoke slowly, "The morning he left, Ossi told me he would never stop helping us. He left because too many people are watching. He's still with us." Femme pulled away, but Meffre continued. "Percie and Pichon know this. We're making plans. I crab with Mr. Julien so I can tell him what Ossi tells us. Papa Luc also wants me to start working all day in the pecan grove with Lucien so we can all be connected."

93

Meffre's maturity surprised and comforted her. His resolve to participate in their resistance and protection eased her anxiety. She thanked him and noted the gratitude in his face. "Listen, come talk to me any time about this or anything. Your people gave you to me as a special blessing."

"Oh! Mr. Julien asked me if I wanted to go bayou fishing this evening, if you don't mind."

"Take anything you need from the barn. Bring back some good dinner for us." After this, Femme thanked the orishas for the message about Ossi.

✝ ✝ ✝

Labas bayed longer than usual when Papa Luc arrived. Femme was collecting and counting eggs and deliberately finished her work to allow him to knock on the front door and wait. She walked slowly across the barnyard and through the gate, rattling it loudly. "Femme, I don't have much time."

She appeared perturbed and unconcerned. "How you can put a fix on your legs and feet to come on my property after what I've been through. White people have finally taken everything a poor woman can hope for in this miserable life. Right now, I'm too hurt to find the right curse for you."

"Femme, you know I didn't run Ossi off. For his safety, it's a good thing he left. We're all working together." He threw his hat violently into a nearby chair and pranced to the end of the porch and back. He pulled at his hair, stopped in front of her, and made as if to leave.

"You didn't stop Hébert. I guess you don't know about the cross-burnings. Maybe you should ask Hébert. Get off my porch. Go."

"I'm not going till we talk. Hébert threatened Ossi and had him followed. Every time Lucien or I go to Mudbugs, we ask about what folks know about the cross-burnings. No one will let on about anything. Even people we trust to be on our side. I don't know how Hébert did it yet, but he has defied my asking him to stay out of your business and this nonsense fight with Créoles and coloreds and now the Choctaws. Father Lorquette told me he just heard Hébert say today that someone saw Ossi coming out of the colored sisters' convent in New Orleans. You know all the nuns here and at that convent. Find out what's going on. Word's spreading about Meffre and Ossi. People know they were part of that Colfax mess. Some people think Carl Keller is right to want his money back." Femme squinted and covered her mouth. He sensed that her anger was building and walked toward her as she held up her hands against his approach.

Without raising her voice, she said, "When you say 'people' you mean white people. Colored and Créole families have kinsfolk of slaves still walking through their lives. We know what you're capable of, but we're capable of fighting too." She turned her back to him and put her hands against the house as if she had the strength to push it over.

"Please, Femme, don't put me in that. Why are you blaming me? I've never been with *them* against *you*. It won't be easy to win against their numbers. Listen to reason. You know I do my best to keep peace. I'll risk everything to make peace for my son and—"

She dropped her arms and turned to him. "Aunt Velma? Me? We want more than peace, and I don't see you giving me any today. Leave my property." A grimace overtook her face.

He tried to take hold of her, but she rejected him by picking up his hat and by pushing into his chest without looking at him. He took the hat, pretending to dust it off. "Fine! You know I'm not in league with those people. Years ago, I sent Hébert to live at Small House because I couldn't abide him. I allow his visits to get gossip about Reginald and regulators. He's a dumbass, but he ain't spilling his guts like he used to. He's suspicious." Papa Luc was nervously fumbling for words but realized he had lost against Femme's obstinacy and willfulness. He fixed his hat on his head and moved quickly down the steps to mount his horse.

Femme watched the fat pig nearing the shade of the old oak and walked in that direction. The pig ignored her and flopped into her accustomed space. Femme leaned against the other side of the tree and slowly moved her back down into a sitting position. She spoke to the oak. "I haven't heard from you, old friend. I know you'll tell me to patch this up with Papa Luc. My own guilt made me take it out on him. I don't want to, but it's easy to forgive the ones we love. Maybe he doesn't know more than he says. Someone does."

The old oak sent a whisper disguised as a cool breeze, *Kumquats.* Femme thought, *What? You're picking my brain, Eshu.*

+ + +

When Pichon appeared that evening, she was waiting for him. After pouring coffee, she asked him to repeat exactly what Ossi had told him. The story was short: "Ossi woke me pulling on my big toe. Percie had already left. He said folks might've figured out about the cross-burnings and that a man, Keller, was looking for him. Lucien heard it from Pike at Mudbug's. When Ossi went to Mandeville to sell eggs, Percie told him. Said he couldn't come back because the bait we set might be traced to him."

She asked sternly, "Oh, my soul! You and Ossi burned crosses? Why?"

Pichon explained that Ossi thought the regulators' planning was too hard to figure out. He did not find out much in Lacombe or Mandeville; setting up fake cross-burnings was a way to make white folks think some northerners were invading their territory—a way to make Hébert or Reginald come out in the open. Ossi believed that Carl Keller had them working for him. Pichon ended: "Didn't seem to work, except to shut folks up. At the sawmill, white folks just stay to themselves and whisper a lot."

Understanding took all the tension from Femme's face. She shook her head affirmatively and paced around the kitchen. "Papa Luc was trying to put it all together. But, Pichon, how could anyone in Colfax know for sure Ossi was here? It's got to be Hébert; he's from somewhere around Cane River. Tell your mama to come here tomorrow. Can you go and tell Charmaine to come tomorrow, too?"

Pichon put both hands on his head as if to turn himself around. "Oh, Lawd. I don't think Julien wants to see *me*."

"Risk it. Julien's with Meffre bayou fishing. Charmaine ordered a springer and a pullet. Take one of those Rhode Island reds. Tell her what you told me and tell her to tell Father Lorquette."

"I was going to leave the Broyard's skillet at Sacred Heart, but I'll deliver everything and the messages right away."

Femme was amused that Pichon welcomed the risk just to see Charmaine. She drank coffee and looked to the pipe stand, noticing that her pipe was gone. *Now that's the second pipe that has gone missing. Meffre and Eshu.*

When Pichon returned, full of smiles, Meffre was on the porch throwing sticks for Labas to fetch. Percie joined him, and Labas ran under the porch. Femme's fish frying had reached the yard and lured Pichon. He headed to the pump to wash his hands. Then he pretended to sneak behind Femme while she ignored him. He grabbed the folds of her apron and dried his hands, kissing her cheeks on both sides. She could not resist because her hands were full of biscuit dough. "Meffre, come in here and put this dog out, please. The beast is trying to steal your fish." There was robust laughter from the porch. Meffre shouted through the screened door, "Here, Pichon, here boy. Come get a pipe to hide."

Femme puffed up and said, "Don't' bite the hand that feeds y'all."

After dinner, Meffre and Percie went to the barn to tend to the horses, a chore Percie relished. Femme and Pichon talked about Julien's impending visit. They also mused about how family must be linked solidly against the general vicious will to tear them apart.

Cutting Slime

T HE NEXT MORNING, AUNT Velma and Charmaine drove up to Femme's in the Broyard's rusty buckboard. They greeted her with fresh okra, tomatoes, green onions, and baskets of "necessities." Aunt Velma announced, "We're making okra gumbo today, ladies. Femme, Pichon said you had ham. Get it from the smokehouse later. Charmaine said Meffre is bringing a mess of shrimp around noon."

"Thanks for the gumbo fixings. Look what I got for Charmaine's sweet horse." Femme waved a bucket of feed.

In a respectful tone, Charmaine muttered, "You're fighting death trying to fatten him. Eats all the time and refuses to gain weight. He hates Daddy. He's trying to starve *us*—buying feed for his stubborn gray ass." The horse started eating immediately. Chickens surrounded the bucket waiting for droppings. This created enough buzz to awaken the fat pig, which ran to enjoy the feast.

They went into the house laughing and took positions at the sink and kitchen table as if assigned. Aunt Velma grabbed Femme's iron skillet and put it in the sink, scrubbed it, and slid it onto the stove. From the stovetop, she scooped a spoonful of bacon drippings into the skillet. Femme had already prepared the fire, and Charmaine washed, chopped, and separated green onions and tomatoes into two bowls. Minced garlic sat alone on the chopping board. She handed them to Aunt Velma, who said, "Thanks, sassy wench."

"Now I'm a sassy wench? I wasn't on the way here."

Aunt Velma pouted playfully. "You told Pichon I taught you to make gumbo in a hurry. That's why mine's better. I believe you said it. I was picking my time to tell you."

"If that makes me a sassy wench, I sure said it. I can't make okra gumbo that's not slimy. But Daddy eats so fast, he cuts the slime."

Aunt Velma said, "Keep talking back, missy. I just might let it slip you saw Pichon last night. Anyway, this is the last time I'm gonna show you wenches how to cut okra slime. To start, use fresh-cut Créole tomatoes!" Charmaine blushed and deflected stares by selecting tomatoes and washing and dicing them.

While they moved to exchanging irrelevant gossip, Aunt Velma stirred green onions, garlic, and tomatoes in one skillet; in another, she browned flour to make a roux. When the flour browned, she drizzled in water to thicken it. Femme and Charmaine had made a good start on the mound of okra they sliced. With the three of them involved in tasks that averted eye contact, an odd silence ensued— caused by a reticence to talk about the real reason they were cooking. Aunt Velma was full of fun though and moved dramatically toward the table with her cooking spoon raised high and indignant. "Did I tell y'all how I get to hear that porker talking to Reginald?"

"You know you didn't tell us," Femme said, smiling at Charmaine.

Aunt Velma walked back to her pot and said, "They go sneaking into the parlor, thinking I can't hear them. But I can." Stirring her pots, she was able to talk out of the kitchen window, punctuating her story by waiting for reactions at strategic points. She described a very small room Papa Luc called a wine cellar—with very little wine and hardly a cellar either—being only five steps below the kitchen. Three days ago, she had seen Papa Luc go down the steps. He stayed for over thirty minutes. Hébert was with Reginald in the parlor and did not know Papa Luc was home. Aunt Velma stored a bank of potatoes and canned stuff out of the heat down in the cellar. This was her excuse to follow Papa Luc, whom she surprised as he eavesdropped. He signaled to be quiet, and they heard Hébert spitting venom against Créoles and coloreds. They also railed against weak men like Papa Luc and claimed white people were going to lose everything. They reveled in having run off Ossi. When they vowed that they were hardly finished regulating, Papa Luc stormed out.

Femme stopped chopping and slammed her knife on the table startling Charmaine. She wiped her hands on her apron and was about to say something when Charmaine's quickened chopping signified *her* angst. Aunt Velma tried to create a distraction by asking questions about Meffre, but Femme sighed and sat disconsolately. She looked from one concerned face to the other. "Whether

I ran Ossi off or Hébert did matters little. The result is the same: he's gone. Don't worry about my tender feelings. Aunt Velma, what do you think they're planning?"

Aunt Velma adjusted her headband and explained Reginald's anger over how the regulators were working all over the South to keep blacks down, but no one had given him enough recognition for watching over white folks' interests in St. Tammany Parish. Reginald bragged that he and Hébert were right to establish their own regulators. She said this while sautéing green onions and tomatoes and thickening the roux. Femme poured lemonade for them and quickly unwrapped ham she and Charmaine set to slicing into cubes. Charmaine ate cube after cube until Aunt Velma popped her knuckles with her wooden spoon, saying, "That gray horse ain't got nothing on your round butt. You two biscuits from fat but keep eating ham, miss." Charmaine threw up her hands and pretended to cower.

Femme wondered aloud how they could fight a force of regulators. Aunt Velma answered that the only prevention was finding out how, when, and where they were planning to do what, and making sure that no one was there to get hurt. The mound of okra dwindled, and Femme and Charmaine began working on a third bowl. Aunt Velma and Charmaine agreed to ask Father Lorquette what he knew.

Femme got up to deliver one of the bowls of okra when she staggered just a little. Aunt Velma noticed first, but Charmaine spoke first. "Lord, today, Femme. What's wrong?" The thought of losing Ossi to regulators intensified her grief and caused dizziness, like the onset of vertigo. She walked around the kitchen, holding on to chairs, cabinets, and counters.

"Femme," Charmaine ordered, "sit down."

Aunt Velma held Femme's face in her hands. "What's wrong, cher? Lawd, today! That Choctaw. Gumbo ain't gonna cure that."

Femme sobbed and, then, fell into a fit of laughter. They laughed in cheer as it resonated against the kitchen walls, which echoed with a noise that minimized the specter of regulators, burning crosses, and lynch ropes. Finally, she blew her nose and said, "I'm light-headed from not eating right. I got to go look for him. I got a lot of questions, but he can't come back here. I can't take that chance, so I have to go. He's been to the convent in the Quarters. They'll tell me something. I'll go on Friday and stay till I can get some answers.

I'll send word from New Orleans, but I might not be back for the wedding. Charmaine nodded in assent."

Aunt Velma held Femme in her arms and said, "Girl, he done some good bed work on you! Got inside you good, huh?"

"Aunt Velma!" Charmaine gently reprimanded.

"I meant inside her head." Aunt Velma laughed. "That's something for a bitch to chase after. I got court evidence on that count—at my house *right now*. Twins!"

Glad for the chance to be sassy, Charmaine preached. "Aunt Velma! You need to remember your place in church *right now*."

"I'm right as religion. This girl can't cut through that Choctaw's slime with tomatoes! Go after him. We'll watch your house and Meffre. Go find your Choctaw!"

Femme nodded. Aunt Velma grabbed her lemonade and moved close. "Now listen. Misery *can* bring happiness too. Let's toast our loves. Lawd, today!" They clinked their glasses, and Aunt Velma went back to putting okra in the skillet, which she had moved off the stove's hottest part to let it simmer. She turned to them, pulled her chair out, and sat.

Charmaine moved closer to her and asked, "You said 'our loves'— plural. Tell us who's looking for you with a candle in daylight?"

Aunt Velma jumped up to go after Charmaine. "See, Femme, I told you she was a sassy wench."

Femme laughed and pulled Charmaine behind her. "We all know you're keeping more than food hot at Papa Luc's. Leave this child alone." Charmaine peaked from behind Femme and dodged Aunt Velma's long wooden spoon.

She went back to her pots and showed no sign of defeat. "I can't help it if my cooking buys me loving. Y'all should be so lucky! Anyway, to get serious again, y'all know why Hébert hates Femme?" Gesticulating with her cooking spoon, she answered, with certainty, that Hébert's animus stemmed from his suspicion that Papa Luc gave Femme money. Femme's house, her couch from a New Orleans' furniture store, and even the inside bathroom evidenced Papa Luc's financing. Her certainty was fueled by her piecing together events linked to Hébert's anger. She recalled Femme's getting electricity only six months after Papa Luc did. Hébert had not finished bragging about Papa Luc's lights and fixtures down at Sacred Heart when he exploded having heard that Femme had electricity, as well.

This triggered Hébert's screaming about no electricity in Small House, which triggered Lucien's going out to his "office." Aunt Velma ended with: "That's what he means when he says you too big for Lacombe."

"What I have, I paid for. Papa Luc just helps me to arrange things." Femme smiled smugly.

Charmaine looked up from the okra bowl. "Well, we don't have any fineries, and we bathe in a number three tub. I guess Dr. Bastard H. Bellocq must love the Broyards. The way I add it up, I've only had a half basket of anything, but one day, with Pichon, we might be able to give a whole basket of something to our baby."

Aunt Velma kissed Charmaine and took the bowls of chopped okra and Créole tomatoes and headed for the stove. She moved the roux pot to the back and poured a layer of cooked okra then a layer of tomatoes into the gumbo pot. She continued this layering of okra and tomatoes until it was full. She covered the pot, checked the fire, and said, "In a minute, got some cayenne coming. Oh, Charmaine, don't eat cayenne pepper. It'll burn the baby's eyes and make him sassy like you."

"That advice is too late. Daddy seasoned and boiled a hamper of crabs last week. I'm craving them."

"Where's your filé?"

"Top shelf on the left."

Aunt Velma reached for the filé and stopped midmotion. "Oh, no. I ain't using no store-bought filé in my gumbo."

Femme hopped up and went digging into a basket in the cupboard. She waved the sassafras root. "Here! Stop your fussing. I bought this so you wouldn't pick on us. Where do you buy your rice and beans and that chocolate you like so much, miss?"

"You so smart. Go over there and grind it fine—finer than you grind your own. I want to taste it without biting it. Young wenches do everything so fast, gonna give us the dérangement."

"Just listen, Charmaine, she's cooking and talking about the flying shits!"

"There's Meffre with the shrimp!" Charmaine yelled.

Meffre appeared at the screened door with a bucket of cleaned shrimp. Aunt Velma took them claiming she had a pot looking for missing prisoners. The boy chuckled through his hungry glances, and Femme cut some ham to put on biscuits he was eyeing. He went off toward the barn, saying that he was going to meet Percie and Pichon at home.

Aunt Velma took the shrimp to the sink and pumped water over them. She was surprised that Meffre had cleaned them so well. "Deveined them shrimp better than my twins could." Charmaine winced and went to the sink to observe how meticulously Aunt Velma washed every shrimp again.

"Get busy, cher, help me stir my pots." In a clean skillet, Charmaine stirred the shrimp till they coiled up and turned into orange-and-white striped balls. She glided around Aunt Velma to move on to the okra frying in the huge gumbo kettle on the front of the stove. As she stirred gently, Aunt Velma sprinkled small bits of ham into the okra. Charmaine eyed the kettle with yearning. Aunt Velma nudged her with her hip and said, "I'm teaching you to cook 'cause Pichon stays hungry."

Aunt Velma rested a bit, sipped lemonade, and perked up. "Julien came by Papa Luc's about two months ago to paint a ceiling. He looks out for the twins. Thinks Percie's the good twin. Now listen. I'm embarrassed to tell this. Percie never said why he got fired from the Lacombe Feed Store. Julien told me. Percie took that sloppy fat DuCette girl to the store after closing and had his way with her. She's a nasty bitch, that one. He had her on the floor, and her big ass took the shine off that white man's tile. Say, no matter what he did, he couldn't get the shine back. They was too stupid to do their nasty business in the dark. Lit a kerosene lamp! That old white buzzard saw the light and ran their black asses out. Fired Percie on the spot." Aunt Velma pulled her headband back and shook her head pretending shame.

Femme and Charmaine laughed and were embarrassed that they had. Aunt Velma gave in and echoed their laughter. Everyone gathered around the stove to watch Aunt Velma put the roux and shrimp into the gumbo kettle. She stirred the mixture, adding more ham. After a heaping spoon of cayenne and a bit of salt, she stirred in the filé and made them wait for a taste. To heighten their impatience, she set out small tasting bowls with a big spoon of rice. The gumbo's scent imprisoned them and had them begging before long. All the while, Aunt Velma described the wedding dress and how Charmaine was prettier with each fitting. She nattered on about the bodice beading, how Charmaine had designed a respectable veil for a pregnant girl—one that did not cover her face. They finished tasting and divided the gumbo into three pots, each suited to its household's appetites.

✝ ✝ ✝

Meffre sat on the porch with Pichon and Percie. Pichon asked, "What they say 'bout the shrimp?"

Meffre said, "Aunt Velma took them and didn't fuss, so I guess they was alright. Your father-in-law says I clean shrimp like I get paid to."

"Good. Teach me. I need his good graces," Pichon said. "Let's go inside."

They approached the door as it opened widely. Percie yelled, "Ossi! I thought you might show up." The others could not disguise their puzzled looks. They followed Ossi to the kitchen. He stood holding a chair's back at the head of the table. The twins sat, and Meffre stood close to Ossi, who spoke hurriedly. His speech was punctuated with directives and warnings. He told Pichon and Percie to keep their eyes fixed on Hébert, tracking where he went and with whom. They were to be vigilant about discovering whomever he talked to and when. Ossi related that Créoles in New Orleans had told him Reginald and Hébert surmised that he had burned the crosses. The most astonishing news Ossi conveyed, looking directly at Pichon and Percie, was that Hébert and Reginald led two groups that joined to shock Lacombe. Carl Keller orchestrated all of this. In finely rendered details, he described Carl and ordered them to spread the word if ever they saw someone resembling him. Ossi directed Meffre to tell Femme. To their surprise, he revealed that he had just spoken to Papa Luc and Lucien. He asked Percie to listen to all conversations of folks embarking on the steamboat train. He told him to continue to listen attentively to buyers at the produce stand. To Pichon, he suggested eavesdropping at the sawmill, especially when loading and unloading lumber.

Meffre pumped water into a pitcher and passed glasses to everyone. Ossi said to him, "Stay close to Percie and Pichon and don't spend time alone. It's not safe. If Colfax people come here, you and I are targets. Practice throwing your knife. Be quick and accurate. Take everything else slow. Whatever you hear, get word to Papa Luc." Meffre nodded. Ossi cautioned, "No one is to *do* anything unless told to. Listening can save our lives; talking and doing too much can kill us." With this, Ossi walked out of the back door, scraped his foot across the bottom step to loosen hard mud under his boot, and rode his horse into the woods.

Pichon pulled ham and bread out of the safe and talked about Ossi's news. The seriousness of the conversation had sapped their energy until Percie started bragging about his new woman. Pichon called him a thin liar and motioned for everyone to leave. Meffre headed out the back door on the path toward the pecan grove. Pichon stood on the porch imagining Charmaine and their baby living in this house. He heard the sawmill whistle blow, mounted his horse, and sped down the trail, thinking about Julien Broyard.

Ruffled Souls

JULIEN BANGED ON THE front door and immediately walked back down the porch steps to survey the house. He looked hard at it, envying how well Aunt Velma had managed. He meandered around the north side to examine the window casing and the straightness of the rafters. He reached the back, scrutinized the shed that doubled as a horse barn, and then started back toward the front, looking, intermittently and with critical attention, to the crawl space. *No standing water; that's good.* He walked across the front again, stopping only to kick hard at the wooden steps, which proved sturdier than they looked. Going down the south side, he noticed a long wooden ladder leaning next to the house. The ladder took him back to his reservations about Pichon marrying Charmaine.

Julien had weakened considerably on these strong reservations because of two conversations: one with Aunt Velma, the other with Charmaine. The conversation with Aunt Velma was simple on two points. One point Julien knew too well: no son of Aunt Velma's was having a baby out of wedlock. She had suffered enough from her husband's fate. The other point had never occurred to Julien, and she spouted it very softly: "Those altar society bitches won't be hiring you to build cabinets and paint for them if Charmaine is prancing around Sacred Heart with a big belly and no husband. Lacombe is too Catholic for that. You make your living as a carpenter and fisherman. Who's gonna buy your seafood?" Julien absorbed this without dispute. Aunt Velma left his shed by kissing him and saying they needed family strength now more than ever. He smiled for a long time and stared at the space where she had stood. He knew she was serious, not only because of what she said, but more so because she had walked right into his shed, knowing his prohibition against intrusions.

When he saw Charmaine standing in the shed door that same day at sunset, he knew he had been primed for the next talk—probably the worst. The conversation was full of shame for them. Although she acted willfully in getting pregnant, she was shameful now for having hurt her father. She confessed: "Love is hard to do by yourself and from a distance, Daddy. I've always loved Pichon, always will. I knew this was the only way I'd marry him. I'm ashamed. I'm sorry."

Even holding her and protesting her crying, which he could not bear, did not soften him. He said firmly, "Like should marry like. He ain't Créole."

At this, Charmaine stiffened. "Daddy, like *is* marrying like. Créoles get their very name from mixing with everyone else. The mix is now mixing again. You can't keep the past. It's left you. Soon whites will just see Créoles the same way they see coloreds. Forcing me to live without Pichon won't make life better for me!"

Julien's head was in his big hands against words he knew to be facts. He drank his beer, walked around the shed banging nail and screw bins. "Please don't marry that nigger, Charmaine. If you do, I'll lose you."

She rushed to face him and said angrily, "Call him that again, you *will* lose me—forever." She turned from him, knowing his anger and beer were conspiring against her. Before she reached the door, he sobbed. Hearing that, she kept walking with more hope than before.

The most powerful motivation in these conversations was, oddly, what Aunt Velma had said about Julien's endangering his livelihood. When his carpenter work was slow, as it often was, he fished the lake and bayou and sold his catch to steady customers, who looked eagerly for his rusty buckboard. Those clients started on Lake Road with Myrtle Picou's bar and restaurant. Picou's served a variety of seafood platters that depended on Julien's catches, and she never bought from anyone else. He also sold seafood consistently to residents along Lake Road, including Femme and Aunt Velma. During the busy season, he hired Percie to fish with him because his many girlfriends would buy seafood. Julien supplied seafood to Father Lorquette for a blessing. Even the famous Lacombe saloon, the Mudbug, was a loyal customer, especially on Fridays during Lent. Up the bayou, Julien sold to residents and to the Carmelite convent that housed thirty novitiates. He knew Aunt Velma was right. Still, it was difficult to offer Charmaine to Pichon without a test.

Julien ambled to the backyard with no particular gripe agitating him except that Pichon had not come out to meet him. Then, close to the woods, just beyond the small barn, he heard and spied Pichon coming out of the outhouse and going toward the outdoor pump to wash. Pichon sang and whistled until Julien yelled and surprised him: "A damn fool leaves a good ladder out in the weather. Must've cost you more than you make. You stole it from the mill?"

"No, sir, Mr. Julien, never stole nothing. Good morning, sir." Pichon ran up to him, his wet hand extended. Julien turned and headed back to the front. By the time Pichon reached him, he was standing at the front door. "Oh! Mr. Julien, that door is locked. I always use the back door. But you stay here. I'll go through the back and"—Pichon ran down the house's south side, stopped to pull down the ladder, and shoved it into the crawl space.

Julien walked quickly and headed down the house's north side. He heard Pichon running through the house. By the time Pichon opened the door, Julien was standing on the back porch. He yelled, "I'm back here, you jackass!" Pichon ran to the back door to let Julien in and noticed he was laughing and smiling.

"Never let another man make you run through your own house, son. No matter what he has that you want." Pichon pretended to enjoy Julien's fun at his expense. Obedience was part of the price for Charmaine. Julien sensed his seriousness and fear. "I wouldn't be here if I wasn't going to let you marry her. So, before you shit on yourself, let that go. I came to make sure you two can make a home here."

As he said this, Julien recalled how he had given Charmaine his decision. She had left him sobbing in his shed. He had watched her run back to the house and heard how she slammed the kitchen door. Immediately, he felt his stomach rumbling—a sign that he had lost control and regretted it. He found her in the kitchen heating an iron to press altar clothes. All he could say was, "That baby's gonna need his daddy more than he'll need me. Marry Pichon. That's right for the baby. All I ask is the respect I deserve. Let me tell him. Not you. I'll let Velma know that I'm going by her house to make sure it's ready for you and the baby. Keep that secret." He ignored her calling after him. She was asleep when he came back, stumble-drunk on homebrew.

He tried to hang on to the gravity of Julien's consent, but Pichon let go and danced a jig right in front of him. Euphorically he stuttered, "Sir, Mr. Julien, I don't . . . I mean, I can't . . . I been keeping up Mama's house since she left for the Coulon's. I only do two things with my money: put it in the bank, and in this house. You can see—"

"Make some coffee, Pichon. And call me Julien." Pichon smiled. They both did.

Their conversation, or Julien's talk about caution, lasted forty-five minutes, and Pichon struggled through every one of those minutes. His nervousness seemed encouraging to Julien, who confessed that he had been wrong. This confession came hard because he had to admit that what he was taught was wrong now—now, as Charmaine and Aunt Velma said, that the world was changing. He hoped that they could be a family. He told Pichon that he had dreamed Charmaine had married a dark man, then a Choctaw, then another black man—all in the same dream. He realized it would cost him nothing to ensure his daughter grew up and left his house happy. Pichon sipped coffee and listened. When he finished, Julien pushed his chair back, took a good look at the kitchen ceiling, and said, "We need to replace those ceiling boards before she moves in. I got enough tongue and groove boards in my shed. Bring your buckboard over to get them. We can fix that next Saturday if you ain't working. Or Sunday. When it gets dry enough, we'll build a wraparound porch on the shady side. Y'all can sit and watch my grandbaby eat dirt."

Inspecting the house had the surprising effect of putting Julien at ease. Being social, for him, extended to *his* shed, *his* tools, and *his* homebrew. He started toward the back door with his hands in his overall pockets. He turned around. "If you ain't got a trough to clean fish, I got one you can have from a job I did. You can put that in the buckboard, too." Pichon held out his hand to shake and pulled it back when Julien said, "Don't shake a man's hand unless you got something to agree on, son." Julien was a five-foot-four, stocky man with thin, straight, graying hair and a pale complexion that allowed him to pass for white. Folks called him a "li'l piece of leather, well put together." He looked up and into Pichon's eyes and shook his hand firmly. Pichon was about to say that he didn't have to work on Saturday, that he *did* need a fish-cleaning trough, and that he was thankful for the ceiling boards, but Julien was down the back steps by the time he recovered from the handshake.

+ + +

Time passed quickly enough. They completed the kitchen ceiling, installed the fish-cleaning trough, and Pichon bought a new mattress. Aunt Velma dressed herself and pulled on the bedroom door for Pichon to come out for her inspection. The last time she knocked, he told her he was naked. This time, she heard him walking hard and uncomfortably in new dress shoes. She could tell he was prancing back and forth in front of the mirror. She smiled and held herself with happiness. She tugged at the doorknob and banged loudly. "Pichon, Sacred Heart Church ain't in this backyard, so we got to go. I heard Julien polished his shotgun last night, thinking you might be late."

Pichon opened the door quickly. "This is how they'll see me. Do I look like a groom?"

"You look like Mr. Felder, the undertaker. Come on, boy. You ain't the first nigger to get married in a bought suit. You got the envelope for Father Lorquette?"

"Right here in my vest pocket. I'm responsible."

"Yes, my darling. You responsible for that baby! Percie, let's go." Percie insisted on riding his horse and added that he was only half-dressed and confused about his tie.

After pinning on Pichon's lapel flower, Aunt Velma put on her hat and stepped out onto the porch to admire the buckboard. Papa Luc had donated white paint Meffre and Percie used to douse the old buckboard. Meffre had especially liked helping Charmaine's girl cousins decorate the buckboard with flowers and ivy. One of them gave him pause when she commented that he was better at the decorating than any of them. This comment tormented him and sent him into a moody retreat that Percie had to nudge him out of with jokes and Muscadine wine.

After eating breakfast, Meffre cleaned up, dressed, locked the house, and set out for the church. For his baptism, Femme had bought a new suit and shirt that he wore for the wedding. As he drove, he again fixated on his attraction to Lucien. How could *they* ever be a family? To be sure, Pichon and Charmaine would be happy, but gnawing threats of regulators and Carl Keller, his undeniable attraction to Lucien, and his preoccupation with his uncertain future, hummed noisily in his head. He struggled to clear his mind.

When he arrived, he was surprised at the number of people standing outside. They all seemed cheerful. The scene was an artistic rendering of contrasts. Old Sacred Heart, with its

110

colorless and dingy white walls, appeared an unwilling backdrop to Lacombe's portrait of exuberant deep reds, bright yellows, pale pinks, flecks of orange, and competing shades of blues and greens on the clothing and hats of smiling and laughing guests—a spectrum of shades all thrown together in an abstract of humanity.

The black women wore their best dresses with matching hats, but each had a worry she bore in her soul, behind her smile, for her children or grandchildren. The men, though wearing their best, without any dirt or sweat, still seemed in their demeanor to be ready to plow fields, cut lumber, or go fishing. For these men, this had more to do with habit and necessity. Even their best clothes sat on them like work clothes. The church represented the core of what Lacombe was and what it concealed. Yet, on this day, no one was drawn to looking on Sacred Heart with faith, pity, or care; today, they all looked at Charmaine, Julien's painted "China doll," who was about to marry Pichon and break down, with love (Aunt Velma prayed), a longstanding Créole defense.

Pichon and Aunt Velma arrived, and Father Lorquette greeted them and escorted Pichon to the sanctuary. Aunt Velma made her way to the front pew. With very few white folks in attendance, she felt giddy about sitting in a prime spot. She spied two of her choir-girls placing flowers on the altar and waved to them. They nodded only—fearing Aunt Velma might catch them doing anything other than what she instructed.

Pichon stood stiffly in the very spot that Father Lorquette had put him. The organist began playing softly, and the church noise turned to murmurs. Then a loud pulling and yanking on the side church door produced Percie as the worst-dressed ring bearer ever to enter a church. His white shirt was too tight against his chubby arms and chest. His pants were too loose with one leg longer than the other. His tie was knotted inside out. Such a shabby presence made Sacred Heart look spiffy. Aunt Velma covered her face. Pichon nodded to his brother and pointed to a spot for Percie to stand.

Seeing these two together, no one would ever guess they were related. That they were twins would have tested credulity. Pichon was tall, muscled, and dark skinned. By any standard, he would be considered handsome. He resembled his mother and inherited her small waist and lean body. Pichon was thick, but there was no fat on his body. Percie, however, was a replica of his father: short and stubby, with a ruddy complexion capped by a full head of auburn curly hair—a true briqué. No matter the haircut or attempts at combing his hair, Percie always appeared disheveled. His plump face, however, was never without a smile.

Pichon fiddled in his pocket for his handkerchief and felt the rings. He handed them to Percie without looking at him. The rings reminded him of Femme's kindness when they went to Covington to buy them. He regretted her absence, but before he could fall into deeper reflection, the organ grew louder, and he could see Julien standing in the back door. Over that long distance, their eyes reached each other, and Julien nodded.

Julien's oldest sister was beelike: fussing and buzzing around Charmaine, who was clearly in a state of torment. Julien's younger brother Ralph and his wife Ellie stood off to the side awaiting the signal to march in as official witnesses. Aunt Velma arranged for this best man and matron of honor without consulting Pichon. "The boy ain't got no people 'cept me and Femme, and we ain't standing up for him. Percie can bear the rings; your people from Slidell can stand up for the bride *and* groom."

Julien was proud that they had succeeded in making Charmaine appear as beautiful as a "China doll"—although he had ever seen one. As he looked on admiringly, Charmaine thought only of Pichon and their baby. Julien pulled at her arm and announced, "Time to get married. Pay attention. Dreamers don't make good wives."

Charmaine said, "Maybe, I'll break that rule too."

Julien's older sister puffed out her cheeks and turned to Ralph and Ellie, ordering them to go in and stand in line. Tearfully, she kissed Charmaine and arranged the short tulle veil down her back. She looked at Julien and ordered, "Don't drag her down that aisle like a Jersey calf to slaughter. Take your time and don't walk on her fucking dress. Ralph and Ellie, wait until I get to my seat before you start walking."

With Charmaine kneeling at the altar with Pichon, Aunt Velma's attention drifted to her choir. The children filled the pew behind her and took every advantage to show off their skills at being sneaks. Aunt Velma, without looking, could pull hair from what seemed to be longer distances than her arm's reach. She did so with such polish that observing mothers were determined to try her skills. Although Father Lorquette spoke eloquently about the sanctity of marriage and how love is the blessing that makes everything last longer, Aunt Velma heard very little. Coughing, pinching, and hair pulling occupied her throughout the ceremony.

When Charmaine and Pichon stood and turned toward the congregation for the first married kiss, seven members of the children's choir were asleep; the rest were moaning and crying over their aching heads and bruised arms. Julien was bored, and Aunt Velma exhausted. Pichon looked at his new family with a surprising optimism, and Charmaine surmised that things had surely gone better than the average Mass with the choir. With the organ's booming invitation, they walked out, blasted with rice from everyone everywhere.

After doing his duty as ring bearer, Percie joined Meffre, leaving the church quickly for the Broyard house to help set up for the reception. They turned onto Old Oak Road, which was built around very old mossy oaks that were respected and venerated. Percie babbled about how high yellow girls were no prize. He promised Meffre an introduction to his "kind of women." He jabbed Meffre with a pointless and symbolic brag that hardly drew his attention. He enjoyed just being with Percie, who was full of mischief and fun Meffre thought attractive only in others.

Even with the wedding's cheer, Meffre's spirit was dampened with a curious disturbance. He sat in the rig and prayed to Eshu for happiness—the kind that would connect him to Lucien. Lately, when he pressed himself, he admitted that even troublesome feelings for Lucien had become a major part of an imagined future. How could this yearning become real? Especially when he had curtailed his impromptu visits to Lucien's bungalow. A sudden hole in the road jarred him just in time to avert overturning the entire rig.

He turned onto the road at the Broyard place and parked. Percie jumped out, pointed to the shed, and sprinted to Julien's homebrew. He yelled to Meffre, "Come on, boy." This alerted Meffre to where he was. He imagined Julien's hands at work fulfilling his family obligations. Some might view his attempt to give his daughter a beautiful wedding as just another country free *allée*. Meffre believed otherwise. The meager decorations, the wooden tables and chairs all prepared for the meal, and the barrels of drink made ready for the reception were a father's love and dedication made tangible. He envied how family looked here. He also thought about Femme, alone in New Orleans. He prayed to Eshu to keep her safe.

Vieux Carré Rounds

THE DAY BEFORE PICHON and Charmaine's wedding found Femme trying to quietly fix breakfast so as not to wake Meffre. She wrapped herself in a woolen shawl to prepare for Lake Pontchartrain's chilly March breezes. Even with the sun getting hotter, March could feel like winter on the lake.

Percie tried to rub the sleep from his eyes as he guided his horse into an empty stall in Femme's barn. Labas snored. His nose twitched with each deep breath, and a gurgling growl signified some nightmare. Percie headed for Femme's back steps where he could see a weak light. He knew Femme had made breakfast with chicory coffee that would pop his eyes open. He was happy to drive Femme to Mandeville for her trip to New Orleans. This meant, as usual, he would drive her rig to the steamboat depot. He worked very near there, loading and unloading produce at the outdoor market. Papa Luc rented a stall there and depended on Percie for deliveries from Lacombe, and sometimes to get strawberries from Ponchatoula. Percie rode his horse every day to Mandeville, but when he had deliveries and used Papa Luc's rig, he made extra money escorting and delivering elderly and single black women to the steamboat depot or nearby errands. His stories came from invented exploits, but the truth—a truth many depended on—everyone accepted about Percie was that he was an expert sentinel who tracked travelers. This was easy because he manned Papa Luc's produce and fish stand near the depot's entrance bridge. All travelers had to go by him. The stand's prime location made it lucrative for years. The steamboat left daily at eleven in the morning and five in the evening and, for an hour before each departure, Percie sold seasonal fruits and pecans to travelers. He also sold whatever fish was in season. His position was strategic for sales, but also critical for what he could observe and hear. Careless shoppers and passers-by dropped precious secrets in

114

the presence of a busy black, inconsequential, ignorant vendor who, they assumed, was not interested in them. Although those close to him never doubted that Percie was honest, he had the reputation of a scoundrel. This was protection against getting caught—bad reputations offer good shields. He had a mind that readily and permanently recorded observances, a knack for remembering faces and minor details. Although he fictionalized and embellished his own sexual feats, he reported accurately activities of targeted passengers. He managed the stand with steady profits, disguised as a much-needed detective. In recent months, he had extended his detective business to spying on Hébert and Reginald Eaton for Papa Luc and Ossi.

Femme came out with a kerosene lamp and a plate, heaped with grits, ham, and eggs. "No biscuits this morning, Percie. I had to get my bags together last night and forgot to set them out. This'll stick to your ribs. I'd invite you in, but don't want to wake Meffre."

Percie grabbed the plate and picked up the ham with his hand as Femme took a fork out of her apron pocket. "You'll have a problem eating grits with your hands, son. Coffee is on the table. I'll be right out."

The ham arrested Labas's attention. He followed the scent and stood growling on the step until Percie threw him the ham bone. "I'm eating the rest of this. You ain't heard growling and a good bark. Try coming up them steps." Labas mouthed his bone and trotted under the house.

Femme pushed Meffre's breakfast to the back of the stove. She took off her apron and threw it across a chair before making her way to her bedroom. When she traveled, she always took the statue of Yemanja with her. She prayed and then put it in her dress pocket. With a radiant smile, she picked up a small vial of water with a cork stopper. She pocketed it too and felt good about leaving. The sun began to break. She turned off the lamps and carried her bag through the back door.

By the time they reached the main road to Mandeville, Percie had not told one story, and Femme had not picked on him. When they passed Big Branch, however, she was ready to talk.

"Percie? You awake yet? You haven't been storying this morning."

"Miss Femme, I had a bad night last night dreaming about fires all around, but mostly the bayou burning. Them dreams kept me up."

"Try getting up and walking around. Give yourself something else to think about." He smiled as if the idea made sense. She hugged him and asked, "What's going on at the depot?"

He looked her way, knowingly. "Things been quiet except Doc Bellocq took a trip two weeks back to New Orleans on the five o'clock. Reginald brought him to the depot. I don't like that red-face old buzzard, and he never even looks at me with the respect you'd give rotten fruit. That day he was eyeballing me hard."

"What did they talk about?"

"Old Doc Bellocq talked about risking the trip to see some man named Keller. Told Reginald they needed to work for him together. He ordered me to put strawberries and kumquats in two different bags. Never looked at me." Percie frowned.

Femme was too startled to respond. She just looked forward onto the long road flanked by pines. She thought of Ossi and held herself and her sadness close. *Kumquats? What's brewing with Reginald, Hébert, and Keller?* Percie noticed her seriousness.

"This mean something to you?"

"Did you tell Meffre about all of this?"

"No, only told Papa Luc last week. Didn't want my mouth to get my ass in trouble."

He grinned and before he could apologize, she said, "What else?"

"Well, was funny him going on a trip with only one little bag. He dug in that bag a lot and fussed to Reginald about a letter. Said it was from Colfax. I kept eyeing him on the sly. I know how to play dumb. Just busied myself fixing fruit and bending down below the crates like I dropped something. When I handed him the two bags, he gave me a pair of eyes and told me, 'You know who I am, boy. Don't fix your face to ask for money. Tell Papa Luc I stole it from you.' "

Femme thought, *Hébert's hiding this trip from Papa Luc too?* This turned Percie's report into a puzzle. *This must be Carl Keller Ossi and Meffre talked about. And he was in New Orleans.* Unnoticed by Percie, she took out the small vial of water. Percie was doing his best to dodge holes scattered on the road. She opened the vial and wet the tips of her fingers on her right hand, praying, *Yemanja, he must give me all the pieces so I can put them together. Help him.*

She gently reached over to touch and rub the moisture on his right hand. "Daddy said when two right hands touch in friendship, we tend to go the right way. Maybe you'll miss some of these holes."

Percie smiled and said, "This horse is smart but don't see too good. I got a time keeping him on track. You know, it was funny that day that I saw Doc Bellocq, Lucien was coming from New Orleans."

"Lucien?"

"Yep. And, Doc Bellocq had to know too, 'cause he told Reginald he had to hurry to board the trolley so he'd make sure 'the boy' saw him. I didn't know who 'the boy' was till Lucien came stumbling along with that bag of kumquats. He always comes to Mandeville and gets drunk at the Bend-in-the-Road. Used to bring me drinks too, especially when he wanted to tell me about some colored jazz players. Invited me to go with him. Like I could. I like him. One time, he gave me all the coins in his pocket, nearly six cents, and asked me to keep his secret from his 'holy' uncle. I'd never kill that secret, but he didn't know that, so I took his money. That day I saw him, all he said was, 'Old bastard doesn't know me. Thinks I'll keep a secret for kumquats. I hate fucking kumquats.' He was drunk as Cooter Brown and cussing like firecrackers on New Year's. Dumped the kumquats into a crate and headed to the Bend-in-the-Road with the paper bag in his fist."

Femme mulled over connecting Lucien to Eshu's kumquat puzzle. She released her hold on the vial of water and asked Percie about working for Papa Luc, when he was getting married like Pichon, and whether he wanted children. Percie became animated in his many responses. He talked incessantly till they turned onto the road leading to the lake.

She saw the Mandeville Hotel in the distance and smelled the lake air getting heavy in the morning breeze. People gathered in the market, armed with empty baskets. The trolley sat at the pier's end waiting for its passengers. "I'm early today. I'll take my load off after I get you put down by the fruit stand. It's shady there. I'll park the rig in the back and be back in a minute."

"That's fine. Here's my fare for the ride and good conversation. When you go back, please check on Meffre for the wedding." He pocketed the money and pulled up to the stand. Several black boys ran up to the rig to help Femme down. Percie ran most of them off and told three small boys to go sit on the back of the rig so they could help him unload. She stood in the shade, thinking of Hébert's plotting and Eshu's kumquats. Somehow, Lucien was a key.

Percie put three crates of strawberries and kumquats in front of the stand and drove away. Femme noticed how whites stood patiently on the pier under an ivory-colored canvas awning. They were busy ignoring or shooing away begging black children. Often, men ran them away by threatening them with walking sticks. The children dispersed only to congregate in another area of the pier, relentlessly begging for pennies. Femme heard that these children picked pockets, and she did not doubt it, looking at their desperation. Percie returned and walked her to the pier. She kissed his plump cheek and headed to the trolley for the ten-minute ride to the steamboat.

+ + +

At exactly eleven o'clock, the steamboat roared its departure in an inelegant and boisterous noisemaking common to Lake Pontchartrain's north shore. Passengers covered their ears, and several older refined women muttered their rosaries. The day was humid, but there was an inviting blue sky that almost lured passengers to stay outside, hugging the rails as Mandeville's shore moved sluggishly away. Femme's mind raced with conflicting thoughts of Hébert, Ossi, Lucien, Papa Luc, and Pichon and Charmaine's wedding.

She sat on a sunny bench away from the loud music on the upper deck. Comforted by the lake's lulling chatter, she enjoyed the peace she needed to go over her plan. She had written to Sister Bernadine that she was coming because she was in trouble. That was just enough information to get her a room at the orphanage. She recalled her classes in literature with great affection. The nuns never prohibited borrowing books, and her reading had been a huge part of imagining worlds other than Louisiana. She also enjoyed long conversations with Sister Bernadine, who once told her the poor, unfortunately, had short, unremarkable lives that could only be lengthened by telling their stories.

Voices in the distance pulled her from her thoughts. She saw two men fishing in a small boat. As one man dropped an anchor, the other flung his baited line into the lake. She could barely make out the line, but she knew a tiny lead sinker pulled the hooked bait into the water. The men's busywork indicated this was a good day for fishing. Their frequent glances at the steamboat registered annoyance at the unsettled waters and robust current it created.

This innocent scene sparked in Femme an eerie sense of calm *and* danger. The vial of water in her pocket called her; she took it out and took a quick sip. Then, she walked, with meticulous balance, to the boat's railing to pour a little water into the lake for safe travels.

She held the railing tightly and thought of Ossi's strength and love. Her entire face tightened with the thought of Hébert's deceit. She returned to the bench, sobbing deeply into her chest. She sat, accompanied by sadness for an hour until a fluttering wind stirred her. She prayed to Yemanja.

The wind roused her and fortified her resolve to risk danger to find Ossi. Yemanja recoiled the fluttering breeze and slid it gently over the lake's surface. Femme felt serene. She had brought *The Prince and the Pauper*, a gift from Sister Bernadine that she had not finished. She set it on her lap and was immediately entranced by the lake's calm. She looked for the fishermen, but they had disappeared.

Having read some twenty pages, she felt hungry and searched her bag for an apple. Just then, a very black woman turned from an outside corridor with two baskets filled with a variety of edibles. She called out, "I got sweet and salty like you like right here. Ponchatoula strawberries and candy; the best pralines on the lake; the best French bread and cheese; and, plenty salty nuts—got them all. I got roasted pecans and too much stuff to mention." Her voice grew louder and louder. She sat her baskets right in front of Femme and stopped. "Now, I can sell to pretty ladies just like ugly ones. What you want, pretty lady?"

Femme marked and closed her book, knowing conversation was unavoidable. After buying bread and cheese, she talked for a long time with the woman, who claimed to be from Mobile, where her kinfolk ran her off for having babies from two married men. She looked sad and muttered, "Couldn't help myself with those men. They couldn't help themselves either. I just took what life gave me. They took my babies back to their wives though. I was ready to fight, but my people put me out. Had to keep going somewhere. Shame's too big. I made candy for a week before I left Mobile. I sold that candy on the Cape Charles Ferry one day six years ago. This boat's my work now. Been here since they took the Cape Charles off."

"You've done well. Proves good hard work takes care of us."

"You talk pretty, too. You can read, huh? Was a nice white man come here and give me a nickel after I told him about my babies. Gave me a small book too. See? Told me I should read it. I ain't told him I couldn't read. Maybe he knew. He pointed to that lady's picture who wrote it. Said she was a great colored lady. It must be worth something. I tried to sell it to colored folks. They just looked away. Take a look." She handed Femme the pamphlet.

The title read, *Southern Horrors: Lynch Law in All Its Phases.* Femme paused over the cover and the author's picture. "Miss Ida B. Wells." She opened the thick pamphlet and started to read but was interrupted.

"Pretty lady, I gotta go make money on the other side."

Femme looked at her with pity and said, "This is a speech about lynching in the South, how white people kill Negroes without reason or justice. It says here that it has a price of fifteen cents. I'll pay you a dime for it, if you want to—"

"For a dime, pretty lady, put it in you grip. God bless."

She plopped the coins in her apron pocket, gathered her baskets, and skirted around the corner. Thinking about the hate in Lacombe and all over the South, she opened the pamphlet and read voraciously. What happened in Colfax was prominent in her memory as she read accounts of black people lynched for, in most cases, no crimes at all. The steamboat tugged along, and Femme was captivated by the speech, which described harrowing inhuman brutality, written by a woman she had never heard of. She imagined the words recited over the murmurs of an incredulous audience. Several times, she found herself fearing for Ossi, Meffre, and all the others, especially for Pichon and Charmaine's baby. Why would anyone bring a child into this vicious world? Yemanja threw resolve again in her direction and, instantly, Femme vowed to continue fighting.

The boat's cacophonous whistle snatched her from the speech. She spied New Orleans poking its presence into the distance. People had started to leave inside seats to come on deck for the landing. They docked at Spanish Fort, where she would take the Smoky Mary train into town, which was nearly a five-mile ride. Sister Bernadine promised to send the orphanage carriage to pick her up at the Marigny Decatur Street station. She collected her things, put the speech in her bag, and moved toward the railing to watch New Orleans enlarge itself.

For most Lacombians, New Orleans was a foreign place that could only be described sordidly. Femme held no such opinion: she enjoyed being a part of the vivacious activity painted on every corner. She lived comfortably with New Orleans as part of her past while Lacombe was her future. Her father had been engaged in a constant fight against the Catholic Church in protesting Femme's education at the hands of the nuns; yet, he was extremely proud to be able to send her to an all girls' private school. She had been educated at

St. Mary's Academy, an excellent school, run by the Sisters of the Holy Family—an order of black nuns. Bragging about this, affirmed his equal status with *gens de couleur libre*, Créoles, and even whites. He also believed that Femme's Catholic education would move her into those circles where good, moneyed gentlemen would find her suitable as a wife. The Mother Superior, on the other hand, hoped that the nuns would educate Femme and assume her into their order.

After her first year at St. Mary's, Sister Bernadine assured Mother Superior that Femme would never be a nun. In her words, "The good Lord has another vocation for Numa Labat; that I can assure you. The girl talks to trees; worse, they talk back, and she answers."

Femme also adored the Vieux Carré, where she spent a great deal of time at her father's cigar shop, listening to stories of his brother, who, he claimed, lived in Salvador, Bahia, in Brazil. Femme loved her father's talks about orishas, and he kept a statue of Eshu on a high shelf over his worktable. The wooden statue of Yemanja, which Femme now owned, he kept in front of him next to a very small bowl of water. He told Femme that Yemanja had saved him as he crossed the ocean.

After he died, she redressed Yemanja's statue. Unlike Eshu's, Yemanja's wooden figure had its original attire. Over the years, the dress had become tattered and discolored. Femme had taken a week to remake the dress (with three layers of skirts), a jeweled crown, undergarments, and lacey white train that trailed down the gown's back. Once, Aunt Velma had commented that Yemanja, all dressed in white and blue, looked like the Catholic Blessed Mother Mary. Femme tried to explain that outside Africa the orishas took on aspects of other religions and cultures, even Catholic saints. Aunt Velma lost interest quickly. However, whenever she saw statues of Mary, Femme immediately thought of Yemanja.

The streets were satiated with forbidden life that had held Femme's interests, as a young woman, more than anything school or her father's business could. She loved to meander through the Vieux Carré, spotting people selling goods in shouting matches at the French Market. There was everything one could imagine buying, and there was every kind of vendor to shout out how his eggplants or her celery were the best that day and every day. Her father's shop was on the corner of St. Peter's and Chartres, just two blocks from the market, and he often sent her to get his favorite snacks: olives or pickles. She came to know many shop owners on her route to the market.

Leaning on the steamboat's rail, she recalled when she was thirteen and had been sent on an olive-and-pickle errand. The vendor's stall was close to the end of the open-court building, which meant she had the pleasure of walking the entire length of the market, looking at every stall, abundant stores of amazing and colorful treasures. When she finally came to the pickle vendor, she placed her order, noticing a small girl eyeing her from behind her mother's dress. The woman shooed the girl away repeatedly as she wrapped the pickles and counted out ten olives. The woman seemed friendly and, to return the favor, Femme took one of the olives off the wrapping paper and offered it to the girl. The child dropped her mother's skirt and vehemently shouted: "Mama don't allow me to eat nigger dirt." The woman did not stop to even look down at the child. She held the paper with nine olives and said, "With the one in your hand, that's ten. Anything else?"

Femme did not answer, but popped the olive into her mouth, stripped its flesh from the pit, and spat it in the child's direction. "Tastes good, nigger dirt and all," she said as the child disappeared into the folds of her mother's dress again. She looked at the woman and said, "I'll pay two pennies for that olive, and you can keep the rest and the pickles." She slammed the pennies on the pickle jar's lid and left.

She returned to the cigar shop and lied that the regular vendor was not there. She later told Sister Bernadine the story, embellished with how she had remained unafraid. The nun simply shook her head and asked, "Are we teaching you those 'sassy' ways!" She remembered, however, that it was her father's standing up to condescending white men, who came into his cigar shop, that taught her to be flip with pride.

The steamboat neared the dock, and there arose the usual rush to disembark. She moved slowly toward the exit stairs. The long line moved steadily, and she could hear New Orleans coming alive. Spanish Fort was a famous resort, and a brass band played loud music as children danced all around. Black children commonly danced for pennies from anxious adults, who tried to avoid them.

Femme negotiated the crowds noticing the crisscrossing of electric wires against the cloudy sky. She also noticed many more horse and mule carriages than when she lived in the city. The big hotel bustled, and the corner barrooms, of which there were many, brimmed with loud patrons holding beers and cheering at the women. She walked quickly past shops that led to the train station where she boarded the downtown trolley. The volume of train noises made her long for her porch's quiet for the entire ride to Decatur Station. Still, she marveled at this city with all the different complexions, languages, and accents.

As they arrived, she could immediately identify the smells of the Quarter. The river, seafood, cooking aromas, scents of fresh flowers, fruits, and vegetables all combined to welcome her. She walked out of the station and saw the convent janitor waving. She knew he would ask about Lacombe and why they had moved there. No one in the city seemed to think her father had made the right decision—except, of course, those thieves who robbed his shop and the police they paid to ignore complaints.

After about ten minutes and twenty odd questions later, the janitor deposited Femme in front of the Holy Family motherhouse, next to what used to be the Quadroon Ballroom before its days as St. Mary's Academy. Since her last visit, the convent and the school had been painted. The janitor let her know, in emphatic and almost religious description, that the church's good colored men volunteered to do the painting, and their wives raised the money for the paint and brushes. When Sister Bernadine appeared in the doorway, Femme secretly gave the janitor five cents despite his protests that he could not accept the money. When he spied Sister Bernadine, he slyly pocketed the money.

Sister Bernadine had gained considerable weight. Her wimple could barely contain her happy face. When she smiled, she looked like a balloon on the verge of popping. She hid her hands under her habit, which made her look heavier still, and rocked back and forth on her feet as if she would topple over. Once Femme was out of the carriage, she said, "Girl, put those grips down. I need a squeeze of God's love." Stout though she was, she was agile still and ran to Femme grabbing her.

"Sister, there seems to be a bit more of you to love," Femme tried to say with some degree of earnestness, but Sister Bernadine would not hear it. She simply sucked her teeth in defiance.

"Shucks, girl. I nearly raised you. I won't break you. Come in. The others are at vespers, and I must join them after I get you settled. How, in God's name, are you?"

"I'm well, Sister, but we need to talk tonight."

Sister Bernadine noticed Femme's seriousness. "Yes. We can eat alone. Come, you know where everything is. Only the outside paint is new. Welcome home." She opened the door to a small room, which Femme dutifully entered. She sat on the bed and thought about how alone she felt without Ossi. She asked Yemanja to help her find and hold on to him. She rested her head on a pillow and dozed off into a sporadic sleep made troublesome by the lynching speech. Fire and storms populated uneven dreams from which she tried hard to wake. She saw herself always on the brink of losing fights to extinguish burning crosses with only drops of water. She was thankful to be interrupted by Sister Bernadine's banging on the door. The portly, toffee-colored nun said through the closed door, "Lots of folks out here waiting for you, Numa."

"I guess the trip tired me out."

The nuns had already assembled for supper when they arrived. Hierarchical order gave preference to the older nuns, who sat at the front table. Other nuns, of lesser rank, stood near chairs along rows of tables. Three nuns escorted Femme to where Mother Superior sat. A very old nun pushed up behind Femme, dropped her cane loudly, and poked her. "I made some of the young ones pick flowers." Femme turned quickly knowing that it was Sister Regina, who used to run the kitchen. She bent down to kiss her and noticed tears. "Let's not get too sentimental, girl. It's probably a sin, and they're watching us." Femme smiled, and a novice handed her flowers. Another gave Sister Regina her cane, with which she slowly hobbled away. After an exchange of kisses, hugs, and compliments, Sister Bernadine ushered Femme to a private dining room.

Sister Bernadine piled food, higher than she could eat in one sitting, on a plate for Femme. The one she fixed for herself was not modest. They ate crab cakes, fresh corn, green beans, and dirty rice—all the while, Sister Bernadine recounted the progress the nuns made teaching and caring for the poor. She was especially proud to be director of St. John Birchman's orphanage, which had grown due to an increased number of abandoned children—mostly black and Choctaw—found at church doors around the city. Yellow fever swallowed far too many parents.

Femme listened attentively but ached to talk about her conflicts with Ossi. She finished eating and sipped tea, thinking about

Yemanja. Sister Bernadine observed that Femme lacked her usual spark. She moved her plate aside and asked dramatically, "Is this when you're going to confess your 'trouble'?" Before she could answer, Sister Bernadine hopped up and headed for a china hutch near the garden window. She reached far inside and fisted a bottle of cognac. She delivered it with a bang, noting Femme's surprise with a sly smile. She fetched two cordial glasses and asked, "You *do* want a nip, huh?"

Femme's mouth stood open too long. Sister Bernadine filled half of one cordial and declared, "Numa, listen, girl. Try being a nun. You need things to confess every week." She handed the glass to Femme and poured hers to the top. "This gives me a good sin to tell Father."

Femme laughed, drank a sip, and turned serious again. She told Meffre's story and the worsening situation with the regulators. Finally, she came to her relationship with Ossi. With her head bent in genuine shame, she divulged her love. Sister Bernadine did not flinch, for she expected that this visit, as so many others, had to do with a man's running off. Femme remained dignified, explaining her shame not for the relationship but for her guilt over Ossi's disappearance. She talked animatedly about the turmoil and the risks they endured. Sister Bernadine raised her eyebrows questioning how strong-willed Numa was full of fear.

"Numa, you heard something you're not telling me. You heard he was here?"

"Yes, Sister, but I couldn't believe it. I want to see him, talk to him. Fix things with him." Sister Bernadine's face betrayed no surprise or shock. She guarded Ossi's secret as he had asked. With Papa Luc's help, Ossi visited Sister Bernadine pleading for help with plans to fight Carl Keller.

"Stop your fretting. Of course, we'll help you find him. That's settled. Now, why are you so fearful and angry even?"

"I heard Ossi was connected to groups fighting for the rights of colored people in New Orleans. Why would he do that and leave me? When he came into my house, I fell in love and believed he respected me just as I am. I misjudged, Sister. Men don't share their manhood easily. I want to convince him I'll change and ask him to come home. And I'm angry. Yes. I can't get killing Hébert Bellocq out of my mind. He's part of the reason Ossi left. On the way over, I read a pamphlet on lynching. I'm certain that kind of evil is behind all this."

Sister Bernadine remembered another time Numa had been just as angry. Femme's first sexual encounter was in defiance of Mother Superior, who wanted her to enter the convent. Femme violently refused. Instead, she allowed herself to be courted by Sister Bernadine's brother, Emile, who came to the Quarter often. Her father would disapprove of him because he had no money or means. Thus, she hid this distraction and battle from Albion.

After six months, Mother Superior, convinced Femme had no religious vocation, had insisted that the courting should advance toward marriage, and that Albion must know. Femme did not love or even like Emile, but she knew she had to get rid of him before her father got involved. Being married and loveless was far worse to her than the nunnery. She divined that her reputation was an easy price to prevent both options. The event occurred at the convent. Emile would never be suspected of any impropriety because his older sister was a nun. Femme tricked him into coming to her room there, and shortly after, Sister Bernadine arrived, unwittingly, at an appointed time, to catch them. The brother moved to Mobile, and Femme was made to repent that summer in the convent. Femme confessed her scheming to Sister Bernadine, who helped her to learn forgiveness and control. By the time they moved to Lacombe, Numa had resigned herself to respect her Christian upbringing while abiding by her father's religion in private prayers to the orishas.

Sister Bernadine moved closer to Femme and said, "Numa, control that anger the way you learned after your spin with Emile. Anger is an internal fire that burns the soul. It'll control you. Pray it away or you'll fill your soul with inextinguishable fire. That'll prevent you from loving Ossi. I've read Ida B. Wells: don't confuse action with anger. Maybe you need to live here with us again to purge yourself."

"Oh, Sister, I can't leave Lacombe now. A man from Colfax is brewing trouble."

"I knew that would be your answer but focus on love instead of being just a warrior. Love, not hate, breeds our success at the orphanage. How long will you stay?"

"A week, I think. I want to spend some time in the city."

Sister Bernadine stood up and blew out the table candles. She motioned to Femme to help her carry the dishes. "You want to go scouting for your Choctaw too! Let's let all that simmer. We'll talk.

A lot. But only to each other. I'll talk to Mother Superior about Ossi. Other than me, she's the only one who talks to him."

+ + +

Femme longed to use the convent library, in which there were far too many books to make choosing easy. Having finished the Dickens novel, she went to the library and was engrossed by novels and biographies not mentioned in the *New Orleans Bee*. Sister Bernadine found her, immersed in this happy dilemma. With a giggle, she asked, "No library in Lacombe?"

Femme shook her head. "Lacombe and good literature aren't acquainted, Sister."

Sister Bernadine was happy to see Femme at ease. The first three days had been filled with tears and tension. The revelation of how much the nuns had helped Ossi inspired calm. That Ossi hid several times at the convent proved to be the most surprising. Knowing this allowed her to sleep better.

Sister Bernadine suggested several books by female American authors. Femme put two in her shoulder bag and said, "Sister, I think I'll venture out to the Quarter to see old friends and shop."

"Good. I didn't want to push you out. Walk up Orleans to Decatur to the market. That way, you'll see your daddy's friends. Rain comes when it wants to, so go now and enjoy yourself." She hugged Femme tightly and winked, which gave her hope.

She walked up Orleans toward the river, intending to go straight to Café du Monde. Many times, she and her father had closed the shop to enjoy strong chicory coffee. She wondered what he would make of the racial fights going on now. It was easy to remember him on these streets. Instead of veering toward the market, she turned onto Bourbon and walked slowly to St. Peters where his shop had been. Memories flooded the street. As soon as she turned onto St. Peters, she spied Les Fleurs Shoppe. She adored this shop and its owners, French sisters named Marilyn and Murielle Les Fleurs. To her surprise, the shop's windows were dark, and doors bolted. She looked across the street to see whether Mr. Barthé was still open.

Her father used Mr. Barthé's shop to get his cigar cutters sharpened. Before she could cross over to the cutler's, she heard, "Hey, la bas! Who is that I see?" Mr. Barthé turned and dropped his broom. His face grew joyful as he ran to meet her. "Numa, my

127

girl. Looking like your papa. You're his spitting image, girl. Well, you're prettier! I miss him. Nowadays, I've got to make it only with those old chiffonniers cross the street. The skinny one's been after me since my wife died. Been sporting through here with a lapel gardenia for me every week. I ain't touched her. She's got gypsy feet. Not two weeks ago, she came with a fruitcake full of liquor. Listen to me, gaggling like a goose." Femme embraced him with affection. She kissed him and saw his tears. He wiped them and took her arm and led her inside.

Femme tried to hide her surprise and responded, "I just arrived and saw the flower shop's closed. But, how are you, Mr. Barthé? Your shop's larger."

"Oh! I added that area. Used to be the glover's shop. Sit here. I got coffee ready with some shortbread."

She had to oblige him through his exuberant memories, but she also knew that too much talk of her father's hard times would dampen her mood. He came back with the coffee tray. He placed it on his workbench and summoned Femme. "Numa, I got a gas stove! It was too small for the Madison Street Hotel, where my brother works. The hotel let me have it cheap, and I built a little kitchen where I had the storeroom. Been so many robberies in the Quarter, I started living here a few months before my wife died." He talked about how his business was great and attributed the robberies to the city's negligence against lawlessness and too much disease. He asked, "But, how you doing out there in Slidell?"

"Lacombe, Mr. Barthé. Well. I have a small chicken-and-egg business and sell a lot in Mandeville and Covington markets. In the spring, I even sell to the French Market. Mostly pullets."

A deep seriousness crossed his face. He sipped his coffee and ate a large chunk of shortbread. He looked at Femme and then up to the ceiling and down at the floor. He scraped the top of his grinding stone with the knife he had used to cut the shortbread. After taking a deep breath, which he exhaled in a huff, he said, "Numa, I used to tell your daddy that those north Louisiana white folks were going to be the ruination of New Orleans. I'm sixty-eight. I knew times when this city had open arms for everybody. I danced with my wife at the Quadroon Ballroom. I've been to dances and balls and Mardi Gras with all kinds of people—from Guadeloupe, Martinique, France, and Africa too. We all got together for any free *allée* we heard about. Me and your daddy went to eat oysters and drink on St. Charles Street for lunch. It's all changing. They make us fight and hate."

Femme put her coffee cup down and folded her hands in her lap. "Things in St. Tammany Parish are dangerous too. I fear all the time for violence spreading. My life's complicated now because I'm helping some folks from Colfax."

"Colfax? That's a coincidence. Last week, a Choctaw bought six big cutting knives from me. Said he was from nearby Colfax. He didn't want to talk about that place, but he let me know the knives weren't for carving turkey."

When Ossi visited the shop, he was disturbed by Mr. Barthé's many questions. He had asked, "What you going to do with all these long knives? Start a war?"

Ossi had stood stoically and, even after more interrogation, said only, "I need them to do some good."

Mr. Barthé stared at Ossi and said, "Lots of folks been trading knives for guns. I keep to myself, try to make money just to have a good meal and fine wine. Life don't give us much more nowadays." Having waited for almost two hours, while the knives were sharpened, he found it odd that Ossi did not talk. He sat patiently and watch the cutler work. When their business was done, Barthé surmised that the knives could only be weaponry.

He related this story to Femme and noticed her expression change from curiosity to concern. She had instantly amassed a store of questions but was perplexed by the contrarieties of feeling: frozen against speech and heated by a soul sparked with Ossi's energy. Mr. Barthé sensed what he could not understand. He knew a talkative, animated Numa. Now, her face was marked by sullenness. Twice he asked her questions that she had not heard at all. He decided that any subject about the Choctaw, for whatever reason, was better left to silence. He picked up the coffee tray as two men entered carrying bundles wrapped in newspaper. He and Femme welcomed this convenient way to end their visit. After quick kisses, Femme blinked in St. Peter's Street's sunlight and walked quickly toward Decatur and the French Market. *Yemanja, let me know where he is; let me see him.*

A drizzling rain brought pedestrians into the covered French Market. Without thinking, she walked down to the far end away from Café du Monde. She needed to corral her emotions and distinguish them from one another. News about Ossi buoyed her spirits, but uncertainty over his secrecy and leaving her weighed lead-like in her chest. Somehow, remembering her father on St. Peter's Street gave her courage and strength.

After she stepped past the produce, she could smell the approaching scents of expansive bins of oysters, crabs, shrimp, and varieties of fish from the lake and river. Booth owners were in constant but steady chaos that allowed them to pitch sales while they threw huge pails of water under pallets that covered the market floor. No owner wanted a reputation for a smelly booth.

At the end of the market, there was a booth run by a fisherwoman, whose husband was reputed to be the best crabber on Lake Pontchartrain. Femme's father always said that was a skimpy lie, but they never visited this end of the market without buying boiled crabs. The crab pot there always boiled with something: shrimp, crawfish, or crabs. The boil's luring aroma was intoxicating. Femme always liked the fisherwoman's pretended rudeness as she yelled at customers with raging impatience. The woman saw Femme approaching and assumed that she aimed for the crab pot. "Come on, Missy. This is a busy booth. I ain't got time for you to look pretty. *My* pots got the best-boiled crabs in this market. For you, they're two for a nickel. Hurry before my mind changes."

Femme knew quarrelling was pointless. Coming face to face the woman meant all was decided. By the time she said, "I'll take two," the fisherwoman had wrapped the crabs in yesterday's *Bee*, saying: "Gimme money. I put some shrimp in there, some lemon to clean your hands—for you, Missy. Lagniappe." Femme turned and was astonished that a long line had formed behind her.

The sun was out again, peppering the stands and stalls with bright, broken lines. Femme followed the light and meandered back to market's entrance. Tables and chairs were packed along the street with folks eating nearly everything the market offered. She found an empty table and ate the crabs and shrimp. They had a cayenne sting, which conjured up her father's warning: "That pepper's going to burn you twice." She cleaned her hands with lemon juice and smiled—a smile that faded as thoughts of Ossi invaded her peace. *Can this brief love be this strong?*

Sadness pushed her to shield herself against this ominous feeling. She reached for Yemanja's water vial when someone touched her arm and said, "Hello, Femme." She looked up into Lucien's handsome face.

He immediately sensed her sadness; it contrasted heavily with his cheeriness. Yet, she had no defense against his blue eyes and smile. He wore a green-and-white striped shirt with shiny white buttons. His black pants were cinched, with crisscrossed leather straps, at his small waist and tucked tightly into his boots. The belt of his satchel cut across his upper body revealing an imprint of his firm chest. He was refined but not in an ostentatious way.

"Why Lucien, I can't remember the last time I've been surprised by such a good-looking man. What are you doing in the Vieux Carré?" His cheery expression invaded her mood.

"May I?" He motioned to a vacant chair as she quickly cleared the table. Lucien sat and put his leather shoulder bag under the table in a very decisive move that Femme interpreted as his foray into conversation. "I'm here to escape my uncle and do some spying."

Piqued by the idea of Lucien's spying, she thought of kumquats but set that aside to smile at the conspiracy against Hébert. "Don't find trouble that's not looking for you."

"I'm searching for fun, really. Here, it's on every corner. Can't stop loving this city. Lacombe's good for a rest. New Orleans is good for making you need that rest."

"Changed a great deal since I lived here."

"That's what I love. Never the same twice. I've begged Papa Luc to come and hear jazz. He's always too busy."

"Lucien, Papa Luc said that you were going to Tulane."

Lucien focused on his satchel. He wanted to tell the truth about only wanting to play piano with jazz musicians in Milneburg and the Quarters, but few agreed with that idea. "I've visited Tulane and inquired about the music program. It's attractive but focuses on history. I like that, but New Orleans music is making its own history, and I . . . well, I want to think more about Tulane later."

"Somebody told me she taught you some songs you can't play or sing in church."

Lucien became animated. "Aunt Velma loves jazz and blues. We love it as much as my uncle hates it. She comes to my pecan shack and sings while I play. And dances too! She's got me addicted to music. When I'm with her, I just forgot all about Tulane and classical piano."

Femme enjoyed Lucien's unusual openness and honesty. He had been an elusive child, who preferred sequestering himself. Everyone, on either side of the fence, could hear his pounding the old upright piano with jazz sounds he played like church music. Pichon joked that Lucien had swallowed some lost drops of black blood. Aunt Velma said Lucien learned jazz to grieve for his mother and torment Hébert. Papa Luc claimed the boy needed to mature his own way. Despite how others saw him, Lucien used his privileged freedom to define himself.

"How's Meffre? He used to drop by to hear me play jazz, but he stopped." She was surprised that he asked this nervously, biting his fingernails.

"Meffre's fine. He's worried, as we all are, about those regulators, but he's fine. He told me y'all are friends. If you think something's wrong, just talk to *him*?"

He scrutinized Femme's eyes, her ebony tint, the smallness of her nose and mouth, and the prettiness of how her dark fine hair fell so agreeably against her face. He was comfortable because she exuded kindness. He bravely posited, "I should talk to him, of course." He blushed and reluctantly let the subject go.

St. Louis Cathedral's bells tolled three o'clock—a convenient interruption for Femme. "I have to get back to the convent. I'm staying with the Holy Family sisters near here on Orleans."

"I'll walk you there."

"That would be nice, but I have to get a gift for them. They adore pralines and say eating them is the only time they sin."

"Amazing! We have a good friend who owns a praline shop on Decatur. We sold pecans to his family for years. But, how about we eat beignets first at Café du Monde?"

"Sure. After that spicy seafood, that's good dessert."

After coffee and beignets, they strolled through the market, pointing out various familiar and odd items. From fresh catfish to eel, from cherries to Georgia late peaches, from imported olive oil to smelly hair pomade, there was an endless array of things to observe, laugh about, and puzzle over. At huge bins of peanuts, pecans, hazelnuts, and walnuts, Lucien pointed out the Coulon name on barrels that were half full. A stand owner, whom Lucien knew, bragged that this was the second barrel he opened that day. He offered free tastes of all the nuts, even the salty Brazilian cashews.

On their way out, they passed a citrus stand whose owner claimed that his fruits were the best in the market because they came by train from faraway Florida and California. Femme and Lucien ate slices of oranges and mandarins. She then spied kumquats and said to the vendor, "This young man doesn't eat kumquats though someone thinks he loves them." She waited for Lucien's face to show his surprise.

He laughed heartily. "Percie?"

"Yes. Percie proves that what great ones do, the less will prattle of."

"Shakespeare must've inspired him, then. It's true I hate anything sour. Like Uncle Hébert. Just thinking of him makes me want a praline."

They walked out of the buzzing activity, talking about Lacombe's slowness. Lucien wanted to ask more about Meffre, but he erred on the side of restraint. They were, however, at an opportune juncture as they neared the praline shop. He allowed, "Sometimes, I see Meffre walking along the fence returning from his deliveries. Like I said, he used to stop by. Just waves now. Maybe you could tell him I've got new jazz to play."

Femme listened attentively and felt this was about more than an invitation. She knew friendship between Lucien and Meffre had unwritten restrictions. However, she puzzled over Lucien's hesitation given Papa Luc's bold risk-taking streak with her and Aunt Velma. What more did this invitation entail? She responded, "Sure. I'll deliver your invitation." They both knew a plot was being laid and left it at that. The subject, however, made Femme inquisitive.

They arrived at the half door of Reynaud's Praline Shoppe—a small shop, with walls of candy tins, stuffed animals with praline bellies, and jars of toffee, chocolate, rum, and bourbon flavored pralines. On a short stool behind a long counter sat Anatole Reynaud. He was tall, his torso elongated—even seated, he sat chest-high over the counter. His complexion seemed blanched, without even the slightest tinge of color. With sparkling blue eyes and slick straight blonde hair, he was the picture of an overdressed French fop. He eyed his customers through the half door and, in a high-pitched, ladylike voice, said, "Lucien Coulon, Jr., bring your lady friend back here and shut the top half of that door. It's not closing time, but I'm in the mood for entertaining. If anyone with money passes by, I'll open again to rob them. Who's this pretty one?"

Lucien took Femme by her hand, which he placed in Reynaud's and said, "This is Miss Numa Labat. We call her Femme. I'm happy to introduce you to Anatole Reynaud, proprietor."

"Such formality. Reynaud. Just Reynaud. Charmed, Femme. Labats owned a cigar shop down the way. Years ago. Nice people. Any kin?"

"My father's shop. You knew him?" Femme politely pulled her hand away from Reynaud's.

"I did. Kind man. Papa Luc told me he had a lovely daughter. True enough. He and that nasty-acting cutler would come for pralines."

"Daddy's passed on now, and I live out in Lacombe."

"I know. And you know my dear friend Hébert, Lucien's saintly uncle?"

Femme could not disguise her anxiety until she sensed Reynaud's disquieting grin. Before she could answer, Lucien grew animated. "Reynaud, stop interrogating. He's baiting you, Femme." Lucien saw that she was not altogether comfortable with Reynaud, but he registered her curiosity. He decided it would be best to story him into the conversation again. "Reynaud, you've known these people for years. Know any *secrets*," he said, hoping for alleviating gossip.

"No fool, no fun. This boy's full of fun when the elders aren't here. Pretending to be good now. Fine. Let's pretend over afternoon sherry. It's true your dear uncle Hébert thinks he's still my friend. Never was. Never will be. See, I knew him from way back in Colfax where he belongs. Colfax, the river land of lynch mobs and mosquitoes. Back then, Hébert was nice and innocent; that is, till his wife divorced him and he became a bigot, *publicly*. She took up with a good-looking, tall Créole. Almost killed Hébert. Now he's down here drinking himself to death. Gets dumber as he gets older. Came in here recently spewing filth about Papa Luc. I just took it all in. Don't mistake his frown; he's far worse than that. We pretend friendship in exchange for secrets. And those, he *never* gets from me."

Reynaud walked prissily to a huge breakfront covered with every sort of silver tray, all laden with wrapped and ribboned pralines. He opened a side door and pulled out a tray with a crystal bottle of sherry and matching cordial glasses. "I know now, but didn't know then, that when I introduced all of them years ago, Hébert regretted, probably still does, that Papa Luc married his sister. But, as I said, he, at the time, was running after a wife who left his fat . . . enough of that."

Femme noticed, with marked inquisitiveness, Reynaud's refinement in setting the tray on the table, arranging pralines next to the sherry cordials in exact and uniform placement to each other, and his pouring sherry to the same level. He motioned to them to be seated by simply offering the tray like a piece of art.

"We don't have such refined presentations of pralines and sherry in Lacombe," she said with mild mockery. Lucien enjoyed witnessing Reynaud's antics.

"Well, then, invite me to bring my city culture to Lacombe," Reynaud retorted in earnest. Femme caught on: this prissiness was who he was unashamedly and boastfully. With reservation, she admired him.

Lucien was deliberately crude in unwrapping the chocolate praline while slurping sherry too quickly. He licked his lips to taunt Reynaud, and Femme's head was all a-swivel trying to understand what their glances meant. Even if the language of their shared motions eluded her, she was sure they cared deeply for each other.

Reynaud sipped the last of his sherry and said, "I know secrets about you too, Lucien. He's finally in love or thinks he is. Secrets run in Coulon blood. But, today, I'm entertaining and giving you pralines as gifts. I'm giving advice too: beware of your uncle's friends from Colfax. Told your daddy that, too. Especially Carl Keller, the assassin. He'll try to kill anything a shade darker than he is, especially if he thinks they're after his money. Hébert was by here two weeks ago trying to wring gossip out of me. Got nothing but gave too much. He was silly enough to let it drop that he was in town for a meeting with Carl about some financial business. Hébert's always been one to drop names to give himself importance. We keep up this fake friendship only to trade gossip."

Reynaud rose, turned toward the counter with a flourish, and said, "The clever survive, son. Especially against the likes of Hébert and Carl. Been clever against all that since my days in Colfax. That's what keeps this shop open. Only *evening ladies* seem to be working longer in the Quarters than Monsieur Reynaud."

"I'd like to take some pralines to the nuns where I'm staying. What's your recommendation?" Femme waited for Reynaud's response, but he hopped up and was busy reaching for several boxes from the top shelf behind the counter.

"Those ladies like the same three kinds of pralines. If you buy smaller boxes, someone will be upset. So, take them all. I'll only charge you half. They're regular customers." He looked out of the front window and could see customers peering in. "Guess I'd better let these folks make me rich." Lucien took this as a cue to gently escort Femme out. Reynaud accompanied them with great courtesy while he ushered in three customers. "Adieu, my loves."

Lucien walked Femme back to the convent, telling her a story about his father and Reynaud. When Lucien was a boy, Papa Luc spent a lot of time in the French Quarter establishing himself as a businessman by selling pecans, chickens, pigs, ham, eggs, and whatever produce his land yielded. In time, he had to depend less on a variety of products and more on a staple like pecans. He grew the pecan business without much competition, and merchants favored his prices to enlarge profits. Everyone who did business with Papa Luc exclaimed that his wealth was deserved because he was a man who came by it honestly. Even as a boy, Lucien accompanied him and was introduced as the "little Coulon" in training. When Papa Luc was too busy to tend to Lucien's curiosity, he would deposit him in Reynaud's apartment. There he would observe praline making and hear stories about wicked Créoles whose religion did them no good. Lucien prayed to be taken to New Orleans against his mother's will. Papa Luc gently coaxed Alinnie into letting the boy enjoy his so-called "apprenticeship." All of Aunt Velma's pouting and Alinnie's begging still resulted in Lucien's dragging his little grip behind his father. Lucien especially loved spending time with Reynaud.

After Alinnie died, the early years of Papa Luc's dealings with Hébert were fraught with turmoil and the unexpected vicissitudes of Hébert's blatant dishonesty. When all this was too much for him, he announced that business called in New Orleans and that Lucien was going with him.

On one such occasion, when Hébert had screamed unnecessarily at Aunt Velma for cutting Lucien's hair too short, Papa Luc arbitrated the fight by taking Lucien to Reynaud's for two weeks. To let everyone know that he had finally given up, Hébert quarreled only long enough to spout loudly: "Good! Go to New Orleans. I'll have peace by moving out of here! I'm going back to Small House for good." To which, Aunt Velma said to Lucien in a whisper: "Boy, remember peace don't keep itself. He'll be back. Start praying against it." Lucien laughed too loudly and grabbed a menacing snarl from Hébert. That was the last day Hébert lived at the Coulon mansion. From that trip to New Orleans, Lucien recorded permanent and cherished memories. He always slept with Reynaud in his huge bedroom overlooking an enclosed courtyard shaded by blooming magnolias. He also enjoyed playing with Créole children, who filled the courtyard during the day as their mothers worked for white families, hotels, or restaurants nearby. Reynaud's French Quarter apartment was a refuge—a refuge sealed in strong friendship with the Coulons.

Femme's attentiveness assured Lucien that this was Coulon history she had not heard. He hoped that this inspired her to trust him. He also hoped that she would carry his message to Meffre. The convent was near, and Femme's thoughts of Ossi returned. Lucien was a perfect escort, with all his father's charm, stamped with his own brand. They walked up to the convent gate, and Lucien wished her a good trip home.

Femme was happy to see Sister Bernadine standing in the front door. "I have a present for y'all: pralines."

Sister Bernadine took the box of chocolate pralines—which she did not intend to share—and told Femme to distribute the rest. "I put a present on your bed for you. Since you're leaving in the morning, I thought I'd give it to you now." She unconsciously fiddled with her wimple and waddled away.

Femme unlocked the door to her room and dropped her packages when she found Ossi standing bearlike with outstretched arms. His face was streaked with elation. He danced over to her and scooped her off her feet and into his arms. Doubt tainted her undeniable happiness at seeing him. Her first thoughts were his announcement, when they first met, that he never wanted to take a wife and have children. Though she had come to save their relationship, she wondered whether she was trying to create something that could never be. Her excitement, however, overshadowed these nagging reflections.

"Sister said she left me a gift. Are you my gift?" She welcomed his kissing her neck passionately; yet, lurking questions and answers prevented swift forgiveness. After a loosely connected conversation that rambled through their perceived rights and wrongs, they concluded that blame was no prize. For her, however, commitment—even marriage—was a treasure. Ossi's anxious expression, however, signaled how ensuring permanence for their future troubled him. For him, their falling in love was fraught with unsettling present and future risks. For her, his reticence was unnerving. She felt compelled to ask, "When you leave me, is it me you're leaving? I know you're concerned about danger you think you brought us. We had that kind of trouble long before you. I know you feel responsible and are trying to protect us. But, when I first got to know you, you said you never wanted to have a wife or children. I wonder . . . are you running away from me?"

He sat of the bed and puzzled long enough over these questions that he fueled her doubt again. Then, with his hand extended to her, he spoke softly yet sternly, "You separate these things. I don't. I brought you danger. It's my duty to protect you because now I love you. I'm confused about what comes first. I can't be the man I was when I first met you. I still want that free life. I can't be that man because you changed me. Just give me enough freedom to trust me. I can sneak up on innocent rabbits and bring them home live for supper. Let me work on putting guilty animals in cages for what they're trying to do to us. That's how I love. The guilty can't see me coming though. I'm not running from *you*. I'm hiding to trap *them*. Please, Femme. Trust."

She fell back on the bed and exhaled her exasperation. Romantic notions rode away on the reality Ossi breathed into his answer. Oddly, she felt somewhat conflicted about settling for his explanation. Her independence and romanticizing love into a fanciful affair were more appealing than Ossi's pragmatism. She knew, however, that to love him meant compromising as much as he had. She held him around his waist. "At least it wasn't another woman."

Ossi laughed and said, "One woman is a tribe to me."

"Well, good. I'm your tribe. I love you and will trust you. You risk your life for me, the twins, Meffre—all of us. Let me know only what I need to know. I'll try to be patient and understanding." He answered by gently pulling her face to his. Respect for the convent allowed them to only lay listlessly yet blissfully in the afternoon's muted light and talk about their mutual obsession with safeguarding their lives and future. They knew it would be painful for her but agreed that he would, of necessity, remain a specter in Lacombe.

+ + +

The next morning, Lucien surprised Femme standing in the train station as if waiting for her. Although he was pleasant, his smile and playfulness had gone. They boarded and agreed to sit together in the back. Lucien's silence hung awkwardly between them. Femme sensed this as they arranged luggage and settled into their seats.

Femme could not resist. "I thought you were staying in New Orleans?"

"Aunt Velma left the mansion."

"No! What happened?"

"Something about a gas stove. Aunt Velma won't cook on it, but there's got to be more to it. Papa Luc's beside himself," he said with genuine confusion. He looked out of the window, down at his hands, and concluded, "I got a telegram from Papa Luc. He's in a state without Aunt Velma. Reynaud told me to go home." Lucien bit his nails and grimaced. Though not entirely true, he knew this explanation would have to suffice.

"I'll check on Aunt Velma as soon as I get home, but this is disturbing." She opened a book but was distracted by Lucien's news. She relived her time with Ossi—time checkered with questioning but marked with love. This reflection made the trip home far better than the trip to New Orleans.

An Interfering Gas Stove

WHEN THE STEAMBOAT MOORED in Mandeville, Femme instantly noticed tightness in the air. She and Lucien had traveled back together in silence, sleep, and lots of pretended reading. Their quiet journey had changed with the swift movements and loud agitation of the pier train's jaunty trek from dock to market. She continued to feel an undeniable tightness even in the ground as she stepped off the train. Absent were the sweet smell of fruits, aromas of seafood cooking, or lovely scents of flowers. Only an unsettling stillness—the air itself, angry and taut. It was particularly queer that Percie was missing from the produce stand.

Lucien discovered Julien sitting in the driver's seat of Femme's buckboard. He greeted them with a forced grin to Femme and a knowing nod to Lucien. When she asked about Percie, Julien again looked at Lucien and then at the horse. Femme thought this was Julien's uneasiness with Lucien's presence and said, "I offered Lucien a ride to the stable. He boarded his horse there." Without a word, Julien got down from the rig and helped them with their belongings.

They rode to the boarding barn in silence until Julien, whose cheeks were puffed up with anger, said loudly, as if directed to Lucien, "Percie's gone missing. Nobody knows what happened." Femme was shocked and insisted Julien tell the story. His eyes were mixed with sadness and protest. For him, Femme should know. With a heavy tongue, he said, "Lucien, you know some of this."

Lucien looked at Femme and answered, "The telegram from Papa Luc said, 'Bad news about Percie and Pichon.' "

Julien reported Papa Luc's sending a big crock so that he could make homebrew for the wedding. Afterward, Meffre and Percie delivered the empty crock to the Coulon's. Both boys were drunk, but they put the crock on the back porch. Hébert was on the front

140

porch and told them to leave. Percie told the doctor that there was a horse with a toothache that needed him in the barn. The boys ran to the rig and sped away.

The next day, Hébert called Sheriff Blake and accused Percie and Meffre of destroying Papa Luc's crock, which had been found in pieces under the back porch. They arrested Percie, but Papa Luc got him out of jail and told him to stay at Femme's. Julien could hardly breathe. As they pulled up to the boarding barn, he said, "Percie was riding home with Pichon last night. Pichon was caught and beat bad. Percie hasn't been seen since. Papa Luc's been looking for him. Everyone is. Pichon's at home and getting better."

Lucien jumped down from the rig and grabbed Julien's arm. "If I find out anything else, I'll let y'all know." He collected his bag, looking with concern at Femme.

"Tell Papa Luc I'm back," she said. Having been gone only eight days, Femme was astounded by the news.

After Percie's incident, Aunt Velma decided to stay at Femme's with Meffre. Papa Luc had come by every day to check on them. He begged her to return home. Aunt Velma would not. She said she loved the invitation but lied that she was afraid of the gas stove. Julien recounted this nonstop and ended saying that Papa Luc had heard about a plan for a "big sign" coming to Lacombe to let niggers and Créoles know how little power they had. Everyone expected whites to start burning houses or lynching. Femme was silent. She thought of Ossi and observed stillness in the pines along the road to her house.

+ + +

When they arrived, Femme found Aunt Velma cutting Meffre's hair on the porch. Labas came running to her barking his version of the story in a haunting baying that signaled bad feelings all over the yard. It seemed to Femme that the pink pig had turned into a hog overnight, for she was solid all around and moving slowly toward her spot under the oak tree. She plopped herself into her comfortable hole, grunting that she was carrying another litter. The oak tree fidgeted, welcoming Femme, signaling that private chatter awaited her.

Aunt Velma brushed hair from Meffre's shoulders. She looked deeply into her eyes and gently nudged Meffre, who stood and embraced Femme. "Glad you're home; we're all worried," Meffre said softly. The tightness in his face revealed fear and anger.

"Seems we have a lot to talk about. How's Pichon? Aunt Velma, thank you for being here. How bad is it?"

Aunt Velma kissed Femme and opened the screened door. Meffre carried Femme's bags, and everyone waited in the kitchen. Aunt Velma went to the stove to stir a pot of red beans. She looked quickly in Femme's direction and returned to stirring. Femme positioned herself face-to-face with Aunt Velma's only long enough to get her attention and notice her wet eyes. She grabbed the wooden spoon and said, "Sit down. These beans don't need stirring. Talk to me." Meffre left, sensing the women needed privacy.

Aunt Velma wiped her eyes with her apron. "We ain't seen Percie, but Pichon is healing fast. Never seen anything like it. There was no mercy—the way they whipped and cut my child. Strange that no wound was deep. Charmaine keeps him clean and rubs him with ointment. His back is knitting itself together already. He's strong, that one." She then related how Hébert unknowingly hired one of Percie's girlfriends as a cook. On her way home from Small House, the cook occasionally met Aunt Velma on the footpath and told her everything she had eavesdropped. Hébert talked about two groups of regulators: one was named the Camellias, led by Mary Eaton and populated with women from the altar society. Father Lorquette continued to watch that group. What surprised Femme was that Hébert now led the other band of regulators. He became their captain because others claimed Reginald was too slow. They met regularly in Big Branch. The cook heard Hébert say that soon there would be "signs enough" against any toleration of "disturbances like in Colfax." Aunt Velma's tears fell without restraint. "Child, they ain't just after us. That porker had Ossi followed in New Orleans. Men from Colfax are looking for him. Papa Luc's doing what he can. Can't say what I'd do without him." Femme started shaking, but she held Aunt Velma's hands.

"Aunt Velma, Ossi's safe. I was with him. Mother Superior's been hiding him. Ossi and I have a new understanding. I realize I must let him handle things his way. He's fine."

"Oh! Thank you, Jesus. Still, Hébert done convinced them regulators to cut down Papa Luc, too. They're madder than mangy dogs and call him a traitor."

"I saw Lucien in New Orleans. We came back together."

"Papa Luc sent him to talk to Reynaud about Hébert's plans with Colfax."

"Hébert was there about two weeks ago, meeting with Carl Keller. For sure, they're planning."

Aunt Velma stiffened in her chair. "We still don't know much. I told Papa Luc I'm afraid to be alone in the mansion. Now you're back, I'm gonna go live with Pichon and Charmaine to help when the baby comes. They beat Pichon to near kill him. My leaving ain't nothing about a stove. Truth is I miss my bed and Papa Luc. Too dangerous. Hébert got rid of his cook. Now I don't know what he's up to. Come by and hear Pichon tell his side. God protect Percie. Nobody rides like him. I pray he got away and is hiding."

Femme's anger intensified. She remembered Sister Bernadine's warning and tried to calm herself. The old oak shook in a gentle violence that she did not like. She kissed Aunt Velma on the top of her head and walked out onto the porch.

Meffre looked up with the creaking of the screened door. She reached for his hand and asked, "How're you doing?"

In her absence, the violence against the twins and his personal turmoil had forced maturity. He told Femme that Pichon had been asking for her. He also knew that Papa Luc had sent Lucien to help them. Meffre looked at her anxiously till she said, "I'm glad we have Lucien on our side. First thing tomorrow, I've got to get word to Ossi." Meffre finally relayed a message from Pichon: he had forty-three candles and wanted to know when to bring the moccasins.

They watched the oak tree resist the mounting wind. They talked about the wedding and how that joy was ruined after Percie disappeared. Femme loved Meffre's melodious voice. Even when anxious, there was always the hint of song in his words. He possessed a gentle soul, easy to discern behind his strength and virility. As he was talking, she remembered Lucien's request. "Oh, by the way, I'm carrying a little gift-like message. Lucien wants you to drop by his 'office' again. Says he's got new jazz for you. You should go. He's wondering why you don't stop by anymore." Meffre's bemused look turned to a smile. She said, "Go! Enjoy yourself."

Meffre left to clean for dinner, and Femme lit her pipe and called to the oak tree, "Now it's your turn, old friend. Who's causing all that bother for you?" The oak's agitation scattered through the yard. The magnolia near the barn hurled its large glossy leaves in shivers that blew angry air through the chicken yard. The roosters and hens flipped their wings and cackled and crowed loudly. Every creature that could move the air united to create one huge swish that came Femme's way in a deep whisper that sounded like a growl: *Scarred boy. Dead tree. Dead man.*

Femme dropped her pipe and walked to the porch's northern corner. She again felt swelling anger. "Eshu. What's this?" Her question caused a flurry of leaves to collect in a swirl at the tree's base. The magnolia sent leaves and dry petals from its large flowers. The hibiscus sent dry brown and yellow leaves to join the growing pile. The roses, camellias, and geraniums dropped leaves and petals that carried themselves dutifully onto piles that stirred toward the oak. Femme could barely cross the yard before a hill of debris had taken its place where the pink pig had rutted. The debris resembled a grave mound. She walked to the oak which exuded strength, and Femme clearly heard Eshu, almost songlike, pronounce, *Scarred boy. Dead tree. Dead man.* The oak's cool embrace called her. She sat atop the mound of leaves and petals and leaned against the rough bark. She could feel the tree's life, which created a sensation that mitigated all fear. *Yemanja took me to New Orleans and back. Eshu, don't make me pay for happiness by giving me this worry. Who must know this?*

Meffre came out and walked directly to her. He said, "I heard. I've heard it all day. Maybe this time it's not a riddle. Hope I'm wrong. Let's take Aunt Velma home and eat our red beans with Charmaine and Pichon. I'm praying this isn't about Percie."

Rest and Aunt Velma's red beans, biscuits, and fried perch reinvigorated Pichon. He smiled broadly over his second helping. "I don't know what's wrong with Meffre, but I won't be thinking about him when I eat his fish."

Meffre said, "Well, you look like you need it." Pichon laughed, but Femme feared that the laughter and lightness in the kitchen was a disguise for what Pichon felt and what the others were not talking about.

Charmaine, with red eyes, said, "Eat as much as you want, honey. Aunt Velma's food will get you out of this rut."

Femme took Pichon's arm and said, "Tell me what happened." This turned the entire room somber. Aunt Velma's face slackened with the weight of fatigue; she left for bed. Femme waited patiently for Pichon to begin. His story was short because it had happened with amazing speed on a frightening night. He pieced it together in flashes of disjointed memory and punctuated it with the sadness and fear of never seeing his brother again.

Percie and Pichon had ridden home on Lake Road in a slow trot. Every black man along the bayou that evening talked about fires in the swamp. Only one house had burned, but everyone knew to get home and stay armed with the knives or loaded guns Ossi supplied. Percie had an order for bayou perch from Miss Hazel, who paid well and had also ordered his presence for dinner. This had become customary when he made fish deliveries for Julien. Pichon did not believe his brother's dinner invitation, but he had caught most of the perch and meant to get paid. Just at the curve in Lake Road, they heard horses behind them. When the horses sped up, gaining on them, they raced off. They knew well the shortcuts in these woods. Riding in different directions against attackers was always preferable to trying to fight together. Percie hurled the perch into the ditch he had just jumped over. "Meet me at the church."

Pichon estimated the distance between himself and the two horses heading toward him. He took off into the woods, seeing that Percie stayed on Lake Road riding toward a light in the window of Hazel's house. Pichon rode on and lost sight of Percie. Two riders pursued Pichon, but he could not tell how closely. He rode toward light in the opposite direction. The light could be a lantern, campfire, bonfire, or—in his growing fear—a burning cross. Yet, he rode on with pursuers fast behind him. He thought it best not to head directly for the fire but to come on it from behind. Tabby allowed the jerking of her reins and understood this ride was different. She felt Pichon's nervousness in his mount, his movement, and mostly in his indecision about their destination. He rode past the Banner's house, flew behind the Cabbot's place, and circled around the open pasture behind the Meadow's farm. They all had dim lights, and his hope was that the presence of these families going about their evening rituals would deter his pursuers. Tabby was full of agitation.

Whenever he slowed a little to look behind him, he could hear violence in the quickening pace of the oncoming horses. Hoping he would find help at the firelight just ahead, he turned toward it, approaching from behind. He prayed for a band of black faces.

He rode straight for the fire. Then he passed it because no one waited for him. He no longer heard the horses behind him. Silence. He thought the chase was over. With heaving breaths, he dismounted and walked toward the fire. Tabby resisted, but he held her reins tightly in one hand, and in the other, he held his knife. The silence grew and forced him to look in every direction in quick fits of fear. Tabby resisted again. Pichon swallowed air deeply until he was standing over the fire. He spotted footprints that had crushed and broken dry pine needles. He heard movement. He spied a huge pine that was lit by the fire and moved toward it as if being called. As he sauntered to the tree, he felt the whirring of a lasso descend on his waist. Then, it started to tighten—so much so that he fell breathless against the pine. His knife fell out of his reach. When he looked up, it was into the faces of five white men, armed with knives, whips, sticks, and guns.

He sat helpless at the base of the pine and let go of Tabby's reins. She sped into darkness. Pichon surveyed the faces as they merged into one he knew well but hoped never to see. At that moment, he realized that two pursuers wore masks, which they now removed. They were teenagers, one he knew to be Todd Eaton. The three white men, older by many years, were barefaced and smiling. The boldest of the lot moved forward slowly and peered directly into Pichon's eyes and said, "You ain't gonna die tonight, nigger. You gonna be a stamped letter to everyone who thinks you can make trouble and get away with it. We gonna send your black ass first class postage." Then, as if issuing a blessing, the red-faced, short, and shiny white man ordered, "Put a first-class stamp on him, boys!"

They went to work: the leader sat and watched as eight fists pummeled Pichon. His tattered shirt, ripped from his back, fell to his feet. The rope they tightened around his waist cut his breath further, and he winced in pain. They used the same rope to bind him tight around the pine. His face and chest were cut by the bark. The tall one with the whip threw the first blow to straighten Pichon upright against the tree. With this first lash, he was left with no choice but to hold on to the tree in an embrace that looked as if love bound him there.

Pichon held on. He wrapped himself, arms and legs, around the tree. With the coming lashes, he felt calmness in his muscles as he reshaped himself into the tree's surface. Oddly, though he knew the lashes cut his skin, he felt no pain. The tree took him in. With the next lashes, the vicious tip never touched him but stung relentlessly behind the circle of the pine. Yet, he spied, with each strike, his blood pitching itself against the tree's bark. Below, he saw pine

146

needles colored red. Smelling the bark's fresh scent, he focused on his knife, which sent off a shimmer in the distance.

Pichon uttered not a word. Nor did he scream. This was intolerable for his tormentors. They, therefore, continued their stamping by knifing his arms just enough to tear flesh. The whipping continued, but all was intensified with repeated blows to his skull with a barbed stick. And, finally, a gunshot was fired just above his head into the pine—the shock of which deafened him.

The leader, in what appeared to be total exhaustion, lifted himself from beside the fire and said in a high-pitched voice, "That's enough postage. This ain't that perch-mouth bastard who talks too much. That one is the real problem. This one's a throwaway." With that order, the tormentors untied the rope from his waist and left him, dripping red from his matted hair to his boots. The anthill, he unwittingly stood on, was soaked in his urine, and the ants were fleeing in an unbroken line to other side of the tree. Pichon continued to stand solidly in the pine's embrace. The tormentors mounted their horses, cussing and swearing for Pichon's death.

They rode away slowly, and Tabby returned just as slowly. She circled the pine and continued to do so until dawn when Julien calmed her. The pine shook all its branches in disgust, but its angry movements did not move Pichon from its trunk. The tree did not release him until Julien and Eshu stood behind him and caught him to break his fall.

Charmaine cried through the story before and now cried again. She held her hand up and said, "Femme, Papa Luc was by here and wants to tell you what they know about Percie, but Pichon's got to go to bed now. He has nightmares, so I give him brandy to make him sleep. I'll get it."

With Charmaine out of earshot, Pichon beckoned Femme to come near him. "Femme, when they cut and whipped me, I saw my blood but felt only a touch of pain. I'm only sore now. I believe it was the pine they tied me to." His eyes teared over, and Femme pulled at his chair to help him up. "The rest of them won't believe me." Femme kissed him. Charmaine returned, and he obediently followed her to their bedroom.

Femme and Meffre went home. They, then, immediately went to the oratory to pray. They prayed separately to their orishas. Meffre became convinced that Eshu was arming them for a fight. He told Femme that Miss Hazel was not home that night and had not been home for three days before. She had not been seen since. Everyone surmised that the light in the window that Pichon and Percie saw was a trap. Percie's horse was found dead behind her house. Pichon told Sheriff Blake that Todd Eaton was there; nothing had been done about that. Papa Luc told them this and ordered them to stay at home after sunset.

Femme prayed to Yemanja for a sign that Percie was alive; none came. She and Meffre locked the doors and talked for two hours. She described her trip to New Orleans and smiled through her talking about Ossi. Meffre's attention piqued at her mentioning Lucien. He asked *how* Lucien inquired about him and other questions that, although she answered, made her wander in directions that led nowhere. She finally cut off the questions. "Visit Lucien, Meffre. He'll answer your questions."

Femme left him and went to bed. After asking about Lucien, Meffre felt guilty for something he could not name. He remembered Todd Eaton, who had fought Lucien. About that, he stayed awake. To add to the angst, Meffre regretted not stopping to talk to Lucien. He turned from side to side fitfully for hours. The physicality of the bed and flipping aroused him. He could not rid himself of passionate thoughts. Even the fear of Carl Keller's targeting him did not lessen his desire. His sexual urges fueled insomnia and resurrected the conflicted feelings of excitement and prohibition.

✝ ✝ ✝

The next morning Femme found him sleeping soundly with his heavy, muscled arms spread band-like across the bed. Her presence stirred him. "Sorry I slept late. Haven't slept since . . . guess I'm worried about Percie like everybody."

Meffre cleaned up and ate breakfast. Femme filled three bowls with water and asked him to help her put them on the oratory. She left him there praying.

She sat drinking coffee when Papa Luc rode up to the front steps yelling at Labas to stop barking and get under the house. "You ought to teach that damn dog I'm not the enemy."

"But you look like the enemy," she said mockingly.

Papa Luc seemed frustrated, agitated, and angry. "Lucien told me that y'all heard very little from Reynaud. I've talked to every decent man in Lacombe about Percie and Pichon. Hell, I talked to sick, hateful bastards, too. Even went to Small House and interrogated *that* bastard. No one's talking. I shocked Hébert, though, by asking him what he knew about Reginald's son Todd and what happened to Pichon. He knew more than he said. Had the nerve to say, 'The worst is yet to come.' " Papa Luc held her by the shoulders and said, "I just don't think they've killed Percie. Hébert's stupid and careless. He would've boasted about that. I've got men looking out from here to Covington. Ossi's got men armed with guns and knives. Did it a while back."

"Come inside. Just made fresh coffee. Aunt Velma will be here soon." He took off his hat and followed her, smiling at hearing Aunt Velma's name.

After Aunt Velma arrived, Papa Luc told them that he thought they were holding Percie for information because they knew he was spying. "Father Lorquette thinks it's time to unite with Sheriff Blake against those regulators before someone gets killed. I just don't trust Blake though." He moved his chair closer to Aunt Velma and put his arms around her. She let her head fall on his shoulders and started sobbing.

"That means you have to include *all* of us in the fight. Ossi and I agreed to that yesterday," Femme said. "He's staying at the convent."

"No, he left," Papa Luc said lovingly. "He's at Reynaud's. It's safer."

Burnt Bassinette

SIX TEDIOUS AND TORTUOUS months passed. Aunt Velma, full of spite, muttered a refrain: "Fear's just dancing 'round us, mocking us." Pichon had recovered, and the drudgery of working at Coulon Sawmill offered him protection. Work and family responsibilities kept him occupied. Uncertainty about Percie, however, prevented even the semblance of peace.

At home, Charmaine made certain the ever-present and unyielding torment over Percie's absence was tempered by happiness. She laced her stories with exaggerations of baby Kebbi's new feats. She made him new clothes and fed him into chubbiness.

Aunt Velma appointed herself a "specialist" in lifting Pichon's spirits by cooking his favorite dishes. She kept everyone hopeful by preparing dishes Percie begged for. "You never know when he'll show up with an appetite bigger than his shirt."

Lucien became a frequent visitor, bringing Aunt Velma her favorite chocolates and any news he had swiped at Mudbug's. She cherished his visits and made him eat while "picking him like a chicken" on what Papa Luc was doing. She especially wanted to know if she was asked for. Lucien howled at this question because Papa Luc visited Aunt Velma more frequently than he did. "You miss cooking for Papa Luc or *something else*?" She slapped his arm and pretended to be insulted. His joking made her happy.

One Friday night, Aunt Velma made codfish balls because she had a premonition that "Percie might smell and come running. My codfish patties been known to make sinners pray. Way I fix 'em can turn whores into church ladies." As the official taster and verifier, Pichon shouted "amen." Her kitchen duties eased her suffering; yet, the bottom of her white apron was rarely dry of her tears.

Since Percie's abduction, the only clues they had on his whereabouts came from eavesdropped conversations at Mudbug's or unusual sightings of Reginald Eaton at Myrtle Picou's Seafood Shack on Lake Road. Sheriff Blake had reported to Papa Luc that the regulators were "keeping low to the ground" and not talking openly. Such unsolicited news from the sheriff gradually built Papa Luc's trust.

Against Papa Luc warnings and outright disapproval, Lucien had resolved to play piano at Mudbug's to spy on regulators. Pike eagerly agreed. He liked having another set of eyes and ears in the saloon, especially after work hours when he was busiest. So far, much of the piano playing yielded only speculation on who fit the regulator profile or not. Lucien and Pike worked out a system that buying the piano player a shot got the buyer a song of his choice. The system operated well in keeping the saloon animated and conversations loose. From time to time, Sheriff Blake passed through for a quick drink with Pike. He never gave Lucien anymore notice than a nod. Patience eased Lucien's angst and bolstered Pike's commitment to his Catholic duty.

Julien, for his part, frequented Myrtle Picou's more often. There would be no suspicion about his presence because Myrtle was his longstanding client. Myrtle's was a favorite lunch spot for lumberjacks who worked with Reginald Eaton. They were a boisterous and undisciplined pack of bigots, whose intimidating giantlike bodies alone gave most men pause. Even sitting on the *colored* side, he could clearly hear the lumberjacks brag about their participation in lynchings and other unlawful affairs. On one occasion, about three months after Percie went missing, Julien had no intention of stopping at Myrtle's, but he had seen Reginald's horse hitched near the side. He had never seen this before. He was emboldened to sit on the Whites Only side, which Myrtle allowed when Julien was alone. When he walked in, the table of lumberjacks greeted him with frowns and cussing. Reginald stood infuriated and said, "Is the other side too crowded for you, Julien?"

Before Julien could answer, Myrtle pulled her shotgun from its rack and cocked it. She picked up a beer and set it before Julien and said, "This is a stupid gun. It's got names on bullets for any bastard that goes up against *my* authority in *my* place. Want to collect your bullet? Come fuck with this gun." Reginald gulped his beer, slammed the glass upside down on the table, and stormed out. Myrtle lowered the gun's cock and shuffled around the bar. She put the gun back in its rack and poured herself a glass of beer. She joined Julien at his table and groaned defiantly. She said, "Don't need to even waste a bullet on him. A few words to his fat-ass wife about his visits, and his party's over." From that episode, Julien felt assured that spying at Myrtle's would not raise too much suspicion. To build his son-in-law's hope—with any news that even slightly suggested that Percie was alive—he shared his plan only with Pichon.

After dinner, Pichon sat on the porch waiting for Meffre. Ossi called a meeting in the woods behind the church at nightfall. He dreaded leaving his family alone and became distressed and agitated. Charmaine and Aunt Velma could certainly use the guns Ossi brought them, but that only quelled his fear slightly. Thoughts of what Percie might be enduring, if alive, stoked immense dread in him. He caught sight of Meffre coming through the woods carrying a small basket and a lantern.

As soon as he saw Pichon, Meffre heard, *Scarred boy. Dead tree. Dead man.* His mood changed instantly. He walked to Pichon. "How you holding up, old man? These eggs are for Aunt Velma. Femme said she's expecting them. She's coming soon with some cleaned chickens. She'll be toting her gun too." Pichon was about to respond, but Meffre fidgeted with the basket and went inside. He placed the egg basket on top of the safe, kissed the women, and fell to his knees in front of the bassinette to cuddle Keb. Aunt Velma found it odd that Meffre had very little to say. When she approached the bassinette to start a conversation, he jumped up, said "good night," and walked out to the porch. This puzzled her, but she attributed it to the general anxiety they were all feeling. Alone with Pichon, Meffre said quickly, "Went to the grove to hear Lucien play jazz today. Papa Luc dropped by and told us he thinks there's going to be trouble soon. We need to meet tonight. Femme knows, and she's coming to sit with Aunt Velma and Charmaine. She'll let them know what's going on."

Terror lined Pichon's face. "Mama always talks about fear. How can I leave them now when things are getting worse? They might see us down at Sacred Heart."

"We're not meeting at Sacred Heart. Mister Julien asked me to come help him bait his crab line and drink some homebrew. We're going crabbing in the morning. We're meeting at Mister Julien's because Papa Luc heard, from the sheriff, they're watching Father. Tonight, if they follow us, they'll just see us baiting a crab line."

"Jesus, thanks for the truth to beat a lie." They laughed in quick grunts, respecting the danger they faced. "Let me get my horse ready."

When they made it to Julien's house, he had already stretched the crab line between two thick pines and was baiting it with pieces of cow ears. A mound of split ears sat on a stump with a hatchet, and Julien yelled to Meffre that his job was there. Julien washed his hands at the pump and went into his shed. He came out smiling with a pitcher of homebrew and a bucket of mason jars. "Y'all just in time for a beer break," he said. They all grabbed jars and poured beer. Julien was in a good mood and moved closer to Pichon. "How's Keb?"

"Keeps me up at night kicking to make space for himself. Don't like his bassinette much." He was at ease with Julien. Charmaine mildly cautioned Pichon against talking to her father about fighting between whites and blacks. However, Pichon had had just that conversation shortly after the baby's birth. He had to know that Julien would fight with him for his family. Julien eased his mind when he recounted his spying at Myrtle's.

They talked through the baiting, aided by enough homebrew to make Meffre lose his footing and stumble over the crate where the salted cow ears had been. Julien pumped water while the baiters washed first with lemon then soap. After another "quick" beer, Pichon talked about growing up with Percie. Their mother always referred to each twin as her best child, but never in the other's presence. Pichon's memories were happy ones, but his storying was solemn, accentuated by the steady beat of approaching horses' hooves. Ossi had entrusted Meffre with a new pistol, which he fingered as assurance until he could be sure of the riders.

Ossi, Papa Luc, and Lucien had met at Sacred Heart. The ride from the church was just over a mile, and they rode slowly to pay attention to any sounds coming from the woods. Ossi carried knives in his saddlebag for anyone in need. Pichon led them to the shed, where Julien had lit kerosene lamps. Excepting Ossi, they all went in and found stools to sit on or workbenches to lean on. Julien offered everyone cold homebrew. Ossi did not enter. Meffre noticed his silhouette against the lattice of the wisteria arbor and went out to join him. He sat on a bench and stared at the sky. He did not acknowledge Meffre until he pointed into the shadows next to him. From there, he smiled at a rabbit nibbling gingerly at grass. Meffre was immediately calmed by the scene. Ossi, in his peaceful way, embraced Meffre. "You look good, my boy. I can feel your heart beat. I miss you."

Meffre sensed a feeling of home. He pulled away from Ossi to wipe tears and moved to sit on the bench. Ossi sat next to him and said, "Your manhood's on you and getting strong. You'll need it. Here, take this gift." He handed Meffre a beautiful knife encased in a decorated sheaf. "This was my daddy's. Called it *Quickness*. Yours now. Don't thank me. It'll keep you alive, and I'll be grateful."

Meffre was transfixed but awkwardly said, "Guess I won't need the pistol anymore."

They laughed, and Ossi rejoined, "Keep both close. Till you master the knife, you might have to depend on being a good, quick shot."

Papa Luc and Lucien emerged from the shed to summon them, both eager and serious. Meffre looked directly at Lucien, whose gentle smile enlarged. They went in, and Ossi faced Pichon. "They'll stir soon, but we don't know against whom. What I heard from Reynaud and the nuns is the same as what Papa Luc and Father heard from the sheriff. Some men from Colfax are roaming around New Orleans. They're working with Hébert and Reginald and claim they're only after Meffre and me."

Papa Luc moved in toward Ossi and said, "Lucien told me the same thing Percie told me months ago. Both heard Hébert talk about meeting Keller in New Orleans. What else, Lucien?"

Lucien did not know where to focus. He had been staring at Meffre, remembering the hour they had spent enjoying jazz. He stuttered through how he heard his uncle talking about "their friend from Colfax" who was "directing the show." Hébert also mentioned the Eatons. Everyone stirred at this. "I've been playing down at Mudbug's. Pike and I listen to everything. We watch folks we know are regulators. Yesterday, a lumberjack offered me a drink to play a song. When he walked back to his table, I heard him say, 'Reginald's got to keep moving *him*. Sheriff's watching us.'" The shed exploded in shouts.

Pichon screamed, "Percie's alive! We got to find him!"

Ossi put his hand firmly on Pichon's shoulder. "Listen to Julien now."

Julien scratched his eyebrows and swallowed the last of his homebrew. "I've been stopping at Myrtle's for about three months. Seen Reginald's horse there a few times and stopped to listen. Nothing. I trust Myrtle but not with this. Seems she's a bedmate with Reginald. So, I never asked her nothing. When I seen Reginald there, he was with his lumberjacks during lunch. Today he was alone with his son Todd." Lucien and Meffre traded uneasy glances. "I sat on the *colored* side. He told his boy they'd get caught if they 'kept moving *him* back and forth from here to Mandeville.' I went straight to Father with that news. That's where I saw Ossi and told him." Julien looked at Pichon with sad moist eyes. Pichon, with his lips taut, went over to him and took his glass to refill it.

This news was immense and tiny. Papa Luc and Ossi explained how they were connecting these pieces. They knew Hébert was trying to launch a plan. They also knew that it was time to let Pichon and the rest know what Lacombe was calling "trouble" had grown far larger. They took turns talking about remaining vigilant, about strategies for staying safe, about how to protect while remaining secretive. As quickly as the meeting had convened, it was adjourned. Everyone pledged to wait to hear from Papa Luc or Ossi and act accordingly. Before they left, Papa Luc said emphatically, "This is about more than whites hating blacks; it's always more than that."

Ossi nodded and said, "This *is* Carl Keller's work; it's about money. Reynaud is our ears in New Orleans, and he's certain Keller is behind this."

✝ ✝ ✝

Two days later, Pichon and Charmaine decided they needed to try leading normal lives in the face of escalating tension. They went picnicking with Meffre on Guinea Beach while Aunt Velma took care of the baby. They brought a basket of fried chicken, sausages, vegetables, and sweets. Aunt Velma gave them a Coulon quilt she swiped from one of the big four-poster beds. Now it provided a cushion against the uneven earth and sand. The bayou flowed briskly, the warm sun hidden behind the huge limbs of the lone pine. When they showed Meffre the powerful pine, they bragged about how it was under this pine they had fallen in love. Pichon's timidity about his past under this tree had long since gone. "Boy, this is what I call my 'love tree.'" Charmaine shook her head, feigning unease.

Their romantic reminiscence inspired Meffre to daydream. He thought about how Lucien played the piano as if it belonged in a juke joint along Cane River. Piano playing and blue eyes drew him to Lucien, and he contented himself with these fantasies. Charmaine and Pichon looked at him quizzically as he smiled to himself. He surmised that Lucien's soul was painted with the color of the blues. When Pichon asked what he was smiling about, Meffre responded that he was happy they named their baby Kebbi after his father. In truth, he was imagining what it would be like to meet Lucien under the longleaf pine.

They stopped at Julien's, and in less than five minutes, Charmaine shooed the men outside to the shed. He met them with ample jars of homebrew and showed them he was again busy baiting a crab line that stretched in lengths tied to four pines. Pichon fell right in place and started baiting. Julien swung his hatchet rhythmically cutting cows' ears into pieces and, with a slight pause, chopping loop holes in the middle. The loop hole had to be centered to knot the meat tight enough to hold for several runs of crabbing. Pichon coaxed Meffre into a bet on who could bait the crab line the fastest, and Julien smiled to see tradition take hold. He invited them to go crabbing in the morning out on Lake Pontchartrain. There was no way to refuse, and Meffre agreed first. Every occasion for crabbing, drinking beer, and telling stories, cemented the idea of family for him. It also helped to divert their worry about Percie.

The baiting went quickly. They took the line down, and Julien guided its placement carefully in a large tub. He walked in circles over the tub until the line filled in the middle and then the perimeter. They put a block of ice on top of it and threw an old tarpaulin over the tub.

"All right, there's a bunch of cut-up lemons for washing those cows' ears off y'all. Use the pump on the side of the shed. I put soap over there too." Julien liked to direct these young men in the same way his father and uncles had taught him—with lots of cussing and beer. The evening sun had snuck away by the time everyone was cleaned up. Charmaine came out to say goodbye. Julien looked at her proudly and asked, "How's the husband and baby?"

"That Pichon-looking thing is a busy one. Aunt Velma's spoiling him too. We'll have full arms for a long time."

When Julien arrived at five thirty the next morning, Meffre and Pichon were sitting on the bottom steps. They put the crab line in the rig, readied the gray mare, and drank a second cup of coffee. They ate Aunt Velma's ham and biscuits greedily. She also gave them a bottle of Muscadine wine—in case the lake decided to be chilly and breezy. Pichon ran into the house to kiss Charmaine and Keb goodbye while Meffre helped Julien load their boots. The crab line roller was the last thing to go on the rig because of its length. It was built with a two-by-four, long enough to fit across the boat—a roller, made from an old bicycle axle, stood up on one side. As Meffre loaded it, Julien explained, "This roller is a lazy man's friend. The line's held up by it to keep it out the water while you're batting crabs in the boat with this net. I know you've seen how it works, but today you'll lose your cherry on that roller." Meffre puzzled over this but was too excited to ask any questions.

The ride up Lake Road was full of Pichon's lies about the time he almost burned to death when he fell asleep at the foot of the sawdust pile. "I was there with Percie drinking wine. He left me fast asleep. Said he couldn't wake me. All I remember, to this day, is I dreamed I smelled smoke and started choking in my dream. Next thing I knew, I got hot. I jumped awake and, man, sure 'nuf, my pants were smoking. I ran my drunk off and got to the sawmill pump sober as an undertaker." Meffre and Julien hissed and took turns swigging Muscadine wine as Pichon said, "Ain't lying. Nearly every year that sawdust pile catches fire. They say the devil gets restless under that sawdust. Mama says when the sawdust fires up, somebody done something bad to trees—like cutting 'em up for lumber." Pichon laughed and asked for the wine.

Bayou Lacombe ran serpentine along Lake Road, which was populated with fishermen lined up to catch perch. Julien and Pichon yelled hellos to nearly every fisherman. Several held up their wine bottles in salute. When they reached the lake, Pichon hopped out to find the boat, which Julien kept tied to a cypress on the bayou. As the clouds scattered to reveal a bright warm sun, they filled the boat with the rig's load.

With Pichon and Meffre rowing, Julien dropped a big red buoy into the lake and started lowering the line. The lake had a glassy calm, an occasional breeze creating slight ripples. They glided along and placed the line through an area Julien called his lucky crab depot. They dropped the big blue buoy at the opposite end and turned the boat around for the trip back to the red buoy.

It was a great day for crabbing. Although a novice crabber, today, it was clear, as Julien went to work, Meffre would have to prove just how much he had learned. Just pulling the red buoy up to cross the line over the roller revealed that every loop was heavy with large male and fat female crabs. Julien handed Meffre the wire mesh net. "Time to bat like a man, boy." Meffre took his place and batted crabs from the line into the bottom of the boat. The crabs were more than plentiful, and his arms got tired, but he was determined to impress the others with his stamina. Pichon offered to bat, but Meffre survived the entire run.

After twelve runs, each had taken his turn batting crabs, and they had filled the boat's bottom with a huge catch. By the end of those runs, Meffre was crowned "expert." By noon, they had loaded the rig with the catch and washed out and secured the boat in the bayou. They stopped at Myrtle Picou's and sat on the *colored* side. Myrtle was Julien's most reliable customer, and he brought in a hamper of big male crabs. She was elated that he always remembered her during crabbing season. She served them cold beers and promised hot fried perch and salad if they could give her just a half hour to fix it. They knew a black woman in the kitchen did all the fixing, but they humored Myrtle. They ate, and after one cold one for the road, they left, telling Myrtle she would probably see them again soon while the lake was running crabs.

They had also filled three straw bushel baskets with females to sell to the seafood store on the bayou. By two o'clock, they had sold crabs at the Bayou Market, the Mudbug Saloon, and to four customers along Lake Road. By three, they had loaded two big blocks of ice on the back of the rig to keep everything fresh at home. Stopping at the icehouse turned into an occasion for another round of beer. They were then on their way home with five hampers of crabs for eating and four dollars in profit. It all seemed so easy, Meffre pronounced, "Now I know what I can do for a living!"

Julien laughed loudly. He patted Meffre on the back. "Late September and October give you the lake's best crabs. Your next trip the catch might change your mind; they do that when it ain't their season."

At Julien's house, the yard was alive with activity. Charmaine had made a hot fire under the boiling pot sitting on a circular brick-and-mortar structure Julien had built. The fire crackled and spat its heat upward in a fury of flames. When Julien saw the pot, he pronounced: "Yeah, a whole lot of folks are hungry." Pichon scurried over to the woodpile to haul more oak to keep the fire hot.

"Look here," Pichon said. "She's even got the purging tub ready! Somebody's really hungry!" Meffre lumbered over to the tub, carrying a heavy hamper of crabs. "That's right, Meffre, let's not keep these guests from a salty bath."

Julien checked that everything was done just right. He went to the rig and pulled out the metal tub that held the baited crab line. It had already started to stink; the cow ears and rope now dripped nasty lake water through the holes in the tub. He dragged it to the side of his shed and smiled knowing Pichon would complain that he had to unbait it. He covered the tub and put two large cement blocks on top to keep the dogs from making a bigger mess.

By the time he washed at the pump, Aunt Velma and Femme had arrived and started a parade out the side kitchen door. They carried large bowls, and Charmaine carried large wooden spoons, cloth towels, and several trays. Aunt Velma's next burden was a box of spices from salt to cayenne. After setting everything on the table next to the boiling pot, Charmaine went over to Julien and Pichon, kissed them, and said, "Y'all smell like old goats." Everyone laughed after Julien said loudly, "But you like these old goats!"

Meffre and Pichon emptied two hampers of crabs into the purging tub and guarded against jumpers—spunky crabs refusing to be subdued by salt. Pichon's jokes giving rise to Meffre's laughter animated the scene as Julien started preparing the boil by dropping in all the chopped contents. His effortlessness was legendary—a natural at catching and cooking all kinds of seafood. The women had cut up all the seasoning in wedges. They had also cut up every-thing else in bite-size portions. He always poured in two cups of oil or two heaping spoons of bacon drippings. This kept the crabmeat from sticking to the shells. Afterward, he added lemon wedges along with four chopped onions. Everyone loved corn on the cob, and when in season, he always put in an ample amount. They also loved and cursed the way small potatoes imbibed the pepper when settled into the boil. Today, the big treat was smoked sausage—Julien's favorite and Femme's contribution. The spices went in last, and they were added with a constant stirring. In a matter of minutes, the boil had turned a bright shade of reddish orange. The last bowl held chopped bell peppers, which were added when the crabs were just about boiled.

Julien went to his shed, which everyone noticed. Pichon and Meffre followed him, and all returned with jars of homebrew. "When that pot comes to its first boil, Mr. Meffre, you can put your crabs in. Then, when the pot comes to its second boil, we let Mr. Pichon take them out. Remember to set them in the pans belly-up. We don't want that good juice seeping out. The last batch we'll let soak so they'll be cayenne bombs." Just then, Femme and Aunt Velma came out with a mound of old newspapers. At such crab feasts, Femme was always responsible for newspaper, and Aunt Velma supplied the dessert.

Femme lined two picnic tables with several layers of paper. Aunt Velma came out proudly holding her grandson. She talked to him as if he understood: "Now look here, you won't see no wood on these tables. Auntie Femme gonna put enough sheets down to soak up all that crab juice."

Everyone worked until Julien whistled loudly. He drank a good long swig of beer. Aunt Velma nudged Femme. After an obscene belch, the entire yard looked his way. Pichon applauded, and the women uttered their disgust. Julien announced, "These crabs finished their hot bath. Time to eat! One of you church ladies pray over the catch."

Pichon netted crabs and put them on trays. He and Meffre stopped long enough to eat two claws to test for pepper. They ate two more to test for salt. Before they could keep testing, Julien belched again and stopped the testing. Each table was set with a big tray of crabs. Aunt Velma and Charmaine came out carrying large pitchers of lemonade. They patiently waited for prayer. Aunt Velma smiled and said, "You bastards got quiet quick. I *better* pray. Lawd, thank you for our beautiful lake that feeds us from your loving hands. Amen." The yard said "Amen." The women sat at the lemonade table; the men, smelly as they were, sat at the other with their homebrew. In seconds, every hand was full of crabmeat, potatoes, and corn.

Julien and Pichon sat at the ends of the table. They accommo-dated Femme, who begged for a homebrew and said with no shame, "I like beer with boiled seafood. Daddy used to say, 'That go good with that.'" Aunt Velma moaned over the potatoes and smoke sausage. Pichon cracked crab claws with his teeth and made sweet eyes at Charmaine until Aunt Velma kicked her under the table and got everyone's attention. She said loudly, "Y'all need to stop that winking and blinking shit. Keb don't need company. His li'l fat ass is two handfuls."

"Granny, you've fallen for Keb. I think you like his color—choco-late—a flavor you like," Charmaine teased.

"Aw, cher. Don't make me cuss your ass out in front of the family."

Julien said, "Didn't you and Charmaine go to Sacred Heart today? All this cussing, Aunt Velma!" She quickly turned serious and said sternly, "Mary and her ladies were there, but only half of them. They prayed the rosary and left. Something's brewing. Pass me two fat male crabs, don't want another female crab near me today!" Everyone caught her meaning and laughed.

They raked through crab shells, looking for potatoes, corn, and sausages. Their laughter was testimony to all that could be good in life before life itself set in. Femme loved being there with Aunt Velma and Julien because most of what happened in their houses was not planned or fretted over. When everyone finished, the uneaten crabs were gathered onto a large tray to take inside. Pichon made his way toward the house with a heavy tray when he heard horses. He took the tray into the house quickly and walked back to the table. Julien was on his feet when he saw Papa Luc and Lucien. They dismounted and walked through the gate carrying undeniably sad faces. Papa Luc held out his hand to Julien and looked directly at Femme and said, "I'd say 'good evening,' but it ain't good. I just got word that they found Percie. At Pichon and Charmaine's house. All you men better come." The yard's lightness turned dark as doom. Every face lost its humor and color. A collective nervous heart thumped.

Femme went to Meffre, held him tight, and said, "Looks like you were right. Eshu didn't give us a riddle." Femme knew from Papa Luc's face that Percie was dead. She went to him and asked, "Ossi?" He replied, "Don't worry."

She sat next to Aunt Velma, who had begun to shake. Then the men were in motion. Julien went to his shed to get something that no one wanted to speculate on or acknowledge. He returned with a hunting rifle. Seeing him go, Femme invited the women into the house. They locked the doors and windows.

The ride to Pichon's was tortuous because Papa Luc knew he could only say that Percie had been found. Against constant questioning, all he would say was that Father Lorquette told him to get Pichon and take him home. Even if this did not confirm Percie's death, everyone anticipated the likelihood. Papa Luc hated dishonesty. Yet, he believed this was the only way to keep unity until they saw the truth.

They rode past Church Road. Afterward, with only the clocking of the horses' hooves and screeching from the rig's wheels, they started down Lake Road. When they neared the road to Pichon's house, all hearts became heavy. Pichon could not contain himself.

The slowness of Julien's rig and his riding mute alongside was too much. He took off and yelled, "Meet me home."

Meffre and Lucien immediately chased after him against Papa Luc's orders to return. When they caught up with Pichon, he was standing at the base of the large magnolia in front of his house. He was full of rage and screaming as he circled the charred remains of Keb's bassinette. Just above it, a blackened noose hung from a high branch. The noose had clearly been cut. Lucien and Meffre ran to Pichon, but nothing slowed his fury, nor could they catch him or try to reason with him. His grief and fear generated hatred so fierce that his peaceful soul turned demonic. He screamed and growled at the tree, but mostly at the bassinette.

The rattling of the approaching rig arrested them long enough for Meffre to get a hold on Pichon. "You know that Keb is safe. Stop!" Pichon lowered his head onto Meffre's shoulder. The front door opened and startled them as Ossi came down the steps. He looked at them individually and commanded, "Lucien and Meffre, tie the horses to the pines behind the barn. Pichon, come with me."

Pichon followed Ossi to the kitchen where they prepared four kerosene lamps. "We're going to be here late; we'll need these in the barn." Pichon picked up the lamps, and Ossi said directly to him: "He's in the barn. They lynched him to make us fight. We must be patient."

The men huddled near the barn door. Papa Luc stood alone holding the milking stall railing. Lucien and Meffre stood close to each other. They all shuffled nervously when Pichon and Ossi came in. Ossi handed a lantern to Papa Luc. Pichon handed one to Meffre. They followed Ossi to the dark, far end of the barn to a stall that was mostly used for hay storage. Ossi hung his lantern on a ring that jutted off the post that formed the stall's rafter brace. He walked to the front of the stall. "Put the rest of the lamps on the dirt over there. Y'all need to see how those regulators work. Father Lorquette told me to come here. When I got here, Percie was dead. Before they hanged him, they tortured him. He has no fingers or toes. They brought him here that way. He has cuts all over, and they burned him, all but his face. That forces his pain on us."

Ossi guided them reverently to the stall and brushed away the yellow hay covering Percie's head. He led Pichon in first. His eyes were glassy as he approached the stall. "Percie? No, my Lord Jesus. I'm looking at myself. Should've been me, Lord. I'm next. But not my Keb." Ossi held him.

Papa Luc looked on the charred skin and heard echoing screams. He shook his head and turned his back to the stall. He said, "Lucien, pay your respects."

Meffre followed Lucien. They leaned on each other; still, it was unbearable. Lucien cried openly and said to Pichon, "I'll pray for him. We'll stop this." Meffre hugged Pichon, holding his head firmly against his shoulder.

Ossi gently covered the body with hay again. The men made a circle around the lamps. "Before dawn tomorrow, me, Pichon, and Meffre will bury Percie in Sacred Heart's cemetery. Father Lorquette's having the grave dug tonight. He was here earlier and begged me to leave Lacombe with Meffre. I must stay. We need to trust only ourselves and the priest. He's hiding me in the rectory. Father hid in the confessional today when Hébert and Reginald were in church talking. They said torture didn't make Percie talk."

Pichon stood unmovable. He asked Ossi brazenly, "Why my house?"

Ossi looked at Papa Luc, who stepped back a little and said, "This'll take some explaining. Be patient. We knew, me and Ossi, from my friend Reynaud, that Hébert's been planning, with regulators from Colfax, to teach Femme a lesson for taking Meffre in. They've hated Femme for years. Way before Ossi came. They're mad that she has money, a business, and defies their women. We never had this kind of trouble before. It's worse since, well, since Ossi and Meffre came to live here."

Ossi moved forward and interrupted. "I'm sorry. We brought the trouble. I'm fighting it. This has to do with money Meffre's father Kebbi stole from Carl Keller, who sold Papa Luc pecan trees. Kebbi planted those trees and never gave Keller the money Papa Luc paid him."

Papa Luc interjected, "That's right. Reynaud heard from Hébert that Keller used Kebbi to carry around that cash. It was his way of siphoning money off his family's business in Covington. Hébert and Reginald, and even Sheriff Blake, know Keller." Looking in Julien's direction, he continued. "This morning Aunt Velma overheard Mary Easton say, 'Today, the final lesson gets taught.' Aunt Velma told Father, and I told Ossi, who hid in the woods behind Femme's house and waited. He was at the wrong house."

Papa Luc patted Ossi on the back. He had been busy going back and forth to Femme's empty and locked house all day. When he got home around three, Father was sitting on his porch talking to Lucien. Father told him he heard Hébert and Reginald talking in the church. What concerned Papa Luc and Lucien most was Father's saying he also saw a bunch of men he did not know on Lake Road. Papa Luc rode back to Femme's, looking for Ossi and could not find him. He rode alone to Pichon's and found Ossi cutting Percie out of the magnolia. Papa Luc heaved for air and mustered enough breath to say, "I'm sorry I couldn't tell y'all sooner, but y'all had to see for yourselves."

Ossi surveyed their faces. "I waited a long time in those woods behind Femme's house. I saw Papa Luc come and go but didn't move for fear we both might be trapped. Finally, I realized Femme wasn't the target. When I came here, I was too late."

Pichon ran headlong through the barn doors. He fled to his horse. Meffre rushed after him. After an uneasy silence, Julien sighed heavily and said, "Let Pichon be a man to his wife and son. Meffre needs some time too. Time to stop feeling guilty about what his daddy did. We need to talk to the women." They all left the barn full of useless hate that marred their souls.

Moonlight fell sporadically on the magnolia. The bassinette was barely visible, for Eshu sat atop the magnolia and dropped every leaf, green or burnt, new or old, high or low, to cover Percie's blood. The leaves participated in respecting a life shortened by unnatural acts. The burnt leaves created the perimeter of a circle around the magnolia's base. Moving toward the center, the brown and old leaves started a mound that culminated in all the shiny green leaves. Yemanja blessed Percie's tribute with a mist that sparkled in moonlight.

Church Oak Suicide

DARKNESS ACCOMPANIED PICHON TO Femme's. He could not raise one good thought on the five-minute walk in blackness. He simply dragged along a foul disposition, spiritlessly, to fulfill a promise. He flung a very full croaker sack across his shoulders. That Percie was dead, that his son and family were targets, that he had done nothing to deserve this thwarted all reasoning. Everything conspired against his best wishes for Keb's future, even when Charmaine convinced him their future depended on retaliating. This distracted him, and he almost ran into a huge pine. He knelt and positioned the croaker sack like an altar at the tree's foot. He prayed: *Jesus. Help me make a life for Keb.* Then, he wailed fiercely in grief for Percie. He found solace in Femme's explaining how the pine in the woods absorbed his pain when he was being whipped. She had told him no one faces life alone. Nature would help him survive and thrive as it does. He thought about his loving Charmaine under the branches of the longleaf pine and inhaled pine scent as an invigoration. He dried his eyes on his shirt-sleeve. Spotting flickers of light in Femme's kitchen, he packed up his burden and walked again, this time differently.

He found her sitting on the porch steps drinking coffee by candlelight. She handed him a cup, and he sat just below her on the last step. He drank, noticing the shadows dancing by kerosene lamplight in the kitchen. He got up to face her and asked, "You want those moccasins today? Got forty-three candles here."

"You remembered. Yes." Pichon noticed her slow-talking seriousness. Having been forced to court routine danger, they now buttressed themselves against palpable doom. Femme had spent most of the night and early morning conjuring her part in the resistance. She now steeled herself against a future of Hébert's making. She stared at Eshu's oak, and with practiced calm answered, "Today is moccasins' day. It'll storm tonight. Cottonmouths like a good storm. It's our turn to teach Eshu's lessons. Go home, son. Take your family to church. Might be some inspiration there. Meffre went with Ossi to bury Percie. He should be at your house later. He's worried too. Go take care of them."

+ + +

Lacombe's oldest, full-limbed oak graced reverently with Spanish moss served as the picture of majesty. The limbs were full and muscled, often defying—with only slight movements—the most intrusive winds. It gently greeted summer breezes with swagger-like movements and sparred with hurricane winds by lifting branches discriminately with swift and crafty gamelike punches. Louisiana oaks have a different dignity and presence than pines and magnolias. With an unbridled command for reverence—earned by age and unrivaled strength—the oak shouldered its history thick in richness, sin, and tragedy.

Lacombians built roads around oaks because they held the full spirit of the place. Everyone revered the fact that the oaks inhabited the land first. Catholics especially treasured the lore that the most magnificent oaks lined the roads to Sacred Heart. The largest, oldest oak sustained itself just at the entrance to the church. With its long, elegant festoons of silvery-green Spanish moss, it stood boldly like a guard. It had witnessed every baptized baby at Sacred Heart, providing the shade for the christening celebrations afterward. Likewise, every funeral cortège received its first blessing under embracing, outstretched branches. Everyone was intimate with this tree—Church Oak.

The day after Percie's death, a gloomy Sunday overcast by gray-black rain clouds, full but refusing to burst, Lacombians—nearly all Catholics—filed past Church Oak. This time, their reverence turned from awe to shock. Through gushing wind, they gawked at the tree's limbs, which had turned brittle—every leaf a deep burnt brown. Overnight, the tree had simply started a long slow creep away from life. Many speculated on the reason.

Sacred Heart accommodated its parishioners without harmony. Whites carted in their supremacy by enforcing an unwritten law that guaranteed them several front pews. Créoles sat behind them, and blacks sat in the rear. Choctaws, when they attended, stood

166

in the back near the exits. Whites euphemized this segregation as "tradition." Father Lorquette transferred to Sacred Heart from St. Louis Cathedral in New Orleans, where he enjoyed that all races worshipped together in peace. Consequently, Lacombe's "tradition" was among the first conflicts he was forced to endure. He accepted what he found, tried to avoid old conflicts, and prayed for heavenly support to change the rest.

On this Sunday, Father Lorquette's spine stiffened. He prepared to preach on hypocritical Catholics, who ignored or even practiced sin and evil. As the head of the usher board, Hébert sat in the first pew and felt the searing stares of those behind him. Recently, Lucien had taken to sitting in the pew just before the invisible line that separated whites from blacks. This infuriated Hébert and to exacerbate the gesture, before Mass, Lucien walked up to the sacristy, genuflected, crossed himself, and nodded mockingly at his uncle. Hébert reddened; Lucien smirked. Their eyes locked as he claimed his seat next to Aunt Velma and directly in front of Meffre and Pichon's family. Aunt Velma's grief was stronger than protocol or unwritten laws. She fell into Lucien's arms and cried boisterously as he comforted her without shame. His wet eyes were full of daring and anger that his uncle knew to avoid.

Father Lorquette had no idea his parishioners had nicknamed him "Father Murmur." On the day Church Oak startled them, he surprised them further when, with a loud and commanding voice, he delivered a long, accusatory sermon, full of allusions to Percie's death. "There's no corner in this town for those who witness sin and don't fight it. You who commit sin-laden crimes and sit in this church, be forewarned that you'll sit in hellfire." His voice reverberated off the sagging walls and met the cacophony of a disgruntled congregation. They rebuffed his accusations with hisses, and the lumberjacks and their families laughed rowdily. The blacks and Créoles shook their heads and sucked their teeth. To keep their attention, Father banged relentlessly on the pulpit and ended with: "Take Percie to heaven. We pray. Take Percie to heaven. We pray. Take Percie to heaven. We pray." Choctaws, blacks, and white sympathizers stood to echo the refrain until the organist played the offertory hymn loudly to silence them. Inside, the church's mood, from this point on, was distractingly heavy *and* solidly sad. No one, however, was sadder than the priest, who turned to the altar full of guilt for his failed sermon.

A faint breeze stirred outside, and then the wind stopped

altogether. With its last energy, Church Oak, advantaged by the stillness, wept every one of its leaves onto large round heaps over its roots. Then, instantly, a determined, wild wind made a whorl of the leaves, fashioned them into one furious ball, and hurled it deliberately toward the church. The two large front doors and two narrow side doors near the sacristy were crafted of solid wood panels. These doors always stood closed during Mass. If anyone tried to enter late or leave early, intrusive creaks and squeaks pulled the entire congregation to attention. When the body of leaves arrived at the front steps, it broke into three parts. Two flanks fell off the larger mound and spun away—one to the right door and one to the left. The leaves unfurled against the side doors and created solid walls from top to bottom. The largest mound forcefully climbed the front steps and crashed with a thud against the double doors. Naked and dying, Church Oak lived its last grieving moments.

Frightened parishioners, hearing the commotion outside, stopped praying. Children sidled next to their parents, and the altar candles suddenly threw longer flames toward the ceiling. In the back of the sacristy, the huge stained-glass window, showing the sacred heart, dimmed. Several ushers dashed toward the doors. Father Lorquette finished the Mass, genuflected, and faced the congregation only to find them completely distracted.

The church darkened. Two ushers tried to pry open the doors, but the mounds of leaves sealed them shut. Panic ambled through the pews, and Father called for more men to help. It was not until Church Oak expired that they managed to push the leaves aside. By this time, the church was in pandemonium and emptied onto the front lawn. Some families loaded into their rigs quickly; others steered themselves homeward on foot. No one, however, missed peering at Church Oak—transformed into an unfathomable wooden skeleton.

Pichon, Charmaine, and Keb did not leave. Instead, they went to the sacristy to talk to Father. Meffre found Lucien and stood with him on the altar's bottom steps. Lucien looked over the departing crowd for Hébert. He was gone, he assumed, through the side door. Throughout the commotion, no one looked for Aunt Velma and her choir until they saw her uniting children with parents. When the last child left, she looked to them in the sacristy and yelled, "Lucien, please come drive me home. Bullshit gets me nervous. Sorry, Father."

With his church silent and empty, Father Lorquette extinguished altar candles and went out amid the aggregation of leaves. He tried to conjure a resolution against such ubiquitous hate. He discounted prayers, even his own. With his head in his hands, numbed by his failure, he lamented obstacles that prevented spiritual values to enter his parish. They came seeking redemption only to refuse it by embracing bigoted hate. This shocked him most; this he had failed to overcome. From the road, faint singing interrupted his contemplation. He spied Femme chanting and circling Church Oak.

Candles and Cottonmouths

GLOOMING OVER PERCIE'S DEATH, sympathetic and empathetic Lacombians exchanged accustomed joy for fear. Burning crosses now signified more than threats; they actualized murder for the town's blacks and Choctaws. Further, there was a general fear that whites too had become targets—those who were guilty *and* innocent. What had been casual and civil conversations morphed into quick nods and wary smiles. To cope, many just worked and then hid, fully armed, in the safety of their homes. No matter how they chose to cope, they held a common yearning for peace and a faint hope for reconciliation.

Papa Luc and Lucien made it part of their daily routine to care for Aunt Velma. They hired a young woman to shop so that Aunt Velma did not have to leave the mansion. Papa Luc came home at lunchtime to comfort her, who was given to long bouts of crying. He brought her flowers and chocolates and new recordings of jazz and spirituals. Lucien consoled her by insisting she sit with him while he played the piano. He knew all her favorites and played them until she kissed and thanked him. He also proudly escorted her to church on Sundays and sat with her in complete defiance of his uncle.

This grief was new to her, and none of the death experiences of relatives or even her husband compared with losing Percie. It was a haunting grief for which there were not enough tears or relief from the heaviness in her chest. Oddly, she felt that she was not grieving enough. Papa Luc assured her that this was normal and natural. She found reassurance, in her worst moments, in what he had said when he found her crying loudly and uncontrollably: "Velma, my love, come let me hold you. The only way we'll get through this is to go through it. Time, my love. We need time." Thus, his arms and Lucien's smile and sincerity sustained her.

Keb, unsurprisingly, held grief at bay in Pichon's household. A baby's laughter is an antidote to adult seriousness. Even the sawmill's strenuous work could not erase Percie's chubby face from Pichon's mind the way Keb's giggling could. Still, he remembered his twin's face exactly as he saw it when Percie galloped away for that last time. His face had held no fear and was marked by a determination for survival. Pichon knew his brother's will to fight and live. That he had had to use that will to fight ultimately for his life made Pichon more resolute than ever to protect Keb and Charmaine. On the night of Percie's death, Pichon found Charmaine sleeping with Keb in their bed. She held the baby as they slept, and her streaked face saddened him. He undressed and moved under the covers. He slept in fits until Keb kicked them awake the next morning.

Many folks resorted to riding horses or traveling in buckboards rather than walking along the footpath behind Femme's property. Word spread quickly that all Lacombians should carry guns or knives in saddle satchels or hidden in their buckboards. Ossi and Femme insisted that, because Meffre was too obvious a target for the regulators, the pushcart deliveries along the footpath should end. Meffre and Ossi constructed a makeshift stall near the barn to sell fresh chickens and eggs to customers who came to Femme's. Lake Road provided access and although the business suffered slightly, no one questioned doing otherwise.

Femme's household was perhaps the most somber and unquestionably marked with grief and more so by guilt. She tried mightily to lighten the burden that Meffre and Ossi shared, blaming themselves for bringing suffering to all. The guilt, however, was deep rooted, and no amount of loving or consoling, on her part, could budge them out of their low spirits for long. Eventually, she found their despondency unbearable. Since Percie's death, Labas had taken to sleeping next to her porch chair while she smoked her pipe. Eshu whizzed through the oak shooting cool breezes in her direction and inspired her to focus on Ossi and Meffre. Then, grief spurred not guilt but anger in her. Their faces, their grief, their guilt compelled her to act.

✝ ✝ ✝

Until it was cut down to a stump, level to the ground, Femme paid daily respect to Church Oak. After parish men loaded the last of the tree's timber into buckboards to distribute as firewood, she prayed to Yemanja for rain and drove her buckboard home to find Pichon, sitting on her porch, brooding over how to protect his family. She sat next to him. He knew she had been crying, maybe even grieving. "Hard to see Church Oak die, huh?"

She nodded. "I sang with Eshu and Yemanja, but no happiness. Percie and Church Oak were sacrifices for peace we don't have. I hope it's not all in vain."

"I feel that too. Everything feels undone. Like no one solved anything with all the fighting and death. Did you go to the rectory?"

"No. Ossi's there. Too dangerous for him to stay at home for too long now." She gently pulled away. "We have everything for tonight?"

"Yes, and Aunt Velma sent food. It's on the stove. Meffre's at my house playing with Keb." He rushed down the steps and pointed to three chicken-wire snake traps sitting under the porch. Labas was growling at a safe distance. "I fed these cottonmouths dead mice and have more to use as bait."

"Go on home and get some rest. Tell Meffre I'm here. He and Lucien will take me to Mandeville for the steamboat to New Orleans." It was easy to read Femme's weariness. Pichon put a wet croaker sack over the snake trap and left. Labas continued his growl.

Nine years before, when Alinnie had contracted yellow fever, Papa Luc had sent a telegram to Colfax summoning Hébert. Immediately, he surmised that Hébert could not stay in his house. In three weeks, he had Small House, where he and Alinnie had lived before Lucien was born, refurbished for him.

Small House had been christened so because it was a near replica, though much smaller, of the outward construction of the Coulon mansion, only a mile away. It stood on one acre that connected to the Coulon's main property, but it was off Lake Road on Cold Branch Road. There were shortcut paths that could easily be taken to the Coulon mansion, Femme's property, and even Pichon's house. The paths were used mostly by men who worked at the Coulon Sawmill, which was a mile past Small House.

Small House's porch wrapped around three sides of the house, with a smaller porch off the kitchen. Eight squared pillars and wooden railings supported the main porch roof. The Coulon mansion's porch differed in that its eighteen pillars were round, and the railings were painted wrought iron.

With very little coaxing from Papa Luc and Aunt Velma, Alinnie, though quite ill, agreed that Hébert should move to Small

House—for "his convenience and comfort." At Alinnie's bidding, he reluctantly gave in, leaving the mansion in peace. Aunt Velma was particularly happy because she detested Hébert's constant eating and drinking, hiding in her kitchen to do it. During this time, Lucien acquired his dislike for Hébert. He was especially perturbed by his attempts to keep him spotlessly clean, which he and Aunt Velma ensured would be impossible. For his part, Hébert only pretended to be upset with the move. In fact, he was happy to have a private place to drink, scheme, and plot. Though he moved, he was a constant visitor to the mansion.

Unlike many stricken by yellow fever, Alinnie's battle proved slow. She, over the course of two months, showed signs of recovery only to relapse with more vomiting or dizziness. By the time jaundice showed on her limbs and face, she had felt stronger for a week, only to weaken considerably afterward. Hébert became a useless physician. His only remedies were to induce vomiting or to suggest giving Alinnie mercury, which Papa Luc forbade. After two debilitating months, Alinnie died while everyone slept around her.

Lucien was eleven, and he remembered his mother well. He also remembered his uncle's promise to care for his "young soul." This false promise gave Hébert a reason, or rather, an excuse, to extend his unwelcomed stay in Lacombe.

Hébert used a back room in Small House as his medical office, where he made money to sustain himself, without much dependence on Papa Luc. He hung his office shingle over the front door. It read:

Hébert Bellocq, M.D.
Appointments:
Whites: 9–12am
Coloreds: 1–3pm

He rarely had white patients, which was convenient, for he was usually heavy headed with liquor's aftereffects. He became a fixture at Sacred Heart and was in "cahoots" with those who succeeded in getting the bishop to remove two pastors who blatantly catered to Choctaws and blacks. Thus, Hébert became a *bona fide* Lacombian, attracting many like-minded allies.

Occasionally, Hébert returned to Colfax because after Alinnie passed he inherited the family home there. When he visited, he was Carl's guest and loyal confidant. Because Carl believed Kebbi had stolen his money, he depended on Hébert to spy for him. Still, the relationship was one sided. Carl detested Hébert, especially after he lost his wife to a Créole.

One Sunday, after another of Father Lorquette's ineffective finger-pointing sermons, Hébert decided to stop at Mudbug's for whiskey and gossip. Pike had been primed by Father to sponge as much information as he could from Hébert. As one of his best and most frequent customers, Pike invited Hébert to vent his frustrations about his regulators and their attempts to suppress resistance. Hébert railed against how badly and slowly his regulators were at taking control. He had several drunken predictions, which Pike absorbed in full agreement.

When Hébert finally reached Small House, he was full of sweat and dirt. He spied someone pacing on his porch. After tying the horse to the watering trough, he marched through the house to the porch where he found a messenger. The telegram read: "Carl in Mandeville." He thought, *Reginald needs to know this.*

Behind Small House stood a newly constructed shed that held tools and ladders and other items that could not be kept outside. These items included a sizable stock of wine and liquor. Hébert took his private time away from the house in this shed, where he had installed a living area for reading, drinking, and relaxing.

After his bath, he found his peace in the shed and in a bottle of port he had been saving for an impending triumph. He tinkered with a model ship he was building and congratulated himself, as the others had, for his good idea on hanging their "sign" in Pichon's yard—a sure way to threaten those on Lake Road, from baby Keb to Papa Luc.

The port seduced Hébert into a deep sleep. He woke to shouting and followed it to find Carl sitting on his porch swing, smoking. He had parked his suitcase next to the front door, and it stood open, revealing a whiskey flask. Hébert spotted it, smiling mischievously. Childishly, he sidled up to Carl to beg a sip. Carl nodded in disgust.

"Thanks for that. This past week's been trying. I had to stop at Mudbug's after church to get a nip for my nerves. There are a lot of people like us at Mudbug's. You're early. That drunk priest made a whole lot of racket in his sermon today."

Carl got up and darted to the front door. "Yes, I'm early. Left Colfax two weeks ago. Stopped to check on things in New Orleans,

Covington, and Mandeville. Been resting in Mandeville for two days. I know, from Reginald, that y'all been regulating. None of your shit is getting my money back."

Hébert disappeared into a bedroom with the suitcase, and Carl made himself comfortable in the parlor. He returned with more talk of recent and impending lynchings. They drank more, and the conversation took a sudden turn from regulators plotting to Carl's personal agenda. Hébert confused the two schemes and miscon-strued that Carl had come to provide leadership. Carl sensed the bewilderment and ignored it.

✝ ✝ ✝

Femme paced until she saw Lucien and Meffre ride up. They tied the sweaty horses for watering and led the old mare, pulling the rig, into the front yard. Her luggage sat near the front door, and Meffre and Lucien came in with quick greetings and took her bags to the rig. When they returned, Femme sat at the kitchen table with big cups of coffee. She invited them to sit, and they noticed that she held the valise. Her eyes were red, but it was clear the crying was over. From where Meffre sat, he saw that the oratory was closed, which was unusual. His puzzled look was her cue to begin. "I'm going to St. John Birchman's in New Orleans. I'll be helping at the orphanage. Meffre, you'll need to manage things here. Pichon will help with selling the eggs and chickens. Call on Julien if you need him. Lucien, let Papa Luc know, and please watch out for Meffre. Keep in touch with Ossi through Father Lorquette. Pichon will come by every day. We're not going to survive unless we stay knotted together. A big storm is going to roll in soon. Keep all the windows closed." Meffre nodded. He asked simple questions dealing with where to bank money and minor details Femme handled routinely. She answered all questions the same way: "Just ask Pichon."

Finally, she unzipped the valise and pulled out a document. She explained to Meffre that Papa Luc had deeded to him the two-acre pecan grove and its little house. The deed transferred on Meffre's nineteenth birthday, which would occur before she returned. Therefore, she wanted him to know. She said cautiously, "Meffre, Ossi believes a clue is in this valise to guide you to your inheritance. Guard it and talk to Ossi. Papa Luc can explain these documents."

She stood and smiled broadly. The afternoon sun shone in weak spurts, but it brightened the yard into its customary animation. She descended the steps to Labas's baying at the roosters and clucking hens.

+ + +

It was dark and raining when Meffre and Lucien returned to Femme's. The only sunlight they had seen was that earlier glimmer at Femme's. Her predicted storm arrived with precision-like musical timing: the wind howled; the rain punched the house's tin roof in syncopation. Lucien lit candles and kerosene lamps to inspire romance. Meffre sat on the sofa and rifled through the valise, where he discovered Eshu's statue. He smiled and held it tightly until interrupted by Eshu's, *See electricity.* He looked at Lucien, anxious that they were again alone in a perfect setting to act out what they both wanted. Their mutual attraction had grown as much as the danger that thwarted their acting on it. He wanted to move into Lucien's arms and knew that he wanted that too. Instead, he went back to fiddling inside the valise.

Lucien saw the need for levity and sat next to him. "May I ask a favor?" Meffre studied his blue eyes—not pulling away this time. He simply nodded. Lucien grinned. "Since you own *my* office now, do I get to visit my piano?"

Trying to control his chest's thumping, Meffre put the valise down and answered, "Start visiting when I move in. For now, let's just have some Muscadine wine." Before Lucien could get too hopeful, Meffre searched further in the valise.

+ + +

At nine o'clock, Carl announced he was tired of hearing about "regulators and niggers" and was going to bed. Hébert was glad to hear this. It would give him an excuse to drink out in the shed. He never took patients on Mondays. Sundays were his days for drinking late and working on model ships. With lightning violently cutting the sky, Carl held on to finish most of a second bottle of whiskey. Hébert slurred through a second telling of Percie's torture, elaborating this time on how niggers had a huge tolerance for pain, which proved they were inhuman. "I tell you," he said, "I chopped off every finger with a cleaver on a stump, and that son of a black bitch never even squeaked. Hell, we ended up chopping away his fucking toes before we got even a moan." Reginald warned them that they were going to kill him before the lynching. They finished their work on the old magnolia. Or they thought they had finished. Percie's spirit had left in triumph before they could practice their last humiliation on him—hanging and burning his body. Hébert concluded, "Anyway, tomorrow is my forty-third birthday. Let's toast."

Inspired by alcohol and evil, Carl yelled, "Fuck you, Hébert. Fuck all fat asses and their birthdays. You think you've done something great killing a nigger boy? Your fucking wife is living with a near nigger because you were too weak and stupid to keep her. What do I have to do to convince y'all that all I care about is *my* stolen money? Get my money back!" He slammed the whiskey bottle into Hébert's chest and trotted off to bed.

When Carl slammed the bedroom door, Hébert mumbled, "*Fuck you.* You want too much. We're doing our best to protect ourselves *and* your interest. Hell, we're doing better protecting your ass than the *president's* men. McKinley's a dead man. Fuck your complaining." Hébert lit a candle and staggered outside. The storm had drenched the back porch and flooded the path to the shed. Rain thwacked and put out the candle, making it useless. He lurched back to the kitchen, traded the candle for Carl's whiskey and a kerosene lamp.

The rain volleyed, paused as the wind created a fury of howls and pounded the tin roof mercilessly. Hébert had, of necessity, invented a clever system of outside and inside lights near and in the shed. When lit, the first light, next to the door, automatically sent a flame through glass tubing in the wall, which then lit a small lamp in the shed. This automatic lamp prevented past whiskey slips and falls.

Once inside, he extinguished the kerosene lamp and adjusted the automatic one to prevent excessive heat or wasted fuel. He managed all this dexterously so as not to drop the whiskey, which he set on the shipbuilding table. To get a glass, he reached into the shadows and heard a dragging movement. With a foul belch, he cursed all rats and mice. Too much liquor and vertigo told him to sit. He steadied himself and gripped a chair. He fell into it and came face-to-face with a cottonmouth. With its mouth wide enough to show solid white, the moccasin's intentions were more than evident. Hébert's head spun too widely to prevent the moment when the snake snapped into his hand, released its venom, and fell to the floor.

In plodding movements, he pitched the chair backward and tried to stand against the table. A younger, swifter, greedier cottonmouth startled him. This sneaky one hid on the open shelf just below the tabletop. It aimed for and connected to Hébert's protruding gut with a force that hammered him to his knees.

He crawled toward the door, where the cleverest cottonmouth lurked to enact the final blow. Nausea backed him against the door. Unwittingly, by extending his arm upward, he chanced upon the tail of the third cottonmouth, which had wound its form into the shelves of a nearby hutch. The snake's abruptness was colored by its brisk precision: it sprung forth and perforated Hébert's jaw with twin piercings. This torture produced only grunts and moans. He was too airless to scream—the girth of a vile assassin reduced to snake bait. He died braced by a door that trapped him, bleeding in three places that burned like blue flames.

The rain's drumlike pounding sounded hellish. The nearest pine tree caught the beat and, with the wind, added the stoking of its limbs to the natural cacophony. Inside Small House, Carl snored and sheltered himself in dreams that ignored the storm. Several times, he considered closing the banging storm shutters, but dreams conspired against his waking. The multipaned French doors let in a hellish glow.

Outside, the pine, no longer satisfied to just brush the shed's tin roof, felt compelled to play a bigger role. With the next wind gush, it hurled one of its largest branches through the roof to spear Hébert's chest. Several kerosene lamps popped and delivered fuel everywhere. Eshu danced on the flames and tossed them into every corner. He used the miniature ships as tinder to blaze the worktable, the wine and liquor rack, and especially the rafters and ceiling joists. Inside, Carl snored, only hearing in his dreams the fury of crackling and popping wind.

Through the night, the shed burned into nonexistence. At about four in the morning, when the storm had dispersed its energy, Carl coughed himself awake. A reddish-yellow glow traveled with putrid smoke through the house. He sat up in bed as the light moved menacingly. He went to the French doors to observe the calm of the past storm and gasped. Through the open doors, the morning's wet coolness invaded his nightclothes. He choked again on the thick smoke that lingered outside. In all this, he found only one place on the porch to focus. He stood transfixed, soaked in an evil yellow light, and counted forty-three candles, fully lit and burning as if rain or wind had never touched them. Forty-two of them lined the porch just below the railing. They were white, five inches tall, and quart sized. A lone black candle stood in the middle at the entry to the steps. It glowed the brightest. He scurried through the rooms calling for Hébert. Small House mocked him with silence. He reached the kitchen, where, through the screened door, orange flames peeked out of shed's embers. He did not venture out into the wooly and acrid smoke; instead, he straightened up and said, "Stupid, luckless, fat bastard. Dumber than a stump."

Later that morning, Small House was chaotic inside and out. Carl had packed to return to Colfax. It was far too risky to stay. After the sun had risen, after smoke had dissipated, and after he had kicked every candle from the porch, he armed himself with some courage to get close enough to see Hébert's skull imprisoned under charred wood. The sight did not inspire even an obligatory prayer.

A brilliant sun governed the morning, and everything glistened after the rain's cleansing. Carl unbridled the horse from the rig and went in search of Sheriff Blake. He assumed his previous alliance with the sheriff and Reginald Eaton would allow him to leave unquestioned.

Sheriff Blake arrived with two deputies. It took two hours to examine the backyard. Although the scattered candles were perplexing, he focused on the shed. He ordered his deputies to finish surveying the site and walked deliberately to where Carl sat on the swing. Without hesitation, he climbed the steps, stood before him, and said he determined that the storm caused Hébert's death. He punctuated his explanation with lighting a cigarette and blowing smoke. He detailed how the large pine branch cut through the shed's roof and landed right where Hébert's skull and belt buckle were found. The deputies only found parts of his skeleton, coins, and remnants of his watch and chain. He also determined that the fire was so intense that it cremated everything. He bluntly dismissed Carl's claim that Hébert was murdered. His investigation discovered no sign of that—certainly not those "birthday candles." His final assessment was that all the liquor bottles that the fire exploded would evidence what they all knew about Hébert: he was a drunk. This, he said, explained the accident. He concluded, "I need to inform Luc Coulon. He owns this house."

Carl shouted, "Those candles weren't there when I went to bed. You're useless against these niggers. For all you know, Coulon's a part of Hébert's killing. I've written to Coulon for years. Sent telegrams about money stolen from me. He never answered. Hébert wrote me many times about Coulon's involvement with niggers." He was losing ground with the sheriff. *This incompetent bastard is as stubborn as Maude the mule.*

Sheriff Blake was expert in twisting lies and always ended up on the winning side. He knew that Carl was no match for him. He was smug and dispassionate in telling Carl that if lightning had not torched Hébert, Mudbug liquor would have. As if stating a fact, he preached, "With the explanation I'm giving you, we're gonna live in some peace here long after your old skinny ass is back in Colfax." Carl stood defiantly, ready to physically engage the sheriff.

Before Carl could even sigh, Sheriff Blake threw down his cigarette, stomped it out roughly, and said, "I know all of them that whipped Pichon. They tortured and killed Percie. I know, too, that he told them nothing. The worst thing is that Hébert led those regulators, who forced this fight for you. Too many times I told Hébert that trying to scare niggers don't work, especially in Lacombe where too many of them have too much money and own land and businesses." Carl's impatience pushed him down on the porch swing. His hate for the sheriff caused him to sweat. Sheriff Blake ignored him. "You take Femme—she's richer than most peckerwoods in this town. The fucking big mistake was letting niggers get too much. Now they're fighting back with guns and knives. Take my caution, Carl. Don't forget, with the Choctaws, they outnumber us. So, I'm not making a case out of no case. It's a good idea to get back to Colfax before someone starts pointing fingers at you."

Carl understood this reasoning and acquiesced. "Well, I'll be back. If *I* don't make it back, I've got people who will. Let thieving Kebbi's nigger boy spend some of my money. Let him waste it like stupid niggers do. That'll nail him and give you evidence. I'll come back for him and my money. I'm justified in getting my money back. Reginald will let me know when." Carl went into the house and slammed the door.

Sheriff Blake repositioned his hat and stared at Small House. *Hébert got his hell on earth. Yours is coming, Carl.*

See Electricity

FOLLOWING PERCIE'S LYNCHING, all of Father Lorquette's prayers for peace seemed to be answered: Hébert's death by fire and venom; Femme's return home; Ossi's return to Femme, hopefully, for good; Carl's retreat to Colfax; Sheriff Blake's secret proclamation "no more fires" to regulators, especially Reginald; Aunt Velma's return to Papa Luc and the gas stove she adored; Pichon's promotion to foreman at the sawmill; Lucien's contentment to play jazz with Meffre at his side; and Meffre's settling into the pecan grove's little house, named Yana Place.

After five very long months, Femme and Ossi returned to hear Aunt Velma's claim that "prancing" back and forth between the mansion—to cook for Papa Luc—and to Pichon's—to take care of Keb—was too tiring. Thus, the very day Ossi and Femme put down their bags was the day she packed hers and waited for Pichon to take her to the Coulon mansion. She claimed, "I'm just trying to spread peace." They all knew that Hébert's death and Papa Luc's daily visits lured her back to the mansion.

Meffre had moved to the pecan grove in early spring. Of the many changes Femme observed, the most pronounced was in him—in his association with her and in his demeanor. She detected signs of maturity even in his walk. He had written to her about his move to and renovation of Yana Place. There was always mention of Lucien and all they were doing together. What Meffre did not say was *all* they were doing. That had started with a trip to Guinea Beach two weeks after Femme left. Unknowingly, Papa Luc sealed a partnership by taking them to survey Yana Place's property. He had fenced all his property into parcels of several acres planning for the time when he might sell. Even the Coulon Sawmill, on six acres, had been fenced. It was important, given Meffre's deeded two acres,

181

to explain the fenced pecan grove. The fence not only legitimized ownership, he explained, it became the symbolic marker of necessary separation. He did not like it, but Lacombe required fences between blacks and whites. Meffre understood and accepted the distinction.

"Lucien, tell your children, and you too Meffre, when they're old enough, to respect and protect these fences. Make sure folks say, 'That's the Coulon place. That's Barjone's pecan grove.' That way, there's a *public* understanding. And you two, when I'm gone, need to honor these fences too. Femme and I have that understanding. I respect her property, and she respects mine."

Their youthful idealism stood guard against all this seriousness. April was unusually warm, and they were eager to go swimming at Guinea Beach. Yet, Papa Luc explained how Meffre should tend to the pecan grove and the little house. Lucien studied his father's face for the anger that was nowhere in his tone but everywhere in his meaning. He knew the Coulons had struggled to own and keep this land. He also knew that his father hated losing and that, part of his sternness, had to do with the perennial undercurrent of racial strife in Lacombe. When he finished instructing them, he gave Meffre a set of keys, shook his hand, and told him he had great respect for his father. He rode toward the mansion using the path behind the property. He left them standing together, feeling more connected than separated. The talk had infected them with a caution that killed the excitement of the Guinea Beach trip. They agreed to go soon but set no date.

Meffre thought about the fence and how little it mattered, before Papa Luc elaborated on its necessity. He interpreted it as a barrier he would have to cross or ignore to really know Lucien, who, since Femme left, had occupied the largest part of his life. In the quiet of Yana Place, he thought of how he must make the fence invisible. He thought it best to confront Lucien about the fence *and* what really happened the day he rescued him from Todd Eaton's waving a hatchet over his head.

A week later, after fishing with Pichon, he cleaned up and was ready to risk being deeply honest, with himself and Lucien, for the first time. He walked to the back fence on the Coulon side of the grove and waited on a post rail for Lucien. Eshu found a devious opportunity to play trickster and, from a nearby pecan tree, mumbled, *See electricity.* Meffre laughed loudly and asked, "See electricity? Again? I only see Lucien."

Indeed, Meffre saw him riding slowly toward the grove. Yearning between men needs a battle line. The way they looked at each other welcomed the fence's insertion. Their bodies warred with unwilling minds while the fence provided a dividing marker for eyes to connect and swiftly separate. The fence allowed the pretense that everything between them had to do with jazz, piano playing, and Muscadine wine.

Papa Luc's praise of fences incited this battle, but Meffre focused on honesty. Their eyes lengthened from a few spotty catches. What had once been a glance wanted to be a look that would grow to a touch that, in turn, invited a lingering magnetism. The fence conspired against them with everything written and unwritten. Without agreeing to, each slowed his passion to be sure that what he wanted was also what the other wanted, which was something men should not want with each other. Certainly, whites and blacks were forbidden to have this something. Thus, the fence forced passion to make space for reason.

Yet, on this day, Meffre, the more daring—Eshu and ownership of Yana Place arming him with pride and privilege—glared at Lucien's confused smile and determined that no fence was going to separate them. Lucien's blue eyes, however, pitched their gaze in a tit for tat of muddied intentions. Without words, this gazing failed to translate into Meffre's willingness for physical contact. Papa Luc's speech on fences prevented Lucien from dismounting his horse and hopping over the fence. He honored the barrier more than he was willing to say; he simply rode away.

The next day, same time, same show, same magnetism. Blue eyes pulling one way; black pulling the other. This time, longing to talk to Meffre motivated Lucien. Never taking his eyes away from the fence, he dismounted slowly, slyly checking for Meffre while picking at leaves on low pecan branches that reached across the fence. When Meffre jumped from the post rail, Lucien faced him, the short distance between them losing its power. They created an unrehearsed two-step, right up to the fence. This two-step—no matter how much it reminded them of their first dance to the chair in Lucien's room—was ridden with reasoning instead of passion. For an hour, they argued vehemently about the fence. Meffre despised it as much as Lucien adhered to honoring it. It ended with Lucien's riding away.

Slowly, day by day, they lengthened the fence battle. It eventually became a graceful, sweet banter. Lucien felt pursued; Meffre felt pursued. In the pursuit, they both felt not only the urge, but also the need to touch. No more words!

Nature plays its role, in staging and production, for anything that grows. Inevitably, the fence and all its blockading restrictions loosened its hold. Lucien rode to Yana Place and to Meffre, who, at their appointed time, appeared hugging the fence post. This time, to Lucien's surprise, Meffre took a leading role and walked toward the woods. Lucien quickened his steps and followed him. Their mindset and actions were emboldened by the spring heat. By the time they walked abreast, some carefree, daring spirit overtook them and told them to run and to laugh. They laughed, ran, and ran deeper and deeper, along the footpaths, into the woods. Vague actions and gestures had been their only language for days. After the run, nearly breathless, Meffre took Lucien's face into his hands and kissed his lips. He said meekly, "Let's ride to Guinea Beach to see Pichon's love tree."

When they reached the lone, longleaf pine, at the gateway to the bayou hideaway, it was twilight. Nearly two years of awkward glances congealed on that heated spot, in late April 1902. On that spot, without words, without shame, they just embraced with unbridled youthful vigor. They held each other hard against every-thing that threatened to pull them apart. Nothing was delicate. It was a near-breathless attack fueled by muscularity and athleticism. In the darkness, under the longleaf pine, they let their souls talk through thick heartbeats. After hard embraces weakened their limbs, after their souls connected, after their lust could bear no constraint, they kissed harder to recharge their lust. They tongued until they suctioned saliva.

Kissing in the open was a daring prelude, but they felt only peace. With the next kiss, the sand shifted under them. They paused to find the smiling pine offering flickering moonlight, like a blessing. Eshu, on a slight breeze whispered to Meffre, *See electricity*. Immedi-ately, the bayou's water took its cue and splashed eagerly. Their fluid movements complemented their honest play: rough male gestures more fully aroused them in the crazed light thrown by a full moon. They ran to the bayou and, looking back at the tree, found each other for the first time by knowing each other's eyes, acknowledging each other's breath, perceiving each other's arousal through thick pants, and most of all accepting each other's soul. These discoveries led to an altogether different kind of daring. Meffre washed Lucien's face with bayou water telling him that Yemanja gave this blessing to create their love. Back under the shortleaf pine, with the bayou singing, the precious scene played itself out with soft kisses and hard wet frottage.

Lucien, who had never lifted anything heavier than sheet music, was slight but firmly built. His hold on Meffre's muscled body was reverential. So fiery was their passion that he entered another spiritual place he had never been. Meffre held Lucien as something rich that he wanted to treasure. He gently led him across the bayou, on the flimsy bridge of a fallen tree, and up the cliff, both clinging to exposed roots. From there, they had a full view of the lone pine, their witness. Lucien finally spoke. "No fences for us. You were trying to teach me. I couldn't bear the separation, felt wrong."

"I know. That tree is perfect: straight and tall without bending. That's our tree. It's like us." Clouds made the moon stingy with its light, so they meandered back to the pine where they sat and kissed until Eshu whispered in cautious chilly breezes. They rode back to Yana Place to enjoy closed windows and locked doors.

Shamelessly, Meffre undressed and pulled at Lucien's clothing. This undressing was a strategy. His hope to attract *and* mollify Lucien was easy. He asked, "What happened between you and Todd Eaton?"

Lucien smiled and did not relent. He did not lie. "I paid him to fake it a few times. I'm sorry. A low point for me. I was running from my uncle *and* loneliness."

Meffre yanked Lucien playfully. "You'll never be that lonely again."

The next morning, while Meffre slept, Lucien grew aware of the cliché he created by watching him sleep. Still, he marveled at Meffre's deep blackness, surprising, for he recognized it for the first time. It was an alluring blackness, undeniably a mark of beauty that entranced Lucien. He was aroused in observing that Meffre's sleeping maleness pulled every one of his features into perfection.

What Lucien could not know was that orishas, as a determined collective, had first imagined Meffre's beauty into reality in Africa by means of a chance distraction. As Yemanja and Eshu imagined this beauty, a bare-breasted woman carrying water to nowhere down an endless road distracted them. When orishas are distracted, all that is left is art. Thus, they gave Meffre, beyond their plan, a richer blackness—no simple opposite to whiteness—a million measures beyond a color contrast.

When Lucien first saw him, this beauty was buried. In his sick bed, when Ossi first brought him to Femme's, Meffre was masked in filth from the Red and Mississippi rivers. Having arrived at Simmesport, they did not have time to clean themselves. A Mississippi freighter had been loaded and ready to depart. They could not miss it. At Femme's, his hair was a mess of soft curls matted in an affliction of lint, dirt, and debris from grasses and trees. His forehead held dignity at bay. Shame lined his brow. But his eyes! Even then, his eyes absorbed Lucien. How different could white and black be in the same space? The relief one gave to the other captivated Lucien as he heard about Colfax. As he listened, he imagined Meffre well and clean. Now, at Yana Place, he gazed on this blackness and fully allowed that this could be his salvation and entrée into happiness.

Gazing led to arousal that became animated with touches that sent sparks in currents across Meffre's hairless skin. He woke to Lucien's roughness with a smile. There was a slowness and quickness about how their love became real. The slowness was easily explained by their deliberateness about the efficacy of love between them. The quickness was not theirs to control: it involved their lovemaking, which mostly ended in naps followed by questions about each other. On one occasion, Meffre asked, "What are you like with a woman?"

Lucien answered: "A sensational pleasure. Easy, easy work, but I've only been with two streetwalkers. It was very wet and slimy and slippery. I loved it." Lucien then asked: "How about you?"

Meffre answered: "Well, I was picking green beans once, and this old white woman, who gave us our pay, called me to the office and told me lay on the floor with all my clothes on. Said she only needed one part of me. She unbuttoned my pants and sat on me. Kept telling me I'd better not finish till she got up. Said I had a 'nice thick pole' and left me soaked. Couldn't finish 'cause she smelled like fish." They howled and fell into their phoenixlike lovemaking: exhausting themselves just to start all over again.

At Yana Place, they loved quick and slow, sometimes to the point of rawness. When they advanced to euphoric entry into their bodies, they experienced common satisfaction. It never mattered who entered whom, for mutual ejaculation and deep sleep always followed. Unbridled loving induced sleep, a powerful tool in preventing hackneyed or pessimistic conversations. Good lovemaking warded off the haunting impossibility of a life together. To counter this, they simply made love and went to sleep. At times, they just held each other and hummed common jazz melodies. Once, Eshu was amused and agitated Meffre, saying, *See electricity.* Not knowing whether this was invitation, commentary, or warning, Meffre simply thanked him. They passed time together for weeks, and no one ever caught a sniff of their love. When she returned from New Orleans, Femme detected a changed Meffre, which caused a scent to travel shillyshally through the woods. After a year, the scent became a smell and spread current-like until it lured Femme, and she strolled over to Yana Place unannounced to find Meffre studying a map.

Darkly Read Maps

Y EMANJA HAD BEEN HER strength when Ossi left. During that time, Femme lived in fear that she would lose Meffre *and* Ossi. Recently, every prayer to Yemanja elicited the same response: *Sweet cocoon.* She sat, with Labas, on the porch smoking her pipe and fretted over the meaning of the nagging *Sweet cocoon.*

Ossi had been in the hen house all morning repairing nesting boxes. They had decided to sell only eggs. Selling chickens was too much work without Meffre. Now that Ossi worked with Pichon at the sawmill, Femme knew they could manage easily. She whispered to the old oak, "I fretted too much. Ossi never left me." The oak sent a comforting breeze her way. She had come to love the routine that tightly knitted their souls. Still, a nagging worry was that Lacombe's peace felt flimsy. No one had forgotten that Percie was a sacrifice for the tentative peace they now enjoyed.

Papa Luc and Ossi had reassured her, many times, that Carl Keller remained under watch in Colfax. If he tried to create problems in Lacombe, everyone would be better prepared than before. Over the last year, Ossi and Papa Luc had ensured that all willing black men had sharp knives, guns, and ammunition to fight against lynchings. Pichon still believed his home was a target and, with Meffre, he became a leader in uniting blacks.

Ossi had enlisted the help of his Choctaw friends in Abita Springs, who arranged to have schooners ready for anyone who needed to get to New Orleans in a hurry. Because the Choctaws were largely left alone, Ossi and Papa Luc decided to store weapons and ammunition, for easy access, with them.

Femme was satisfied and proud that Meffre's relentless work on his pecan business resulted in marked successes. She was overly curious, however, about Lucien's frequent piano playing at Yana

Place. She explained away the change in Meffre to expected independence but regretted that there was a conspicuous and widening
chasm between them. She gnawed on her pipe and, for the first time,
puzzled over Meffre's lack of overt interest in young women. Having
surprised herself with this, she sat up straight in the rocker. She
drew on her pipe deeply and prayed to Yemanja. There was a sudden
rattling in the house. It came from a tiny calabash on Yemanja's side
of the oratory. Femme went there directly and picked it up. In an
echo, Yemanja said: *Sweet cocoon*. She allowed the riddle to slip away,
promising to resurrect it later. It clearly was not a warning and in
truth, her nervous curiosity primed her against interpretation.

Later that evening, Ossi and Meffre rode into the yard with their
catch of shiny, speckled trout. Meffre also held Keb on his horse. He
rode up to the porch and said, "Look who's here. He came to tell you
that everyone at his house is coming for fried trout tonight."

Keb laughed and fidgeted to get down to run to Femme. Meffre
had Keb wobbling and running awkwardly from one end of Femme's
porch to the other as soon as he could walk. He had grown into a
tall boy who adored Pichon and Charmaine, but he had taken to
Meffre, who spoiled him and became his uncle and fishing instructor.
No one could make him laugh as Meffre could; no one could stop
his crying more quickly. Porch fishing was one of their favorite
pastimes. One day, Meffre set a cane fishing pole on the corner of
the porch. As soon as he turned away, Keb meandered over to the
pole and, without a lesson, grabbed it with two hands and hurled
its string into the yard, startling a bunch of resting hens. Meffre
laughed. "Guess I don't have to teach you to be a fisherman. Got a
lot of grandpa Julien in you."

Keb became the focus at family dinners, and Meffre inspired his
clowning around. Aunt Velma taught him to dance, and any song set
him to stomping his feet. Femme was her happiest when they were
all together, eating and laughing, and waiting for some tale Pichon
or Ossi would inevitably tell about the sawmill. Even the promise
of a family gathering eased Femme's fretting. Lynching continued
in areas not far from St. Tammany Parish, but there was no such
activity in Lacombe. Although the Eatons kept gossip alive about
her involvement in Hébert's death, Femme's enlarged family was left
alone; for that, they were all grateful.

After dinner, the women cleaned the kitchen, and Femme noticed
that Meffre constantly checked the time on his pocket watch. She

asked if he had to hurry home. Her questioning caused surprise in the kitchen. Meffre, however, seemed undaunted and responded, "Lucien is bringing some paint over. Tomorrow, we're painting all the rooms. We're moving furniture out of the way tonight."

Aunt Velma and Charmaine went back to dishwashing, but Femme dried her hands on her apron and stared at Meffre, searching for something she could not locate. "Well, maybe you'll invite me over to see Yana Place when it's all done," she said, not taking her eyes off him.

"You're all welcome. Maybe wait till the painting's done." He kissed Femme, waved quickly to everyone, and left through the back door. The three women busied themselves, cleaning in an awkward silence.

+ + +

When Femme decided to visit Meffre, she arrived unannounced on a Saturday afternoon. She walked along the footpath, ruminating that the change she had first noticed in Meffre had now changed again. Ossi had gone fishing, and she picked the occasion as a good one to appease her nagging curiosity about Meffre and Lucien. She knew she was spying and felt bad about it. However, she rationalized the visit by convincing herself that she wanted to see Yana Place firsthand. She heard piano playing when she knocked. Meffre came to the door shirtless. He grabbed his shirt off a chair and ushered Femme in. "Sorry, I thought it was Pichon."

Femme looked around admiringly and asked for a tour. They went into the living room where Lucien was playing. He too was shirtless. Meffre reached around her and handed Lucien his shirt. She nodded with a smile and headed for the dining room. She saw papers and books on the table and tried to read them, but Meffre was too close. Because it would be too obvious that she was spying, she moved on. She continued surveying, commenting in every room on how nice the wall colors were. Each room had vases with flowers, and Meffre had set up a small oratory in his bedroom with the statue of Eshu she had given him. Her tour ended in the dining room at the French doors that led to the porch. She opened one of them and stepped outside to notice that the porch on that side had been freshly painted. She asked, "Oh, now you're starting on the outside, huh?"

"We thought we'd start here and work our way around. Lucien helps a lot."

"It's good you two have stayed friends. I was wondering who 'we' referred to, but—"

"Well, we is Lucien and me. We're painting and doing other work. Pichon comes by too." Meffre could read some disdain in Femme's face. However, part of the change she could not pinpoint in him was his obstinate refusal to divulge the truth living in Yana Place. At that moment, this stirred in them an unsettling feeling of distance, but it had its genesis shortly after he moved from her house. Her pulling him back against his pulling forward and away showed in minor infractions, surprises, and secrecy. Somehow, they knew that there would eventually be something that would tip their relationship away from her mothering and into his independence. Neither knew that this tipping would happen on this June afternoon.

Meffre led Femme into the kitchen, where she accepted some lemonade. She fussed about dirty dishes and windows that could use a good cleaning. Admiring flowers on the kitchen windowsill, she finally complimented him on how well the place looked and how proud she was of his being on his own.

They went back into the dining room. Pretending interest in books on the table, her eyes landed on a map, which had markings all over it. "You tore this map from a book. Why? I hate when folks destroy good books," Femme said with disgust.

Meffre knew the lie he had to tell was far too thin for Femme's intelligence. He looked down and said firmly, "One day I'll have to check on how well my pecans are selling in the French Market. I have to know the route to New Orleans—lake and train routes." He folded the map and put it in his pocket, hoping that Femme would read this as a sign that he wanted privacy. His obfuscation was a ploy for time and Eshu's menace. Femme could not connect her loose suspicions, but she knew Meffre had lied. This motivated her urges to spy further. Yet, she could not fully read Meffre's hiding of the map. He was certainly aware that hatred could come from anyone anytime, including Femme. Did this stop him? No. The very prohibition animated him. Thus, he was as motivated to hide as she was to discover.

By the time Femme noticed Meffre's map, the lovers had fully planned a trip to New Orleans. Lucien insisted on the trip because Meffre had not left Lacombe since he had arrived from Colfax. He wanted to show Meffre what a real Catholic Mass looked like at St. Louis Cathedral where all races worshipped together. He wanted to show him the French Market and Vieux Carré and how they could be freer in the city. They spent many evenings finalizing plans. It would be easy for Meffre to blend into the anonymity of New Orleans while he and Lucien went about the city. In the privacy of Reynaud's apartment, they could sleep, bathe, eat, and love together. Lucien took trips alone to New Orleans often. Therefore, he needed no excuses. Meffre had no plan other than to be with Lucien and convinced himself that the reckless risks were an expensive price worth paying.

Imagining the trip was as enjoyable as actualizing it. They relished creating this fiction, but imagination is a sanctuary for play in an unyielding reality. Meffre rode his horse long distances to prepare for the trip to Mandeville. Lucien, who had connections in New Orleans, wrote about bringing a friend to the theatre next spring. He showed Meffre the responses and enjoyed his smiles. They also played out their insecurities. In their plan, they would leave separately and meet in New Orleans. In melodramatic concern, Meffre would exclaim, "I can't be without you from night to daylight! How will I wait so long to meet you?"

All of this was said with deep affection, and Lucien plotted fictional alternatives just to keep Meffre laughing. They knew the complexity and hazards they were playing with. They knew their ages were no match for the longstanding tradition and culture of bold, rigid lines prohibiting what they were trying to commit. Yet, their collective arrogance would not recede. They planned the trip to the point of setting a date near the anniversary of their meeting under the longleaf pine on Guinea Beach.

There was, for Meffre, something sacrilegious about Femme's trying to read a map that meant so much to him, as if it were only about destroying a book. His long talks with Lucien had always concluded with the same refrain on secrecy. Although they wanted to trust Femme, they were unsure of the consequences. Her inquisitive visit unnerved them.

Two weeks later, Meffre visited her. He stood, searching her face for an expression that would lead them into conversation. He intentionally fixed his face without a show of emotion so that the reaction would be hers alone. Her face, however, was expressionless, and he read this as dissatisfaction. He walked slowly to her and held her shoulders and kissed her. A blush quickened her cheeks, and she said, "Meffre, you're keeping secrets. You're a man, so it's understandable." She moved away slightly. "Will you tell me what's going on between you and Lucien."

Meffre bristled and tilted his head a little and said, "You're asking for an explanation for something you already know and won't accept. Ossi knows and never asked. Really, he told *me*: what we find in nature, take as natural. We know others choose not to do that, and so we can't be honest with everyone. You love me. I love you. You know this. Can't that stand for now?"

Femme was unable to suppress her agitation. Her face was a tangle. She needed to be alone. Shame swelled in her because she believed she had betrayed him. She lied: "Meffre, I need to walk over to Pichon's. She kissed his forehead, and he left completely dismayed.

Meffre recounted his visit to Lucien. In his usual way, Lucien dismissed the episode by exclaiming it was only Femme being motherly. He also reminded Meffre that Femme had asked that he look after him. He said this with a big grin and added, "I'm a-looking."

From time to time, Meffre and the map unhinged Femme, all over again, into a near-frenzied state. This gave way to undisciplined imaginings of Meffre's trafficking with low-life women, as had been rumored about Lucien. She stirred her own anger thinking that many of Lacombe's young women would be good company for him. She fixated on rumors that Meffre went with Lucien to Mandeville jazz bars. For all her deliberate speculation and wrongheaded imaginings, what Femme ignored was that Eshu guarded Meffre. They had accepted each other, and Meffre was, thereby, protected by a trickster who enjoyed a good strong lie as a part of male energy.

Such a spirit, in a questionable map, can spread scents or strong smells that linger in the nostrils of those who refuse to imagine and accept what stares back at them. Some folks just follow those scents, making their imaginations greedy and fat. Femme was on this scent. Meffre refused to tell the truth about the map, and that denial was a scent Femme wanted to follow so she could be there grinning knowingly when Meffre would explain his running after the loose women Femme invented. And, Eshu, Janus faced, skipped through both their houses enjoying their mutual angst.

After her continual prodding—especially halfhearted attempts to make Meffre feel guilty—did not lead to a confession about the map, Femme began gathering evidence on her own. She used her egg stand to gossip with young and old black women from the quarters. She planted sticky questions that would trap some bit of testimony and lead to a clue. It did not work. None of the women ever talked about Meffre coming after them—a sure sign, said the older women, that he was getting "his satisfaction" from some low-life woman away from Lacombe. Having heard her own suspicions thrown back at her, Femme accepted how absurd this venture was.

On the other side of the pecan grove, Papa Luc also became inquisitive. He questioned Lucien on what was so entirely important about taking evening walks to Meffre's. Why did Lucien change his habit of spending time with him over brandy talking about the sawmill or other parts of the family business? Papa Luc interpreted this as rebellion, which he expected because it was rumored that Lucien was keen on black women. When he raised the subject with Aunt Velma, she shrugged and said it would be better not to look too hard for stones to throw at anyone else. She recalled, after one of Meffre's visits, that Lucien asked her about falling in love. She knew then what Papa Luc was fishing for now. With one sincere conversation, Aunt Velma convinced Papa Luc that Lucien was a grown man who had fallen in love with Meffre. She was surprised that there was no shock on Papa Luc's face.

Femme, however, veered in the opposite direction. She was not heartened by Ossi's warnings not to meddle or Papa Luc's advice to let Meffre and Lucien exhaust themselves before they would have to become serious businessmen. She protested this counsel and, therefore, took on a diligent campaign to unearth the map's secret. She paid Pichon to trail Meffre daily to find out anything he could about the map or travel plans. This would not seem unusual because Pichon was a frequent pest at Yana Place. His daily visits continued for three months, without results, until December 14, 1903, when he stopped at Meffre's after rabbit hunting. This time he masked his spying by the pretense of sharing one of the rabbits he had killed. He saw Lucien's horse tied to a post on the back porch. It was unusual that the kitchen door was locked. He thought about his pledge to Femme and walked quietly around to the side porch doors, which opened out from Meffre's bedroom. He could hear voices inside and decided to hide and eavesdrop. He pulled his pint whiskey bottle out of his satchel and crouched just below the porch's floorboards.

From this vantage point, he could not hear as much as he could see. He drank two good mouthfuls and looked up to witness a kiss between two slender, muscled, naked men. That sent him running, with two rabbits dangling at his side, without a destination, toward Lake Road. If his aim were to go yelping to Femme, the path behind the pecan grove would have been shorter, but Eshu distracted him entirely. A meandering path through the pecan grove lit up before him and took him swiftly to Lake Road.

With the kiss planted firmly in his eyes, he planned to get to Femme's and stutter his way through to a convincing portrayal of Lucien and Meffre. As he started to run up Lake Road, Eshu pushed Julien, his rig, and a quart of Muscadine wine between Pichon and his plan. Julien was coming from the lake with only a few bayou perch when he caught sight of Pichon looking lost and almost running into the rig. Julien was surprised to see him—so much so that he did not notice Reginald Eaton riding into the woods toward Yana Place. Pichon was as surprised by Julien's rig as he was about his being on Lake Road. He always took the footpath. Julien invited him into the rig, offered him a swig of Muscadine wine, and started talking nonstop about how cold weather could starve you. Eating from the lake and bayous was a version of hell, he claimed. Pichon felt the whiskey and Muscadine wine and held up his rabbits. Julien laughed and said that the rabbits would be plenty enough to keep everybody skinny. By the time they passed Femme's house and slipped by Pichon's, they both had dozed off. The rawboned horse, however, was hungry. He knew his way home on Old Oak Road and kept walking long after Julien had dropped the reins. When the horse pulled the rig into Julien's yard, Pichon was snoring louder than Julien. They slept in the rig until the horse's neighing woke them in the early morning hours.

Pichon found his way home and begged Charmaine not to yell because he had been with Julien and they had too much wine. He cleaned up and insisted he needed to see Femme. Charmaine's cooking and Keb's begging for food proved distraction enough for her.

Pichon walked to Femme's and stood in her kitchen—confused over something urgent he knew he had to tell her. Ossi and Femme sat in the parlor near the fireplace. She questioned Pichon about what he saw at Meffre's, and he could only answer, "I don't know. They were there. I just don't remember what I saw. I guess nothing.

But since then, I can't seem to get this noise out of my head. Like a bee buzzing in my ear." He said this loudly and confidently—yet completely unsure of himself. Eshu blew out a candle next to Femme, and she looked outside at the old oak and smiled as Pichon walked home on the footpath.

Ossi eyed her suspiciously and said, "Meffre is claiming and owning his privacy."

Femme lit the candle again, took Ossi's hand, and said, "It's hard for me to accept what I don't understand."

Femme would not own the truth she knew lived between Lucien and Meffre. For Ossi, the truth was real and sacred and could never be disguised. That evening, sitting near the fireplace full of love for Femme, he reiterated his promise to protect Meffre and ensure his happiness. He decided to ease into a conversation she would not broach. He talked in low tones, in reverence for the subject, and in respect for Femme's concern. He put her head on his shoulder and said, "In my tribe, we've always had men who do not take wives and women who do not prove happy as wives and mothers. These people live as a part of our life always, doing what their responsibilities demand."

"But this is unnatural."

"You were taught to be a good Catholic. I told Meffre, and now I tell you. Nature is what we find in nature—not what we *want* but what we *find*. Remember the pink pig's first litter? Remember, she was the one that rutted near the trees' roots? You don't have a black hog in your yard, but she had three speckled pigs. Those spotted pigs—they're not unnatural. Beauty in nature is what you know is different too."

She looked into his shiny black eyes and whispered, "Meffre told me you said this. I think he was trying to be honest, but I wouldn't listen. Even Yemanja told me: *Sweet cocoon.*"

✢ ✢ ✢

When April started warming the days and nudging quiescent nature, Meffre and Lucien decided their trip to New Orleans was overdue. Lucien had written notes and directions so that Meffre would travel alone with ease. When they were not together, Meffre read the notes and studied the map. Although they would never risk traveling together, Lucien assured Meffre that crossing Lake Pontchartrain from Mandeville to New Orleans would be easy. Meffre, however, anguished over every detail. Which stable in Mandeville would care for his horse? Would anyone question him? What if he could not find the meeting place in Spanish Fort? What if they could not attend a theatre in the Vieux Carré? What if someone recognized him? What about Keller's regulators? Yet, with these doubts, he journeyed alone, full of energy. Pichon agreed to look after Yana Place. The only detail he could not handle was confronting Femme with the news that he and Lucien were going. He, therefore, confided in Ossi that he was going to Reynaud's in New Orleans and asked that he let Femme know. Ossi assured him that Femme had found a big place in her soul for his happiness.

While Meffre was away, unbeknownst to anyone, Reginald Eaton passed by Yana Place every day. Pichon never saw him.

+ + +

When he landed in Spanish Fort, to Meffre's surprise, Lucien was waiting with Reynaud. The five-hour trip to New Orleans allowed him to sleep a bit, only to be awakened by noisy steamboat activity. When he saw Lucien and Reynaud, his quickened heartbeat caught the thriving pulse of New Orleans. The electric streetcar they would take to downtown stood ready, and Lucien waved to come quickly. He hugged Lucien and looked around for disapproval. Reynaud sensed Meffre's anxiousness and walked up to him, took his bag, and said, "Look at this, smiling all over yourselves. Well, in this case, I'll say y'all have good reason. Looking like something in a love painting." Meffre laughed heartily while Lucien shook his index finger at Reynaud. They walked to the streetcar with Reynaud's yapping about his plans for them.

At Reynaud's apartment, Meffre talked excitedly about tall downtown buildings, the many Canal Street electric streetcars, and the various complexions in the French Quarter. Reynaud chuckled at Meffre's excitement and promised more surprises. He showed Meffre the room he and Lucien would share and, then, invited them to lunch in the kitchen. He returned to the praline shop.

The new happiness filled their chests. The city promised a different freedom, one without debilitating caution and hiding. Their love found expression in eyeing a splendid palm tree in the courtyard below. Embraced by the large window, they held on to each other and commented on the greenness of the palm and how healthy it was. Lucien said, "I will keep you just as safe and healthy. With me." Meffre stopped him from biting his fingernails and kissed his hands.

When Reynaud returned, with a bag of soft-shell crabs, he found them asleep and spent. Strong lovemaking weakened them, and they could only sleep and snore. He smiled and closed the door to make supper.

Supper conversation included Reynaud's accounting of "too needy or not needy enough" men he had put out. These men provoked his single, independent life. He also claimed that those "suitors" refined his choices. Meffre was amused with Reynaud's openness even when it riveted him. His prim vocabulary suited his personality. Studded with double entendres, he showcased expressions that only fit men like him. Lucien cued and saved Meffre from his confusion over when to laugh or not. After they coaxed Meffre into eating the last of the crabs and remaining green beans, Lucien insisted they go out to hear Buddy Bolden.

Reynaud agreed excitedly. "I saw him last week with my friend Millicent, and that man played with me too much. I never go to those dance halls, but I did last week. Miss Millicent was shy at first, but I made her get up so I could really see that good-looking Buddy Bolden. Even with his cheeks full of air, he was easy on the eyes, cher—the picture of a man, who'd make a blind woman swoon. For sure, he could give a girl a good time. Me too! Lord, today! That is one fine horn player. Go see him. He's playing at the Funky Butt. They say he goes into a trance and will put you in one. He did me! Millicent too. Y'all be careful. Told Lucien I'd take him one day, but he's nabbed his own beau now."

Lucien was adventurous and lived for jazz, especially Créole and black jazz. He wanted to take Meffre through the Vieux Carré to Congo Square to hear the African influence in the music, which he had heard during Mardi Gras. Reynaud cautioned against it: "There's still a Code Number 111 in effect, cher. You're still white, Lucien. Or you look like it. You can go anywhere, but your Meffre should be guarded. The Quarter is different from downtown." He suggested that they hire a carriage to take them to the Funky Butt dance hall and to save Congo Square for daytime.

At the Funky Butt, Lucien dreamed of when he would be able to play with such fine musicians. Before Buddy Bolden came on, the brass ensemble played loud dance music, and the audience covered the floor. Lucien and Meffre mused on how Aunt Velma would enjoy being a part of this scene. Meffre added, "Keb, too." As the drinks circulated, the audience shouted titles, and Buddy Bolden played every song. Lucien could not sit still and often jumped up to cheer the band. Meffre enjoyed every moment Lucien enjoyed. He also enjoyed all the different people bound together, swaying and dancing to the music.

The next day in Congo Square, Meffre came alive, seeing black people dressed beautifully in African colors. They sold everything: produce, nuts, clothing, drums, calabashes, sugar, coffee, freshly baked French bread, and liquor—especially rum from Guadeloupe and Martinique. There was music everywhere in Congo Square. Lucien focused on improvisation from drummers and trumpeters, which answered each other in a marchlike jazz. This call-and-response became his fast favorite. They listened for over an hour till Meffre begged Lucien to leave. He wanted to see the Mississippi River by day.

They decided to walk to the river through the Quarter. Lucien pointed out Royal Street apartments and shops, famous for antiques, courtyards, and jazz and blues. He showed Meffre Femme's treasured Holy Family Sisters Convent and St. John Birchman's Orphanage. Finally, they arrived on Chartres Street in Jackson Square. Meffre could smell the muddy river and hear the ships' whistles. They passed through the square promising to take in St. Louis Cathedral and the Cabildo another day. The cloudy day made the river look even muddier than usual, but Meffre's mind was on their ultimate plan. Lucien sensed that his silence was not just awe of the mighty river. He asked, "This river is a giant compared to the Red River, huh? Is the Mississippi what you expected?"

The question surprised Meffre. "Oh, I remember both rivers from when Ossi brought me here. I wanted to see the Mississippi again to imagine our trip going north. I don't think I can do it alone." Meffre could tell this made Lucien sullen. He looked around and pulled Lucien to him. "I always dream about this because I really love you."

Lucien's smile was reassuring. "Remember that dream when you're on the train! You'll have to be calm, not jittery. You'll hand your ticket to the conductor, find your seat, and eat and sleep till you get to Cairo. The conductor will call out when you need to change trains. Before you know it, we'll meet in Chicago. You got here just fine; Chicago will be easy too. We might even take the same train. Don't worry now." They stayed in the French Quarter until nightfall. Meffre wanted to walk down Canal Street to take in electric lights, streetcars, and the city's energy.

Reynaud's was sitting in his drawing room sipping brandy and listening to music on a gramophone when they arrived. Although Meffre had seen the Coulon's gramophone, he had never heard one. He savored the sound, and Reynaud noted his wonder. "You found a lot to marvel at in Funky Butt? Not much of this going on in Lacombe, huh?"

"Lacombe's exciting too—in ways that make you want to leave. New Orleans has a live fire that won't go out, and it's big enough for our big sin." Reynaud and Lucien shared an approving glance.

Lucien said, "Reynaud's been to Chicago. Says New Orleans is nothing compared to that. I told him when we go, we might stay." Allowing space for his worry, Meffre took Lucien's hands and kissed them.

Reynaud mocked their affection and dispensed advice. "Well, yes, Chicago awaits you turtledoves. You'll still have to be discreet. But, surely, you'll find life tolerable enough to keep this loving y'all got burning. Now go wash your muddy asses, so we can go to Millicent's and get fed well. If anybody stares at you there, stare back. Créoles scare easily."

Eshu's North

LUCIEN TOOK THE TRAIN from New Orleans to Hammond, where a disaffected stable boy delivered his horse. He was a tall, grimy black boy, who snarled when Lucien smiled and passed him a nickel—more than most would offer. Even this did not evoke a pleasant reaction. Lucien looked at the sky. "Think it's going to rain?"

"I ain't studying no rain, sir. Don't mean no disrespect, but a man, near where I lives, was hung and burnt last night. Everybody's afraid." He backed away from Lucien and sat on a stump near the boarding barn. Lucien tipped his hat, muttered he was sorry, and rode away angrily. The thought of Meffre's coming home alone on the ferry through Mandeville alarmed him. He dismissed the risk of anyone seeing them together and decided to go to Mandeville and wait at the pier train. There was only an hour of daylight left when Meffre disembarked. Seeing Lucien there alarmed him. They rode swiftly to the Coulon mansion.

They arrived in darkness and did not recognize the horses tied to the front hitching post. After caring for their horses, they entered through the kitchen. Cigarette smoke hung in the air. Hiding near the parlor door, they heard arguing voices. Papa Luc, Ossi, and someone else talked about "trouble." A booming voice explained, "This week, we've had two in Slidell, one in Mandeville, and one in Covington—all at night with crosses. I've done all I can to keep peace. Luc, you know this. I've worked with you, Father, and this here Choctaw. Small House might've been the start of it. I talk to y'all, but y'all don't talk to me. Like I said, that Keller bastard claims he's after his stolen money. Y'all can't solve this shit without the law." The man's tone was angry. They could even hear his blowing smoke fiercely.

Meffre and Lucien heard Papa Luc pacing. "Listen, Blake. His name's Ossi. In my house, you respect him. Anyway, no one knows what happened at Small House. You called it Hébert's drunken accident. That's what I call it. Time's passed, and I'm not worried about that anymore. You're making more money than St. Tammany Parish pays you. Keller's paying you, probably more than I am. To keep peace, you can't allow things to get out of hand. You always come in at the end, and nobody gets charged. By then, the worst has happened. And those Eatons? You don't have anything on them? Pichon was brutalized and saw Todd there! You're ignoring Percie's murder? You know Hébert and those Eatons were behind that."

Sheriff Blake was full of bluster. "I questioned Todd, and he had an alibi. No way to trace the others. I took Pichon's word against the Eatons? Now they call me a nigger lover! Losing their trust is losing their secrets. We ain't gonna win if I don't have their trust. You know where I stand. Didn't I send word to Ossi through Father? That's why Lacombe's peaceful. But trouble's coming from Colfax. Percie's death's the beginning. Keller's sure Ossi and that boy have his money. Folks siding with him think he's justified in getting it back. Reginald Eaton told him nothing's changed here. But talk to that boy. Getting biggity!"

Ossi then raised his arms with fisted hands. He punched the air in Sheriff Blake's direction. The eavesdroppers could not interpret the silence that followed and what seemed to them a lack of activity until Ossi said, "We won't live every day with fear taking our spirit. We'll fight here as we fought in Colfax. Meffre deserves a life here. He works that pecan grove and sells at market. He's doing nothing wrong. Percie did nothing wrong."

The clear reasoning defeated Sheriff Blake. He stubbed out his cigarette and held on to his chair as he rose. "I know," he said roughly, "but, go slow and don't start the fight. I'd better be going. I'll come by if I hear anything."

Meffre and Lucien could tell that Papa Luc was accompanying the sheriff to the front door. Their eyes mirrored confusion. Unlike Meffre, who was afraid, Lucien was overwhelmed with anger. When he heard the front door slam, he marched into the parlor, in a rage. "Papa Luc!"

Ossi stood and faced the young men. Papa Luc moved over to them and said, "Oh. I'm glad to see you two made it back safely. I telegrammed Reynaud this afternoon, and he wired back that y'all had left. Sit, have a brandy." Lucien's anger abated, and Meffre looked at Ossi, waiting for a reprimand about taking unnecessary risks. Instead, he simply slapped Meffre's back approvingly.

Lucien told the stable boy's menacing story and confessed that they heard the conversation with the sheriff. Papa Luc called the sheriff a "stupid-ass idiot" and explained that everyone needed to work on getting messages right and to their destinations quickly. Lucien asked about threats against Meffre, and this time Ossi answered that no one should be afraid. Papa Luc and Lucien had given Meffre strong assurance that he would be protected to do with his property as he pleased. Of this, he was convinced. Otherwise, there would be no progress for black people and the fight would continue. They finished their brandy and Ossi rode alongside Meffre through the woods until he left him and headed home. Femme greeted him, and they sat on the porch while Ossi told her everything. Eshu shook the old oak's branches to dapple the porch with intermittent romantic moonlight.

✠ ✠ ✠

Meffre's return from New Orleans added more changes to those Femme had registered. Ossi noticed this too because Meffre asked for and heeded advice. Everyone thought the changes originated in Meffre's dedication to the pecan grove. Yet, it seemed to be more than that. Early one Saturday morning, Ossi woke Meffre to go with him to Abita Springs. He readily agreed because Ossi had often talked about the Choctaw village there. He did not disrespect Ossi by questioning the trip's purpose. When they arrived, many greeted Ossi with near reverence. One of the young men took their horses, and an older man, who appeared to be a leader, took them to a small house near a shallow bayou. Ossi introduced Meffre. Nito, the older man, knew Meffre's story—from Ossi, no doubt. There was also a younger man, busily preparing food. Nito talked to Ossi about how their women were doing very well selling their wares—herbs, beads, decorated leather, and baskets—in the French Market. He described their schooner trips on Okwa-ta, the wide water, over to New Orleans from Mandeville.

The younger man, Chukfi, served rabbit, peas, corn, and beets. Meffre expected the guest to be served first, but Chukfi gave a full plate to Nito, then to Ossi, and to Meffre last. When he returned with second portions, he cut the largest rabbit parts for Nito. For dessert, he set a fruit bowl before them and carved a pear into pieces for Nito.

After they ate, they sipped tea, and Nito talked about his role as a tribal spirit interpreter. He was a religious elder called Chahta Ima, the spirit of the Choctaws. The young man, beautiful and dutiful, caught Meffre's attention, for he never left Nito and seemed entirely devoted.

Later, when they went out on the lake, Ossi explained to Meffre that Nito and Chukfi lived as man and wife. Meffre absorbed this respectfully just as Ossi offered it—without overt emotion. At the same time, the reason for the trip became evident and boosted Meffre's resolve to stay with Lucien. Since his arrival in Lacombe, Meffre wrestled with the question of what family would mean for him. Watching these two men go through mundane activities schooled him in what a different kind of family could be. Meffre was enthralled with their interactions, their caring for each other, and the respect they offered naturally. They reached the landing for boarding the schooners to New Orleans, and Ossi said, "Meffre if you are a man like Nito, love yourself. Read nothing dark in you."

With his eyes on his lap, Meffre simply nodded and said, "Thank you."

Ossi instructed him to remember Nito in Abita Springs if he ever needed a place to hide. He should also remember the Mandeville schooner landing as a safe route to New Orleans, which Ossi used frequently. For the first time, Meffre felt the calmness he envied in Ossi. In odd inexplicable ways, the danger of Keller's threats shadowing him emboldened him and gave him the resolve to resist. He was conscious, all the way home, of sitting differently on his horse.

Any residual adolescent timidity faded and allowed Eshu to become more present. Through Femme's caution, Meffre knew that Eshu was a trickster. He would often sit on his porch and hear pecan trees buzzing with movement when there was no wind. Eshu, Lucien, and his solitude were the fabric of his peace. For hours, he enjoyed such movement as his father's spirit running among the very pecans he had planted. In his playful imaginings, he believed that Eshu gave Kebbi chase among the pecans.

The pecan grove was a masterpiece of symmetry: it provided vistas of straight lines at any angle. The branches created an interlacing canopy that became an arbor on even the hottest days. If it never produced one pecan, the grove was worth its every inch as a love incubator and garden refuge. It was impossible to gaze through these trees and not be moved. Meffre was never afraid here, and after the freedom he had felt in New Orleans, where he had been able to love Lucien freely, he now felt that nothing could prevent that love. The trip to meet the Abita Choctaws presaged a future with Lucien. He shouldered his manhood, and with the firmest determination, shouted into the grove: "Eshu, show me my next road!"

There was an erratic rustling that continued for three long, electrified minutes. Then, after a swift and meaningful silence, the magnolia next to the porch, threw a breeze his way, and he heard, *North.*

A Lyncher's South

ON OCTOBER 14, 1904, three years after Small House's shed burned, Papa Luc, soaked from a downpour, received a telegram in the sawmill office. The telegram contained a direct message: *Tombstone shipped—Hébert Bellocq.* The signature: *C. Keller.* Papa Luc felt absolutely nothing. He slid it to Lucien, who sat behind the desk adding numbers in a ledger. He looked up, read the telegram, and went back to the accounts that were a trial for him. He mused, "Well, at least, we'll know where they put Uncle Hébert's bones. It was hard finding a grave marker to put candles on Les Toussaints les Lumieres du Morte last year. Couldn't remember if we buried him to the left or right of Mama. Pity uncle left no one to grieve for him."

"Respect the dead, please," Papa Luc said, making a clumsy sign of the cross. Lucien mocked the gesture with a phony blessing. The drumbeats of pounding rain distracted him from his accounting. It was as good a time as any to broach a controversial subject. He pushed back his chair, opened the small desk door, and pulled out brandy and two snifters. He poured two good shots, gave one to his father, and said, "A toast to the heaven-bound soul of Uncle Hébert." Papa Luc smiled. He knew Lucien wanted to talk seriously. Brandy incited seriousness, no matter the initiator or how fleeting the subject. They stood staring and sniffing long enough to smile knowingly.

"Papa, I need to ask about an idea I have, or really, an idea Meffre and I have."

He held out his hand to Lucien. "Let's make a gentleman's shake on whatever you're going to ask. I'm always outnumbered against you, Meffre, and Aunt Velma."

Aunt Velma and Lucien relied on each other as silent and effective buttresses. When she thought they should get a phone, Lucien convinced Papa Luc they needed it for business. When Lucien wanted a newer model gramophone, Aunt Femme made the idea Papa Luc's gift to her.

"We want to open a produce and seafood store—an indoor market, within walking distance of Sacred Heart. Meffre already talked to Femme and Ossi. They think it's a good idea. Julien and Pichon are going to supply all the seafood from the bayou and lake. We'll buy produce from local farmers. We know we'll be watched, and that Keller is dangerous. It's going to look like my store—everything named Coulon. On legal documents, it will be in Meffre's name." Papa Luc's seriousness was unmasked by his smile. Lucien bit his fingernails and waited for the most important question: who would finance building the store. He preempted him. "You don't know how well Meffre has done selling pecans to every market around here and in New Orleans. Months ago, we rented a stall right in front of Café du Monde. Reynaud, who checks on it for us, had to hire another vendor to run it. They've been selling three barrels a week. Meffre has made enough to start the building, and he—"

"—found the money his daddy stole from Keller."

Lucien made no attempt at dissembling. "Yes. *We* did. We thought it best to invest in a store."

Disappointment pushed a deep blush into Lucien's skin, and Papa Luc saw the shame. He, Ossi, and Femme knew it would happen. He did not think it would be so soon. He paced from window to window in the long office, trying to invent a way to advise against the store. Lucien saw trouble in his father's pacing and sighing. The more brandy they drank, the more rattled Papa Luc seemed. Really, he was distracted remembering how Aunt Velma and Ossi had teamed up to convince him that separating these young men would be akin to, or even harder than, rooting out regulators. The pacing continued and, several times, Lucien wanted to abandon the proposal altogether.

Then, suddenly, Papa Luc turned toward Lucien and said, "No! Ossi's right. We lose everything if we're afraid. We'll never have peace if Keller fences us inside our own yards. Kebbi, Yana, Percie, and all the others we don't even know paid with their lives for that store. We must honor that! Look, we already shook, and I made light of it, but I stand with you two. Obligation always elbows me into these deals. I just want to know one thing: Did that valise lead Meffre to the money?"

It had. Lucien knew that, if the store was built, it would be evident that Meffre had more money than selling pecans could produce. He poured more brandy and focused on the valise and his life with Meffre.

When they returned from the first trip to New Orleans, Meffre and Lucien agreed to design elaborate plans that were feasible and practical. As Pichon could drop in anytime, they had to devise a way to open and close Yana Place to him. When he visited, their abrupt silence, which annoyed Pichon, hastened his departure. Without knowing exactly how he knew what he knew, Pichon read welcome and avoidance signs quite accurately. Signs were sometimes simple: Lucien's horse tied to the front hitching post was a welcome, especially if accompanied by loud jazz improvisation. A clear avoidance sign was Lucien's horse boarded in the stable. The most blatant avoidance sign, however, was when either appeared shirtless. On such occasions, Pichon simply made a toast to Percie, took a quick drink, and left. None of this bothered him because what he could not *name*, he could not hate. As his son grew, so too had his responsibility. He had fewer hours to spend in the pecan grove because Charmaine protested. In his view, the responsibility was an earned honor. Still he was the most frequent visitor at Yana Place, and his absence was never longer than a day or two. Meffre treated him as a brother; Lucien entertained him as a friend.

Thus, more Lucien visits meant fewer Pichon visits. Oddly enough, it was one day, when Lucien's horse was in the stable, that Pichon—sent by Femme with freshly baked mirlitons stuffed with crabmeat—was brazen enough, against warnings, to march right through the back door and into the kitchen. He surprised Lucien and Meffre, who were pouring over documents and a map, strewn over the table. Pichon merely lifted the checkered towel to release the mirlitons' aroma. Meffre started folding papers and stuffing them into the valise, and in his haste, he unraveled threading from the inside pouch. He continued to fill the valise till the table was cleared. They sat to eat, and Pichon did not leave until Meffre took off his shirt.

With Pichon gone, Lucien could tell that something was animating Meffre, who looked puzzled until he collected the valise and hurriedly emptied it. They stored the many city, state, and inter-state railroad maps they had amassed in the valise. It was full and hard to manage without taking everything out. Meffre was looking for an Illinois Central Railway advertisement, which Reynaud had mailed to Lucien. They treasured all this information as a vital part of their dream of leaving the South. In his haste to find the advertisement, Meffre again snagged the long thread and inadvertently tore open the valise's lining. The lining fell easily as the threading loosened. Inside the lining, he found a letter and an envelope with a diagram. The letter was from his father and stated simply: *Talk to Eshu every day. This money buys your future.* The diagram was very easy to understand: it was a roughly sketched replica of the grove's hundred pecan trees just as they had been planted in a ten-tree-per-row square. The riddle at the bottom of the diagram was a bit more difficult to decipher: *count five in any direction—use six in the middle—find the middle again. Between 46 and 56.*

Reading this Meffre said, "This is an Eshu-like riddle so its simplicity could be a trick." They were giddy over discovering the letter. They opened a bottle of Muscadine wine and drew the grove's trees by designating each as a numbered dot. After half the wine vanished, Meffre was useless. Lucien studied their drawing as he plucked the table like a piano. Finally, he figured it out, kissed Meffre hard, and insisted they pick the best time for digging unnoticed.

For two days, they dug gently around the roots of pecan trees. Eshu whispered buzzing clues to Meffre, which tricked him away from the money. Finally, annoyed by Eshu's tricks, they chanced on the money's burial ground. It was nowhere close to Eshu's pointless clues and exactly where Kebbi's puzzle led them. They hauled thirty mud-covered mason jars into the house. When the counting was done, Meffre had inherited nearly three hundred dollars.

Papa Luc's enjoyment was measured by his boisterous laughter. He was, however, shocked that they had found the money over a year ago. That they could keep the secret was no surprise; that it was not spent was. Knowing how they frequented jazz bars, he applauded that they had not squandered the money. Their discretion, he noted, had duped the regulators. He sipped the last of his brandy and said to Lucien, "Let's go home. Planning that produce store will have to happen another day. Aunt Velma's cooking filé gumbo; it's sure ready now. We won't get filé gumbo till Thanksgiving. Let's go."

+ + +

By the time Pichon and Ossi painted the final coat of white enamel on the store's weatherboards, Lucien and Meffre had hired several hands from around Lacombe, who worked with Julien to build produce shelves and bins. They also built large seafood coolers that would hold block ice. Julien supervised the entire project, and all had gone well. Even the electric wiring, contracted out to a Slidell man, proved easy to install. Lucien ordered a chest icebox for the porch so that they could sell soda and beer. They put two large ice chests in the back so that the iceman would have easy delivery access.

Even if it took, off and on, over a year to finish, the entire family circle was excited to participate in building and stocking the store. Meffre wanted everyone to supply and sell goods to him so they could share the profits. This idea came from Ossi, who impressed on Meffre the importance of keeping family far ahead of greed. Meffre accepted this as long as it did not interfere with his goal to one day live in Chicago with Lucien. He was determined not to inherit the life his parents suffered. Nor could he see a future in the shadow of Keller's vigilance.

With shelves fully stocked, the sign went up, and Lacombe Seafood and Produce was ready for its opening. On Friday, Femme, Aunt Velma, and Charmaine had stocked shelves with canned fruits and vegetables. Julien filled the cooler with beer called "Julien's Homebrew." Three crab lines had been baited for an early Saturday morning fishing trip, and Ossi and Pichon had crated twenty dozen of eggs, brown and white. So that there would be fresh fish, Ossi and Pichon planned a trip on Sunday morning to catch white trout and bayou perch. Aunt Velma and Charmaine did a final cleaning and arranging on Saturday. Meffre, Lucien, and Papa Luc busied themselves with the paperwork and cash register details. The plan involved Meffre as stock hand and Lucien as the counter sales-clerk. On Sunday, April 22, 1906, after eight o'clock Mass, Father Lorquette blessed the store, and it officially opened.

That Sunday was animated for all sorts of reasons. It seemed that everyone entered the store willing to buy something, especially the plentiful white or speckled trout. When the trout was gone, folks bought perch, crabs, and even the crawfish that Pichon hauled in a wheelbarrow. The shelves nearly emptied by three o'clock, and Lucien looked shocked that all the produce sold. Many Lacombi-ans raised their own fruits and vegetables, but the store's produce variety and reasonable prices made everything attractive. The pecans sold rapidly as well, and Meffre happily weighed out a bit of lagniappe for customers.

There was a great deal of talk that day about a San Francisco earthquake, many saying that they would rather tolerate a hurricane. These conversations gave Lucien the idea that they should sell newspapers, and after the clients had gone, new ideas for commerce were hatched over beer drinking and laughter. Papa Luc stopped by for a celebratory beer and offered that they should get a telephone to make more money. This went on until nearly five o'clock when Sheriff Blake knocked on the screened door.

"Coulons got another successful business, huh?" he asked in a tone more mocking than congratulatory. Meffre grabbed a broom to clean the store's backroom. Lucien and Papa Luc changed the subject to "trouble" in Ponchatoula—two lynching victims were found in the woods near a strawberry field. This immediately put the sheriff in a negative mood. He said, "Seems those boys stole tools out of somebody's barn. That's all I know. At least, it wasn't here." He tipped his hat and left in a fake hurry.

After cleaning the store and preparing for the next day, Meffre and Lucien rode to Yana Place with the money they had made and the pride in ensuring, as Kebbi wished, that the future could be theirs to buy. When they got home, Lucien left Meffre to read over papers Papa Luc had given them about the Canal-Louisiana Bank and Trust Company. As usual, from the valise, he pulled out information to plan the Chicago trip. This always energized him and allowed his imagination to create dreams of jazz and blues clubs, about Reynaud's tantalizing prediction of a freer life, and about his future with Lucien. He spent his evening and night putting together that future, held together with Eshu's advice, *North*.

+ + +

By the middle of September, Lacombe Seafood and Produce had blossomed into a major success. It had profited from the good fortune of place in the center of a triangle of land where three roads intersected, making it visible and accessible from well-trafficked roads near Sacred Heart. Folks from Slidell, Mandeville, and even Abita Springs found lake and bayou seafood bounty and rich produce from Lacombe's farms. The greatest irony was that most people accepted this as a Coulon enterprise. Therefore, whites shopped there regularly.

Meffre and Papa Luc had convinced Lucien that they needed to deposit money in the bank, and they decided to open business and personal accounts at the Canal-Louisiana Bank and Trust Company. The September weather was agreeable, but it was also unpredictably changeable. Hurricane season had already started with several brutal storms. Lucien decided to take the train from Abita Springs to New Orleans, stay with Reynaud, and return quickly after completing the banking. The trip would take three or four days, and Meffre would keep the store closed while Lucien was gone.

When Lucien left on September 20, 1906, dark clouds and sharp winds threatened St. Tammany's north shore. Three days later, a storm rolled into the Gulf of Mexico, and for six days, the hurricane made good on its threat. Pensacola and Pascagoula were devastated by its wrathful blasts. Lake Pontchartrain overflowed and flooded the north shore and New Orleans. Lucien was cut off completely from Lacombe because telephone and telegraph poles and lines were down or destroyed. When Ossi reported that the lake had flooded Lake Road and the bayou had disappeared, Meffre secured the store and nailed tight all the storm shutters. The land owned by Papa Luc, Pichon, and Femme was on high enough ground. If the floodwaters did not get any higher, they would be safe. Meffre rode through a pitching rain and got to Yana Place to find Pichon nailing shut the storm shutters. He told Meffre that Femme wanted him to come to spend the night at her place. They left together, on foot, down the woods path in spikelike rain. As soon as they left, Reginald and Todd Eaton rode up to Yana Place with intended devilment. Yemanja accelerated the storm's intensity and thwarted their plans.

When Meffre and Pichon arrived at Femme's, it was hard to imagine that a hurricane was pounding down on them. Femme had cooked a large pot of red beans with ham and Andouille sausage. The table was set with bread and fried chicken and fresh salad. She was steaming rice when Meffre grabbed and kissed her. She hugged him and asked whether they had seen Ossi. Pichon answered that Ossi went earlier to Sacred Heart to help Father Lorquette put up storm shutters. "Well, he'll be home soon," she said, "and he'll be hungry after protecting everyone else in Lacombe. Forgot all about me. Good thing Pichon took care of my windows."

"Well, I can hear Charmaine fussing through the thunder. Better get on home." He opened the door to a relentless rain and cried, "Oh, miss, here comes trouble dragging mud across your porch."

Pichon left and Ossi came in, soaked and laughing that Father was only good for taking care of souls. He described how Father watched Julien closing off the church window and doors. Meffre enjoyed this time with them, but Femme noticed that he suddenly became quiet. He and Ossi drank lemonade and talked about how the storm could be good for fishing and crabbing. Ossi agreed that the speckled and green trout could still run fast this fall. Ossi made more fishing predictions, but Meffre became disinterested, and Femme called him to her bedroom. "You're worried about Lucien. He'll be fine. Papa Luc said Reynaud knows how to weather a hurricane."

Meffre, surprised, welcomed Femme's interest. He took her hand and thanked her. His eyes penetrated hers. He said, with no shame, "I love him."

Femme held his shoulder and rubbed his head. "I know. It's natural to feel this way. I thought I lost Ossi, so I know. Lucien's safe. He'll come home to you."

"Eshu keeps telling me, *North*, and I think I know why. Lucien and I are planning . . . I mean we're trying to leave for Chicago. Reynaud knows someone there who can help us get settled. He thinks it'll be better for us there. Is this what Eshu's telling me?"

"I don't know. Eshu's a trickster. He gives and takes. Could as easily mean trouble's coming from the north. Hard to say."

Meffre turned to the window. His concern was not only for Lucien but, more deeply, it was anxiety over uncertainty. Femme went to her dresser and dug out the pamphlet on lynching. The Ida B. Wells speech taught her a lot about what was happening outside Louisiana, even in the North. She wanted Meffre to place his dream in a realistic context. Yet, she did not want to cause him to despair. She described how she bought the pamphlet from a woman who had overcome tremendous hardship. After reading it, she was resolved never to give up resisting hatred. She urged him to read and study the speech. He would find, she said earnestly, that Lacombe's hatred was widespread. Although lynching continued, she assured him that it could be defeated. "What you and Lucien are doing is dangerous. When you love someone, it's easy to forget reality. Read this speech. You'll see what you'll have to endure here or any place. You and Lucien want to leave. I surely don't want you to go. If you believe

Eshu is guiding you, and if you two can bear it, go." Meffre's mood lightened. He took the pamphlet and promised to read it.

Lucien returned to the store with a small bandage under his left eye. Meffre had no opportunity to question him because he offered immediately that a magnolia branch in Reynaud's courtyard had nipped him and scratched a tiny tear under his eye. Meffre's excitement over Lucien's return displaced suspicion about the story—but only for a short time.

When they reached the bungalow, Lucien could feel distance in Meffre's reaction to him. He tried to pull Meffre to him, but he pulled away. Then Meffre stood close enough to stare at the bandage and asked, "What really happened?" Lucien colored and turned away in a pretended pout. In that short time, the bandage became a wall between them.

Meffre turned him around and yanked the bandage off to reveal a healing black eye with no tear in the skin. He balled up his fists and said angrily, "Same eye Todd Eaton blackened." Even though Lucien felt trapped, he stood firm and braced himself. He moved closer to Meffre and tried to kiss him, knowing the move would fail. Meffre's lips tightened over clenched teeth. They stood over the bandage on the floor. Its presence between them foiled Lucien's every attempt to get Meffre to look into his moist eyes. Finally, Meffre's anger sent a fiery impulse through his leg and slammed his foot on the bandage. "I asked you what happened. Tell the truth this time."

Lucien remembered Reynaud's advice to lie when the truth is damaging. "You're jealous, Meffre. Jealous of nothing. The wind flung a branch at me during the storm. Let it go."

"Leave now. Leave my house—"

"—*Your* house. That's a lot to—"

Pointing to the kitchen door, Meffre's voice was growl-like. "Leave, Lucien. Liars cheat, then steal, then kill. I won't be a part of that." Lucien sat defiantly on the piano bench in tears. He could not bear the lie's weight and its cutting into his love for Meffre. Though he thought it was too late, he told the truth.

He and Reynaud were relieved that the storm had passed and celebrated by going to a nearby Vieux Carré bar. They drank and listened to blues and jazz until the bartender started sweeping. Lucien drank whiskey and talked all night to a tall man from Charleston who was also stranded in New Orleans. Reynaud cautioned Lucien about flirting when drunk, but the drinks gave him another idea. When he whispered an invitation to Reynaud's apartment in the man's ear, he accented it with a nibbling kiss. Luckily, the man was as drunk as Lucien, and his fist grazed Lucien's eye with a sloppy pop. Reynaud and the bartender handled the man like the day's trash and hurled him out the front door. They returned to find Lucien on the floor holding his face. Lucien capped the story: "Nothing happened, Meffre. Don't be jealous over nothing."

"Nothing happened but you wanted something to happen. Leave and leave now."

For seven days, Lucien left gifts on the kitchen porch at Yana Place: flowers, fruit, chardonnay, cognac, Aunt Velma's cookies, strawberry jam, Femme's pralines, and finally a letter that said, "I can't stop loving you. Talk to me." Meffre took in and enjoyed all the gifts. That night, Eshu woke him with a buzz of *No locks*. He was certain this was no riddle and interpreted it as an order to forget and heal. It took him four more days to collect more gifts and love notes before he stopped locking his bedroom's porch door.

When lovers quarrel, the bed is not always a curative. With these young lovers, however, passion was a gateway to reconciliation without lots of useless explanation. Meffre slept soundly the night Lucien slid next to him and held him tightly with arms and legs. The bed's emptiness had become self-imposed punishment. Aroused from his sleep, Lucien's warmth freed him. In the darkness, he said lovingly, "Leave me before you lie to me again. Promise."

As he undressed Meffre, Lucien said "I promise" repeatedly until, sex exhausted, they fell asleep. The next morning, Lucien was full of stories about the hurricane and the tangle of wires along Canal Street. Many of the electrified streetcars were not working, and it was impossible to send telegrams or get phone calls through. By the time they walked into the store, Meffre was happy to assume his previous role but with a difference. He resolved to work very hard solely to prepare for Chicago. Lucien became ecstatic and willing to work just as hard. Meffre told him that the Ida B. Wells speech taught him that hatred moves quicker than love. He had come to realize that his parents' death left him in control of his life, but this was a blessing and a burden. With only his eyes, Lucien found a way to commiserate and finally said, "I'll read the speech, for sure, but only if I can play Chicago jazz after, so we can stay in a good mood."

"Then, you'd better read it drinking some Muscadine," Meffre replied.

November's dampness and chill came in a snap, but it was endurable. The hurricane did indeed stir up the bayou and lake and even the swamps. Fish, crabs, and crawfish were plentiful that fall, everyone making more money than they imagined.

Even Julien made money, which spared him from working extra carpentry jobs. He claimed he had enough money to save a little. To pick at him, Aunt Velma asked about his painting his house. He responded, "Why waste paint?"

Charmaine and Aunt Velma enjoyed sewing towels, napkins, and table clothes to sell in the store. On a dreary and chilly Friday afternoon, they left Sacred Heart, after delivering altar clothes, and went to the store to set up a display of Thanksgiving napkins Meffre thought would sell well. As usual, they entered through the storeroom, and to their surprise, they spotted Mary Eaton making a long-distance phone call. Aunt Velma could not believe that any Eaton would come to the store. From behind the heavy timbered shelves, they tried to hear the conversation. Through muffled chatter, Charmaine heard Mary say, "I know, Carl—the sheriff told Reginald." Carl's response had to be unpleasant. Mary's cheeks swelled with impatience and she bade Carl a loud "goodbye." Aunt Velma and Charmaine retreated to the storeroom, and Mary summoned Lucien to pay for her call. Lucien asked whether she would like to buy fresh trout, and she responded that she only shopped for food in Slidell. She thanked him with a snarl and left, yelling at her stable boy.

Charmaine and Aunt Velma told Lucien what they heard, and he confirmed that the call was made to Colfax. "She couldn't hide anything," he said dispassionately. "I have to ask the operator for the charge amount, and she tells me the destination and price for the last placed call. No secrets. She wanted me to know she was talking to Carl Keller."

News spread quickly about this episode, and everyone remained cautious. Lucien and Meffre, especially, became deliberate about their comings and goings. Ossi alerted everyone that no one should go anywhere alone until he figured out what might be going on. Even a long-distance call to Reynaud produced no news. Although Ossi continued to search for clues, he uncovered nothing.

+ + +

A cold Louisiana winter could blink itself into a warm day overnight. At the beginning of December, Pichon sweated heavily as he knocked on Meffre's kitchen door. When Meffre opened the door, Pichon pushed a capped bottle of Julien's homebrew into his chest. He held another bottle for himself and searched around the kitchen for something to open the beer. Meffre said, "I'm glad your father-in-law invested in a bottle capper. I used to get a big gallon bottle from him, and it would go flat before we'd drink it all. Unless you came around. I guess we ought to sell openers at the store."

Pichon found an ice pick and opened their beers. He talked about how Julien always tried to do everything he could for Keb. After several swigs, he turned serious and asked, "Much as you love Keb, you ever gonna marry and have children?"

"Don't think that dog will hunt, and you don't either. Anyway, I got other plans. Here, I always feel like a rabbit running from hounds. I need to be somewhere else." Meffre drank a long swallow and looked to the grove. "I'm planning to move north like so many folks."

Pichon knew about these plans from Femme. He also knew that Meffre was being secretive and felt guilty about baiting him. "Wherever you go and whatever you decide, we're your family. Come, go, do as you please, but always remember your family. Charmaine and Keb love you. She might not say a lot, but she constantly surprises me. She insisted I teach her to shoot my shotgun in case I was at work and someone came on the property. She's not the girl I married any more than you're that kid that came here all cut up. What's the same is we're family. Remember that."

The awkwardness of this frank conversation ran in full capacity until Pichon and Meffre knew that there was little else to say. The rest resided in what they felt, which, between men, often lived better unsaid. Pichon rescued the conversation with the reason for his visit. "I hear there were two lynchings in Slidell last week. What you see in the newspaper always makes it seem like black people have done so much wrong that the only way to deal with us is a rope. I'm sick of it. Been sick of it since Percie. Mama's been sick of it since Daddy was lynched. But we go on. We're meeting at the sawmill tonight. I'll see you then. Better go check on your nephew."

Meffre was glad for this conversation. He pulled out the valise and traced station stops on the Illinois Central railway line from New Orleans to Chicago. Someone riding in a full gallop from Lake

Road to Yana Place's dirt road interrupted his study. It was dusk dark, but he could make out, from the draping of his cassock, that it was Father Lorquette. The priest got off his horse, completely exasperated. He grabbed Meffre by the shoulders and cried, "Carl Keller is in Mandeville. Reginald told him he saw you and Lucien digging in the pecan grove. He and Todd were drunk down at Mudbug's and told Pike that you found money. Seems Keller is here to collect. These are sick, demented people. They're telling everyone that you and Lucien have crossed a line worse than stealing money. Meffre, they're coming after you. Sheriff Blake told Ossi and is on his way to tell Papa Luc."

Meffre grimaced at the mention of the sheriff. Father sensed his discomfiture and said loudly and firmly, "Listen, Meffre! I baptized you and buried Percie. You must trust me. I trust the sheriff because we have no choice." Father's eyes had turned glossy as if some unendurable grief had broken his soul.

Receiving this information incited confusion and suspicion about the sheriff. Meffre was paralyzed and could not tell him that Pichon had just left and that there was a meeting at the sawmill later. He thanked Father and shook his hand. He needed to get to the sawmill immediately. Father Lorquette blessed him and fled Yana Place.

Meffre rode with a small lantern along the footpath to the sawmill. He could feel the knife Ossi had given him dangling at his side. He was calm and fearless, cautious and attentive. When he reached the sawmill, he found everyone in the stable behind the office. There was tension in their expressions. Lucien walked straight to him, grabbed the lantern, and guided him out to the office porch. A charred and smoldering cross, as tall as they were, stood there like something forced into deliberate evil. Lucien put his arm over Meffre's shoulder and turned him away. He held him firmly and said, "Let's get back to the meeting, making plans."

When they returned to the stable, they found Ossi pointing to a spot on the ground where he had drawn a map. Ossi smiled at Meffre and Lucien, and said to everyone, "That cross is meant to shake our spirits, and this little map is how we fight back. We must have a plan to pick them off, one by one, so that we can hide them. If someone comes after us, we take him to this place we call Iti. Iti is the lone longleaf pine that Pichon and Charmaine always talk about on Guinea Beach. Julien, Femme, Charmaine, and Aunt Velma know all about this. When we leave someone at Iti, Julien will find them and keep them there in his shed till I take them to a hiding place in Abita Springs. This is our plan so no one gets hurt. It can all change quickly if we're forced to fight."

With the mention of the longleaf pine, Meffre and Lucien looked knowingly at each other. Pichon was moved and proud of Julien's involvement and for the selection of his love tree as Iti. Papa Luc agreed with the plan but feared any one of them could be followed. Ossi said that he would teach everyone a different way to get to Iti through the woods or using the bayou. Meffre came forward and explained what Father Lorquette had told him.

Papa Luc said that Sheriff Blake had come to warn him about Keller. He grew angry and claimed that this explained the cross on his property. He believed that Meffre was no longer safe in Lacombe. It would not be long before he would have to leave to save his life. For the first time, he stuttered through an admission that he agreed with Father Lorquette that they had to risk trusting the sheriff. Still, he reminded them that Keller paid the sheriff, and no one should forget that. Speculating that the sheriff could be meddling in Keller's business too, he cautioned them to be careful what they said to him. He instructed them to spread the news about the cross-burning. "It's not safe for Meffre to be alone. Lucien ought to move to the pecan grove and stay with him. If we follow Ossi's plan, we might be able to control this."

Pichon looked around at the group and said slowly, "I take Meffre as a brother. I'll check in on him day and night. Just keep some Muscadine wine ready." They laughed, and Lucien suggested that they drink some brandy.

The Upside-Down Tree

TIGHTLY BUTTONED IN a winter coat, Carl smoked and waited in the Fontainebleau Hotel's lobby for Sheriff Blake and Reginald Eaton. He thought about the eighty-acre pecan tree farm his family owned in Covington. The business was lucrative: they sold and shipped trees, by train or steamboat, all over the South. His family had become wealthy in Covington, but his mother detested being uprooted from Colfax origins. They maintained the pecan business but moved back to Colfax the year Carl was born. After his parents died, he managed the business and enjoyed strong profits. It was from this property that he sold Papa Luc the trees Kebbi had planted. These reminiscences disquieted him because freeing slaves lessened his profits and power. What was once a norm became a battle prize.

A black waiter came to offer drinks, which snatched Carl from his musings. He ordered a whiskey and could see, through large double windows, a carriage wheeling up Lakeshore Drive. He also requested a bottle of whiskey and two glasses in a private salon with a small fireplace.

Sheriff Blake climbed the steps with a grimace, and Reginald followed lackey-like, red faced, and puffing. The sheriff greeted Carl with a limp handshake. "Good place to meet, away from that stupid priest and other spies. Got the priest in my palm. For him, I'm the law that's gonna keep the peace. I'll do it, for you, by finishing your fight with those niggers."

Sheriff Blake's vacillation between fighting blacks and keeping the peace unnerved Carl and inspired mistrust. He poured whiskey and stood up to crack his neck and back. He saw idiots before him, but miles of separation forced his dependence. "How was the cross-burning?"

Reginald responded eagerly. "We set it on Coulon's property so him and his ginny-woman son could see we're serious. Passed by there early this morning. Cross was gone. Nigger lovers got the message."

Sheriff Blake guzzled his whiskey in one loud swallow. He scratched mud from his boot onto the salon's fake Persian rug and poured another whiskey. "They ain't afraid of crosses. They bold enough to build and run a store in the middle of town. Rubbing it in our faces. Making so much money, they ain't afraid of nothing. They know what regulators are doing before y'all do. Hell, you lynched one of them, and they got stronger! *Lynchings* ain't scaring them. They got guns, ammunition, knives, and transportation. Worse, niggers got help from peckerwoods like those Coulons. Catholics too! Even looks like freejacks are helping. Julien Broyard's selling shit down at that store. Used to be Créoles didn't mix with niggers. Now they marry." Reginald nodded his dumb assent to the sheriff's pronouncements.

This report drew neither wince nor whimper from Carl. His back hurt, and the whiskey was no remedy. His slackened cheeks lacked color, and his eyes were a dirty yellow. He rolled another cigarette and listened in disgust. It surfaced quickly that the sheriff had convinced Reginald and his regulators to avoid Lacombe, which had caused enormous friction. The sheriff argued that the fight must happen at the right time with a solid plan. Because many people were involved, just killing Meffre would not solve problems or get Carl's money back. Percie's killing exemplified the regulators' incompetence and propensity for failure. He insisted that the law needed to control the outcome. Reginald puffed up in resentment, and Carl's hostility erupted. He faced the sheriff and said emphatically, "I paid you! Now you admit you're doing nothing? Either you return my money or do better than you did with Hébert's mess. That young nigger's the thief his daddy was. Sad when the law protects the lawless. Time he pays with his neck."

Sheriff Blake took his hat off and wiped sweat. He sneezed, blew his nose, swigged down whiskey, put his hat back on, and yanked at his crotch. "It's fucking unfair to say I did nothing. *Your* Hébert planned a lot of shit, but I did damn near everything. *I* moved that boy from Lacombe to Mandeville. Hell, Myrtle never knew *I* hid the boy in a skiff under her place. That's how *I* can get things done.

I kept the boy alive as collateral to get your money back. Reginald's jackasses killed him. *Lynching is against the fucking federal law!* Courts are changing too. Whites are getting caught and tried. Niggers are revolting." The sheriff's anger hid dexterously his true motive of preventing Percie's death and sustaining peace. He sensed Carl's impatience. "I got a wife and seven children. I got to do this *my* way. Can't be obvious. Associating with regulators was a bad idea. *You* wanted that. Maybe it worked in Colfax; it won't work here. These people are tight as virgin pussy." The sheriff filled his glass, but nervousness spilled his liquor. *I've said too much. Carl's in knots.*

Carl nodded patiently during an extended accusatory argument between the sheriff and Reginald. When he had heard enough, he said, "Blake, thanks for all you did. Seems I've put you in a delicate position. Do what you can. Patience's a fault of mine. But I want my money *or* that black bastard dead. Good afternoon, gentlemen." When they left, Carl went to the front desk, pulled his pants up, and ordered a horse for seven the next morning. He then sent a telegram to Reginald's home.

By seven thirty the next morning, Carl had dressed warmly, eaten a hardy breakfast, and was on his way to Lacombe. He had not taken this ride since visiting Hébert, but once he passed Lakeshore Drive leaving Mandeville, he remembered the landscape's density. The roadsides were lined with oaks, magnolias, and longleaf pines. He felt as if the trees were encroaching enemies. Since that tree had burned when Avery Barjone asked it to, he had harbored a distaste for trees. Burning trees populated his nightmares, and selling trees was far better than sitting in their shade. He only appreciated branches sturdy enough for lynching.

Eshu and Yemanja haunted Carl; they instigated trees into easy swaying and spiteful, cold breezes. The road was busier than he imagined. Two large rigs desperately tried to avoid holes and puddles. Choctaws and blacks lumbered by with huge loads on their pushcarts and wagons. With experienced drivers, stagecoaches drove by with speed. Several hired carriages, with decorated horses, managed to stand out as signs of class and luxury. There were many lone riders, who avoided the traffic that inevitably spooked their horses. The more adept simply steered horses off the rode while freighted rigs rolled by. He was disgusted most, however, with how the so-called natural beauty suffocated him. He envisioned trees falling everywhere to be used as timber and imagined a hurricane or drought that would wipe away all loathsome fanning palmettos. He passed Big Branch's swampy areas, with mossy cypresses growing straight through tall grasses and, for these, he visualized their rotting till they fell. When he reached Lacombe, he had had enough harrowing visions and yearned for barren land. Although anxious to see Lacombe Seafood and Produce, he went directly to the Eaton's.

Their arrogance was underscored by living on up-the-bayou property, which sat just above the road that led to Slidell. Their house, however, contradicted and mocked their pride. Painted green with white trim, its ordinariness was an intrusion to the thick pines surrounding it. Reginald worked for a rail freight company that cut lumber and shipped logs. When trains rumbled in and out of Lacombe, he supervised loading and unloading timber. Mary was proud that her cooking made Reginald and Todd enviably strong and tough. They owned an unearned and unshared boast for being a powerful family in town.

As Carl approached, he despised their awkward posturing on the porch. He knew that they beamed because he had chosen them as confidants and operatives over the sheriff. Grinning, Reginald greeted Carl and escorted him into the house where Mary had prepared fried, fat-lined pork chops, a withering cucumber salad, mashed potatoes laced with underdone onions, and butter-drenched hard biscuits. She served dutifully and then searched for compliments by apologizing for food cooked on a new gas stove. To accomplish his goals, Carl would have to praise and cuddle the Eatons. He fancied rescued money or a dead Meffre Barjone as more important than integrity or pride. He complimented Mary with such a sideshow that she blushed.

After lunch, Carl was direct. He pulled three bills from his jacket pocket. Reginald eyed the fives. Mary knew her part in the scene required an exit. She collected dishes and moved to the kitchen to listen. Carl rolled a cigarette and tapped it vigorously before lighting. He leaned forward and said sternly, "I need you to do three things. Today is Wednesday. Tonight, burn a cross in front of their store. Shoot out all the windows Thursday night till there's fish in the road. Friday night, torture that Barjone bastard till you get my money. If you can't, let his ass swing and burn on a tree near that store. Here's my word in cash. I'll pay you double that when it's done."

Reginald's protruding gut could not contain the pride that bloated him. He imagined himself leading the charge against those stealing power from whites. It escaped him that Carl could not care less for the welfare of Lacombe whites. Carl was ready to go, but Reginald offered, "My son Todd's here." On cue, Mary ushered him in. Dressed in overalls and a homemade, checkered shirt, he was a caricature of the clumsy simpleton and brute. "He's a first-class regulator, watching those Coulons. We don't mix with niggers except down at that nigger-loving Catholic church. We ain't Catholic, but Mary's got to pray somewhere. Really, she goes there to spy. Eatons stand with you." Carl did not respond or even look at Todd. Instead, he darted to a hanging rack to fetch his coat.

Reginald read Carl's disinterest with spite. "Go see that store: electric lights inside and out, toilets for customers, window curtains, and flowers all over. They even got produce shipments coming on my lumber trains." Todd and Mary stood silent and useless.

Carl could not abide this patronizing. Yet, too many futile exchanges with the savvy and duplicitous sheriff convinced him that Reginald was his last resort for revenge. He pretended earnestness: "Where's this store?"

"You passed it coming here. The big place right in the triangle—painted white and surrounded by three old oaks. Directly across from Mudbug's. Todd can show you."

Carl faked deliberating, put on his coat, and lied that he remembered the store. He thanked them for lunch and kissed Mary's cheek, which titillated her and annoyed Reginald. "I leave Thursday from New Orleans for Memphis. I want to take the Louisville-New Orleans line. I hear it's a comfortable train. Let me know your success by telephone. Here's the number where I'll be staying in Memphis. Of course. say *nothing* about this to Blake." After Carl left, Reginald immediately rode over to Sheriff Blake's house and enlisted help *only* with Friday night's lynching. He promised the sheriff "good money" if the law exonerated all regulators and made the lynching fade away quickly. Sheriff Blake agreed readily.

+ + +

Fate escorted him as he crossed the bayou and happened upon Mudbug's. Carl was glad to be rid of the Eatons and decided that, on his return to Mandeville, he would stop at the store to assess what his money had bought. He blithely confessed to his horse that now he needed whiskey to wash out Mary's food.

Pike was behind the bar and stepped constantly on and off a stool to grab everything he could not reach. When Carl walked in, he was swiping a smudged glass from a shelf above him. Carl immediately interpreted the name Mudbug: everything was grimy, including Pike. As he approached the bar, Pike showed hospitality by wiping a clean space for Carl with a dirty dishrag. He then used the same rag to clean the glass he planted in front of him. In his version of politeness, he asked, "What would the gentleman like?"

Carl laughed and responded loudly, "I'd like a clean glass from that upper shelf with as much whiskey as it'll hold." He muttered, "Place is muddy as crawfish." He threw his coat across a bar stool and stood, constantly pulling up pants that had never slipped.

Pike came over with the whiskey. "Oh! I see. Another prissy tourist. Locals don't care *what* they drink out of, but I'll treat you better."

Carl downed several whiskeys and proffered concocted examples predicting how blacks would ruin the country. He made Pike suspicious when he begged his perspective on Lacombe Seafood and Produce. Pike said, "Coulons seem to be good Catholics. They give plenty money to the church. Once a year, me and Father Lorquette make a breakfast for poor niggers. I don't like it, but I do it for Father. Coulon's store got more folks coming in *here*. I like that."

Carl pressed Pike about who ran the store. He simply added, "Coulon's son runs it. Gossip has it that young Coulon's sharing the business with niggers." Pike snarled, trying to avoid the stranger's questions.

Prodded by whiskey, Carl seized on Pike's observation. His tongue was looser, his demeanor less rigid. "Well, like I said, blacks are taking over. Ropes, chains, and fire can stop that shit. I got folks to prove it right around here. Soon."

Pike was perturbed but agreed. He escaped with a whiskey bottle to refresh drinks for other patrons. This gave him time to think about what he might say to entice the prissy man to say more. Back behind the bar, he stood on his step stool and said, "Listen, Mr. Pretty Suit. I ain't no nigger lover, but I don't like no lynchings either. Catholic Church don't allow it."

At this point, Carl could no longer manage what the whiskey would not dull. He shouted, "Fuck Catholics," grabbed his coat, paid Pike double the bill, and left. Pike bowed over the bar, sick to his stomach. The bar emptied after he told his customers he was sick and had to close early. He locked Mudbug and headed for Sacred Heart.

With fate guiding him again, Carl rode across the street to Lacombe Seafood and Produce. Three large oaks looked on protectively while he tied the horse to a painted hitching post and surveyed the building. It disturbed him that it was quite attractive. Before he could get inside, the three oaks mustered a frigid breeze that pierced his bones. He shuddered but marched up the steps and met Lucien. He tipped his hat when Lucien greeted him: "If I can help, just call on me." *Got to be Coulon's son. Barjone's bastard can't be far.* He walked down the aisles, stopping periodically to handle peaches and pears. He could hear a child's laughter.

Pichon promised Meffre and Keb that they could spend Wednesdays together. They were playing a favorite fight game on the back porch. He punched in Meffre's direction trying to connect with his open palms, which were in constant motion. Keb was smart and quick, and he hit much more than Meffre anticipated. Any smack incited shrill laughter that Carl heard as he ambled light headedly through the store. Impressed with the store's variety, he grew angry. He walked back to the counter and asked bitterly, "A fine store like this and you don't have Ponchatoula winter melons?"

"Yes sir, indeed we do. They came in dirty on the afternoon train. Meffre just finished washing them." Lucien skirted the counter and called Meffre. After quite a bit of noise, Meffre appeared with two cleaned and shiny green melons. Keb ran beside him begging for candy.

When Carl's and Meffre's eyes met, Eshu sped through everything electrical, sparking hot energy in Meffre and icy stasis in Carl. Meffre heard only, *North*, and dropped the melons on the counter. In contempt for Carl, he unscrewed the candy jar unhurriedly and handed a treat to Keb. "You first, little man. This is for being a *good* boy."

Carl glared at Lucien. "I don't want melon after niggers pick over them!"

Carl's tone was a provocation. Keb held his candy in one fist and ran up to Carl and punched him soundly in the leg with the other. Meffre laughed and called out, "Kebbi!" He pulled the boy away, but his eyes told Carl not to venture a move. Lucien hopped over the counter to usher Carl out. He said irately, "Sir, you'd better leave now!"

Carl slurred his drunken anger at Meffre. "Kebbi? Well, this'll be the last time you save his black ass—like your daddy tried to save yours." He headed for the door, but before he left, he looked at Lucien and barked sarcastically, "Your uncle Hébert was as worthless as he was fat. Somebody did us a favor by burning his sloppy ass." Carl left chilled by an invasion of freezing air on his face.

Meffre held Keb close and said, "That's Carl Keller, Lucien. Call Papa Luc!"

Aunt Velma answered the telephone and promised to tell Papa Luc to alert everyone. They hurried to close the store even with customers trying to get in. They emptied the safe, locked the storm shutters, and bolted the front door. Meffre pulled the buckboard to the front with Keb sitting close. Lucien came out carrying a portfolio and a moneybag and jumped into the buckboard and pushed himself behind Meffre. They rode past Mudbug's and onto Lake Road. Meffre saw Sheriff Blake riding toward them with Pike running besides, waving frenetically, panting, and sweating. He shouted to Lucien and Meffre, "Father said for y'all to go Femme's. The Choctaw is gonna meet you. Go!" Sheriff Blake nodded in agreement.

A cross, eight feet tall, burned that night in front of Lacombe Seafood and Produce. Ossi prohibited its removal. Thursday night, the storm shutters were no protection for what guns unloaded on the store: all windows riddled with lead. Again, Ossi instructed no response.

Friday morning, Lucien and Meffre hid in Julien's rig under a tarp. Femme climbed into the seat, holding a lantern. Julien smiled and fastened the lantern to the front of the rig. They left Ossi, Pichon, and Papa Luc at Femme's house drinking coffee and planning. A bit past nine, they arrived at Nito's in Abita Springs. Lucien and Meffre held each other for the entire trip, rehearsing their plans. When the rig stopped, Meffre got out and Lucien stayed. Few words were spoken; everyone knew what to do. Meffre said his goodbyes in tears and went with Nito.

Julien drove the rig to Mandeville's steamboat port, from where Lucien took the steamer to New Orleans. He went directly to Canal-Louisiana Bank and Trust and withdrew their money in bank notes and cash. He then went to Reynaud's apartment to wait for the next Illinois Central to Chicago through Hammond.

The next morning, Nito fed Meffre and informed him they would have to leave for Hammond. Although sad, Meffre talked to Nito about Lucien. He enjoyed being honest. Nito smiled and called out, "Chukfi." He said to Meffre, "When he first came to live with me, he said that I should name him something that I really loved." Nito had an elegant smile. "I call him Chukfi because there's nothing better than rabbit." They all laughed, and Meffre's sadness moved on. Chukfi carried a basket and told Meffre that he would have to sit on the train where there would be no food. He told him to buy apples or swipe them from parked freight cars.

Nito sat next to Meffre, and Chukfi drove the small rig. For the entire trip, Nito told stories about how trees are protectors. Meffre told his story about love under the branches of the huge longleaf pine. Nito said, "That pine will remember."

+ + +

When they met at the Hammond train station, Meffre left the segregated car and ran to Lucien without regard for appalled onlookers. He carried a small bag as a gift: apples, freshly pinched. "You'll have to wash them again," he said, "and don't forget." At the many stations from Hammond to Chicago, they found ways to meet. When they reached Cairo, they were bold enough to go to the dining car kitchen, extremely late, for a dinner Lucien arranged with the black porters. Although the porters' stares were piercing—clearly, they were expecting a female guest—they could not dwell on the scene with anything more than sniggling. To these black men, all that appeared before them, day to day, defined surprises they cherished or despised. What they witnessed in Meffre and Lucien was just that day's surprise. They pocketed the ten-cent tip that was far more important.

+ + +

That Friday night, as Meffre and Lucien fled to Chicago, Reginald and his regulators set out to execute Carl's final demand. Four regulators prepared the largest oak behind the store while Reginald acted alone to handle Meffre. He tasted glory, and burgeoning hubris made certain Meffre's torture and assured delivery of Carl's money. He approached Yana Place and found the house dim with a lone shadow playing in the kitchen. He wanted to be sure that Meffre was alone. He dismounted and hugged the house all the way to the back steps. He heard pacing and crawled up the porch steps to listen before he stood and drew his gun. When he heard whistling and dance-like shuffling, he barged in with the full force of his weight. He steadied himself and faced Pichon, who, with his hands up, stood with an odd welcoming smile. Reginald pointed his pistol and demanded furiously, "Where's your thieving nigger friend? You don't talk, I'll string you up like I did your brother."

Ossi appeared magically behind Reginald and startled him by slamming his gun across the floor, twisting his arm behind him, and forcing a sharp cane knife under his chin. Papa Luc broke out of the shadows with a drawn pistol. He cocked it and aimed the barrel at Reginald's forehead. Reginald could not focus until Pichon screamed, "He admitted he killed Percie. The sheriff's got to know!"

Papa Luc answered, "I'll go to Sheriff Blake right now. Y'all take care of him."

Ossi drove Reginald to his knees as the cane knife drew a trickle of blood. They tied his hands behind him, blindfolded and gagged him, and hoisted him into Pichon's buckboard. An unassailable silence accompanied them to Guinea Beach until Ossi said smugly, "Tonight, Iti."

✝ ✝ ✝

Sheriff Blake and his deputies secured their saddles with guns just outside his barn. Papa Luc rode up to them and reported, "We caught Reginald at Meffre's house. He confessed to killing Percie. Ossi and Pichon have him. Looks like you got work to do with a lynch mob at the store. They're working out Carl's plan." He tipped his hat and rode away.

✝ ✝ ✝

With two lanterns at his feet, Reginald, tied tightly to the longleaf pine, prayed his regulators would appear. Ossi spoke first, wielding the cane knife. "You chose punishment because you won't stop killing. You've turned unnatural and against the earth. There will be a storm tonight worse than the one in your soul."

Eshu and Yemanja shook the pine branches above Reginald's head. He could not move. Even positioning his head, from side to side, was painful. Ossi nodded to Pichon, who picked up his lanterns

229

and left for Julien's. Ossi looked at the moon mullioned by clouds. Reginald felt the tree's life through its bark. It meant more than timber now, and he sensed a confusing strange affinity to it. He cussed and railed incessantly, his will refusing to subside or give in to his fate.

Ossi raised his lantern slightly. "It's peaceful here. There's a rabbit eating grass. He's not used to our smell. He'll keep eating, knowing he can outrun us. If we share space, he won't be afraid or run. If we want to eat him, we'll have to catch him. It's a fair natural fight. Trees fight hard, but they don't win against unnatural weapons—your saws. You're close to that tree now. Ask forgiveness. Ask Percie's forgiveness too."

Reginald cussed and spat blood as Ossi took his lantern and walked to Julien's. The rain started to fall, and Yemanja opened wide her white-and-blue gown to engender pouring outbursts. Eshu sent flashes of weak lightning high across the sky. He perched atop the pine looking down on Reginald, laughing in puffs that the prisoner thought was wind. As he twisted himself against the pine's bark, his back started to ache and bleed. He cried out, and the rabbit looked up then returned to foraging. Reginald thought of Mary, who had convinced him to become a regulator. He hated her now for it, for letting Carl kiss her, for being fat, and for not giving him a daughter. He regretted not marrying Myrtle. With each scattered thought, the pine swelled in a pulse that tightened the rope. Reginald screamed to his only audience, a disinterested hungry rabbit.

✝ ✝ ✝

Aunt Velma cleared the dining room table in an odd silence. She was sullen after Papa Luc returned with news of Reginald's capture and threats of a lynch mob; she could not shake her haunting worrisome past. Papa Luc held her and begged playfully, "Sing something jazzy."

"I can't stop thinking about what's going on. Fighting fire with fire just gets us all burnt. Maybe talking to them—"

"I tried talking to the ones I trust. Father and Sheriff Blake did too. It's hard to stop them from hating when they think they can make money off it. Let's pray we've seen the worst." He saw that this did not appease her. He put a Buddy Bolden record on the gramophone and clapped to the beat. This made her smile. She stopped her sweeping periodically to shake in front of him while he sipped whiskey and shook his head. His feet tapping under the table lightened her mood. When she teased him about eating two bowls of shrimp bisque, he teased her about the cayenne pepper working on his old stomach. Papa Luc loved this banter and thought it was meant to be this way—easy to love those who loved him.

After two more whiskeys, more Buddy Bolden, and a lot of Aunt Velma's dancing, Papa Luc begged her sit on his lap, and she was glad to accommodate. He held her around her waist and asked, "Did Femme ever tell you a secret about me?"

"We share lots of secrets. None *just* about you."

"Well, for years, she's been holding it over my head. I'm going to ruin it for her. Guess what: I'm a freejack!"

She jumped up. "Man, what the hell you saying?"

"I mean my people were freejacks from the time of the Battle of New Orleans. We've been hiding our colored blood for a long time. I told Femme's daddy; she's known for years."

"Oh! No! Stop! Now listen. All my life, I dodged colored men. They boss you. Take your money and youth. Once they get half-a-pocket of money, they won't work even if they ain't got enough shit to stink up outhouses. You could've kept your secret!"

Papa Luc bent over in laughter to counter Velma's feigned snit. He clapped to the jazz beat and begged, "Come on, Velma, dance with this old colored man." He got up and swirled her around. She held him close and thought, *No wonder he's always on our side.*

+ + +

When Ossi reached Julien's house, he did not knock. He just walked in smiling. Keb was running through the living room with a half-eaten praline. Pichon and Julien were drinking homebrew and lying about who trapped the most rabbits in one day. Charmaine, cleaning the kitchen, complained about how hard it was to raise a spoiled child. They all waited for Ossi to speak. He said, "I think I'll drink some beer, please."

Charmaine went to the icebox and handed the beer to Pichon. "Where's your manners?"

To relieve their anxiety, Ossi said, "Nobody needs to go back to Iti tonight. Papa Luc went to Sheriff Blake, who must've stopped the regulators like he promised. No one came for Reginald. Let this wintry storm save Reginald's soul or punish him."

Keb begged Ossi to hold him and fell asleep in his lap. Charmaine pricked her finger on a knife she was drying. Pichon bandaged the cut while she looked at Keb in Ossi's arms and cried loudly. "I'm so afraid my baby won't be safe growing up here. We can't keep fighting." She sobbed into Pichon's shoulder while Julien tried to console her. They passed the next hour talking awkwardly about reopening the store, which Julien thought might bring people together and invite healing.

When the wind started to howl, Ossi left to watch its violent judgment. The rain fell like glass blades, and he reached Reginald just before the wind cracked a branch off just above his head. He eyed the lantern in Ossi's hand and screeched, "Cut me off this fucking tree, you filthy bastard. I'm white. Did you forget what they'll do to y'all?"

Ossi walked closer to Reginald and noticed blood coloring his head and back. "You're not listening to this tree. It's fighting you because you're destroying its peace."

"Fuck trees. Cut me loose, and I'll get the sheriff to go easy on your ass."

Ossi grinned. "Sheriff Blake? Trusting *him* put you here. He wants peace. You want money and killing. Tonight, you get punished. Forget money." He led his horse away from the lone pine. Eshu popped a loud streak of fired lightning straight into the ground next to Reginald. Then he swam through the tree energizing its sap into a fever, which burned Reginald and forced him to babble. Yemanja called a thick downpour to drench the entire scene with water, which mixed with blood and made a path to the bayou.

Ossi moved still farther away. The storm's sway was vengeful and exacting. It ripped here and tore there, but when it focused on its mission, it plunged into rage and surged with peels of rain and deafening thunder blasts. This storm would be remembered, but the orishas united to mark the spot forever in memory through story. Reginald's head bobbed and fell to his chest; his every attempt to look skyward failed.

Ossi witnessed the storm of all storms rain down on Lacombe a cleansing Yemanja fixed for permanence. The majestic longleaf pine, where love had grown protected by its branches, swayed to a bending. Eshu pulled one side of the tree. Then, in a flash, he pulled the other. Reginald raised his head, opened his eyes, and fire blinded him. Eshu held fast to the largest branches until a vicious and violent bolt pierced the tree's middle. Its force cut apart the captive's ropes and split his skull. He fell, burning hellishly as his panicked spirit drifted haphazardly away. Ossi left in a very slow trot to notify Pichon (in private on Julien's porch), the sheriff, and Papa Luc.

The huge, majestic pine looked as if the fatal split had taken its life. Eshu left it to die, but Yemanja stood over it and engendered life again through the rain. That perfect, straight tree succumbed to bending in the most bizarre posture nature would allow. Its branches were forced to transform into roots, shooting downward like spikes to the ground. The pine's soul seed, borne to nurture love, lost its strength, making it, once again, a weak sapling. Spring after spring, with some hope to be a tree again, it sprouted thick, green branches, with long pine needles, downward where the roots should have been. Though life returned, it bore a death mark.

It took Yemanja a long and wet spring two years later to urge green shoots to look upward on the bare branches. Old branches turned gray and ossified. New branches raised their needled arms to the sky. In two more years, the old bent branches turned yet a darker gray and looked like roots all around the new growth. As children passed across the squeaky sand to throw themselves off the hanging rope into the bayou, one would invariably say, "Look at that upside-down tree!"

Thus, with a single shot of unregulated electricity, the storm pounded the lone longleaf pine and recreated it into a trophy that marked the spot where Pichon and Charmaine had loved to create Keb, where Meffre and Lucien dared to express their love, and where Reginald lost his chance for natural salvation.

✝ ✝ ✝

Femme waited for Ossi to come home with news and was full of remorse for the actions they were compelled to take. Although she enjoyed time alone, she spent it ruminating on whether the lynchings would end or whether they had made the situation worse. She hoped for a future without strife. At the oratory, she sprinkled her hands with Yemanja's water and remembered Meffre's request that Ossi work the pecan grove. He and Lucien might visit one day but living in Chicago meant she would miss them for a long time. Meffre had told her to visit Yana Place to listen to the grove talking.

He instructed, "Start by finding a special tree. Sit and rest and listen. Don't just hear—*listen.* The trees will guide you." She then remembered Percie's smile and was deeply saddened until Yemanja inspirited her with chatter that led to laughter about Keb.

Eshu blew a breeze of drowsy sleep across Femme's yard, and the animals rested undisturbed as Ossi walked his horse into the barn. He was tired and felt dirtied by the night's work. As he closed the barn door, Yemanja delivered a tender rain to wash his face, hands, and even the dirt from his shoes. His tiredness washed away as well, and with the night's ugly past behind him, he headed inside. Eshu accompanied him—two warriors finding home as its own reward. Without a sound, he entered with outstretched arms. Femme filled his embrace with more love than he imagined the South could hold. "When they take the train back home, it'll be safer than when they left." His presence soothed her and temporarily eased her angst about the future.

✝ ✝ ✝

In the last week of December, three days after a debilitated Carl had returned from Memphis with pneumonia, his butler lost hope for improvement. One warm morning, a special postal clerk delivered a postage-due letter from Mary Eaton. Carl winced and directed the butler to read it. The officious butler refused to honor the Eatons with a verbatim reading of the four-page letter; instead, he summarized "her foolishness" to what was minimally disturbing. She reported that the sheriff betrayed her by posting a warrant for Reginald's arrest. She included a brash warning that the butler was obliged to read: "My husband ran off. My son, Todd, has tried repeatedly to contact you in Memphis and Colfax to collect the payment balance for services rendered. If the money is not sent at once by Western Union, Todd will arrive in Colfax, to collect."

Laid flat and staring at the ceiling, Carl gasped and nearly choked trying to suppress laughter. From Lacombe to Memphis and to Colfax, he had carried a persistent piercing chill that the day's warmth could not assuage. The butler headed to the fireplace to dispose of the Eaton rant, when Carl groaned hoarsely, "What else?"

"A *New Orleans Bee* clipping. More nonsense, sir."

"Read."

The butler stood closer to him, resenting all that had been foisted upon them, and read the clipping Sheriff Blake had reported:

December 14, 1906. Today a nigger was hung in St. Tammany Parish in the up-the-bayou section of Lacombe. Never tried or juried to the crime of unnatural acts, the nigger was hung from the tree nearest to his crime. The nigger was witnessed forcing Lucien Coulon, Jr. into sodomy. The first time the nigger was hung, he didn't die. He was dropped again to ensure the deserved death. Nature responded by burning the nigger past recognition with lightning. Lucien Coulon, Jr. has not been seen since. Reginald Eaton disappeared and is a suspected lawless regulator responsible for the unlawful hanging.

In a jittery but definitive move, the butler agitated the fire with the balled-up letter and clipping. Carl coughed blood into his handkerchief and mustered a whisper: "Finally, justice. Kebbi's bastard is dead. They can't trace that to me. If an Eaton steps on my property, tell the groundskeeper to put a bullet in his head. Dumb as stumps."

Yemanja's Baptizing Sermon

I
N THE ARMS OF a whimsical and ambivalent peace, the next year's passing was restive *and* quick. Draped in a weird silence, Lacombe tried to heal only to relapse and fester. Folks moved by the half-ruined Seafood and Produce Store as if it were a tombstone *or* a victory monument. No one was sure whether peace would hold tight or crack open. Though Lacombe was spared violence during this time, there were still ominous lynching reports to the north and south. Even when Sacred Heart Church was packed and lively, folks gathered and segregated themselves as if avoiding a looming pestilence. Even so, the past's venomous vengeance could not win out over the shame both sides tried unsuccessfully to hide. Only Eshu buzzed with energy and enjoyed this dangerous ambivalence.

With the impetus of Femme's nagging prayers, the time came for Yemanja to do a heavenly dance. She gathered dark clouds and filled them with holy water. For three weeks, she paraded them over Lacombe, the darkest over Sacred Heart Church. The folds of her blue gown opened and closed and presaged rain's arrival. The time, however, was not right for baptizing. Since Reginald's death, Femme had prayed for a way to heal and cure Lacombe souls, including hers, from the deep-seated and malignant hatred. Though the response was slow, Yemanja heard.

One chilly night, Ossi held her close and noticed her tears. He turned on his side to face her. "You pray to Yemanja more now," he said and kissed her forehead. She was a bit surprised and wondered if he knew the reason. He wiped her tears. "Why?"

Such questions strengthen bonds, galvanizing how lovers know each other more deeply than their words. She said weakly, "For forgiveness and for peace to last."

He kissed her lips gently and made her smile. "When we had our trouble, you prayed to Yemanja. You told me *we* had to act first. *We* had to pull a lot of weeds to make our garden. *We* wanted what we have now. Each gave in to keep the other. Difficult for a town to do this. Someone must lead them. Lead *us*."

He was unsure whether this moved her. A long pause pushed her thinking inward. After being lulled by his breathing, she put her head higher on his chest. "We caused too much of this. Hébert. Reginald. I wanted revenge. That's not right."

He took a deep breath and blew it softly through her hair. "I have a story for you—about a sow. When I was a boy, living on Cane River, my chore was feeding hogs. Once, I watched a big black sow deliver a litter. Soon, the pigs started to suckle, but a puny one couldn't find a teat or didn't want it. In one big gulp, the sow ate the pig. I ran to my father crying. He laughed and said, 'Nature takes care of its own sick.' *Nature* took care of two sick men, not you. We wanted them to pay for their crimes, but we took no payment. We don't have that power."

Ossi's breathing and heartbeat created a lullaby rhythm. She felt herself dozing, but conflicting thoughts, inspired by Eshu, the Janus-faced trickster, prevented sleep. Her inner quarrel peaked with, *Revenge is not justice.* Then, her eyes brightened. She sat up, full of energy, and said, "You're right! *They* didn't want to save their own souls. Others might. We've got to talk to Papa Luc, Aunt Velma, Sheriff Blake, and any good people on the other side—especially through Father Lorquette. Wishing and praying won't make peace hold."

Ossi smiled and sighed. "I need to tell more hog stories."

✝ ✝ ✝

The next morning, Femme interrupted Aunt Velma's kitchen cleaning by knocking anxiously on the screened door. She threw her drying towel over her shoulder and asked, "Lawd, today. Something bad had to drag you here this early. What happened?"

"Nothing. Papa Luc's gone to the mill?"

"An hour ago. Come in. I got fresh coffee. What's this all about?"

Femme's explanation went faster than expected. Papa Luc and Aunt Velma still blamed themselves for Meffre and Lucien's absence. She told Femme that, in the past year, they had only received two phone calls from Chicago. These were "happy calls," full of good news, but they felt sad afterwards. Papa Luc said absence and death become too similar too soon. After two cups of coffee and Aunt Velma's distracting headband adjustments, they agreed that the two sides needed to talk. They envisioned a dinner to devise a plan. Papa Luc, Ossi, Julien, Sheriff Blake (a critical representative from the other side), and the two of them would discuss what could be done. They also agreed that Father Lorquette was key to any solution.

Aunt Velma chuckled knowingly, which Femme questioned. "Might not be so easy for Papa Luc and Father to agree on much. Last week, he went down to Sacred Heart and asked Father to marry us. I told him don't do it, but hard-headed bulls gotta buck. Came back with his fists balled up. Father was right: if the law's against it, the church can't do much."

Femme covered her mouth to suppress laughter but could not contain herself. "Well, paper and a blessing won't make y'all *or* us any more married! Anyway, Papa Luc and Sherriff Blake ought to lead us. We gotta make it look like the rest of us are staying in our place. When white folks run it, folks believe it."

Aunt Velma pulled at her headband, raised her eyebrows, and said, "They'll even believe *colored* folks they *think* are white." She winked at Femme.

"Oh! Papa Luc told you, huh? Good. Now you know who you're cooking for. Gotta go. Charmaine's coming for a hen and eggs." She left, urging Aunt Velma to focus on the dinner.

Over the next few days, Papa Luc's resolve to lead the peace effort came from people who encouraged him from various corners of Lacombe. Sheriff Blake had asked many of them to talk to Papa Luc and, in the end, all agreed the dinner was a good start.

Aunt Velma prepared a "puny" winter salad, a rich seafood filé gumbo, a tender skillet roast with carrots and potatoes, buttermilk fried chicken, fluffy biscuits, and chocolate crème brûlée. To Sheriff Blake and his wife's surprise, Aunt Velma sat at one end of the table with Papa Luc at the other. They all drank fine wine from California or beer Julien contributed.

Sheriff Blake spoke first, exclaiming emphatically that he remembered a time when Lacombe was a quiet little place incapable of generating enough trouble to warrant a sheriff's notice. He chose to settle in Lacombe as a good place to raise his family. His only regret was that outsiders had influenced St. Tammany parish residents into regulating against blacks. He swore he never supported regulator work and claimed many mistrusted him and had suspicions about him as a neutral peacekeeper. He speculated that such suspicions were surely worse with blacks and Choctaws. He owned that, as a lawmaker, having folks question his loyalties was useful. Papa Luc raised his glass to toast Blake's questionable loyalty. Everyone laughed, especially the sheriff's wife. The sheriff laughed too and said, "Right now, we need each other to fix this mess once and for all. Only Father Lorquette holds enough trust on both sides to make a change."

They toasted Father Lorquette, and Papa Luc and Sheriff Blake agreed to go together to talk to him. Aunt Velma, while serving dessert, reported on how a "sick sadness has come over Father." It bothered her that none of her food or joking could muster a smile out of him.

Julien verified this. He had gone to work fixing a string of leaks on the church's roof above the sacristy. A line of rusty nails had popped up and loosened a sheet of tin. "Father didn't seem worried about those leaks. Didn't say he'd order tin to fix them. I pointed to the stormy sky. He just nodded. Charmaine made pralines for him. Barely parted his lips in thanks."

Ossi shook his head and said, "He needs hope. I brought him fish, and he couldn't stop talking about being a failure."

To change the table's mood, Aunt Velma served brandy, after which the sheriff and his wife shook everyone's hands and left. An uneasy silence ensued until Aunt Velma mentioned that they had a call that morning from Lucien and Meffre, who complained about snow and ice. Femme and Ossi surprised the table with news that they received a telegram signed "Iti." The message was: "Pecans and Kumquats." That amused everyone, and Aunt Velma ran to put on a Buddy Bolden record and wiggled her way into a brandy inspired dance. Papa Luc acknowledged that it was smart for the boys to send cryptic messages that would not run the risk of circulating through gossiping clerks at Western Union or the post office. Still, everyone was happy for positive news.

+ + +

Wrapped in his winter coat on Friday, January 24, 1908, Papa Luc rode Lucien's horse to Sacred Heart's rectory. He missed his son desperately and fixated guiltily over his role in effecting his absence. Even if he helped to save their lives, he, nonetheless, grieved over the vile separation that goaded him to act. He rode courageously past the Seafood and Produce Store thinking of its fleeting triumphs. As he passed Mudbug's, he saw Pike sweeping dirt out of the front door. He waved, remembering Aunt Velma's admonition that sweeping anything out of the house was bad luck and meant money was being thrown away. He arrived at the rectory just as the sheriff pulled up in his rig. They walked in together.

Sheriff Blake was full of impatience over an argument with Mary Eaton. He gruffly puffed out his grim status report, preempting what would have been Papa Luc's more gentile approach. Through all his bluster, he never sat or put his hat down. "Father, you know Luc and I have tried for years to stop this crazy violence. Even citizens working with the law can only do so much."

Father's eyes settled momentarily on a withering ivy growing in water. The sheriff spoke loudly and brashly; Papa Luc spoke softly and elegantly. He told stories of people being afraid that cross-burnings and violence would return. Fear kept everyone close to home, and parents complained of their children's unhealthy behavior. Papa Luc could not discern the priest's level of interest. "Father, please help us unite the parishioners. At least, let's try."

Father neither agreed nor disagreed. Several times, he wiped moisture from his eyes or arranged papers on his desk. He reached for his pipe and put it down. After the sheriff and Papa Luc represented their sides, the priest stood. Everyone knew the conversation was over. The only words Father uttered were: "The two of you weren't in church when I preached reconciliation after Percie's death. Only the walls heard that sermon. Thank you for your faith in me, but I've failed too many times."

After saying that the peace they now experienced was proof of Father's success, the sheriff left, tipping his hat. Papa Luc felt guilty for his recent talk with Father about marriage. After Father had rejected the request, he had pointed his finger in the priest's face and shouted, "If I could, I'd ask the Pope and Teddy Roosevelt myself. I'm never stepping foot in Sacred Heart again." Now he looked at a priest aching with defeat. In the doorway, he shook his hand and said, "Forgive me, Father, for what I said about marrying Velma. If you preach a sermon for Lacombe, I'll be there. So will the sheriff *and* Femme."

+ + +

Six weeks later, black clouds, heavy with rain, arced over Sacred Heart Church. Word spread that Father Lorquette had a big announcement and urged all parishioners to attend Sunday Mass. By nine thirty, the congregation assembled, and there was very little space left even for standing. Only the front pew, on the Blessed Mother's side, was empty, guarded on one end by Sheriff Black and by Pike on the other. Without saying a word, neither guard allowed anyone to enter. The sheriff's immensity and scowl spoke loudly, and Pike's unusual clean appearance—slicked-back hair and a crooked green bow tie—signaled no nonsense as well.

The church was awash with chatter, anticipating what message the taciturn priest could possibly give to justify having amassed such a crowd. The number of rarely seen attendees shocked those who never missed their Sunday obligation. Aunt Velma sat, as usual, in the last pew with her unruly choir. Papa Luc, in defiance of protocol, sat boldly next to her and elicited unbridled stares. Charmaine, Pichon, and Kebbi were in the middle of the church in the first row allowed for blacks, Créoles, and Choctaws. Ossi, Femme, and Julien sat behind them, which distracted Keb into squirming.

Mary and Todd Eaton filled the first pew's far corner on the pulpit side. Olga Glapion, Pauline Breau, and Eva Doucette and their families filled out the first three pews. To Mary's chagrin, other members of the Ladies Altar Society and their families sat on the opposite side just behind the empty first pew. A crew of lumberjacks—Reginald's friends—and their families filled in several pews in the church's midsection. Amelia Plachette, the Pellicer sisters and their husbands, Sheriff Blake's wife and seven children, and Myrtle Picou sat in the third pew on the Blessed Mother's side. Myrtle occasionally looked back to smile at Julien—a puzzle for most onlookers except lumberjacks who frequented her bar.

Choctaws and blacks occupied the remaining back pews or lined the church walls. Those who fancied a seat crammed into the choir loft. The constant shuffling for space ceased by the time Father Lorquette followed two pimple-faced altar boys from the sacristy. To everyone's surprise, the altar boys sat, and Father came down from the altar through the short door of the communion rail. With his hands raised, he drew the church's attention by yelling, "I need your voice, Jesus, to invade these souls. Come through me to them." In measured steps, he blessed both sides of the aisle and walked directly to Aunt Velma. "Come with me Velma. Bring your choir.

Today, and from now on, these children will sing God's praises from the first pew." Dutifully, Aunt Velma followed Father and ushered her choir forward. Papa Luc proudly trailed them as they assumed their places with awkward smiles that agitated most parishioners. He shook Sheriff Blake's hand, looked over the pews behind him, and located known sympathizers. He nodded at them and took his place on the center aisle. Before the agitation from Mary's side could erupt, Father shouted, "Silence. You've all said too much. Not today!"

Mary Eaton was past toleration and stood. "My husband's lost and—"

"I said 'silence!' " The redness in Father's face signified an anger no one had seen in him. He faced Mary and said loudly and confidently, "Today, you'll listen, or you'll leave this church permanently." With his robes bellowing, he strutted back to the center aisle. "Today, I will not preach a gospel sermon. Your sinful souls are unworthy recipients of God's words. This black morning, I, a sinner like you, will talk to your souls." The church's uneasiness was mirrored in the priest's constant amblings from the center aisle to either side and back. He peered into the eyes of anyone who looked his way. Long pauses stretched out his seriousness.

Yemanja released an irksome tip-tap drizzle with the cadence of a funereal song. Femme heard it and thanked the orisha. Ossi nodded knowingly. Julien sat nervously, looking to the rafters for the first sign of leaks.

Father centered himself below the altar and preached: "At one time or another, I've heard confessions from nearly all of you. I'll never betray those confessions, but today, *I'll* confess to you. I came to this parish with a clean soul. It's now full of filth, hatred, and violence you've confessed to me. *My* confession is I have failed to save your sin-packed souls. Because I can't save you on earth means I'll burn with you eternally in hell. None of us will see St. Peter at heaven's gate. Your hypocrisy, murderous hatred, vile attitudes, and unholiness has doomed us. I've given you penance and forgave you in Christ's name. But you return to confess the same crimes against God and nature. Earthly confessions won't get you into heaven. You must bleach sin from your souls." He breathed heavily and felt strength pulsing through his muscles. He had prayed for the physical vigor and fortitude needed to move this crowd. Hope stiffened his spine.

The storm's full rampage started with Eshu riding a single furious lightning bolt. Next, echoing thunder. Then, Yemanja opened the clouds, turning the lugubrious drizzle into pounding rain. The church's tin roof braced for the assault.

The roof dripped rain through the sacristy's wooden beams just above where Father stood. The string of leaks seemed to beckon him to walk just below them. Instead of finding a dry spot to preach from, he stalled under a streaming leak and allowed it to drench his curly hair into slickness, which he pushed back in strident moves that emphasized his speech. He paused long enough to observe the congregation. Many eyes were moist, red, or full of tears. Shame bent heads downward. Children sat in fear of what they did not understand. He raised his arms and, exclaimed, "I couldn't save your souls because I've helped you sin. For this, I'm guilty. But all of you should have a collective guilt. I wanted peace. But instead of leading you, I followed and helped Satan create violence. I confess and ask your forgiveness and God's."

Yemanja swept the rain in torrents from the altar to the vestibule. The water moved in blasting waves against the very winds that caused the fury. The stained-glass windows lost color and turned gray. Sprinting and beating rain did not abate even when the wind began to subside. The weather empowered Father, whose voice boomed and magnified his message. "I helped welcome death's pain and sorrow. My work should've prevented Satan's ravages, but I escorted him while he carried pieces of hell into our lives. After Percie's murder, I preached against your hypocrisy and hate. You wouldn't hear me because I was weak. Not now! Forgive me, Jesus! Now you'll change or take your damned souls elsewhere!"

He fell to his knees, as if in a fit, and pounded the wooden floor to echo his rage. "No more! No more! No more torment from Satan." He froze there, on his hands and knees, lips moving in prayer. With only the storm breaking the silence, the church watched him pray for what seemed much longer than the minutes it took. Sheriff Blake stood to help him up, but he motioned against it. With soaked vestments, he found his way to his feet and moved to the dry bottom step just below the altar. From there, he wiped his wet face with his scapula and said, "Before we have Mass, I vow to work from now on to save your souls from damnation. But you must promise me and God that you will become good Catholics who love rather than hate. Look at Jesus on that cross. Some of you burned this, the holiest of symbols."

The lumberjacks interrupted and voiced their pride at taking part in cross-burning. He fiercely confronted them, "Look at your children here! Is your hate their inheritance? You're damning them to hell as well. Sit or leave!" The disgruntled lumberjacks sat and mumbled invectives to each other.

Father marched back to the center aisle, "You must also love and protect nature in Lacombe. You build roads around godlike oaks, then you abuse their limbs by unjustly hanging your fellow Christians. Never again! You may laugh and ridicule, but I will no longer give the sacraments, especially communion, to anyone who doesn't abide by this pact. Don't come to this altar rail to receive Christ's body unless your soul is clean. I will not put Christ in souls full of hate. No more! No more! If you can keep this pact in Christ's name, welcome to our *new* Sacred Heart Church. If not, leave now. To take Christ's body today, you must say, 'I pledge peace.'"

Todd Eaton, against Mary's protests, left, punching the air all the way to the back doors. Several lumberjacks cussed loudly and kicked kneelers up as they exited, pulling reluctant wives and children. From the vestibule, the boldest shouted, "Nigger lovers swing from trees too!"

Father stood on the altar steps undaunted and blessed the congregation in spectacular motions that caused a distinct murmur which subsided only when he turned to the altar and sang the "Kyrie eleison." Aunt Velma's choir stood on cue and sang the entrance song *a cappella* in melodious harmony to start the Mass.

At communion time, the line to the altar was robust. Papa Luc, the Pellicer sisters, and their husbands were the first to kneel for communion. Next, Femme, Ossi, Julien, Charmaine, Pichon, Aunt Velma, and choristers—who had reached the age of reason—knelt with bowed heads. Pike and the sheriff knelt next to Myrtle, and to their surprise Olga filled out the last space on the kneeler. Behind the first communicants, two lines stretched to the back of the church.

After preparing his chalice with bread, Father turned and was astounded at the many bowed heads before him. One of the altar boys followed him to administer communion, and when Father held the host before each kneeling soul and said, "Corpus Christi," he heard, "I pledge peace."

When the last person had received communion, Mary Eaton, in tears, rose and went before Father. He waited for her to kneel; instead, she turned to the congregation, pointed to the priest, and bellowed, "I've lost too much to pledge peace to this drunk, to this traitor of a sheriff, and to y'all who lower yourselves to be equal to niggers. I'm leaving, but I'm not finished. I'll go to the bishop and elsewhere with this."

Father moved to face her and ordered loudly, "Leave! You've never been baptized Catholic. You don't belong here." The church shuffled at this news. Mary stormed out abruptly and frightened the altar boy, who dropped his platen with a clang, loud enough to create a distracting juncture for Father to resume and end the Mass.

A weak slant of sunlight marked a path down the church steps. It appeared, disappeared, and reappeared, growing stronger each time. During the dismissal song, the church emptied slowly with parishioners throwing cautious glances and even smiles at each other. Sheriff Blake and Pike soldiered the front doors and nodded goodbyes.

The Pellicer sisters stopped to talk to Charmaine while Pichon shook hands with their husbands and tried to quiet Keb, who pulled him down the aisle to get towards Julien. The taller of the Pellicer sisters said meekly, "Charmaine, we hope you will join the Ladies of the Altar Society. Some won't like it but, after Father's sermon, *we* welcome you."

Amelia Plachette eavesdropped and added, "Looks like we got a vacancy. I'll be there to welcome you too."

Charmaine looked to the sacristy and replied, "Well, I'm usually here dressing the altar, so I'd like to accept your invitation." One sister patted Charmaine's shoulder; the other shook her hand. Pichon beckoned to her, pointing at Keb. The women walked out and commented on the storm and how the sun was now brightening the stained glass.

Aunt Velma, Ossi, and Femme stood on the church porch and waited for Papa Luc to drive the carriage around. Femme complimented Aunt Velma on her pretty new hat—a lovely substitute for her "ratty" headbands. Before Aunt Velma could start cussing, Ossi spied Papa Luc and led the women down the steps. Aunt Velma brusquely invited them to sit in the back seat so she could show off her "expensive" new hat in the front.

After changing into dry street clothes, Father raised kneelers and returned missals and songbooks to their pew caddies. He enjoyed a healthy satisfaction as he reflected on today's sermon. Regrets over Percie's funeral sermon started to fade. He smiled repeatedly as he finished tidying up the church. Out in the sunny church yard, he ran his fingers through his damp curls and mused on Sacred Heart's fragility. He turned to the road and peered out to the young oak the Usher Board had planted to replace Church Oak. He stood there for a long time, with hope, and prayed that words could still make a difference.

Acknowledgments

To appreciate the heavens, we must recognize the stars.

For the most part, writers function best in solitude. Producing a book, however, involves a concerted group effort. Thus, I happily tender thanks to those in my writing fellowship. Thanks to my friends and colleagues Bob Fish and John B. Mason, who were unwavering beta readers, offering suggestions that strengthened subsequent drafts. Throughout the drafting and polishing of the novel, Carol Beran was generous in her commentary and support. To her, I extend my full-throated gratitude.

Ernesto Mestre, a fine novelist, was an early editor for this work. His fingerprints are everywhere in the manuscript, and his perspicacious comments goaded me on to revise sentences, paragraphs, and entire scenes. His knowledge of the Yoruba religion Vodoun informs the orishas in the novel; this saved me hours of deliberation on the use, efficacy, and authenticity of this religion in the book.

Two very accomplished novelists, Chris Helvey and Lou Berney, supported the development and publication of my short stories and agreed to affirm *The Upside-Down Tree* as readers and critics of the final manuscript. I am truly grateful for their continued recognition of my literary efforts.

Having wished for an ideal reader, I found her in Cosette Puckett at Aubade Publishing. She played a pivotal role in criticizing the novel's ending, for which I am enormously appreciative. I owe a gigantic debt of gratitude to Joe Puckett, Aubade's executive editor, for the book's final presentation.

Living with an avaricious and indiscriminate consumer of African American art, history, and literature is perhaps the best luck I have had in constituting my writing community. Aside from being my lifelong soulmate, Darrick Lackey is the one reader and critic whose unbridled honesty shaped and reshaped my intellectual spine with his inspiration and confidence. Dedicating this work to him is meager thanks indeed for all he has done.

Alden Reimonenq is a New Orleanian transplant, who lives and thrives in Palm Springs, California. He writes reviews, poetry, short fiction, and has published the collection *Hoodoo Headrag, Poems. The Upside-Down Tree* is his first novel.

Learn more about Alden and his work at www.aldenreimonenq. com, and on Twitter at @AldenReimonenq